J(

THE SEA
SAM SMITH

Cover Photo Maksym Fesenko

This book is a work of fiction. Any reference to historical events, real people, or real places are used fictitiously. Other names, characters, places, events, and incidents are products of the author's imagination. Any resemblance to actual events or places or people, living or dead, is entirely coincidental.

Copyright © 2024 by Sam Smith

All rights reserved. No part of this book may be reproduced in any form without written permission from the publisher or author.

For My Kitty Ollie

You light my path and,
like a good servant, I follow.
I love you,
Mummy
My furry friends in Georgia
Lulu, Laci, London,
Lolly, Lync, Lyam, and Lilly.
You are immortalized within my heart.
A massive shout out to...
Lynda J Lyle
Aside from being a gorgeous Southern Belle,
You are also
My Best Friend. My Confidant. My Rock
&
The Sister I Always Wanted.
I love you, Shugah xx.

JUPITER
BY
THE SEA

To reveal the agony deep within
is possibly the most brutal act
I have had to bear.
~ Sam Smith ~

I WATCHED BEN BARRYMORE standing in the center of the dance floor, charming a blonde and a brunette with his effortless smile. Conversely, I watched from the shadows, my frumpy dress and mousy hair keeping me anchored to the corner. Still, my heart ached as I watched him so close yet a world away. Suddenly, our eyes met across the room, and for a heartbeat, I felt seen. But then he turned away, and the moment vanished, leaving me with longing and regret.

LUST

PLATO BELIEVED THAT every heart sings a song, incomplete, until another heart whispers back...

I saw Ben Barrymore in Palm Beach late Saturday night, and though I had millions of reasons to say hello, I did not. Instead, I swayed to the music and mimed a popular song, ignoring a man I have known since the dawn of time.

Still on the clock at my current job, I am eager to complete my assignment with the abrasive man whose torment lingers. In despair, I yearn to separate myself from all his demands. As I look around the room, all I see is happiness, and I cannot help but envy it.

Ben was the biggest attraction in the room, and I would ask him to dance if I was not working. Although he was not the wealthiest man here, he was the most handsome I had seen in years, and I have seen many men. He dressed in a black tuxedo and looked as dashing as ever with his cheerful smile and sparkling eyes that shone as brightly as the midday sun.

I reference his eyes, identical to mine, as they reflected the same emotions and lustful hunger, we both once held for each other deep within our souls.

In an earlier life, I recall an incarnation where a stranger caused my death and affected Ben's life, and I groaned as Ben held the conviction that I had acted recklessly, which was unfounded. Nevertheless, his fury was immeasurable, and it was now up to destiny to decide if we would embark on another journey together. Over time, I have known this magnificent man as my friend, lover, and tormentor. I pondered whether he sensed my passion tonight or was still clueless despite my sending hundreds of signals.

The soft murmurs of conversation and the tinkling of glasses echoed throughout the ballroom's elegant dining area, intensifying my sense of exclusion, as no one had invited me to join them for a meal.

Disgruntled, I eyed Ben with suspicion and jealousy. The bitterness that shook my body inspired me to replicate Hadrian's Wall in England. It was a desperate attempt to protect myself, as I saw that Ben had chosen to ignore me, refusing to understand that I was merely a pawn in a chess game, and unless our King avoided checkmate, we would be at the mercy of a feisty Queen.

Saddened, I sighed and faced the opulent ballroom, where I admired The Carlisle Resort's hand-crafted statues, impressive waterfalls, and tropical flowers. The five-star hotel offers Palm Beach County's wealthiest residents the best hospitality and services.

On my last visit, I stood beside a tall marble statue of a man resting a palm on his knee, with hardened facial features and a non-expressive look. I looked for the exact location that night.

Since I had arrived alone, my inconspicuous stance proved challenging as predatory men roved throughout the room and gawked in my direction. I surmised that this party host lacked friends with the class status quo as most men could not resist their urge to proposition me. Though troubled by the alarming number of mature men requesting discreet favors, I stayed composed and politely declined their advances because it would never happen. If I could vomit, I would. Still, I smiled and strolled to an empty corner of the room, stopping once to nod at a group of women sitting at a table, awaiting an eligible suitor to ask them to dance.

In my experience, I have learned that men are dogs, if not worse, as I have a dog, and he is a darling little male who would mistreat no one.

Applauding the massive chandeliers and the decorative artwork adorning the ballroom walls, I tried adding each fixture's cost, which was challenging, as I still needed to pass math and finish my art degree. Still, my low-income day job and rich connections afford me the luxury of seeing how Carlisle's developers spared no expense, spending upwards of millions of dollars.

The Carlisle Hotel is one of the fanciest resorts I have visited in South Florida. However, since I live in Miami Beach, I seldom accept invitations to bask in its glory. My trips to this opulent town were exhausting, especially during weekend traffic when more drivers were on the road. Besides, I preferred engagements closer to home, as I saved money on gasoline. The long drive also added an extra three hours to my schedule, making my disappearance more noticeable to my friends and boyfriend, Harry.

A cheerful, mature server interrupted my thoughts and offered me a vintage coupe glass from circa 1955. The crystal flute, adorned in yellow gold engravings, sat amongst others beside a bottle of Louis Roederer Champagne. Although I enjoyed Cristal, I declined this light-bodied French beverage even though my mouth was salivating to sample the peach, fruity drink, as I had to drive back to Miami and was still on the clock. So, no boozy night spent drinking the world's finest champagne for me on that spectacular evening.

Remorseful, I watched with envy as the hotel employee soldiered on to a group of men who accepted the import, toasting each other before gulping it down in two mouthfuls.

In better times, I thought and focused on a mature couple dancing together as a love song echoed throughout the room.

Suddenly, a romantic thought about Ben entered my mind. Without further ado, I rebuked my devilish yearnings and forced myself to applaud the grandeur of The Carlisle despite its renovated walls holding me captive.

On that bustling Saturday evening, the paint still smelled fresh, as did the upholstered chairs and the centerpieces of candles surrounded by flowers decorating every table. I could not help but admire the shimmering silverware, plates, and metallic ornaments illuminated by the clandestine light fixtures.

The majestic resort welcomes royalty from as far away as London, Denmark, and Dubai. And though I have stood within its walls six times, I am not one of Carlisle's wealthy occupants or visitors. I am a pauper who sneaks through the city streets unseen in the darkness of night.

True to form, the historic building and all its finished construction were on full display, as were the people attending this function to honor local entrepreneur Clive

Owen, a longtime resident who had commissioned a team of engineers and architects to restore the dilapidated structure into the palatial hotel it is today.

Right now, I want to clarify one thing for you. I confess to creeping through Carlisle's expensive crafted four walls six times over the past two months. So, trust me when I say I mean it. Though I am not in disguise or hiding tonight as the man of the hour, Mitch Carter is up for an award. Aside from being a prestigious guest, he is also the sole reason I am here.

Married, Mitch had requested a paid companion for four hours. Now, I know that I may read like I am a whore or something, but I am not. I am a 'you may look at me, but don't touch me' kind of girl.

The State of Florida recognizes me as a Tour Guide, and two months ago, I paid a nominal fee to get my occupational license to keep my taxes in order. In times of challenge, I can present my license to add validity should hotel personnel question why I am on the property, which appeals to my acquaintances who frequent this resort.

As in earlier visits, my client's fantasy was watching me walk around the room while he tended to his wife. We have met six times but have never acknowledged each other's presence or spoken, except to discuss the date.

Mitch is a mature attorney, and I like that he pays without doubting my worth or rebuking tips, as he is a generous tipper who helps me pay my bills. However, watching him dance to a romantic song with his wife, I caught him glancing my way. I wanted to heave, as his arrogance was nauseating, more so because the attractive middle-aged woman was unaware her husband was a rotten cheat. Not that Mitch has accosted me or asked for intimate favors, but that does not and should not diminish the fact that he is still a pig.

At twenty-six years of age, I have learned little about Palm Beach other than that it caters to old-school family money and tech-savvy men. In contrast, Miami is home to actors, musicians, and other self-made millionaires.

Palm Beach is a beautiful town and a prestigious gathering place for the world's wealthiest people. A haven for Polo fanatics, it also boasts Mar-A-Lago, the home of forty-fifth and forty-seventh President Donald Trump.

Inside the venue, the hours ticked by at a snail's pace, and I struggled to avoid conversing with people and battled extreme boredom while resisting the urge to express a colossal yawn.

In Miami, if out with friends, I could sigh loudly, raise my hand, and exhale a painful groan to signify I wanted to leave. However, this is Palm Beach, and unladylike actions are taboo. Besides, the one thing I have learned is to do as others do when in plentiful company. If not? The snobs will cast you aside and never return.

Such is Palm Beach.

The locals understand everyone has a price, and like them, I have mine.

By day, I attend classes at a local college and work as a copy editor in Miami, earning a salary one step up from minimum wage. In my cheap-paying occupation, I do as I please and do not care what my cheapskate boss, Bob the

Knob, thinks about my reckless attitude to the terrible articles that he thrust on my desk every Monday morning.

"I need these proofread by Friday," he would snarl like a rabid dog who had escaped an abusive owner. He made me angry, and I only stayed because it was more of a cover for my secret occupation than the lousy pay.

My dream was to become a bestselling novelist, and editing other writers' work was helpful as I learned grammar, plots, characterization, and what the fuck not to do. Trust me when I tell you that you could not fathom the poorly written scripts on my desk from my boss, Bobby Adler. I would be putting it politely if I told you they read like a five-year-old had drafted the story or, worse, a junkie who had lost touch with reality.

I am the first to admit that I have a pathetic existence. Please understand why my manners are appalling at work. If you knew Bob, like I know Bob, you would behave the same or worse. In contrast, when I am on assignments, I am on my best behavior without one word, foot, or pose out of place. Despite fatigue, I stand tall, hold my head high, and never slump my shoulders. My military stance and technique are what I call them. While in London, I saw the King's guards in front of Buckingham Palace, focused on their surroundings and nothing else. I admire their ability, and even though I have a talent for concentration, I am not superior to those who have honed their skills for years to achieve greatness. I raise my hat to anyone with abundant discipline and the ability to fade out because their work ethic is strict. Those gifted people are who I envy most, and expressing my gratitude is something I would like to scream from the rooftops.

Ouch! Out of nowhere, I felt a painful cramp surge down my right leg, and I tried to shake it out as discreetly as possible. Still, while doing so, a rambunctious admirer approached me, mistaking my discomfort as a subtle sign that I wanted to dance.

Dance?

With YOU?

Are you serious?

I wanted to laugh but smiled and turned to stare at one incredible piece of art hanging on a wall. Since my face was not visible to others, I kid you not; I yawned so profoundly that I thought my windpipe would dry up.

Composed, I returned to the crowds and saw the busy dance floor. Since I enjoyed the current song, I could have had a quick twirl and blended in amongst hundreds of people. However, knowing my client would be annoyed, I stood my ground.

Along with the generous funding I received from Mitch came rules, instructions, and lectures reminiscent of the Spanish Inquisition. As his secretary, Greta, reminded me, I could not flirt, dance, or talk to another man. "You're to look ravishing, so make sure you are," she had quipped early Friday morning.

A lady bowed to a man and waved a fan across her face, waiting for him to lower his knees and raise her back to standing height. It was romantic, considering most men here were hungry for a little more than a dance partner. They put a new twist to the saying, looking for love in all the wrong places. Still, as mundane as these events are, I try to look cheerful and smile for no reason other than that I would look ridiculous prowling the room with a sour expression.

The problem with stuffy social gatherings is that they cannot arouse interest and bring little-needed enthusiasm. A more comprehensive assortment of entertainment, such as a traditional Middle Eastern belly dancer or a small ballet performance, would stimulate people's minds and encourage them to donate more funds.

In my travels across Florida, Palm Beach has no fond memories in my heart, as the superficial people living here are narcissists with egos the size of one of the world's geographical continents.

Aside from judging, I like to analyze the glitz and glamor at events like these. I can instantly spot the mega-wealthy instead of those who live on a budget higher than most but still cannot brag about their multimillionaire status, as most Palm Beach County funds have spread from generation to generation.

To the left of the room, I spotted the public bathrooms. I surmised the ladies' room would be an excellent place to retreat and would allow me to rethink my role here and even wake up from the monotony of idle chatter that did not hold a sincere word in any sentence I had overheard. I hoped the change of scenery would add something interesting to my dull itinerary and ease my tiredness. But, as I walked in that direction, I saw a line as long as those at Walt Disney World. I realized there was no prospect of my gaining access to the bathrooms and no chance to chat with the attendant, if only to have at least one genuine conversation.

Not that my evening had not been stimulating because there had been four or five crazy exchanges of rivalry between the men. Yet, through it all, I felt as ignored and neglected as a lone angel atop a Christmas tree.

Disgruntled, I traced the outline of a large marble slab on the floor, desperately trying to hide my boredom with the idle chatter shoved my way, as my interest was elsewhere. Besides, the light conversation drained my energy. It reduced my positive thoughts to zero, forcing my active mind into a snooze zone with no rhyme or reason to think of anything but an escape plan.

Noticing that the bathroom line was moving slower than I had hoped, I returned to the ballroom. I regretted that decision and choked up when I saw a familiar face whose good looks had haunted me for years.

Goodness, why was he still here?

Yes, he lives in Palm Beach. But he was too young to socialize with people old enough to be his grandfather. Yet, there he was, standing two feet away, and all I wanted was to run for cover.

I inhaled and swallowed hard. Ben Barrymore looked bored but engrossed in conversation with the group of people before me, and that scared me as I have known Ben since childhood. We were never friends, far from it. Our paths had crossed because my mother worked as a servant at his parents' home in Jupiter, Florida. As if that was not embarrassing enough, Benny Boy was also involved in an oceanic fishing venture with my boyfriend, Harry Higgins, who owns a home fueling company that specializes in filling up rich people's boats that aligned the waterways throughout Miami.

Worse, yes, the situation gets worse.

Ben knows of my Miami lifestyle, even visiting Harry's home for occasional Sunday football parties and car sharing at boating events like the Columbus Day Regatta. So, our paths have crossed over the past few years.

Now, I am aware I am not cheating on Harry, but just knowing Mitch had reimbursed me for my time filled me with guilt. I lowered my head and counted cracks on the marble floor to avoid eye contact with Ben. Just before I was about to erupt like an active volcano, I threw caution to the wind, pushed my feet in my heels, and raced away to another corner of the room.

Regrettably, I focused on nothing but Ben and the potential nightmare that would begin when Harry heard about my attendance at The Carlisle Hotel. Still, I did not freak out or even sweat. I was too busy praying and begging the Lord above for this uncomfortable and garish evening to end.

And if so?

How soon?

A slim gold watch, my grandmother's gift, adorned my wrist. Though small, it glowed under the glaring bulbs of a low-hanging chandelier, and I discreetly checked the time. It was close to midnight, the witching hour, the end of my date, which was comforting. However, I planned to leave five minutes before twelve because I could not stand being here, knowing succulent Ben Barrymore was mere feet away.

Nervous, I licked my rose-colored glossed lips, and just when I regained my composure, I almost choked on my saliva as I saw Benny Boy approaching.

Oh no!

Dear Lord, make him disappear, I pleaded and held my breath. Then, I searched for a place to retreat, but the dance floor had emptied, and no seats were available.

My only distraction was a friendly conversation with an elderly lady named Beatrice, who looked to be over ninety. Still, I was delighted in her mannerisms and enjoyable in her chitchat. Darling Beatrice wore her blonde hair in a bun and had various clips displaying the world's finest emeralds. She had a tanned complexion, rosy cheeks, and a gallant smile that caused her mature eyes to twinkle each time she laughed. As gracious as she was, my first attraction to her strong Southern Accent wore off as her pronunciation was challenging to interpret, and more maddening was that the old dear spoke in a low tone.

Georgia-born Beatrice was a Southern Belle in all senses of the word. She was reminiscent of Scarlet O'Hara in Gone with the Wind, with her coifed hair, colorful makeup, and attire. All that was missing was a fan wafting in her direction should she find the Florida humidity stifling.

I listened to the stories she shared about her life in Georgia, where water flowed from mountains down to valleys and into lakes across the State, particularly Lake Lanier, which was popular with the locals and visitors alike. I enjoyed the small talk about her years in Albany as she spoke affectionately about her hometown. Though I had never visited, she almost convinced me to go. Mind you, she left me wondering why she had moved away and, of all places, settled in Florida since she believed Georgia was such a wonderful place to live.

I longed to ask but decided against it, as I did not want to offend Beatrice, as she was such good company. So, why spoil the fun? Besides, she handed me her business card, and since I was desperate to have a friend, the delightful, mature lady was worth her slender weight in gold.

"Bella, my partner, Emily Parker, has retreated from the ladies' room. Since we arrived together, we shall remain at each other's side. I hope you understand," she said. "Please give me your contact information so I may call you."

I recited my telephone number, watched her write it down, and lowered my head.

Astutely, Beatrice noticed my disposition. "Do not be sad, young lady, for I will be in touch. And we will continue our conversation about all these sleazy men. A word to the wise, now that we have exchanged phone numbers, let us not play games about who should call the other first," she told me confidently. "I look forward to becoming friends with you. Once again, allow me to introduce myself. I am Beatrice Ryder, a Georgia transplant enjoying life in South Florida, and I cannot wait to converse with you again in the not-too-distant future," she added, and just like that, she was gone.

I could not resist feeling profound sorrow as I watched her reunion with Emily. I felt guilt for placating the older woman, and I became remorseful as I was once again all alone.

Soon after Beatrice left, I searched across the room for Ben. I spotted him conversing with an alluring blonde in a revealing dress, highlighting her impressive bosom and shapely figure that could rival Kim Kardashian's. I deduced that you are a pig, and a wave of jealousy consumed me, leaving me unsettled with a single plea.

Curves! However, more than a voluptuous figure, I need to stop this awful habit of gnawing at my lower lip. A fixation I adopted last year after quitting smoking. A decision that made Harry happy and me miserable because I still miss the taste of tobacco. I regret adopting this lip-biting self-mutilation, as it causes me more distress than smoking ever did right now. I am so keyed up that I would give anything for one puff on a Marlboro Red or a packet of twenty. In fact, I could smoke an entire carton of cigarettes at rapid speed. Such was the level of my anxiety.

Stop being negative, I cursed, listening to a familiar tune on the stereo system. And before I could stop myself, my right foot was tapping to the beat of the music as I swayed from side to side.

Just stop fidgeting! I cursed again while watching Benny Boy, still schmoozing with the chesty blonde. I wondered what he might say to Harry upon seeing me here tonight. Would Ben mention my presence to my boyfriend?

Of course, he would, I concluded.

Get with it, Bella. I cursed for the third time in minutes.

You are a fool if you believe Ben will not call Harry as soon as the sun rises across the Atlantic Ocean if he can wait that long.

Can he?

Probably not.

Like most men, Benjamin Barrymore thrived on gossip, especially about women. He would use his cell phone to call Harry the first chance he got. Then, Benny Boy would banter about seeing me here and inquire why Harry had not gone with me to the ball.

I imagined the conversation already. "Hey Harry, I saw your girlfriend Bella at an event in Palm Beach on Saturday night. Who does she know in that crowd, and why didn't you come?"

Darling Harry would choke on a Bud Light, his favorite alcoholic beverage, and after chugging a fresh can of beer, he would bombard the tittle-tattle Ben with a hundred questions.

Deep in my heart, I prayed for Ben to be quiet and not divulge to Harry that he had seen me there. If he did? I was in deeper trouble than I already was. Though I am a decent woman, I had a sinking feeling that, like Harry and Ben, the Heavens above would not be too pleased with my current occupation.

The gods would throw me to the wolves.

I predicted that to be correct every time I earned this income. When I considered how risqué my secret life was and my love for money, it was only a matter of time before someone exposed my trash.

What I am doing is a sin in the Bible.

Thinking about my strict religious upbringing, born to a mother who preached biblical quotes all day, particularly on Sundays while attending our local church, I wondered when everything in my life had gone wrong.

How had I succumbed to this sacrilegious lifestyle in which I thought of nothing but money?

I honestly did not know.

All I know is that I lived, breathed, and dreamed about dollar bills, and should my mother see me now, she would tear me apart, for the love of money is a sin in the eyes of the Lord and the only place I was heading to after this life was hell.

A young man appeared in front of me. "Would you like to dance?" he asked, a hopeful smile on his face.

Though tempted to tell the punk I was not that desperate, I mustered a friendly smile instead. "Thank you so much. I appreciate your invitation, but I had foot surgery and cannot dance," I lied and rolled my eyes as I watched him walk over to another girl standing alone.

You are so bad, I chastised, and sadly mistaken if you believe good karma will come from all the lies you have told over the past two months. I slipped my hand into my dress pockets and gnawed at my lower lip, deep in thought of how tempestuous I had become. Then, noticing Ben was now edging closer, I experienced a faintness and wished I had eaten supper. Recognizing that I would experience a sense of obligation to create fairytales to explain my existence to all these wonderful rich folk, I averted my gaze.

I realized that my story to Ben would be better if it were a whopper of a tale; if not, he would question me to the end of days.

Would Benny Boy keep quiet if I spun a good yarn and tried to fool him, or would he inform Harry? I wondered nervously.

Time will tell... I groaned.

Benjamin Barrymore will either be discreet, rat me out, or throw more drama into the equation. I hoped not, but I was sure he would tell my boyfriend. Ben would be afraid not to, as he would worry that I had informed Harry of my attendance tonight, and his saying nothing would make him perceive himself as conniving.

I could implore Benny Boy not to speak of my appearance. Still, I do not want to ask him to lie, as that would create tension, which could open a new assortment of problems. I knew the latter was correct because they were intensely involved in similar interests, such as embarking on boat trips to Bimini and snorkeling expeditions off the coast of Key West. Overwhelmed by a sense of hopelessness, I let out a groan, unable to see any escape from this catastrophe.

Benjamin Barrymore would unequivocally expose my appearance tonight, regardless of what I wanted. Unlike most men, Benny Boy would not take my aloof stance to heart. He would push and shove until he knocked down my protective walls, and none of my nearest and dearest friends could help me overcome this adversity.

I kid you not. If I could ask an angel above to open the ground that held me transfixed in this torrid nightmare and swallow me whole, I would—if only to help me escape the curious expression across his face. But remembering the earth underneath the flooring held nothing but rocks, soil, and bugs, I cringed, stood my ground, and pretended not to notice Ben Barrymore approaching my tranquil space.

I sank my hand into a nearby fountain and splashed my fevered brow, willing it to cool. The chilly water did nothing to ease the heat from the soles of my feet to the nape of my neck. As I gazed at Benny Boy, I doubted that even Holy Water would quell the intense passion inside my body.

His handsomeness glowed like a beacon in the night as he narrowed the space between us. At that moment, I begged for death, critters, or no critters because right now, I welcomed them more than what I saw less than two feet away and nearing closer to my side.

In ten breaths, he was facing me. A rueful smile etched his mouth. Full lips exposed perfect white teeth, and a brightness in his almond-shaped eyes held warmth. Then he removed a hand tucked inside his trouser pocket, extended it towards me, and embraced me in a tight hug, which gave me the sensation of having passed away and transcended to Heaven.

Slowly, I opened my eyes, peeked at Benny Boy, and grimaced. Ah! I was still standing here but wondered if his next move would send me to hell.

The unforeseen future will let me know.

Aside from Ben's obvious good looks, I could not avoid noticing the fragrance of his cologne. It was a crisp scent that, in any other circumstance, would have hypnotized me off my feet and straight into his bed.

Yes, I am aware. I read like a tramp. I am not, but you only learn that as you uncover more in this story.

"Bella, it's so good to see you," he greeted genuinely. "I cannot tell you how boring I find these events, but my mother insisted, so here I am," he whispered and winked. "I was almost ready to leave until I saw you standing alone. So, let me admit that I may have pulled a leg muscle in my haste to get to you as quickly as possible. I am joking, of course," he told me and smiled.

I was about to answer with my made-up story, but Ben did not give me a chance to practice my bullshit on his ever-so-fancy persona. Before I knew it, he started shooting questions at me, which I mostly disregarded because of my inability to deceive him, which frustrated me.

"How are you?" he asked, a broad smile etched on his sun-tanned face, accentuating three or four distinguished lines around his piercing blue eyes.

The same color mirrored my own, except my eyes held no wrinkles, mainly as I live a more gothic life than a sun worshipper. I am proud to announce that sunscreen has left my skin wrinkle-free, for now, anyway.

"You look incredible, Bella, so stunning," he said admiringly. He held my arms outstretched as his eyes caressed my body. "I don't think I have ever seen you looking as beautiful as you do tonight," he paused as if struggling to remember. "Ah!" He grinned again. "The first time I saw you, you wore a pretty blue dress with yellow sunflowers, and your mother styled your hair with matching bows. Well, I fell in love with you that afternoon. Of course, we were much younger, but to this day, I'm so grateful that your mother brought you to play at my parents' home while she worked because seeing you made my life so much brighter."

Most women would be thrilled with his blabbering flattery. Still, I had heard it all too many times—not from Ben but from other men, such as one of my clients, who had spoken similar sentences to take me to bed. Though they failed in their desires, I learned their enthusiastic small talk was nothing but foreplay and lies.

If any man I had met held such sentiments, wouldn't one rescue me from my sordid lifestyle and make me a lady like Prince Charming did in so many fairy tales?

Yes!

Had any?

No!

Would Ben?

Not bloody likely!

I resolved Benjamin Barrymore would end up in an arranged marriage as soon as his family members found a suitable bride. Until that daunting day, Benny Boy would play the field like most other hot-blooded men in their thirties.

"Earth to Bella. Hey, are you wearing an earpiece?" he asked, interrupting my thoughts.

"Excuse you?" I gasped, aware of how closely he stood next to me.

He shook his head. "Bella, not ten seconds ago, I asked how you were doing. And you ignored me, acting as if you did not know who I was?"

Realizing it was impossible to play my bullshit game with Ben, I looked into his eyes and shrugged. "Of course, I heard you. I did not know whether you were speaking to me or another woman. Now that I understand that it was me you were addressing allow me to exchange the same civility." I stood tall and grimaced. "Evening, Ben," I said sharply to conceal my fear. "I'm here with a friend." I paused, pointed at a bunch of strangers, and willed myself to think.

What would my imaginary friend's name be? And what if he wanted to meet this fictitious person? Shoot! You are in trouble, Bella. And by trouble, I mean a big mess because significant problems are heading your way, and there will be no escaping the lies once you explain one of your crazy stories. I shrugged again and offered a sweet smile. "I was born and raised in South Florida, Ben. Yes, I may live a meagre existence in Miami, but I, too, have wealthy friends across the State, particularly in Palm Beach County."

I noticed him flustering at the attack and the indignant tone in my voice, and I regretted blasting his inquiry. My heart sank as I realized my unworthiness, regretting my mocking words. He had tried to make small talk, and I had kicked him to the curb. Unaware of my secret life, Ben would either extend a helping hand or sever ties with me if he became suspicious. Troubled with that knowledge, I moved backward, trying to avoid the intensity in his eyes, which bore into my whimsical soul as if reading my world inside out.

"I didn't mean to upset you," he sighed, gnawing his inner cheek. "I was trying to get you to open up. That is all," he explained. "You're like a sister to me. I would never want to hurt or injure your pride, and I would allow no one else to do so. Can we please be friends?" He then extended his right hand for me to hold so we could shake, an action in his mind that would or could signal a truce.

I wanted to reach for his hand, but I was so fearful that my client Mitch might see my friendly banter as a threat to his masculinity that I had no choice but to rebuff Ben's peace offering. Additionally, his charming demeanor intimidated and provoked me more than I wanted to acknowledge. So, instead of making peace, I turned away and cursed myself to the moon and back.

What is wrong with you? I wanted to scream. You are such a foolish woman; wise up before you lose it all, Harry included—get a grip of yourself.

I faked a cough, feigning a need for water. It was my only weapon of distraction to escape Ben, and considering I was under so much pressure, I needed to recap my story. I sniffled my nose, reached for a hanky, then tripped and fell to the floor like a blundering idiot.

To say I had become the sole entertainment in the room was an understatement. Instantly, male guests rushed to my side. They clawed at my arms, waist, and even my legs to pull me upward and off the marble floor, and with my eyes closed in shame, I could only listen to their cries of dismay.

My head spun with questions such as...

Are you injured?

Would you like to go to the hospital?

Do you need to see a doctor?

One woman expressed how embarrassed she was for me, and another urged her husband to hurry so that they could finish the dance, as the song playing was one of her favorites.

Charming, I thought. Humiliated and shaking like a puppy caught urinating on a brand-new rug, I sobbed, and who could blame me? I should not have created such a scene by falling in front of everyone. Still, it was not something I had done with intent; it was an accident, a situation that humiliated me now and would continue to do so until the end of time.

A stranger tried to straighten my dress, and my mind reeled in dismay. All I wanted to do was cry aloud that I was not too fond of being manhandled, and I wanted to go home. But I stayed quiet as a proper lady should and smiled a gracious thank you to my persistent helper before reaching for my clutch-style handbag, whose contents fell outside my purse and were visible to all. That caused me more distress because others could see everything I concealed.

So much for trying to be incognito, I hissed. Now, my efforts to be elusive had fallen to the wayside, all because of a slip and fall, causing me to become the focal point of the room, a laughingstock. My dismal behavior made the meaner partygoers scoff in alarm, particularly the ladies whose competitive eyes mocked my inexperience and lack of decorum. Hey, I never said I was born into the same class of status as most here. I have tried in vain to blend in, and though I am now a freak show, it was not a title I wanted to claim, especially here.

At that moment, a man effortlessly lifted me to my feet, his hands securely clutched my waist. I wanted to question his strength in my inelegant and clumsy position, but I was too embarrassed to look him in the face. Instead, I glanced at my dress and adjusted the bodice. However, I almost fell again when I saw that my swollen breasts had nearly spilled out of the low-cut décolletage. I lowered my head to avoid others seeing the flush of color that swept across my timid face.

Thankfully, a live band took to the stage and played instrumental tunes. I wanted them to play a song that others would recognize, and instead of focusing on me, they would retreat to the dance floor, but with no such luck.

After regretting my clumsy fall, I saw Ben standing before me. His arms stayed wrapped around my waist, his concerned gaze never wavering. So, you were my Superman, my hero, I mused, wanting to ask, but I was too afraid to investigate the depth of his sympathetic features.

Ben rattled me to the core because he had mesmerizing eyes that were bluer than the deepest oceans and brighter than the sky on a sunny day, which is daily in South Florida. Try as I might, I could not ignore his penetrating gaze, and looking upward, I stared back into hues of blue. As we connected, I noticed how intensely his eyes quizzed my own, and the care he showed made my body shudder in ways I am too ashamed to mention.

I may explain later in this story, but I have more to tell first. I am thinking about Benny Boy. It was an enchanting moment as we locked eyes, a magical connection where blue met blue, and time stood still.

Ben's blueness, filled with worry and apprehension, was the only bizarre token. I had never dreamed or imagined that he would or could care about someone like me. Yet, all I could see was distress in the glint of his eyes.

At the same time, my face expressed my disdain for being so close to this ridiculously delicious man, one of the most gorgeous in Palm Beach County, and for good reason.

Ben Barrymore was beyond perfection. He was tall, sandy-haired, and physically fit from daily workouts. His long, luscious lashes fluttered atop and emphasized the mirrors of his soul.

I tried to fantasize that my attendance at this event was for other reasons and not the reality that slaps my face every chance it gets. If convincing? I might flirt, even risk gazing into the depth of his sincerity, and give him a run for his money because I am an excellent flirt.

Now, heroic Ben may have mastered the art of seduction. But I, too, can play that game, and when I put my mind to it, I can outstare anyone, even sweet, caring Ben, even if his seductive look bores into my heart at a million miles per hour.

Sadly, I could not tell him, as I was on a mission.

I also want to mention that I have a boyfriend who was partying in Miami without concern about my whereabouts. And that worked out fine, particularly on nights like tonight. Though I adored Harry, he cannot enlighten my emotions or soften my hardened heart like Ben Barrymore.

Suddenly remembering that Ben's arms still encased my slender waist, I unfolded his fingers and pushed his grip away before I whispered, "No," which did not go down well, as Benny Boy did not understand the meaning of no.

I watched as he returned his hands inside his trouser pockets; all the while, he watched as I tried to tame the strands of hair cascading over my brow.

"Do you want me to help you?" he asked with a flirtatious smile.

"No!" I snapped. "I'm not a child anymore."

"You sure look like one."

"Gee, thanks."

He shrugged. "I did not mean to offend you, Bella," he spoke earnestly. "I just cannot say anything right tonight, as everything I say to you is an insult or taken the wrong way."

"Ben," I groaned. "You just called me a kid, which I'm not. I am no longer that little girl who played in your parents' garden. In case you haven't noticed, I'm a grown woman."

"Oh, I noticed," he teased.

"Give it a rest, Ben. I am here with my friend Beatrice Ryder," I lied. "Besides, what do you care? I am sure you have brought a date to this event. Knowing you, Benny Boy, you brought half a dozen women, which is so gross. Yuck!" I scoffed and marched away at a fast pace.

I paused before a floor-to-ceiling mirror, stood aghast at the mess staring back at me, and at once tended to my disheveled clothing and fallen hairstyle. At the same time, a tug of rationality sprung from my mind. Despite my attraction to Ben, seeing him, much less talking to him, was one of the biggest mistakes of the night. It was worse than falling in front of everyone because I had brought attention to myself, and knowing men were more inclined to gossip, especially men over thirty who had not settled in a committed relationship or were not married with children, scared me. Sadly, single men had spare time to preoccupy themselves with whimsical thoughts.

I placed a clip on the side of my temple and secured a strand of hair that refused to stay put. Looking at my reflection, I saw Ben standing three feet behind me. At once, I turned to confront the stubborn, spoiled boy who refused to accept that I was not interested in him, least of all his ravishing, good looks, and family money. Let another girl deal with both prison sentences because, in my life, I preferred to fly solo and answer no one.

"You look gorgeous, Bella," Ben complimented and sighed. "I'm sorry we got off on the wrong foot. Can we try again?"

"Ben," I said, a condescending tone in my voice, as I was no longer enjoying his company. "Do you see that woman over there?" I motioned to his right and watched as he turned. He nodded, looking glum, before chewing his inner cheek again. "She has the biggest crush on you, okay?"

Nodding again, he tried to argue, but I cut him short. "Listen, Benny Boy, and listen carefully. I am sorry to inform you that I am not interested in chatting with you. And must I remind you I have a boyfriend with whom you are friends?"

"We conduct business together, Bella," he argued. "I would not say we're friends."

"Well, you both attend boating events in Miami," I said, mindful of their countless trips together.

"That's just meaningless corporate stuff that we have to do because I invested in his company," he said and paused. "If Harry were a friend of mine, don't you think I would have invited him here with me tonight?" he asked before adding. Of course, I would. Think about it, Bella. Is Harry here? No! The reason for that is that he is not my friend."

Instead of listening to his explanation, I turned away and waved to Beatrice Ryder and Emily Parker as they prepared to leave the gala. "Goodnight, and I'll ring you tomorrow, Beatrice," I said warmly. Then, I returned my gaze to this rogue of a man who was becoming a thorn in my side. "Ben,

Harry would be upset if he heard what you said. You realize he thinks you are both friends, right?"

Ben shook his head. "You're wrong. Harry understands we are only business associates. True, Harry and I are together at fishing tournaments across the State. Still, it is only public relations for his company. You are the only fool to believe we are friends. Harry understands our relationship perfectly."

"Then why spend certain holidays at his house?" I asked, confused.

"I attend those parties because Harry invites all his investors, and it would be a pretty shitty thing for me to do if I didn't show up," Ben said, throwing his arms in the air. "Right?"

"I guess," I agreed, seeing the frustration in Benny Boy's eyes, and I felt like a witch for questioning him.

"So, can we be friends now?" I did not answer, as I did not know what to say. I nodded and stared at my feet, swelling in the five-inch heels I had bought for this event.

We stood in silence, and it seemed like hours had passed, but it was no longer than ten or twenty seconds. I was surprised to find myself staring at Ben's dazzling smile as he greeted a family member, and watching how he conducted himself made me weak. I also loved his new hairstyle. Though it was shorter than he usually wore, I could still see the wavy curls cascading down his neck, and he looked gorgeous. For the strangest reason, I found it adorable, as intoxicating as a puppy's first trim.

I blushed, aware that I was staring and becoming spellbound by his magnetism. Then, to knock sense into my visible admiration, I shuffled my feet just as he bid goodbye to his uncle and reached for my arm, which I yanked away.

"I'm sorry," he said as his hand fell to his side. "After seeing you, I became too eager and forgot my place. I noticed you looking, so do you like it?" he asked, his fingers smoothing through a thick patch atop his crown. I was worried the barber had cut it too short, as I prefer my hair longer, but I guess I will learn to like it," he added, offering a friendly smile.

"I don't see any difference," I lied.

"You don't?"

"Ben, I never give you a second glance. So, for you to assume I would recognize a fresh cut is insane. Perhaps a girlfriend or a friend might be more observant, but since I'm neither, I'm sorry, but I don't see any change."

I watched as he ran his strong, long fingers through his hair. I longed to experience the touch of his hand again, but realizing that was impossible, I turned to leave. "It is getting late, and I have to go," I lied again because until my boss, Lisa, messaged me to inform me my assignment was over, I was stuck like a caged animal in a Big Top Circus show on display to all.

"Do you have to go?" Ben asked, puzzled. "Why not stay so we can talk, drink, and maybe even dance?"

My heart ached as I gnawed at my lower lip once again. Ben's earnestness was undeniable, and I longed to spend more time with him. But my conscience, a constant reminder of my professional commitment to this ball, intervened. I was still indebted to Mitch Carter, who had paid for four hours of my time, and I could not ignore the fact that I owed his roving eyes ten more minutes. After bumping into Ben, I liked him more than ever, but the fear that he might uncover my business dealings with the mature man who had hired my services terrified me. "Ben! I have a long trip home, and though I drink, I never drink when I have to drive, and let's not forget, I'm driving back to Miami."

"Come on, Bella. You are acting like a sixty-year-old woman," he teased, and his hunger burned into my eyes. "I'll have my chauffeur take you home, and I swear if you want to spend the night, I won't try anything, promise."

My expression softened because he looked hot with his pleading eyes. His sincerity and inquisitive demeanor seemed genuine, which should have provided comfort, but it left me frantic.

Ben Barrymore was a hot commodity. Born into extreme wealth, he was personable and a genuinely lovely guy who put a capital G in gentleman. His physique was solid and lean. His broad shoulders emphasized a trim stomach, and long muscular legs and muscular arms stressed his height. I can only imagine the beautiful chest underneath his tuxedo and pressed white shirt. In my heart, I could not resist his chiseled good looks and expressive eyes, not forgetting his voluptuous lips that softened as he spoke. He was too hot to manage, particularly for a poor girl like me, and with that reality, I concluded I could not be friends with this gracious man.

Ben was Palm Beach's most eligible bachelor and a local girl with social graces was a better match for him than a woman like me. Prestige and luxury were not the family name I carried. As tempted as I was, I feared rejection, which would be inevitable because Ben's family would not accept me as a future bride.

Mother and Father Barrymore want their son to marry a girl from a wealthy family. I cannot imagine their horror should I have allowed myself to date Ben, who had asked me out when I was in my late teens, but that was baby love, and nothing came from first love. If anything, a first relationship was a learning experience, to teach a person how to correct their naive ways and better themselves for the adult love that would come once in a person's twenties, thirties, even forties, or never.

I blushed as Ben placed both hands in prayer mode and pleaded with me to reconsider. "Come on, Bella. It will be a fantastic night, especially with you here, as you are the most exciting girl in the room. Please stay," he begged.

"Ben, should I decide to stay, please understand that I have no spare clothes here and cannot leave wearing this elaborate dress tomorrow morning. Besides, I have Harry in Miami, who is wondering where I am, and honestly, this is not my scene." I paused, and my heart sank as I saw my benefactor, Mitch Carter, standing nearby. I feared he would be angry. Yet, after seeing his mouth mime thank you and signal, I was free to leave. I was relieved and almost tempted to stay. However, imagining the gossip that would follow, I knew I could not. "Listen, I have to go, Ben. Truly, I do. Though, I am sure half the women here will be happy to entertain you for the rest of the evening. Sorry, but I am just too tired."

Ben sought my arm and grasped it hard, sending an electronic spark throughout my body, and I jumped.

"Awe, come on, Bella. You do not have to go, do you?" He asked again. "Can't we chat? We haven't spoken for over five minutes in almost fifteen years."

"Ben, Benny, Barrymore! Please understand that this is not my scene. You and I are different, and no matter how you want to mix things up, we know there's no future for us or our friendship."

"But why?"

"Because this is not my life, that's why." I snapped harsher than I had intended and regretted my rudeness. Still, it was the truth.

My mother told me the truth would set you free, but it may hurt others or something similar, and seeing Ben's disdain, I realized her words were correct. After noticing his sadness, I wanted to reach out and tell him it was for the best, but I had to be realistic and keep him at bay. I was sure Ben did not know that I was poor. My poverty would mortify him. I rented my gown, my friend styled my hair, and my handbag and shoes were on loan from a local boutique. That salesclerk had yet to learn that I planned to damage both items and return them as soon as the shop opened the next day.

I will admit to another ghastly habit. How disgusting is it to buy items, wear them, break them, and then return the merchandise for a refund?

Did I mention that I would reveal more events as you read along? I will. So, stay tuned, and I will tell you all my secrets.

I noticed Ben's shoulders slumped, and he lowered his head in defeat. Witnessing him become so sad hurts me more than I cared to admit.

What was I doing?

I am on a paid date, a distraction for Mitch Carter, and here I am, encouraging Ben, a friend of my boyfriend and someone I have known since childhood, to fight for me, fight till the end, as if I am suggesting he may win me over.

I was playing with fire, and knowing such flames could burn and torture me if I stayed at this resort with Ben Barrymore, I decided it was time to leave.

"Don't look now," I told Ben, "But there is a gorgeous blonde with an athletic figure, and she is dressed to the nines and eyeing you up from head to toe. If you want an introduction, let me know?"

"Grow up, Bella. I do not need help to meet women," he answered angrily, fists by his side and ready to fight. The idea of a Barbie Doll who spends half her day locked inside the bathroom, obsessively primping until she reaches perfection, holds no interest to me.

"My apologies. I was only trying to help."

"Don't bother, and don't do me any favors. I am not a charity case. If I want one of those fake, high-maintenance chicks, I can get them anytime, day or night, got it?"

"Yes," I stammered, glancing at a tall palm in the room's far corner. "I'm sorry. I did not mean to insult you. Besides, I must go, Ben. Honest. Although I admit it is good to see you, I was shocked and maybe nervous at first, but now I'm glad I bumped into you." I lied again. "In better times, Ben. Other than that, I hope you have a perfect evening."

"Bella, I have so much I want to learn about you and more that I want to tell you. Is it so abnormal to admit that I want to spend time with you, get to know you, and try to understand what makes you tick? Is it so terrible for me to ask for a couple of hours of your time?"

"Of course not. It is just that I live far away, and I am exhausted as I had a lot of manuscripts to proofread earlier today. I'm sorry, but I have to go."

The above statement was the only truth I had spoken the entire evening. Witnessing Ben's anguish was troubling, but I was here for a business appointment. Since it was over, I had to leave this resort, even if that meant leaving Ben lonely and miserable.

Again, I realized Benny Boy would and could become a problem if he needed to own and have someone to love to complete his masculinity, which I suspected.

In all the mindless madness, I pardoned myself, using a need to visit the ladies' room as the only excuse I could muster. Once inside the sterile, white-tiled bathroom, I noticed how brightly lit the room looked compared to the romantic lighting outside. I counted at least one hundred LED bulbs along a vanity mirrored wall and one thousand shining down from the ceiling. Though not to my taste, the illuminated bathroom was a makeup artist's dream, as the harsh lighting emphasized colors that needed blending, unevenly outlined lips, and pimples requiring concealer. To the left was an extensive line of private booths filled with toilets and personal items most women needed. To the right of the room were lounge chairs and massage tables with attendants eager to rub away whatever tension a high society lady may be experiencing. In the middle of the bathroom were gleaming clean sinks and a helper handing out fresh towels to guests needing to dry their washed hands.

Observing a tired-looking woman using a cloth to help a socialite remove a stain from her dress, I decided the overworked attendant needed a break. So, I shoved past the Barbie Dolls, as Ben had called them, and sat down next to the only working-class woman in the entire room aside from myself, who appeared decent. She was a Jamaican bathroom clerk who spent most nights aiding wealthy women who never said thank you or left a tip.

I sat on the only available chair I could find and nitpicked my scrambled thoughts to analyze my current situation, of which I am not proud. Since I knew my precarious activities could unravel in the blink of an eye and have the potential to destroy other people, I concluded I must fly solo.

You may think I am sitting or standing on an easy street but trust me when I tell you I am not. Yes, the double life pays well. Though it is challenging work and only suitable for those who can tolerate being alone, which works for me because despite how close I am to Harry, I am on my own, and the isolation is crippling. Still, I decided to become a professional companion. Initially, I did not think about how hard it would be to keep my occupation a secret, nor did I think about bumping into a man like Ben while on a date. I jumped in headfirst without concern, as it was business and nothing more.

After two months of moonlighting, I cannot stop, as I am addicted to easy cash and involved in the drama. While there is no point crying over spilled milk, I yearned to be free. On my escapades, no one would have been wiser if I kept my distance, did as instructed, and did not have too much to drink, which would have caused a scene. I planned to behave that way tonight, but bumping into Ben had flung my well-laid-out plans out the window, all four floors down to the street below.

A nervous flutter in the pit of my stomach caused me to gasp, and to calm myself, I crossed my legs, leaned back against the chair's headrest, and watched the drama unfold. In all fairness, and perhaps because I work hard, it was overwhelming how rich people acted so cheaply compared to working-class people who were more generous. Of course, rich people have money because they detest spending their cash but would burn through other people's savings without hesitation.

I inhaled and exhaled as the bathroom emptied. I smiled at the attendant, whose name tag read Rosalie. Then I rose from my comfortable seat, fished through my handbag, pulled out a fifty-dollar bill, and placed it into a cup on the bathroom counter.

She raised her hands and gestured a prayer to express her gratitude. In turn, I patted her arm and reminded her that patience is a virtue. We both laughed because we understood what I meant.

At five minutes past midnight, I opened the bathroom door and peered outside to check if Ben had rejoined friends and would no longer be a distraction. I spotted him chatting with an older man, which was my signal to exit the venue.

"Man trouble?" Rosalie asked.

Startled, I rolled my eyes. "No such luck," I replied and smiled.

"Rubbish, a girl as beautiful as you must have men chasing you all over town," she beamed a smile so bright I swear I saw a halo atop her crown.

"You're too kind," I sighed. "But I appreciate the gesture."

"It's the truth!" she insisted as she folded towels. "I wouldn't tell you tales. I have seen you here before, and you have always appreciated me. Unlike most women who come here, you are a pleasant lady, and I'm grateful for your tips."

"You're also a good woman, Rosalie," I complimented.

"Why are you so generous with me?"

"You work hard. Why not?"

"But you always give me fifty dollars every time you come. Isn't it too much money?"

"Look at it this way, Rosalie. It will keep you honest."

"And I will keep you safe each time you visit."

A brief conversation later, and we bid to each other goodnight. I tiptoed over the slippery bathroom floor, and as I struggled to close the heavy door, I saw Rosalie smile as she held her money. Though I longed to give her more cash, I had hidden my earnings inside my girdle. So, I grinned and blew her a kiss. "Be careful driving home, Rosalie. There will be about fifty people driving drunk after this group leaves the building," I cautioned. But before she replied, I vacated the bathroom.

It was eleven minutes past midnight, and as I walked toward the venue exit doors, I was sad that I would not talk to Ben again and patted the wad of cash hidden in my undergarments. In a strange sense, I missed the boy I had known since the beginning of time.

I strolled along the carpeted hallway toward the resort's lobby and reflected on seeing Ben. Still, I cursed myself for forgetting to thank him for saving my dignity. I should have been more direct and explained why I was at the gala instead of acting mysterious and aloof. At that moment, I hated myself for being such a cold fish toward a man who offered nothing but kindness and affection. Regrettably, I urged myself to stop criticizing my mistakes and focus on my exit.

The gossipers at The Carlisle Hotel will pass along everything I expressed to Ben and exaggerate it tenfold before breaking their necks to tell Harry. Somehow, I feared my boyfriend would learn about my night out, and the exposure would kill me, not to mention the inevitable arguments that would follow.

Bella, I told myself. You know that part of your life is something you have struggled to keep secret. You cannot allow a soft spot for Benny Boy to alter your life's journey because this is your making, your disaster, and your karma.

I pressed the elevator button and rushed inside before the doors fully opened. Once there, I leaned against a gold-plated bar and heaved a sigh of relief that I had fulfilled my duty and was free.

Free to do as I please.

I was free to roam the city streets and escape the persistent questions in Benjamin Barrymore's voice.

Others, like you, dear reader, may find my attendance at tonight's ball impressive, as one rarely receives an invitation to such a magical party. Yet, in my mind's eye, all I saw was a living hell of life because these upper-crust people shrouded every hour in deception, and I was not too fond of their falsity.

Plus, right now, I have bigger fish to fry.

First, I am determined to avoid Ben at every future event because Benny Boy appears to have positioned himself as my protector, bodyguard, or potential romantic partner.

Why?

Who knew?

Do you?

I certainly do not.

Seconds later, the elevator beeped to signal a stop on another floor. I stiffened and reminded myself to keep up my guard, as I was not out of The Carlisle yet. I still had a long trek ahead until I reached the hotel's main entrance and the city's freedom below. The elevator doors swung open, and as a couple entered, I darted out of the metal chamber that had promised to take me to ground zero.

You fool, I cursed. It would be best to take the elevator down to the lobby. Now, you are stuck on this floor until another lift becomes available. I leaned against a tall pillar and struggled to regain composure as my hopes shattered, almost causing me to burst into tears as I struggled to adjust my nineteenth century-style dress. And that proved to be my hundredth mistake of the evening. Glancing down the hallway, I spotted unfettered Ben approaching me with a forceful look, and he did not seem happy.

"Please don't try to engage me in another meaningless conversation," I begged, wanting to inform him he was borderline stalking, which was against the law. Instead, I grimaced and shied away.

Ben's eyes focused on my bustier, which was ridiculous because I am not a large-chested woman; the fussy dress gave that impression, not forgetting the excess padding in the corset I wore underneath. Yet, he appeared intrigued, almost skeptical, with a need to inquire if I had had breast enhancement surgery, hence another embarrassing moment, and yes, my skin flushed with color again. However, I wanted to laugh because he would be disappointed should he ever discover that underneath the elaborate dress I wore was a body with minimal curves, for I am straight up and down, a figure like a boy. My mother used to tell close friends that her daughter, Bella, was an adventurous child, preferring jeans, tees, and sneakers. Though she forced me to wear dresses to church and various other places, she explained it was like moving a mountain.

Bless her heart, my mother was not lying in her vocal description of her stubborn, opinionated daughter, as I preferred hanging out with boys, going fishing, playing soccer, and biking. My favorite pastime was jumping from one tree branch to another while yelling words like Tarzan. Activities like dressing dolls, playing house, and dreaming about the latest pop star could not have been more boring.

I was a masculine girl with a phony, uncompromising attitude who hid my meager curves under baggy sweatshirts and fleece pants. The same principle has continued into my twenties, as I still dress in jeans and a casual shirt and wear either shorts or gym clothes. Aside from nights like tonight, I never wear dresses. Still, this evening's shindig was unavoidable. Despite my pleas to my boss, Lisa, to give me a different assignment, she refused and told me to accept and work on the date, which I did with professionalism throughout the evening. It was when Ben showed up that all hell broke loose and gave me no way out, regardless of how off-putting I had behaved toward his fragile ego.

I stood stiffly and frowned at the thunderous sky etched across a skylight. Standing underneath the rolling clouds, I sighed. The roads would be treacherous tonight, I groaned.

My hands shook, and I shoved them inside my pockets. I looked through the glass tomb, enthralled by the darkened rain splattering against the transparent rooftop. It was slightly comforting to see the windy horizon, but it reminded me that the Carlisle was still holding me captive.

I looked down at my shoes. My feet were beginning to blister and sweat. I glanced along the hallway, happy to realize I was alone. Hooray, I wanted to cheer, feeling no more distress from other people's expectations. Then, just as I moved away from the pillar, my thoughts fixed on pretending I had not seen Ben or his determination as he barged closer to where I strolled.

"What the hell, Bella," he said exasperatedly. "I've been searching for you for ages. What is wrong with you?"

I scowled at him. "As I told you earlier, Benny Boy. I am leaving as I have a long drive home. Since we did not arrive together, I have no responsibility to inform you of my intentions, particularly since we are not friends." I replied.

"What in God's name did I do that was so awful for you to treat me with such utter disgust?"

"Nothing!" I yelled, not caring if the people lingering in the hallway overheard. "I'm just not interested in talking to you, Ben. Do you understand that? If so, respect my wishes and leave me alone."

"But," he said, throwing his arms upwards again. "What the fuck did I do to you, Bella? I thought we were old friends. Why are you acting like such a bitch?"

Noticing a group of strangers had stopped talking and were now eavesdropping on our conversation, I lost my composure and trembled as unease shook my body. "Your language is a disgrace," I criticized. "Everyone can hear you acting like a teenage boy having a tantrum because you cannot have your way."

"I don't give a fuck what those dummies can hear," Ben snapped. "I only care about you and am trying to understand what I did wrong?" In a flash, I clutched my handbag and marched away. I would not listen to a drunkard's rantings, even if the words spilled out of Ben Barrymore's mouth.

After watching how my father slammed my mother against every wall in our rundown home, I swore no man would ever put me through such abuse, and that was a principle I have held to this day.

Even Ben, with all his riches, was not getting off easy because I would rather spend time with an ugly older man who treated me like a princess than deal with the belligerent ranting of a drunk.

Early in the morning, my sixth sense told me to refuse this gig because dreadful things could happen. Since I rarely drive to Palm Beach, I almost backed out, as I was not too fond of the long drive. Instead, I preferred boat excursions to the Bahamas, where I am away from anyone and everyone I am acquainted with, particularly people like Ben. But, like an idiot, I caved to my agency's demands and took this assignment. Now, hours later, and while off Mitch Carter's paid timeline, I am borderline enraged as I walk back to the elevator. To add insult to misery, the fancy dress that exposed my hidden curves also attracted the lustful eyes of most men I crossed paths with, and that drove me insane.

Not daring to look back, I pressed the elevator button and focused on the double doors, willing them to open as I instructed myself to keep my cool. If the lift did not arrive soon, I would walk to the nearest emergency exit and run.

Exasperated, I chastised myself for wearing such an uncomfortable outfit. Then I reminded myself that the dress choice belonged to my client Mitch Carter and had nothing to do with my preference, as on assignments like tonight, I could not dress myself, which was frustrating. However, the glamorous gown gracing my body was stunning, and knowing the designer had created a dress fit for a princess, I embraced wearing its silky fabrication, as it provided me with a sense of luxury. Nonetheless, it was not one I would wear because I could not afford it in a hundred years of slave labor.

I pondered if Ben's mind was curious and if he wondered how I managed to afford such extravagant garments. However, I feared the answer because, despite our altercation, I foresaw Ben, and I would meet again. In that instant, I found myself unable to combust any sensible thoughts, which was another reason I dumped Benny Boy like the plague and headed home. Besides, it would only be a matter of time before he would ask who else my friends were at Palm Beach. I cannot think of another person's name besides Beatrice Ryder and Mitch Carter.

I may be a good liar to strangers, but I cannot lie to those I care about, and aside from Ben being the most gorgeous man I had ever met, he was also the most annoying because he had a nosiness that drove me insane.

In my short life, I have found that men can ask intrusive questions so straightforwardly that they can sound like an interrogation and become impossible to answer, and Ben was no exception. I can still hear his queries swirling throughout my mind, and his intense scrutiny scared me to death.

Born on July 1st, 1986, in the year of the Tiger, and ruled by the star sign Cancer, Benjamin Barrymore held a natural curiosity like an Aquarius male, though less intense than a Scorpio. Alongside a burning desire to claim his territory, he was forceful and proud. Ben had planned his ownership map a thousand years before birth, and Benny Boy would not allow rejection to deter his quest for love. Nothing would stop Benny Boy from achieving what he wanted, except the sharp wit tongue of a woman like me, who could send this boisterous crab back inside his shell.

I remember how painstakingly shy Ben was when we first met. Still, as the years passed, he revealed himself more openly, mainly because he was unafraid of emotional depth.

Most women would find this romantic.

I found it frightening because he had become comfortable in my company, and the intensity of his emotion was wide open. His intuitive mind was also always awake and on target. However, his ability to notice my feelings, speak my words before I had uttered them, or knowing that I was trying to hide something was worse. If I allowed him into my life, he would uncover secrets and expose me as deceptive, and Benny Boy detests liars.

There is no such thing as casual with a man like Ben, who is not interested in small talk. He wanted answers to questions to understand and climb inside a woman's heart, mind, and soul because knowing everything and forgetting nothing consumed him.

To put it bluntly, darling Ben was clingy. It was because he was a crab with claws. Intuition tells me he falls in love hard and just as fast when deciding on a partner.

Such is his desire for love.

In love, Benny Boy could not separate himself from whatever or whoever he was obsessing over. Because his sensitivity would lead to codependency, which would open Pandora's box of problems for a girl like me, I had no choice but to rebuff his advances.

Okay, I am aware of what you are thinking, and I will admit I lied when I mentioned I knew nothing about Benny Boy. And for that, I apologize, but from my lips to God's ears, I swear you are the only people in this universe who know I have this delightful man's life path cemented in my soul.

So, try to keep it a secret, like I had.

Well, until now, that was.

Thank you.

Let me go back to Ben.

Have you ever noticed that people born under the sign of cancer have a mindset that runs into overdrive? If so, then you will, without a doubt, have experienced the following interrogation.

I did not know you had friends in Palm Beach.

How did you get here?

Who do you know?

Do we share mutual friends?

The questions would never end.

At the same time, I can often be quick with my fake answers, as I am an excellent storyteller, and I have rehearsed my elaborate tales since day one. However, I do clam up when in the company of someone I care about more than I should, a particular person, such as a man like Ben, who can stifle my well-laid-out plans and leave me vulnerable.

It may be down to an emotional reaction. When you do not hold affection for someone, days, nights, and plans pass by at lightning speed. Yet, the minute your heart is involved, feelings can take you to places your mind has no right to visit. Suddenly, all plans nosedive faster than a shooting star across the atmosphere.

Let us pretend I sought him out, returned to his side, and stood face to face if only to explain the complexities of my life.

Can you understand I would become a rambling idiot who would sink to the bottom of the ocean faster than the Titanic because my mind would not be so sharp? Then, to add insult to injury, I would more likely redden brighter than a ripe strawberry and fall to the ground again because I am tired and withered in shame. I am confident in my heart that defeat would be the only outcome.

Yes, I have avoided intrusive questions and people's nagging inquiries. I will continue to do so until I can become a woman to be proud of.

I orchestrate my life to keep secrets hidden and never risk exposure. Still, tonight, my hardship could all come crashing down. All my dreams could shatter into pieces for all to see, and I cannot allow that to happen.

If I did?

Destruction would prevail.

Not only would I be outcast by all, but I would have to move to a different part of America, to one of those small towns where nobody knew my name, or into obscurity amongst the wildlife tucked away in some State Park where deer, moose, and goodness knows what else roam in the darkness of night. Overwhelmed by a sense of melancholy, I dragged my exhausted feet towards the quickest exit of The Carlisle, an enormous staircase built with a minimum of fifty steps.

The cool breeze from an air conditioning unit blasted across my bare shoulders. I shuddered while debating how difficult climbing down such a steep staircase in high heels could be.

Not as difficult as facing the intensity in Ben's eyes again, I surmised and prepped myself to endure the biggest challenge of the night because from atop the stairwell, it appeared as if I was standing on an Egyptian Pyramid and fearing heights. I froze.

My conscience urged me to return to the elevator, but I resisted. In my stubbornness, I took a step forward, only to realize that descending the steps was not for me or my dress. With a heavy heart, I retreated from the stairs. I hurried back to the lift, hoping to distance myself from all the falsities I had experienced.

I noticed my palms were wet, and my stomach fluttered. Despite my fear, I strolled, mindful not to hurry to the point of attracting attention, which was tricky in this multi-layered Victorian-era dress.

I rounded a corner and whisked past a palm tree whose overgrown, low, hanging branches clung to my hair and dress. I fought my way out of its thick, sticky leaves with vigor. Then I noticed people giggling at my struggles, which caused my heart to pound so loud that I swear it sounded like a drumbeat at a rock concert. They questioned my haste, but I no longer cared. I had had enough of their judgmental looks and needed to leave. Besides, bumping into Benny Boy again, mainly if he had drunk more alcohol, would end badly.

At that instant, I knew leaving was the worst thing I could have done because now, like most men, Ben would want answers to the questions that I knew were burning down into the core of his stomach. His ego would create a reason to contact me if only to ease his curiosity.

I should have never left.

No kidding! I scoffed.

Aware it would have helped if I had pretended, I had consumed far too much champagne and should have smiled seductively instead of acting like a crazy bitch, I cringed.

Why did you not think of that earlier? I hissed before chewing on my lips and pressing the elevator button again.

Why didn't you tell Ben you were a guest of a female friend? A friend, who was also attending the ball, someone like Beatrice Ryder. She was a fabulous Southern Belle with various answers about life's complications. Why, Beatrice informed me, it was not only the male species who had diamonds on the end of their dicks. Women were walking among us who had bigger diamonds, dicks, and balls than most men put together, and do you know what? She was right.

Isn't it frustrating how easy it is to reflect on our mistakes and see the outcomes we could have avoided if we had known the result before we acted like fools? Yes, I agree, as errors in my life were never visible upfront. I am oblivious to my mistakes until I am so stuck I cannot get out, particularly during the million and one questions Benny Boy always flings my way, which is worse than an interrogation from a spy from Red China.

I have never been to China.

The Caribbean and Europe are my usual haunting grounds. Although I plan to walk the Great Wall of China and explore its culture one day, a trip like that will require hundreds more companionship dates than the measly two dates per week I currently accept.

Thinking about how I should have acted tipsy from drinking too much champagne made my blood boil, as pretending drunkenness would have made me appear accessible and not the raving witch I had displayed to Ben, and that would have been a better solution.

But where was that idea twenty minutes ago?

I will tell you, trapped within my stupidity, is where it was. That is where it always was.

In lousy judgment, I had created a mystery that would captivate a man like Ben, who would fight to penetrate a part of my life that I had shrouded for years.

Forget him, Bella. He is not the man for you and will not save you. Only you can set yourself free, so stop dreaming and go home.

Uh-oh! How right was my last statement?

One hundred percent, I sighed.

Before long, I grew tired of waiting for the busy elevator and strolled back to the tallest indoor staircase I had ever seen. Three women gathered in a corner, champagne glasses in hand, engrossed in idle chatter about fashion, hairstylists, and manicurists, stopped and stared at me, but I was too melancholy to care.

Uh! I groaned. Their chronic complaints were more annoying than my own. Nonetheless, I smiled wryly, ignored their judgmental glances, and willed myself to surge the distance ahead. I rushed back to the pyramid I had stood atop only minutes before.

Well, fuck me, Freddy, but the depth that led to my exit was fucking insane.

Resolutely, I stood at the top of what seemed like The Great Pyramid of Giza and looked down at a magnificent glass door that led to the street below. Nervous, I wiped my brow and took a deep breath before hearing a group of aristocrats who, like most, had drank too many cocktails.

Before I took my first step, I calmed my breathing rapidly and descended the stairs one step at a time.

"Nice outfit," a sharp-dressed man called out.

"Excuse you?" I asked, confrontational, gripping the handrail that secured my stance.

"Sorry, I didn't mean to offend," he apologized. "I just want to say you were the hottest chick in the joint tonight."

"Thanks," I smirked. "Although, in my eyes, I saw a lot of attractive women at the ball."

"Maybe so," he said and checked his watch. "But you were the most captivating by far. Your silky skin and natural beauty are the most interesting. My name's Pete, and you are?"

"Tired!" I told him sharply, not in the mood to meet someone new after the chaotic night I had just had. "And, leaving."

"Be careful going down those steps. I would not want to pick you up from the ground for a second time this evening," the man named Pete teased before adding, "Safe travels home."

I ignored his sarcasm and focused on his recollection of my earlier fall, which annoyed me. Besides, I had a more significant situation to contend with because out of the corner of my eye, I could see that Benjamin Barrymore was less than six feet away and moving closer by the second.

I exude confidence, but I am not an arrogant woman. Still, I knew he was rushing to my side. I reckoned he had made himself my chief protector in his responsible mind. Regardless of whether I liked it, I would do as he instructs, as he knew best, which reminded me of Beatrice's comment about men and their big dick egos.

For the first time tonight, I laughed, and I mean, I genuinely laughed. As soon as the sun rises tomorrow, I will telephone my new friend and invite her to lunch, and if that means I will return to Palm Beach to do so, then so be it because I needed a woman like Beatrice Ryder in my miserable life.

A childhood memory springs to mind: I learned a crucial lesson in the church I attended with my mother.

The Lord giveth, and the Lord taketh away.

Blessed be the name of the Lord.

The recollection of that verse sent shivers down my spine. It was as if my Heavenly Father had touched my soul because he may have taken my beloved mother back home. But he has blessed me with Beatrice, who I sensed is a gift from Heaven. So, in reflecting on that verse, my lesson to you is to find fulfillment, trust in God, and understand his plans, regardless of the sufferings we may endure, are for a good reason because God is sovereign. He rules over all creation and has everything under control, and this brings Job comfort.

If you do not believe me, I implore you to check the solace God gave Job in any bible because what I wrote is true.

Do you need to be convinced, or are you too idle to search? Allow me to give you the exact place to read the passage.

King James Version. Job 1:21.

It may be tempting to doubt my words.

Please do not.

I may lie more than a dog who scratches as if covered in a million fleas. However, as I told you earlier, I only tell tales to protect the people I love, and since I do not know you, I cannot love you.

Therefore, you do not count.

Thank you for understanding.

I Focused on the steepness before my weary eyes. Because I was tired, I gripped the handrail, glanced at the corridor to check if any other perverts were following me with an illicit comment or proposal, and saw no one interesting enough for a second look. No one other than tall, robust, and inquisitive Ben refused to let me leave. To say he appeared obsessed was an understatement, as his eyes flashed from rage to lust.

I groaned again and stepped at the highest step before glancing at the daunting staircase that would take me to ground level and closer to my automobile, parked two streets away. Then, on the third step down, my heeled pumps became entangled in the stone, and I almost fell forward and plunged to my death.

In terror, I screamed aloud and willed a solution to appear fast, and I mean fast. The only aid I saw was Benny Boy's outstretched hand offering to guide me down Mount Kilimanjaro, which I ignored.

"Oh, come on, Bella," he urged. "Stepping over these uneven stones in those heels is far too dangerous. You are going to fall flat on your face. At least let me help."

"Go home, Ben," I told him rudely. "The last thing I need right now is a drunk pretending he is sober enough to stop me from slipping and plunging to my death."

"But I'm not drunk," he defended.

I arched my brow and rolled my eyes. "I can smell your breath from here, Ben, and trust me, you reek of alcohol."

"At most, I had one or two drinks, Bella. That does not make me drunk, nor does it make me unable to help you. So, please reach back and take my hand."

"Take it where?" I queried and pulled off my shoes. "Goodbye, Ben. It was nice to see you, to see you not. Adios Amigo." I laughed, relieved of my sobriety, as I was now able to outrun him. I ran down the staircase two steps at a time, which was difficult as I gripped two expensive shoes because, unlike Cinderella, I was not leaving any evidence behind.

Phew! I gasped, finishing my torturous sprint toward The Carlisle Resort's entryway. Still, I marveled at my triumphant finish, as it was not an easy task. Standing beside the elegant main entrance, I basked in the ambiance that I was home free and wanted to jump with joy, but the sight of Benny Boy bolting down The Great Pyramid of Giza brought me back to earth. Indifferently, I stepped into my ill-fitting heels, pushed open the massive glass doors, and exited into the night and the ghastly humidity.

Despite a torrential burst of rain, I was thankful for the Florida heat, which warmed my air-conditioned body and relaxed my alert mind. Suddenly, delighted that my mission had finished, I inhaled deeply and exhaled, no longer caring who was watching.

I was free!

I completed my assignment and outwitted Ben. It brought satisfaction to abandon everything despite the discomfort of the scorching, humid air clinging to my exposed shoulders. The amount of water vapor in the South Florida climate causes uncomfortable stickiness. I could feel it drenching the flesh on my body, causing my hair to frizz and my dress to cling tighter against my body, not forgetting that makeup was melting down on my face.

Mindful that I looked messy, I inhaled again and smiled. In stark contrast to the awkwardness, I had experienced earlier, I felt triumphant and optimistic that my attendance had fulfilled my client's wishes. And I was once again no longer concerned about my appearance.

I rejoiced, even as raindrops pelted my body, and a massive storm fell from rain-bearing clouds. The furious grey skyline hid the stars, and darkness covered the horizon with sadness. Before tumultuous tears fell from the heavens and pounded the city streets below, I basked in the rain as it trickled down my body and splattered over my new shoes, completely ruining both.

In an act of rebellion, I playfully lifted my dress, skipped along the cobblestone sidewalk, and quietly sang a song that had consumed my thoughts for days.

Though I expected a decent tip from Mitch, I had a keen sense that he would not be as generous as on earlier occasions because of the fiasco my fall had created, which was okay, as I am content my paid appearance was over.

Abruptly, I halted my pace, pressed my hand against my dress, and checked that the thick wad of money within a sealed envelope still lay inside the fitted girdle.

It was.

Hooray! I wanted to scream joy to the world. I also wanted to count my total earnings, as I had not earlier when

Mitch Carter's assistant, Greta, handed me the package. I should have, but he was wealthy and would not cheat me. Cunning Mitch would have counted forty-hundred-dollar bills twice before he packaged the cash inside a sealed Manila envelope alongside an explanatory note on his company's stationery explaining his wishes for the evening.

In my haste not to be late, I only read his request, which was, as usual, written eloquently on engraved paper sealed with a wax stamp that had his initials. Despite Mitch being an old creep, my wealthy client delivered a first-class presentation.

Beautiful Bella,

I cannot wait to see you tonight. I want you to enjoy the night as much as I do, and I hope you do. Please keep your distance from my wife but remain close enough for me to watch you, as you know how I enjoy seeing you waltz around the room.

Regards,

Mitch.

On my stroll to downtown Palm Beach, I pondered whether to drive home over Flagler Memorial or Royal Park Bridge across Lake Worth Lagoon. I chose the latter as it was closer to my car and a more scenic route. Plus, the traffic moved faster along Lakeview Avenue, a shorter distance to I-95 and less congested. On earlier trips, I traveled to the highway via Southern Boulevard, which was a preference, though it took longer. However, the route allowed me to bask in my dream of living amongst the riches of Palm Beach, even if it were a silly fantasy I knew would never come true. Since my early teens, I have fantasized about living life as a Palm Beach homemaker who caters to her husband's every need, and though it was a pathetic existence, I could not help but hold that vision within my heart.

I turned left off Coconut Row and strolled onto Worth Avenue, the most famous street in Palm Beach, only to cringe at the expensive shops that flaunted the best money can buy in designer handbags, clothing, and shoes.

In awe, I stood overwhelmed by the window displays of the upscale boutiques, art galleries, and fancy restaurants before I fell back to earth after realizing I could not afford one item.

True, I have earned four thousand dollars and am rich. However, I would be poor again by morning, as rent, car payments, and utility bills were due. After paying all of them, I would beg Lisa for another high-paying job. That realization made me cry because I was not fond of the work. I wish to make money legitimately instead of entertaining men at public functions. There was no stronger emotion than being rich, even if the moment was brief.

My father used to remind me that cash is King, and without it, you are nothing, and guess what? He was right. Sadly, he did not practice what he preached, as my dad spent all his hard-earned money at the local pub, where he drank away his minuscule salary week after week.

Crushed by that reality, my heart sank. Still, I dawdled along the illuminated street, daydreaming until I decidedly ignored the glamorous shops and expensive museums, as the items for sale extended my budget and my entire life's future earnings.

While rushing to a crossing signal, I noticed my feet swelling in the bolstering heat. Not making the crosswalk before the light changed, I stopped and groaned.

"Ouch!" I yelped, feeling my toes blister inside my tight shoes. Do you care if you walk barefoot?" I asked aloud. Though I did look around for nosey onlookers, I saw only three couples laughing and teasing each other, and compared to the crowd I had just left, this bunch appeared harmless.

Ingeniously, I contemplated removing my shoes, as I was not friends with these individuals and would never meet them again. So, I slipped my sweaty feet out of my painful pumps and took a left on Hibiscus Avenue, lingering outside a Chanel clothing store.

And do you know what?

I was no longer envious.

After a brief silence, I rejoiced. I was footloose, fancy-free, and much better off than this morning when I had no cash.

Yes, I mulled. Right now, life's good, and I am on cloud nine because nothing and nobody can ruin the happiness burning within my heart. The only person with the power to destroy this evening would be a police officer, arresting me for not wearing shoes and other things, too. However, local law enforcement would have to prove that, and a client like Mitch would not rat me out."

My face lit up with a broad smile as I bid goodnight to the dazzling buildings along Worth Avenue. Then, out of the corner of my eye, I saw dreamy Ben Barrymore leaning against a gallery window with his arms folded and a mischievous smile teasing his lips.

Surprised, I almost stumbled to the ground.

LIVELIHOOD

RUMI BELIEVED THAT if you are looking for a friend that is faultless, then you will be friendless...

I heard rock music echoing across the calm evening sky, and in my wish to avoid Ben. I focused on the song that burned within my mind. Still, the heavily tuned bass made it impossible to remember the lyrics, so I turned to face the gallant man standing by my side.

Far away, burning rubber wafted into my nostrils, reminding me of a childhood memory when a skunk sprayed me in yellow oil after I had wandered near its den while camping with my father.

Twenty years later, I cannot forget that foul odor or my mother's complaints as she struggled to rid my clothes of the offensive scent in a lake beside our campsite.

A car horn sounded, interrupting my thoughts; I spun around and saw a vehicle speeding along Hibiscus Avenue. Suddenly, I grew tense because I recognized the automobile and the driver.

The Porsche halted at my side. I raised my hand and motioned the driver to wait before returning my gaze to Ben. Seeing him unsettled on the bustling sidewalk, I cringed and took a deep breath. Though intrigued by his concern, I ignored his stance, walked toward the flashy automobile, and peered inside the passenger window. "How are you?" I muttered.

"Why are you standing on Worth Avenue at this ungodly hour?" My partner in crime, CJ Clarke, yelled over a raspy voice that sounded like Steven Tyler. "Where's your Toyota?"

"Hey, CJ," I said, ignoring her question. "Why are you driving on Hibiscus Avenue at this time? Isn't Miami your usual haunting ground?"

"No need to be a smart ass." She said, perturbed.

I glanced at her intently and struggled to make eye contact. "I didn't mean to be cocky. My night is going from bad to worse, and I'm having difficulty ditching a friend who won't take no for an answer." I frowned.

"Who's the hunk?"

"A fool who won't accept I'm not interested," I replied.

"You must have him bewitched then," she murmured smugly.

"What does it matter?" I asked, irritated. "He means nothing to me. I want to get out of here, that's all." I yawned, cringing at CJ.

"Is he bothering you?" she sounded concerned. I shrugged and rolled my eyes. "He thinks he's the shit. Do not mess with him, as he has major connections in Palm Beach," I cautioned.

"I don't care what he's got," she answered. "I am here because I need your help with a client."

"Don't talk to me about work right now," I snarled. I looked around to make sure nobody else heard her last comment. That is when I noticed Ben straining to eavesdrop on our conversation. Swiftly, I looked away and glared at CJ. "And don't mess this up for me," I hissed at her, resisting the urge to slap her smug face.

"Don't tell me what to do! Just get it together because we have places to go and people to fuck."

Mortified, I flung the car door open and sat inside. "Listen to me, CJ. Do not advertise our sordid occupation to everyone," I said, gritting my teeth. "I know that man, and he does not know what I do."

"A new boyfriend?" She teased and honked the car horn.

I shook my head. "You're acting like a child," I pointed out. "Just take me to my vehicle," I implored, struggling to fasten the safety belt. "I'm parked at the Hotel Abigail."

"Who's the sexy stranger?" CJ asked, lighting a cigarette.

"Goodness, CJ," I hissed, sitting pensively on the seat. "He's a friend of my boyfriend's and was at the ball I attended earlier. He is also strange. So, let's leave."

"But what about him? Shouldn't I offer him a ride home or, at the least, take him back to his vehicle?" Not waiting for my reply, CJ lowered the convertible top, rose from her seat, leaned against the windshield, and whistled long and hard. "Hey, stranger, if you need a ride. Now would be a suitable time to get in."

"If he gets in your car, I'm walking," I said, unlocking the door.

"We cannot leave him stranded here," fearless CJ scoffed. "Besides, he looks hot."

"Please don't give him a ride," I begged. "You don't understand that I have been trying to escape that man's fixation for the past hour. So, I will ask you again. Can you take me to my car?"

CJ fell back into her seat, cocked her head, and eyed Ben wistfully. "Relax," she said, snapping her knuckles. "I'm teasing you. But I will say, he is one hot piece of ass. Just look at him. Calm, cool, and collected. Yet he is so dashing and tall. He is almost perfect for me. If you do not want him? I'll take him." She giggled.

"What?" I gasped.

"It's a joke, relax. I am just being nice, but in all fairness, we cannot leave your boyfriend's friend here. The least we can do is offer the poor bastard a ride."

I watched her eyes yearn up and down Ben's length as if debating whether to screw him, and that made me angry. In a fury, I nudged CJ and frowned. "Yes! We can offer the poor bastard, as you call him, a lift. But we're not."

A couple seated on a nearby bench stopped kissing and stared at the Porsche, adding to the spectacle that follows CJ everywhere she goes. Feeling like a fish in a bowl, I lowered my head. "Please, let's leave," I whispered, shamefully aware of others watching, which rattled my core. Ignoring my request, CJ remained pensive. The rhythmic tapping of her groomed fingers on the steering wheel further fueled my annoyance. "Let's get out of here, CJ. I can't deal with any more drama tonight."

"Hey!" she goaded. "Take a chill pill, will you? I was joking. You know, like I was having a bit of fun. For God's sake, lighten up."

"I'm upset," I explained. "You're creating a scene."

"No, Bella. You are the only one creating drama on Worth Avenue."

"We are on Hibiscus Avenue, not Worth," I corrected and secured my seatbelt. "I want to get away from him," I spat, not caring if Ben heard.

"Nobody is stopping you from leaving. As for being on Worth or Hibiscus avenues, I do not care; city streets are all the same to me," CJ scoffed.

I noticed the seductive smile she offered Ben, and I almost hyperventilated. "If streets were all the same, they wouldn't give each road a different name," I said, maddened. "Let's go. Now!" I snapped, watching Ben shift awkwardly in his patent leather Oxfords.

To my horror, CJ continued to taunt me. "Sorry, potential bedmate," she shouted to Ben. "But I cannot give you a ride, not tonight. Still, if I were alone, I'd offer a lot more than a lift, and trust me, I'm a very talented woman, particularly in the bedroom."

Mortified, I felt my face turn every shade of red, and in embarrassment, I prayed for death for the second time that night.

Most days, I liked CJ. Most nights, I hated her vigorously. But tonight, I was melancholy towards the forceful woman trying to land Ben. Still brimming with fury, I grudgingly struggled to grasp her fascination, leading me to soften my stance toward her. In all fairness, CJ did not rain on my parade or judge others, which made her okay in my book. Plus, she introduced me to Lisa, which allowed me to boost my income and get out of debt. For this reason,

I rolled down the car window, glanced at Ben, and smiled. "She's joking," I lied and waved goodbye.

After closing the car window, I raised an open soda can and gulped the warm liquid. I was eager to go to Miami, which freaked me out because I knew it was impossible to spend the night with Harry or continue evading Ben in Palm Beach. If the truth be known, no matter how I looked at it, I was in a screwed-up situation because neither man was going to get me out of this mess, let alone save me from a fate worse than death.

"Thanks for leaving your lipstick all over my drink," CJ said. She sounded annoyed, and I was unsympathetic. I faced my unruly friend and sighed. "you're welcome. Next time I ask you to leave, perhaps you will remember this incident, and maybe, just maybe, you'll do as I instructed." I groaned.

CJ laughed, and despite my desire to choke her to death, I refrained. I understood she marched to a different beat, and while I enjoyed her craziness, I did not want Benny Boy to see it. But I figured he had already seen enough to know I was spending too much time with a precarious girl who may or may not be too dangerous for his liking.

Too bad. I took my bag, sat it on my lap, and rested against the plush automobile seat. Angered, I watched CJ drive onto Chilean Avenue, stop beside a restaurant two minutes later, and check her cell phone.

"I have to text Lisa," she muttered nervously.

"But why?"

"Boss's orders, that's why." CJ moaned.

"I would think Lisa will text when she's ready."

"Maybe so, but I don't want to get into trouble. So, I was checking for missed messages."

"Whatever. Do as you must," I said, feigning a yawn, as I was still more annoyed than ever. My coworker's freshness towards Ben had exhausted me, and I exhaled long and deep, struggling to relax before I mustered up enough venom to begin my rant. "How could you think that man was my date for the evening? Don't you realize you almost broke our one cardinal rule? I believed you were more knowledgeable than to assume a man I was chatting to would be a client."

"You're right. My mistake," CJ admitted. "And I know the rules, as I taught you."

"Of course you do. Then why risk exposing my life to that man when you know it is incorrect? You Know, CJ, I do not think you know as much as you profess, and if you do, please remind me because I do not believe you." I listened as she sighed loudly, and though inwardly furious, I forced myself to calm down. "Let's forget about it," I said in my most forgiving voice. She nudged my arm, and as I turned to face her, I noticed a sheepish grin on her gorgeous face. "Rule number one," she said, pointing a finger. "Never assume that any man we're with is a client. Although you must admit, he is hot. I'll bet he's dirty as fuck in the bedroom."

"OMG! Stop it!" I exclaimed and blushed.

"I'm teasing. Relax."

"Thank you," I said. "Getting back to the rules..."

"Screw the rules. I know them back to front."

"Then why forget tonight?"

"I was excited. That is why. The man's hot, but you are right. I shouldn't have presumed he was the client."

"No shit, CJ. He could be my brother or my father."

"Your father's dead."

"No shit!" I repeated. "I was with my dad the day he died, which was painful as he was full of regret for the way he treated my mother. Still, I suppose, my forgiveness was important to him, as it helped him face his master. The day after my visit, he died in his sleep."

"I know the story," CJ mumbled. "What you did was commendable. I doubt others would be as generous with their affections as you were with him. Why, if not for you, your father might have burned in hell."

"Thank you. I hope my dad is at peace. After all that has happened, it is the least I can wish for.

> "So, who's the raunchy bastard you were talking to?"

"Nobody, CJ," I said and yawned. "He's a friend and not important." I lied again.

"To be honest. I thought the hunk was your date, and it irked me why your date was sexy, and I had to contend with a wretched older man."

"That should have been your first hint."

"True, as no stud muffin would pay for our company."

You would be surprised, I thought. But I said nothing, as I did not want CJ to suspect that Ben Barrymore was easy prey. Though Benny Boy would not hire an escort, I believed he would have paid any money to keep me by his side. However, despite my confidence, I could not help but think Ben would never pay, and if he did? Without saying so, I wanted CJ to grasp that Benny Boy was mine, and I was not sharing him with anyone, least of all her.

I want you to understand why.

And I hope you do.

Back to CJ.

While enjoying a restful moment in her Porsche, I relaxed and closed my eyes as we rounded a corner onto Chilean Avenue. I felt the car jump over a speed bump and instantly sprang back to alert mode. "What the hell?" I asked, astonished. "Why drive so fast? That bump could have given you a flat tire."

"Not really," CJ assured me. "Unless someone slashes them with a knife, my tires do not go flat, and I do not speed."

"You drive fast," I said. "As for your tires, they must be made of reinforced rubber or something, as mine would blow up if I drove my car as hard as you drive yours."

"There's a big difference between German engineering and affordable cars from Japan," she said, pointing out the obvious as she steered onto Coconut Row toward Royal Palm Way.

"Hey!" I joked. "Don't put my Toyota down. It is the only car I can afford to drive. Besides, my Toyota gets excellent mileage and accepts cheap gasoline. Not to be presumptuous, but you have to pay for premium gas to fuel this beast of a machine, so at least my Toyota saves me money."

"Hopefully, you can save enough to buy a decent car."

"Don't be so mean."

"Sorry, that was rude."

"It's okay. Hey, how long did it take for you to afford a vehicle like this?"

"Do you mean, how many dates did I have to go on?"

"Well, since you put it that way, yes."

"Bella, I've been moonlighting for over seven years. Plus, I manage a bank. Though my day job pays well, it is not enough to afford luxuries like a Porsche sports car. I have to supplement my income to cover my bills."

"How long?" I asked again.

"Well, to be honest," CJ said and hesitated. "I am a slave to my image as you are to yours, and that's the pitfalls of life. The more money you make, the more you spend; before you realize it, you are in a ton of debt. The only way out is to take more dinner dates, so the vicious cycle continues."

"Are you telling me you couldn't quit this companion business even if you wanted to?"

CJ nodded and shrugged. "Sadly, that's why I am still escorting. I've been doing this longer than I had hoped, and though I long to quit, I cannot, as my monthly expenses are killing me."

"But you told me the bank pays a decent wage?" I asked, surprised. "Surely, if you wanted to quit, you could?"

"True, my day job pays well, but come on, Bella. Do you honestly believe that working in a bank affords me a condominium at Turnberry Isle Country Club, a luxurious automobile, and a fabulous closet?"

I shook my head. "I guess it was a mistake for me to surmise you are living a grand life," I said. "But, in all fairness, I did not know. Besides, you always seem so together and happy. I did not know you were miserable."

"Bella, I'm not sad. If anything, I'm a slave to money, as is everyone else in this business."

"Sorry," I sympathized.

"Oh, don't feel bad for me. I am financially stable and have a nice life. Perhaps if anything, I wished, I..."

"Wished, what?" I interrupted.

"Well, don't tell Lisa, but..." CJ hesitated.

"Come on, CJ, I won't say anything."

"Okay. But I'm just saying this once."

Seeing CJ blush, I almost rejoiced.

Now, it was my turn to grin.

"Take my advice, Bella. Be smart with your money, and do not buy expensive items. If anything, buy one or two quality outfits, but save money. If not? You will be indebted to this industry for the rest of your life. You do not know how many girls I have met who were delusional to believe they could work for one or two years, get up to date with expenses, and then get out. That will not happen because this business needs to snare and keep girls trapped. If you don't save, you become a slave, and then you're screwed, as there is no way out."

"I don't understand," I said, confused. "Why can't a girl leave this industry if she wants out?"

"As I told you earlier, the more money you make, the more you spend. It becomes a habit, such as gambling or another addiction. You do not initially notice you are doing it but trust me. You will do it just like the others did, as did I. This money is dirty, and the knowledge that you have sold your soul never goes away. Hence, you cannot spend it fast enough to clear your conscience, leaving you penniless again. Does that make sense?"

"Since you put it that way. But why did you introduce me to this lifestyle if it was such a terrible existence?"

"Bella, Bella, Bella," CJ practically sang my name. "I recruited you because you were young and impressionable, and though I regret it, there is nothing I can do about it now. I messed up. Okay?"

I did not answer. Instead, I listened as the car engine roared toward the Abigail Hotel on Lake Drive. The hotel valet parked my Toyota, which I did not like, as most parking attendants rifled through visitors' cars and stole. You will not believe it, but someone took my car's spare tire. I did not realize it until I drove away from the hotel and heard banging noises from the trunk. Honestly, I was creeped out, thinking a person was stuck inside. After stopping and investigating, I noticed the theft.

To make matters worse, I returned to the hotel. I complained, and the night manager contacted the police, who insisted I file a report. This news irritated Harry, who wondered why I had valet-parked at a hotel if I was visiting a friend in the neighborhood.

It was a reasonable question. However, my boyfriend did not know I was breaking every behavioral rule in every relationship advice book I had read. I have also failed every Cosmo boyfriend quiz I have taken. And I know that because I used to sit for hours studying those simple tests about whether I was a lousy girlfriend or a successful partner. Though more frustrating than those romance guides was Harry's cross-examination about the valet service.

What did it matter where I parked my car?

Shouldn't the thief have angered him and not my parking at a hotel?

Thinking about Harry and his questions upset me, but not as much as CJ's comments to Ben moments earlier or her true feelings about this escorting business. Now, I was worried that I would become addicted to making fast money and become trapped.

Was I stuck in an industry that, according to CJ, had ruined girls' lives?

I did not know.

Despite my easygoing nature, people assumed I was a pushover, but they were wrong, as I am tough underneath this whimsical facade. Earlier, when CJ mistook Ben for a client, he spoke to him without consulting me first. I did not let my frustration get the best of me and turn into a furious rage, did I?

No!

I hid my anger and told CJ that we needed to leave without the tall, handsome stranger she so desperately wanted to bed, without the concern of exposing us both as cheap whores.

Admittedly, I was tense, and I almost blew a gasket. But if it had been any other man, I would not have reacted as aggressively as I did. The problem was that Benny Boy brought out my protective side, and aside from wanting to run and hide every time I saw him, I also yearned to unite with him as one, both equal as we were born.

If you find yourself curious about the meaninglessness of the sentence above, I understand entirely. Just give me time, and I will fill in the blanks.

On page one, I mentioned that Ben and I have known each other for centuries, and we have. It is a complicated union, but one I promise to explain.

Trust me when I tell you I want you to know about Ben and me. It is just taking longer than I expected to reveal my secrets, which I need to do if I ever want to return to my home in heaven.

Now, I love my life on earth, and I enjoy the company of friends, particularly CJ, who, though unruly, is the most realistic person in this superficial industry.

CJ's unwavering loyalty towards me was commendable and deepened my affection for her. However, she did not grasp that she had almost exposed my secret life. She would soon, I thought. I planned to explain to CJ why I did not want Ben in her company. I feared repercussions the minute I watched his silhouette disappear as she drove away.

After thousands of years, I knew Benny Boy like the back of my hand in every incarnation we have lived. He would not take kindly to my associating with a woman like CJ, as he would find her reckless. Still, I enjoyed her outspoken boldness. Though the act can become unbearable, like intolerable meanness, CJ was not a cruel woman. The only thing that bothered me about CJ was that she spoke her mind without caring what anyone else thought of her looks, attire, or life.

She was born a free-thinking woman and masqueraded around South Florida every night of the week. Still, as she had explained, she had no choice but to drive a flashy convertible Porsche, particularly one that always shined like new. By day, CJ Clarke portrayed a successful executive in a tailored wardrobe and expensive designer accessories. At night, she drove from one date to another to make money to support her elaborate lifestyle.

I tried to fathom why or how she had made twice as much as me in the past, but that was before she confessed to taking daily appointments.

She was beautiful and tall, slim, and groomed from head to toe, with matching-colored nails on both fingers and toes. Still, her intense brown eyes that quizzed others faster than a rocket scientist gazing into space pulled in the clients. As did the gold jewelry, which sparkled against her half-Latin skin, courtesy of her Colombian mother and American father. Gifted was CJ, as her father from the Lone Star State of Texas had blessed her with six feet of height, and everything she wore graced her figure as if a couturier had designed it.

I met CJ four months ago after a bank teller threatened to close my account because of insufficient funds, which cost me a fortune in overdraft fees.

I argued with the teller, and she introduced me to CJ, who took me into her office and assured me my checking account would remain open. She also invited me to lunch and offered to pay since I had expressed hesitation, as my funds were too low to afford the luxury of eating out.

We began meeting on Fridays, and I appreciated how CJ helped me learn to balance a checking account and avoid bank fees. Two months into our friendship, CJ introduced me to our current boss, Lisa.

Money-wise, I have not looked back, as I can now supplement my income and keep my bills up to date. Not that I could afford CJ's luxuries. Still, my head was above the waterline of monetary responsibility, and I no longer worried about eviction notices gracing my apartment's entryway.

Yes, as I told you before, I know this is immoral, but somehow, knowing CJ was also involved in this triangle makes it appear not so bad, as I am not doing anything more than attending events. I am not having sex with anyone for money. CJ reassured me that there was a significant distinction between a woman who engages in sexual activities for cash and a woman who accepts financial support as a professional companion. The companionship sales pitch piqued my interest, as I had never gone all the way with any man. In my life, I am saving myself for someone special, a man like Ben. Therefore, the strict dating rules of no sexual contact made sense, and I welcomed the opportunity to increase my income. Despite having a boyfriend, Harry and I did not have a sexual relationship. Although he may not have liked my honesty if you had met him, he would have agreed with this disclosure. Now in my mind's eye, and yours too, I am guessing you see any woman in either industry as a skank. You have the right to express your opinion. I, too, felt that way until Lisa said there are three types of women in the dating world.

There is the woman who beds a man after he treats her to dinner at a local steak house. Obligatory sex is nauseating. Then, the woman who flaunts her curves on every street corner, advertising sex for money. Finally, the woman who travels through the night to see a man who will treat her like a queen and pay her for her company.

Who is the smartest of the three? Lisa had asked.

Surmising the Miami Madam did not want to hear my opinion, I shrugged, recognizing the importance of being cautious and silent to avoid any potential wrath from the Miami Madam. I kept a neutral facade during the interview, causing my boss to perceive me as unprejudiced or something of that sort. It suited me, as I just wanted to hold cold, hard cash.

Back to Lisa.

"I'll tell you, Bella." She informed me, bragging. "The girl who goes home with her dignity intact and can afford to live life to the fullest. And, the reason is simple," she continued. "The prostitute is not being paid enough for her body, and the lavish dinner date with a workmate was nothing more than a free romp in the bed to him, which leads nowhere other than being a booty call. Do you get it, Bella?" she asked in a matter-of-fact tone.

I smiled and nodded in agreement, as I needed the job.

"Good," Lisa applauded. "You have the right insight to work for me. When can you start?"

"Today," I answered.

"There's one more thing I need to mention," she said. "I don't like my girls giving out their phone numbers. If asked, your phone is a courtesy service from my agency and not for personal use. I enforce these rules, so don't disappoint me."

I nodded again.

"Now, allow me to explain. I cannot express how badly my clientele may behave. Since I want to hire you, I demand that you work with loyalty to me because my clients will try to sway you to see them on the side, but I find out." She checked her cell phone. "By the way, I'm changing your name to Sarah, as Bella is such an old lady's name—anyway, again..." long pause. "If my client wanted a regular girlfriend, they would have one. They contacted me to rotate between girls because they like variety. So, don't fall for their bullshit love stories because clients do not marry working girls."

I gulped and continued nodding, as I suspected the lecture was not over, and I did not want to distract my future employer from her speech.

My new boss leaned forward on the glass desk inside her home office, crossed her hands, and whispered. "Men want to believe they are your first bedmate. So, if you jump into bed with them, then they think you are doing the same with other men, and no man wants to date a tramp. Do you understand, Sarah?"

I ignored the question since I was not Sarah.

"Sarah," Lisa snapped. "Earth to Bella. Are you listening?"

"Yes," I muttered. "Sorry, I forgot my name."

"Get familiar with it and repeat the name Sarah until it's the only name you answer to."

"Yes," I muttered again. This time, I flushed with color and stared at a phone that would not stop ringing. I counted ten missed calls throughout my interview and suspected the Miami Madam would keep me busy.

"Sarah, don't ever overlook that men want the fantasy. Do not bed them ever. Got it?"

I blushed once more as I replied, "Yes."

I got it, Lisa. I got, as you asked, everything you told me, and I believed you, as I am not a promiscuous woman. However, I still could not fathom how attending functions for cash made me better than my friends who jumped from one man's bed to another every other weekend. Still, I would have to wait before asking that question, as I have not seen her since my interview. The money I owe, I deposit into a corporate bank account, and her assistant, Jamie, gives me my assignments and dress requests. So, I have not had the chance to mention my friend's frequent bed partners to my boss because Lisa believes you are the person you associate yourself with, and I did not want her to think I was worthless.

A hot-tempered Lisa lectured that one should aspire to become equal to the company one keeps. Therefore, pretending to be a lady twice a week and hanging out with sleazy people the rest of the time would cause my boss to look at me with disdain. Besides, Lisa did not own me or dictate what I could and could not do. True, she pointed out the obvious to remind me to better myself. I took her advice because it was easier than her thinking I was difficult. In all fairness, my boss was the first to admit that renting me out to the highest bidder was her job. So, I let her sell the mystery and went along with the program.

One day, my boss informed me I could choose when and where my next appointment would be.

Which was a fucking lie!

Allow me to explain.

Early Saturday morning, I called the agency, and while speaking to Jamie, I confessed I did not want the date. She assured me it was all right to cancel my appointment with Mitch.

Not true.

By mid-afternoon, Lisa telephoned and announced that my job would be gone if I canceled. Then she bellowed for over thirty minutes, telling me I was ungrateful. If I did not appreciate her efforts to give me financial freedom, I could leave the company, which I did not do, as I could not afford to walk away.

Suddenly, aware that the Miami Madam had tricked me, I stretched.

"Are you okay?" CJ asked, concerned, as we stopped at a traffic light.

"I'm fine," I lied.

"Are you sure?"

"Absolutely," I lied again, realizing I could not recall when I started telling so many lies.

"Are you thinking about the boy on Worth Ave?"

"He's a man, and we were on Hibiscus Avenue."

"I was being polite," CJ said. "I would have hoped you'd appreciate my gesture. Lord knows I try to be as accommodating as I can without being borderline rude. How do you know the tall, dark, handsome stranger?"

Shifting in my seat, I glared at my friend. "Are you serious?" I asked. "I don't know him well, but since you propositioned him, I'll bet he's told everyone I know I was here this evening, including Harry."

"Harry is a drunk. Even if that strange man you were chatting with tells your boyfriend, I doubt he will remember, as he remembers nothing. Didn't he forget your birthday?"

Ouch! That was a low blow.

I despise people who hit below the belt.

Why do people lash out and wound one another when the other person is at their weakest point?

It made no sense to me.

It just made me more determined to be strong.

To fight for all I believed in, Benjamin Barrymore included.

At that moment, I regretted entrusting Harry with forgetting my birthday to CJ. But my emotions were in turmoil, and I did not expect her to use it against me months later. Though she was the only person who called to wish me a happy birthday, no other person had remembered; if they had, they would have said.

I did not receive one free card or internet message on my special day.

Not one.

Oops! I lied. A single email landed in my inbox with a message from my boss, Bob, telling me to edit the attached text by Monday. Aside from his demanding message, I received nothing, not even one spam email.

Yes! I lead a pathetic existence, but there is not much I can do about it, not now anyway.

"Screw Harry," CJ soothed. "He doesn't deserve you. Here's hoping the mysterious stranger who owns your heart is a better man."

I jolted upright. "What are you talking about?"

"Just telling it how I see it, that's all."

"You're mistaken. You are also driving the wrong way to my car. So, where are we going?" I asked, noticing we were heading toward Royal Palm Bridge and leaving Palm Beach.

CJ slammed on the brakes. "Didn't Lisa text you to inform you that tonight is not ending?"

I shook my head.

"Well, it's not. A client wants to see me and requested I bring a friend. Guess what, Bella? You're it."

"No way. I have to go back to Miami."

"Listen to me, Bella. Lisa insisted I take you with me because you were the closest to the date. The only alternative would be my waiting for a girl to drive up from Boca Raton or Miami, which could take two or more hours."

"Are you serious?" I asked, stomping my feet. "I cannot go to another appointment. Look at what I am wearing. I am wearing a ballgown, and I have no other clothes. Not forgetting, Harry will be furious."

"Don't you carry a second outfit in your car?"

"No! Since I take only one appointment a night, I had no reason to pack spare clothes," I paused. "Besides, I can't go out again. If I do not get to Harry's party, he will question me for eternity, and I will already be late. Please, CJ, can you find another girl?"

My coworker slapped a hand onto the steering wheel and faced me. "Listen to me," she commanded. "If you don't go with me tonight, I can tell you firsthand that your life working for Lisa will end," she hesitated. "Now, if you want to walk away from making an abundant amount of money, be my guest. Though you would be foolish to do so, it is your life and your bills. Now, you can accept the date and collect an additional five thousand, or you can return to Miami to be with a drunk who only cares about alcohol because we both know that Harry dreams about nothing else."

"Ouch, CJ." I groaned. "You don't have to be so mean. I realize Harry drinks, but he is also doing well, as he has cut back on hard liquor and is only drinking beer during the week. When we started dating, I swore I was in this relationship for the long haul because I adore him. Not so much when he's drunk, but when sober, he is the most charming man and the best boyfriend I have ever had."

"You're selling yourself short," CJ said, raising a hand to cover a dry cough that forced her to cut her lecture shorter than she would have liked.

"Can I at least get my car?" I asked in such a trembling voice that I could not even believe how submissive I had become. That way, when the date ends, I can drive straight to Miami and bypass Palm Beach."

Still coughing, CJ did not answer, but she signaled no, which left me discouraged and feeling like a prisoner of the night again.

This time, not by Benjamin Barrymore.

No, this time, CJ Clarke held me against my will, and it made my blood boil how pathetically weak I was to allow anyone to mistreat me.

Shuffling in my seat, I racked my mind about the laws on holding someone against their will in Florida. Then, I needed internet access to read that statute and figure out if that law applied to my current situation. Still, that would have to wait until I can access a computer. So, instead of battling with CJ, I accepted the appointment and resigned myself to dealing with Harry whenever I saw him again.

Poor Harry. Not being with him pained me, and I could not wait to return to the comfort of my apartment to change into jeans and a tee and arrive at his house before all the partygoers left. His Irish blood may have adored one too many beers, and most people laughed at his drunkenness, but to me, Harry was a hopeless romantic who loved me.

In my heart, I knew he drank himself unconscious because somewhere deep inside, he was, like my father, battling demons. He was a faithful man who could little imagine the horror my secret rendezvous could enfold around his capital life. I could quickly destroy such a lucrative career as Harry owned one of Miami's largest energy companies, and the community respected and liked him.

As for me?

I am an ornament, shy and in awe of the cavalry of wealth flaunted before my poverty-stricken eyes as Harry's customers spared no expense. Frequently, I watched my boyfriend's eyes sparkle with delight as he enthusiastically mingled with consumers at benefits and luncheons. However, I am not fond of parties, the glitz, and all their glamor because I am terrified of Harry introducing me to a former client of mine. So, being my protective self, I slip out of sight. My worst moments are when Harry drinks and engages in too much idle chatter, bragging about my success to his friends as it forces me to come out of hiding. I fear I may recognize one of his clients, or they may recognize me and tell Harry my secret.

At that moment, CJ stopped coughing. "Your cell phone is beeping," she spoke in a low tone and sucked on a cough drop. "Better check it, as Lisa may be interested in our estimated arrival time."

I rifled through my handbag and pulled out my phone. To my dismay, it was not a text from Lisa but a message from Harry, who had plastered ten hearts at the end of his text. I faced CJ and gnawed at my lower lip. "I have to call him," I told her. "There's no way I can avoid not answering. If I do? He will become suspicious, and our union will end as surely as the sun rises tomorrow morning. Besides," I continued, desperate to sound assertive. "I need to stall him for a few more hours, and I can't ring from my phone as I need a local area code phone number to back up my lie, as I told him I would be at my aunt in Palm Beach."

CJ nodded in agreement. Still, I sensed she was furious. "How far away is the Abigail hotel?" I inquired while rereading my text.

"We're not going to the Hotel Abigail; we're going to Hotel Atlantic, and it's two blocks to the left," she replied. "Listen, Bella, I don't want to see your life in shambles, as I consider you a friend, but please, when you're out for the evening on assignments, don't make plans to be someplace else, as we never know what the night can bring."

Grasping my cell phone, I rested my head against the car seat and thought about Lisa, CJ, Benny Boy, and Harry. I also thought about my life and ranked everything and everyone in order of importance, concluding that Harry was number one.

"We're here," CJ announced as she stopped on the parking ramp in front of the hotel. "There's a public phone to the left of the concierge desk. Do you need quarters, or are you using your bank card? If I were you, I would use change as I do not believe in leaving a paper trail. If you do not have cash, there is a roll of coins in the glove box. Help yourself, and please, be as fast as you can."

Thankfully, I opened the small compartment, grabbed the money roll, descended the vehicle, and rushed up the driveway to the revolving front door, aware of the curious looks I received from valet staff and hotel employees. Not that I cared, as I was on a mission to save my life, and their knowing stares could not dissuade me from one of my life's most important phone calls.

True to form, CJ was correct in her knowledge of access to the hotel's public telephone, which was to the left of the concierge desk. I saw the shiny phone booth as soon as I strode past a mature man dressed in a navy pinstripe suit, light blue shirt, and navy tie adorned with gold stars.

I smiled as his keen eyes rose and fell across my ballgown. Still, I ignored his assumption that I was a wealthy socialite and rushed toward the phone booth.

Once inside the private compartment, I plunged a hand into my pocket and pulled out a handful of coins, which I laid on a small wooden stand. Then I debated what I would tell Harry about why I was in Palm Beach before ordering myself to toughen up and dial his phone number.

"Harry!" I exclaimed. "I'm stranded at my Aunt Martha's in Palm Beach. I've tried to leave, but the old dear insists I stay the night."

Yes, I know I tell a lot of lies.

A knot formed in my stomach as I listened to the crackling on the old phone line, dreading the outburst of Harry's anger, but there was only silence.

"Bella, I see on my caller ID that you are up north. I wish you had rung me earlier, as I was worried about you."

I softened my stance. "Harry, I apologize. I could not break free from my aunt or her friends. It was bridge night here, and we were all so engrossed in the card game that I lost track of time. Do not hate me for being late." Even after I spoke the last words, my heart raced at ninety miles per hour as I dreaded his reply because regardless of his drunkenness, Harry was a quick-witted man who, like Benny Boy, never forgot a thing, least of all lies.

Drat, why was I thinking about Ben?

I did not know, though honestly, his handsome face and devilish ways tormented my memory every waking moment. Focusing, I chastised and forced my attention on Harry's heavy breathing and cursed myself to calm down.

"I miss you," he admitted. "I cannot express how empty my house feels without you, Bella. It amazes me how you have managed to turn four walls into a home, and though I love what you have done with my place, I long for your return. When are you coming over?" he asked and groaned.

In that instant, joy sprung into my chest, which caused my troubled heart to burst with love, adoration, and thankfulness that Harry was not angry at me nor wounded by my absence. His worry was clear in his words. Still, if I am honest, I expected anger, and much worse, as I was waiting for him to lose his temper and scream hateful words, such as how I was irresponsible, and because of that, he was ending our partnership.

I-95. Since I dreamt about a car accident last night, drive safe as I do not want you to get into a car wreck, so please pay attention to the roads and get here when you can." he said, yawning.

"But, Harry," I protested, but the tiredness in Harry's voice caused me to moan. "I just told you that my aunt Martha has insisted I stay. She does not want me driving this late at night, and I told you that not over two minutes ago. I would have thought you would be happy, as Saturday nights are notorious for drunks on the roads across any town in most countries. Yet, you're now implying that I should ignore my aunt's concerns and start the one-hour trip to your house, which is shocking because if you had my best interest at heart, you would agree with Aunt Martha that I should remain in Palm Beach."

My reasoning annoyed Harry, and when his attitude changed from amiable to nasty, I prepared myself for the lecture heading my way.

Cue the bitchiness.

Harry yelled on the phone. "Bella, this party was held in your honor because of your promotion at work. How could you be late? I have a house full of guests, a girlfriend, whom I might add is missing, and gossip to seize, not to mention the questions I feel forced to ask of you. You helped plan and prepare every detail for tonight's bonanza. What happened to you, my love? Have you forgotten your obligation to your friends and me? This party is your night, and I shall not allow your absence to silence the laughter; if my heart did not ache so much, I could smile myself, but as I stare around my home, all I see is emptiness. Hurry to my side."

"You cannot be serious?"

"I am, and rightly so."

"But it's the middle of the night, almost Sunday morning. The sun will rise in less than seven hours. Why ask me to risk driving in the dark when my arrival can wait until early morning?"

"I am not asking," Harry corrected. "Get back inside your car, Bella, and drive back to Miami, pronto, I insist," he demanded. Because I have doubts, I will speak with you when you are here and in front of my face, as I want to see your eyes while you talk. Do you hear me?"

"Oh? Let me guess," I fumed. "Did Benjamin Barrymore telephone you and tell you he saw me earlier tonight?" I yelled. I was angry, mainly because of Benny Boy's eagerness to gossip and throw me under a bus. His empty promises shattered my trust, confirming that he did not deserve it like most other men I have known.

The betrayal hurt.

How foolish am I?

How utterly stupid could I be?

Ah! I wanted to scream into the universe and beg for death because even Ben did not have one ounce of loyalty.

Well, not to me, anyway.

Harry's voice grew louder and echoed in my ears as he screamed on the telephone. "What?" He shouted. "When the hell did you see my investor, and if you've been playing cards at your aunt's house, how did you see him? Oh, wait, let me guess. I suppose you will tell me that my client, Ben, also played cards with the mysterious Martha. Are you?"

"No! Of course not."

"Then tell me how you saw Ben?"

"I bumped into him when my grandmother Martha had a friend stranded at a restaurant, and we went to pick her up," I said, lying for the thousandth time. Then, I checked my nose to ensure it had stayed the same size.

"Your grandmother?" Harry quizzed. "You just told me Martha was your aunt. You are such a liar. I am so sick of your tales and so finished with this relationship. Go fuck Ben Barrymore. In fact, fuck the entire town for all I care. We're through."

"My aunt, Harry! Martha is my aunt." I corrected, but my efforts were futile as the telephone line died.

Harry had hung up.

I cannot say I blame him, as my imaginary aunt Martha, in error, had become Grandma Martha because of my confusion with all the fairytales I told.

My screw up.

Not Harry's.

Like a fool, I inserted more coins and called him back. My call went straight to voicemail, as Harry did not answer. I cleared my throat and left a message, repeating that Martha was my aunt, and I could have her ring him tomorrow. My rationale sounded like a plan, as, at the very least, I could ask Beatrice Ryder to play a game called Pretend, where she masqueraded as my aunt. I told myself that Beatrice would solidify my story that we went to the Hotel Carlisle, which is where we spotted Ben. However, realizing how screwed I am, I chose not to. However, I did tell Harry how insulting he was to presume that I was cavorting around Palm Beach with all available suitors. Then, I told him how rotten he was to insult me when I was house-sitting Martha, my only living relative. Satisfied, I placed the phone's receiver back on its cradle and exited the booth. Two minutes later, I stood in the hotel lobby, shivering from fright and the frigid air wafting across my bare shoulders.

Suddenly, a voice spoke to me.

Yes, I mean that someone called my birth name, and shocked, I turned to confront the unknown culprit, only to see Lisa standing less than three feet away. She walked toward me; arms outstretched and did not quit until she held me close. "Do not worry, Sarah," she said.

"Wow!" I said, alarmed. "I thought you were in Miami. Isn't that where you live?" I asked, struggling to elude her grip.

Madam Lisa held me firmly. "I'm sorry, I requested you stay longer tonight, Bella. Er! I mean Sarah," she said, correcting her error.

I blushed, as Sarah was my working girl's name, and it was so my clients would not learn my identity. Though it comforted me that the Miami Madam still remembered I had a real name, I could not help but feel like a prized leg of lamb at a meat packing company. Still, I was not fond of the name Sarah and would have preferred something catchy, like Julia or Candice.

"Don't concern yourself with your boyfriend's abusive tongue. By morning, he will forget his rage."

"It's okay," I mused, forcing a shy smile. My statement was untrue, but I did not argue with my boss, as she believed she had answers for all of life's uncertainties. However, I wanted to tell Lisa that I was tired from attending the ball, but I chose not to, as she would point out that I was still young enough to function without sleeping at twenty-six.

"Are you sure you can double date with CJ?"

"Yes, I can do it. I am just upset because my boyfriend is not happy with my absence, and he just yelled at me, calling me horrible names, which broke my heart," I said and clutched the tissue she offered. "Bella, one day you'll understand that you cannot have personal relationships while working in this industry. It is possible, but I do not recommend it because of the emotional toll it can take on your nerves. So, please remember this advice when deciding if you are working for my company in the long haul or to catch up on your depressing financial situation. I would love to continue collaborating with you. However, I understand that if you wish to quit and live with a boyfriend or girlfriend, depending on your choice of partner, I wish you well. Just know this industry is only for some; you cannot be half in or half out. It's all or nothing, and though I would hate to see you quit, I also want you to be happy."

"I know you do," I sobbed, freeing from her embrace. "I like the money, Lisa. It is just that tonight, I did not expect to be out for so long. I knew I would spend four hours with Mitch, but I thought I could go home afterward as Harry was throwing a party. And while I understand that work comes first," I paused and shrugged. "Well, it's just that," I paused again, longer this time. "I didn't expect to bump into a friend at the ball. That's all."

"I understand that it was upsetting for you to see a friend while on your date with Mitch, and I can empathize with how traumatic it must have felt. Nevertheless, it is crucial to remember that the client invested substantial funds in meeting with you. The money should compensate for all the heartache you endured to entertain my client." Lisa said, checking her watch. "If I didn't understand that you needed to make as much as possible in the shortest amount of time, which were your words on the day we met, trust me, I would not have pushed you for a second date. I thought you would be happy. Seeing that you are not joyous is causing me pain." I watched as she reached inside a pocket for her cell phone and answered a text message before continuing her lecture. "I need a woman committed to her craft, not an up-and-down and all-over-the-place child," she told me. "It would help if you decided. However, examine your ambitions before making choices, as poor judgments can affect every aspect of our lives.

I stood silently and nodded.

"We all have and will continue to sacrifice for the almighty dollar," she said, a twang of bitterness in her voice. "I once had a wonderful husband, Donald, who loved me, but he could not provide for himself, let alone me, and fueled by poverty and desire, I left him. Look at me now. Alone, afraid, and consumed by greed. I would not and do not wish this existence on anyone, ever. I have seen and experienced so much in life that I sometimes want to close my agency. If I could turn back the clock and go back to living in poverty with Donald, I would. She sighed. "Still, those days are long gone," she said, apologizing for her rambling speech.

I did not aspire to be like Lisa, living with regrets. Still, I had bills to pay. I forced a smile because, like Lisa, CJ, and the other girls, I had no choice but to continue collaborating with the women in this devilment game, a charade we all were reluctant to quit. Like it or not, we were all comrades and each other's protectors and losing one would indeed cause the finely tuned steamship to go off course and sink to the bottom of the ocean.

"Why did you call your boyfriend from a public phone, not your cell phone?" Lisa asked, consumed with curiosity.

"I had to have a Palm Beach area code," I mumbled. "If only to make my fictitious story believable."

Madam Lisa appeared to nod, wince, and grimace simultaneously, leading me to believe she understood the search for financial independence, regardless of the cost to personal affairs. "Why not call him back?" she suggested, rechecking her watch. "Enough time has passed since your last call. Perhaps he's calmer now."

"Do you think so?" I asked.

The Miami Madam nodded again.

I regained my composure, poured coins into the phone booth, and called Harry's home again. This time, I was forceful because I had to figure out whether it was a life with Harry or a commitment to my job with Lisa, and no amount of stalling would get in my way. Harry answered on ring two; I jumped headfirst into my sermon without giving him a chance to complain. "Harry, darling. I miss you. I must explain this catastrophe before you hate me forever. After Martha invited me to stay, I told her no, but she pleaded with me not to drive. Then I bumped into my friend Lisa, who had fought with her husband Donald, and like Aunty Martha, Lisa begged me to still be at her side..."

"Bella, if you're at your aunt's house, I understand, but why are you gallivanting around Palm Beach with Lisa?"

Think!

I urged.

I thought long and hard, then my mind kicked into fifth gear. "Lisa is my cousin, Harry. She was at Martha's home before I arrived. She has been staying at my aunt's house for the past week. I was not in town having fun, but with Lisa offering support as she poured out her heart about the verbal insults she had received from her wretched husband." I lied.

A few seconds later, I told Lisa that the line was dead. Harry had hung up on me again. "Fuck him," she mouthed and typed a text on her cell phone. "Perhaps go into the lady's room and fix your hair and makeup, for you look dreadful. Oh, I forgot," she said and looked at me. "I had my assistant Jamie bring you a dress to wear," she glanced at her phone again. "She should arrive any minute. So, please clean your face, and I'll send CJ in with the dress."

I smiled grimly, swallowed hard, and entered the ladies' room.

In the bathroom at Hotel Atlantic, two women talking and giggling about their night events scared me as they stood in a fashionable line with a 'do not mess with us expression' across their faces. "Are you finished with the phone?" a busty brunette cheerfully asked.

I nodded.

"Let's grab it before someone else does," the blonde suggested. I watched the two women rush from the ladies' room. The door slammed shut, and I jumped. Then, I studied my appearance in a mirror. However, I could have fallen to the floor and cried at the sight of my swollen face. Knowing CJ was bringing me a dress, I hurried to make myself look presentable for my next appointment. Gathering all my strength, I prepared myself for the task at hand.

Oomph! Just like that.

Dress, smile, and look happy.

As if life was that easy.

I TURNED ON THE TAPS, let the water pour until it was ice cold, and plunged my face under the faucet until I became too frozen to hold a single emotion for anyone, at least myself. Once wide awake, I slicked my wet hair into a low ponytail, secured strays with hair clips, and applied a uniform contour color to my eyelids, temples, and chin. I blended all three shades, giving my white complexion a tanned look, and then I applied a dab of lipstick, blush, and mascara to emphasize my bone structure before I stepped away from the mirror to check out my transformation.

Not bad, I thought and smiled.

The bathroom door swung open. I jolted and turned to see CJ standing at the entryway, holding a hanger with a sexy black dress in one hand and a bag of cosmetics in another. "Wow!" she beamed. "Had I known you would look utterly fabulous; I would have never lugged my makeup bag in here. You look terrific, simply gorgeous."

"Do I?" I asked. "I tried to do the best I could with the few pieces of makeup I own, but I was unsure if I needed more color, as I'm pale. If you think I need more, I'll add it."

CJ raised her hand. "Are you kidding?" she scoffed. "Stand here, and let's look in the mirror together." She tugged my arm and dragged me to her side. "Look at yourself, Bella, not at me. Can you not see how beautiful you are?"

I grimaced. "Truly, I do not see myself that way, CJ. It is not my thing, as I prefer jeans to dresses," I explained as she thrust the little black dress into my hand.

"Save the casual attire for housework," she scoffed. "Put this on. I think it will fit your slender figure, and it might even add curves here and there," she advised and smiled, prodding my small breasts in a playful, innocent way.

"It looks tiny," I criticized. "I hope it fits."

"Of course it will. You are a waif. I've often wondered if you purchase your casual attire at Baby Gap."

Just then, I burst out laughing.

"It is so good to hear laughter, Bella. I'm glad you are feeling better."

"You and me both," I mentioned as I pulled the dress over my shoulders, across my bosom, and past my hips. A sense of concern washed over me as I contemplated whether it would be too short, but the drape stopped mid-thigh, which was a comfortable length.

"Now, turn and look at yourself."

I saw my reflection and smiled. The little black dress fit CJ's expectations, which made me feel good.

Sleek and sexy, but not too sleazy.

"Wow! Bella. The outfit gives the impression that a designer has crafted it to match your body, and..." she hesitated. "If I were into girls, I'd fuck you myself because you look delicious enough to eat," she teased, patting my bottom. "Nice and firm," she chuckled and hugged my shoulders. "I'm joking. I just want you to feel better. Okay?"

I forced a smile. "Thank you, CJ," I said. "If not for you, I'd be a basket case tonight."

"You sound breathless. Are you okay?"

"I'm still reeling from bumping into Ben Barrymore while on the Mitch Carter date," I explained. "I'm so happy to be off that assignment. You cannot imagine how eccentric a client Mitch is..." I inhaled. "Do you know, he insists on watching me from afar while he dances with his wife and chats with the upper-class men, which was quite taxing on my nerves," I explained, putting my makeup away. "The dress is a stark contrast to the one I wore to the ball at Hotel Carlisle," I scoffed, giving my reflection one last going over. "But at least I'm no longer dressed like a queen from the dark ages."

"Are you sure you are okay, Bella?"

"Of course," I lied again.

Dear reader, I swear my nose should be a mile longer than usual, considering the enormous number of tall tales I have told this early Sunday morning, and that troubles me, as I do not wish for you to think of me as a lying sack of dog poop. I am a nice girl; It is just that being involved with this group of women brings out the worst in me, and I should have run away the first chance I got.

"You're back to being tense," CJ said, using a maternal tone. "I'm just afraid of what is next on this crazy night," I said, noticing my coworker also seemed afraid. Did she, too, fear what our next endeavor would entail, as it was the first time we had ever been on an assignment together? I suspected CJ, like me, wanted to leave. Still, like me, greed had forsaken all dignity, which was why we were miles from home in this godforsaken place.

I finished dressing, and we organized our belongings. However, as we crossed the floor, I was surprised to see CJ follow my lead as we exited the bathroom. She ordinarily led the path in the past, so I found her behavior strange tonight, but I surmised she was tired.

Lisa stood inside the hotel lobby, conversing with a valet attendant. "There you are, my darling girls," she smiled as we approached. "I've asked this young man to fetch your automobile from The Abigail Hotel. That is where you told me you had parked it earlier tonight, correct?"

I nodded yes, but to be frank, I did not recall telling Lisa where I had parked my vehicle. I longed to ask how she knew but thought it was best not to question my boss. Yet, it bothered me, as I parked my car far away from my assignments in case a crazy client might see my license plate number and uncover my identity.

How did Lisa know? I questioned.

Was she spying on me?

I did not know, but it was the only answer I could conjure up, and that freaked me out more than Benny Boy did after I spotted him leaning against an art gallery only one-half hour earlier.

As we stood atop Hotel Atlantic's decorated entryway, Lisa conversed with the valet's night manager and gave instructions while CJ and I hovered in the background. When she finished acting as a drill sergeant, she smiled at us. "It's alright, ladies," she said smoothly. "Your car is coming here, Bella. Er! Sarah. Just so, you know, CJ texted me earlier and said you wanted your car. So, I am arranging for this young man to fetch it for you."

"You did?" I asked CJ.

"Of course I did. I want you to be happy. But arriving in the same automobile is better, as this client likes to party and can become paranoid if he consumes too much."

"Are you telling me that our first assignment together is going to be babysitting an addict?" I dread her reply. CJ's lips turned upwards and downwards as she smiled and grimaced, which told me all I needed to know... Our next client was a man who would make the antics of Tony Montana appear normal, and I shuddered at the thought of dealing with a man whose addiction issues were more significant than my own.

A nudge from CJ brought my attention back to Lisa. "Please fetch my girl's car right away," she ordered.

I thought, "Please drive my Toyota slowly. I did not want the young man to crash my vehicle, as it was my only means of transportation. Still, Lisa thrust a Hotel Abigail valet ticket into his hand alongside a one-hundred-dollar bill and told him to hurry.

"I suppose this is where we wait?" I asked anxiously, estimating the parking attendant would take at least thirty minutes to fetch my vehicle.

"No," My boss replied. "I paid for the valet and gave him a generous tip. Let's see if he keeps his promise to deliver your auto within five minutes." A sly smile etched her lips.

I glanced in Lisa's direction. She appeared calm, I thought, noticing her confident stance. No wonder her ex-husband Donald tore his hair out with frustration. My boss was a complex woman. Though she portrayed diplomacy, I could not help but imagine a tornado was brewing inside. Still, while she was gorgeous, she was older, although just how much older was unknown, as there have been visits to one or two plastic surgeon's offices. Plus, those shopping trips to Bal Harbor Mall, courtesy of a Rolodex of clients and American Express, made age guessing impossible.

Not five but seven minutes later, I saw my Toyota arrive, and thrilled, I smiled, knowing that my freedom was mere feet away. Not that I planned to bail out of the second gig, but seeing my battered older model Corolla parked in front of this expensive hotel felt nice.

"The boy did well," the Miami Madam gushed excitedly, mingled with a peevish glee. I smiled, brimming with pride. Thank you, Lord, I said as I watched the valet attendant thrust my car keys into my shaking hand.

Suddenly, CJ and Lisa rushed me to the driver's side with such haste that I almost tripped onto the ground, just like I had at Hotel Carlisle one hour earlier, which freaked me out. "Am I driving us somewhere?" I asked.

CJ smiled, but Lisa roared with laughter. "Oh, Bella. I love your sense of humor," she chuckled. "And as much as I adore your beautiful face and gorgeous figure, no way am I allowing anyone within a five-mile radius to witness my entering your rundown vehicle." Her blunt explanation hurt. "I'm sorry, but my Rolls are in the shop," I said, upset.

"We're having a quick meeting in CJ's sports car," Lisa said, wrapping her arm around mine. "Let us get inside the Porsche. Come on, CJ, quick to it. Time is money."

As we huddled inside CJ's vehicle, I could not help but admire the splendor of Hotel Atlantic. It is the pride of Palm Beach's most dignified society members and stands tall in a feminine, almost glamorous statuette. The local news featured the hotel because dignitaries occupy the luxurious suites, and security officers walk the grounds like soldiers off to war. The eighteen-hole golf course, a private members-only club, has attracted the world's richest and most powerful men. Every US President has played the course or entertained world leaders by watching others play.

While Lisa and CJ discussed business, I sat in the back seat, mesmerized by Hotel Atlantic's unsurpassed beauty. I peered through the window, admiring every conceivable angle of the hotel. Then, I became sad, as, like most properties along the Florida coastline, a direct impact from a Category 5 hurricane would cause Hotel Atlantic to crumble, which disturbed me because I have loved this grand hotel for years.

CJ began revving up the powerful engine of her black, shiny Porsche.

"Lisa, are you coming with us?" I asked. Since she had yet to vacate the vehicle, I feared CJ's heavy foot might blast us all into outer space.

"No! She is not," CJ told me. "Lisa, we have to go, and you need to leave. I will ring you once Bella and I arrive."

"Sarah," Lisa corrected. "You should call her Bella on days off because, as far as my clients are concerned, Bella does not exist, but Sarah is charming and worth every penny. So, CJ, please do not screw this assignment up by calling Bella anything other than Sarah."

"Yes, Mam!" CJ saluted and revved the Porsche engine again. "We have to go, Lisa, so please leave my car. Bella, you can sit in the passenger seat as soon as she exits. We have to plan our story, which will need much practice before we arrive at his mega-million-dollar home."

"Where does he live?" I asked in bewilderment. "Is he a Palm Beach native?"

"No! He lives in Jupiter," Lisa answered.

I frowned.

"Don't worry, Bella, it's only twenty minutes further north," she soothed as she stepped out of the automobile. "Silly me, I mean Sarah," she grinned.

I yawned, exited the vehicle, and waited for my boss to adjust her pantsuits before ascending to the passenger seat. "I love your blouse, Lisa," I said as she unbuttoned her lavish jacket and revealed a pastel shirt with a lilac floral pattern. "Is it silk?" I asked aimlessly, as I did not know fabrication and was trying to sound like I knew expensive clothes did not come in polyester and cotton. In all fairness, I thought linen was high-end and could never have imagined wearing something like a luxurious silk blouse. Though I am making extra money, I cannot bring myself to splurge on fancy clothes. I should, as looking expensive is the name of the game. Still, I was a victim of my poverty-stricken life and needed to work longer hours to shop in designer boutiques, as they were not something I could afford.

Lisa stood aghast. "Of course, it's silk," she said. "Bella, I mean Sarah," she corrected. "One of these days, I am taking you shopping, and you will spend money on two designer outfits because your choice of attire is dreadful. At the very least, you need a little black dress and a tailored pantsuit. Considering your earnings, you can afford to part with funds. Please accompany me to Bal Harbor shops, where I will pick out a few nice outfits for you, as I cannot continue to borrow attire from other girls just because you don't own decent clothing."

"Lisa, I appreciate the dress," I said. I am still behind on my payments, so tonight's money will be gone within hours. I am not reluctant to buy beautiful items. It is more that I lack the funding, as I was so far behind on my rent, and..."

"Stop making excuses, Bella," Lisa interrupted harshly. "You cannot expect to earn top money if you show up to the date dressed in clothes that look like you purchased them at Walmart. And it will only be a matter of time before repeat clients become tired of spending extra money on you. No client should have to buy your wardrobe, and..."

"But Mitch bought the ball dress because it was a special event. He has bought no other items for me," I argued.

My boss tapped her foot on the tip of my shoe. "Bella," she snapped. "I speak to each client before and after a date.

I listen to excellent reviews and complaints. And you, you have the most negative feedback."

"There's no way," I groaned. "Mitch Carter requests me; if he hated me, he would want another girl to walk the room."

"Mitch likes you, Bella, but he wants a girl dressed richly, so he feels compelled to buy your outfits. However, Mitch will tire soon if he feels he has another wife, as men like Mitch want a showpiece. They do not want a woman who reminds them of their spouse, who complains she has nothing to wear when standing in front of a stacked closet. Do you get it?"

"Yes," I murmured. I cursed myself for making excuses because, in my childhood, my father lectured me that excuses lead to failure.

Thinking about that sentence, I concluded he was correct because I felt like a loser, which was ironic considering I was standing in front of the most expensive hotel in Palm Beach.

"Then we are clear," Lisa snapped. "First thing Monday, you and I are going shopping, and if I hear you have no money left after tonight's dates, I will loan you the cash, and you will work until you pay me back, okay?"

"Crystal," I whimpered and descended into CJ's Porsche.

"Good! I expect to discuss this matter in private tomorrow morning at ten o'clock. So, when you finish the date, go home, sleep, and do not waste your time or energy on boyfriend Jerry."

"Harry," I rectified, and sensing her fury, I buckled my seatbelt, grabbed the door, and slammed it shut.

I faced CJ and exhaled. "Are my clothes that awful?" I asked, twirling the material on my borrowed dress.

She hesitated before answering. "Your attire could use improvement, but you don't need to spend a fortune at an expensive shopping center like Bal Harbor. I know some specialty stores in South Miami that I could take you to, and they have fashionable clothes for far less money than Dior or Chanel."

"Would you?"

"Of course, I would."

"When can we go?"

"We can go any day I get off work." CJ hesitated. "Although, I don't recommend refusing Lisa's invitation, as neither you nor I need to be on her shit list."

I motioned and sighed. "CJ, I'll go with Lisa on Monday, and if anything, just browse the shops, as I can pretend not to like the high-end designs. Then we can shop later in the week."

CJ laughed. "Oh, Bella," she said. "Bal Harbor is a dream place to shop, and there's no way you will leave without falling in love with every item you see, as it's all Gucci, Fendi, Hermes, LV, and every other top-named brand."

"What is LV?" I inquired.

"Are you serious?"

"Yes, I am," I admitted. "Don't have fun at my expense. Tell me what it means?"

"LV are the initials of Louis Vuitton, one of the world's largest and oldest fashion houses. Their handbags adorn the hands of celebrities, rich housewives, and, on occasions, on the hands of escorts like me." She said and held up a small, tan-colored leather handbag."

"Oh," I said. "I thought your bag was a fake Michael Kors, as he also uses initials on his canvas bags?"

"Kors is a fraction of the price of LV," CJ laughed. "An MK satchel is perhaps two hundred dollars, whereas a similar style by LV is five thousand dollars."

"Are you for real?"

"Absolutely. Louis Vuitton leather is top-of-the-line and built to last a lifetime. If one item gets damaged, the fashion house will repair it and refresh the bag to look new again.

"Refresh?"

She explained, "Clean the leather, polish the hardware, and replace the zipper. "

Unexpectedly, a tap on the window jolted us, and we both glanced at Lisa, the only woman I could think of who would dare to do that. CJ pressed a button and opened the car window. "Yes," she asked. "You girls need to get going, or you'll be late." Lisa tapped her gold Rolex watch to signal the time. I raised my thumb to show I agreed. Then CJ shifted her Porsche into gear, slammed her foot on the accelerator, and sped down the ramp.

I glanced back at the Atlantic as she drove away and watched the masterpiece fade. Though a fit for a queen, it was no longer one of my favorites, and I was glad we had left. Still, celebrities praised the splendor of this exclusive retreat in all interviews, saving Atlantis millions of dollars in advertising. A famous actor revealed how grateful he was for the extensive services he had received while staying there to film his latest movie, and he was thankful that the hotel staff catered to their guests' every need.

Can I tell you what I thought of that world-famous actor as he raved about Hotel Atlantic?

Well, even if you do not want to know, I will.

After viewing his five-minute interview, I decided he was a male chauvinistic pig who treasured his visit because the Hotel Atlantic provided every service available. Drugs, escorts, you name it. The concierge had access to an extensive notebook holding connections to the best illicit street drugs and whores in South Florida. However, watching Mister Movie star rave about his healthy lifestyle sickened me, which compelled me to change the channel. To me, he was a pervert, and that is inside information.

Last week, I arrived at his hotel suite, but unlike the other women sitting around naked, snorting cocaine, I left, and it was the best decision I have ever made. So, screw the liar and his enormous ego because I owned one piece of ass that he could not buy.

The sad part of that vulgar ordeal is that I still love Hotel Atlantic and always will, as I have dreamed of getting married in its stunning ballroom my entire life. By day, the hotel functioned like a monastery. Still, as the darkness of night coveted Palm Beach, only hungry monsters prowled the floors in search of fixes that would leave most guests mortified. The daytime staff are robotic in their mannerisms and treat their guests like royalty. In contrast, the night shift ignored illegal activities and favored a hefty tip by supplying rich people with the best sins money can buy.

I had dreamt of living there but knowing that so many vices had occurred over the past two months, I no longer wanted to bask in its glory. Nor did I envision myself anywhere within its four romantic walls. In all fairness to Hotel Atlantic, my only reason for not setting up a home in the monumental building was that I needed more funds. And my dream to become married in its ballroom was just that—a dream. Now, in my mid-twenties, my once delusional ambition had fallen to the wayside, as no one had asked for my hand in marriage. Well, not yet anyway.

One day, hopefully.

I say a girl can dream.

After five minutes of high-speed driving, CJ and I were turning onto the northbound on-ramp of I-95, an interstate that runs north and south through Florida. It is similar in direction to the Florida Turnpike, but unlike the overpriced tolls on the Turnpike, most lanes on I-95 are free to drive. Still, I prefer to pay the Turnpike fees, regardless of toll charges, as it is faster.

A pang of sadness tugged at my heartstrings as I took a quick look out the passenger window, bidding farewell to Palm Beach and succumbing to the overwhelming yearning for Benny Boy, a feeling I could not bring myself to confess. Still, I expected we would arrive at our next gig in less than thirty minutes. Seeing traffic backed up for miles caused concern as a never-ending stream of red brake lights aligned the lanes ahead. The problem was a car accident, a mechanical breakdown, or an automobile problem that had become every motorist's nightmare.

"Bella, do you want to drive?" CJ asked.

Shocked, I nodded.

"I'll stop on the hard shoulder, and we can switch seats. I am just too tired to deal with this traffic. This traffic is too much, and I want to relax."

"No worries," I told her. "I'm wide awake and more than happy to drive. Besides, it is not likely to get past 30 MPH in the current situation. Would you look at all these cars stopped? This mess is worse than a parking garage on a Saturday night at the mall."

"Just take it easy and drive slow," CJ instructed, resting in the passenger seat.

"Of course," I said, placing the shift stick in gear and driving onto the highway. The red lights were stressful, and I was too annoyed to pay attention to the distressed motorist beside the road.

In haste, I no longer concerned myself or CJ about my driving ability. I saw the red line on the GPS screen, and despite the accident, all I wanted was to evade the traffic and reach our next appointment.

"May I?" I asked CJ as I retrieved a packet of cigarettes from the automobile's consul.

"Sure," she said. "Just don't use my ashtray as I use it for toll coins, and ashes mingled with quarters could prove messy."

"Of course," I repeated and focused on the drive ahead.

I sat, lit a cigarette, and searched for a lane with the fastest-moving traffic. Finding none, I imagined Harry was correct, as I remembered him telling me about the Saturday night accidents along Interstate 95. Troubled, I rolled down the car window, inhaled a Marlboro cigarette, and choked on its strength before discarding the tobacco taste, favoring gum as a nerve settler.

The traffic delay trapped, confused, and imprisoned me, and I worried about my friend Adam's dependability. Would he be waiting? Or would he leave our planned meeting to favor free drinks at Harry's party? I have a sympathetic heart that tells me he will stay. Yet I know a love of parties and a desire to parade his masculinity around every fanciful female was a handicap for Adam.

You are mean, I thought. I was judging Adam, who had done nothing wrong. My friend may be a conniving man. Still, he will wait for my return to Miami, not because he wants to get paid, but because I can count on him. Earlier, I reminded Adam that his word was his honor when money was involved. I could only hope that nobility prevailed.

My entire life, my mother taught me not to rely on anyone, least of all a man. "All men are pigs," she had complained. "And each one will be a bigger pig than the previous, and one day, Bella, that pig will ruin your life. You mark my words." As I recollected my mother's words, tears swelled as I realized it was less than two months ago when I started working for Miami Madam, and now I had proven myself unworthy of a pig.

"Bella, are you alright?" CJ asked, interrupting my trip down memory lane.

I nodded my head and focused on the road. "Allergies," I lied and nudged the Porsche forward. "We are going to be late," I added nervously.

"He will wait," CJ said confidently. "He's not going anywhere in his condition, that's for sure."

"Meaning?"

"Nothing! He is a strange man, but he is harmless. I have seen him two or three times in the past month, and he is a generous tipper, so I wanted you to go with me. You will earn double the funds you made from Mitch Carter."

"So, you have met Mitch?" I asked, surprised.

"Every working girl has seen Mitch," CJ scoffed. "He's a longtime client. I heard Lisa used to escort Mitch and that he was the reason she started her business, as he wanted to see different girls. Our boss had to shuffle through a mailing list of female friends and proposition women at local gyms, dog parks, and even bars in Miami Beach. She felt determined to satisfy Mitch Carter and his friend's hunger."

"Wow!" I gasped. "I thought Mitch was a new client. I did not realize our clients lead as complicated lives as we do, which is sad. Though I feel bad for his wife, who must know he calls girls, I bet her life is hell."

"I doubt it," CJ said and yawned. "Most women don't care if their husband is screwing around. I know lots of women who would rather their husbands receive sex from a stranger than be asked to perform the act themselves."

"Wow!" I repeated. "That is so cold. I could not imagine being married and allowing my husband to have sex with another woman. No way!"

"Obviously, not in the beginning, but as the years pass, women lose interest in the bedroom and find it easier to ignore their husband's extracurricular activities. Besides, why would their wives care? If their husbands return home, they are content. There are married women cheating on their husbands with the pool man, the gardener, and only God knows who else. Don't you read, Bella? I know you are a copy editor, but do you ever absorb the content you are viewing? Or do you skim the outline?"

"Of course, I read." I scoffed.

"Fantasy, romance, or the news?"

"Historical romance," I answered.

"You should read some blogs I found on the internet that feature nothing but horny people who are married."

"Um! No, thank you, CJ. That type of stuff is for someone else. I am too romantic and impressionable. So, please don't burst my bubble, as I'm sure enemies are waiting in line to perform that tedious chore."

In the distance, I watched a police officer move a barrier and wave motorists out of the chaos of their hellish nightmare. I sped to where a Florida Highway Patrol Officer stood. Then, I slowed the Porsche before maneuvering the vehicle onto an open lane as rapidly as possible without getting arrested.

While enjoying the fast-flowing highway traffic, CJ challenged me to listen to the reason behind our lateness, focusing on specific keywords we needed to memorize, and use should we no longer want to spend time at our upcoming client's home.

"We need a plan to explain why we're late, and it has to be solid," CJ instructed. "A fictitious story that will turn heads and grab the attention of every curious busybody in the house."

I laughed aloud. "Seriously," I said. "It's late. I doubt your client will have a house full of friends now." Then, I listened as CJ delivered a reasonable excuse and laughed aloud, as her story was funnier than a sitcom. It was refreshing to me that I could count on CJ to provide fascinating crap. I would have never dreamed of such a bullshit tale. Still, she had fooled me with her outlandish stories. I recalled as I sped toward Jupiter Inlet Colony.

I felt refreshed from giggling, but as I glanced at the GPS, I saw our exit was nearing, and I dreaded the realization that we would soon arrive at our destination. I clicked the indicator to signal a lane change, sped across the five-lane motorway, and then slowed down to exit I-95 onto West Indian Town Road. On the GPS, I saw that South Beach Road and Cato's Bridge were less than two miles away. "We'll be there soon," I mustered and soldiered along the road toward 2250 Ocean Drive.

"Are you focusing on the road or listening to my notes?" CJ asked.

"Right now, I'm vigilant on all three."

"Three?"

"Yes, I'm following the navigation system, looking out for drunk drivers, and remembering your story," I replied flatly, wishing CJ would shut up. She was rambling on about such utter nonsense that my head ached. Besides, I had listened to enough lies and told many of my own, and I noted that if CJ would listen for once and stop chatting like a silly schoolchild, the blabbering woman might be surprised to learn that I, too, have ideas, but she did not.

To CJ, I was an unsophisticated girl, much too young to understand the importance of our chaotic life. And what do I do? I allow her to judge me. One day, I would like to shatter CJ's convictions that I can only drive a car. I would mention it now but now was not the time; at this moment, my coworker had no interest in anything other than herself.

There must be something I could do, I thought, noticing rain spots on the windshield. There was and is, I argued, even if it was only extortion. Who did CJ believe she was to put words into my mouth and order me around? I should kill her. No, I shook my head. I could not do that. Lisa would kill me. Rightly so, and if she did not hire a hitman and chose to perform the murderous act herself, we would both be in jail for life.

Bella, accept there is nothing you can do, not in this lifetime, anyway. Though I harbored a secret desire to throttle CJ, I could not help but feel grateful for her role in introducing me to this money-making scheme. She was, as Adam informed me earlier today, a lifesaver.

Thinking about Saturday afternoon when I was moaning to Adam, I smiled as I remembered his advice. "Bella, you would be in financial ruin if not for CJ. The publishing company where you work is no longer getting big accounts, and if your boss lays off staff, you are the first to go. Last in, first out, if you catch my drift?"

Adam, I caught your drift. Since it has happened before, I expect to get my marching papers any day.

In my first job, I held a management position at a South Beach newspaper, which I enjoyed. Well, until my boss fired me one day for behaving combatively and refusing to take a pay cut. Still, I understood my past employer's cutback; though it wounded my pride, the job loss crafted my acting skills as I pretended to go to work every day with Harry and my friends.

I performed that circus routine every morning until I landed my current job at Bob's Copy and Editing Services.

Trust me when I tell you how bitterly aware I am of the job market in South Beach, where talented artists rule the town. Although I have a gift for words, I cannot claim to be as skilled as Ernest Hemingway. I am simply a girl my boss pays to read while sitting at a desk. I dream of writing, but an author needs an idea, writing skills, and time to combine them to draft a bestselling novel. Hence, I refer to one of the greatest literary authors ever born.

Allow me to explain. Regardless of the risks I have taken and will continue, my mind tells me to pretend all is well, even if my world is crumbling. I love Harry, and I do not want to lose him. The knowledge that I cannot hold a job would shock him, as he thinks I am a responsible woman.

Ha!

Now that is funny.

Harry views me as a success in my occupation. To date, he does not know I am a phony who is too cowardly to confront my demons and admit failure.

Admit failure?

Admit, I can no longer support myself.

Admit that I, Bella Bloom, who has boasted my independence since my teenage years, will now accept demise and receive charity from a man?

Never!

I noticed Highway US 1. I turned left and drove toward South Beach Road, holding my breath as we sped over Loxahatchee River.

We were getting closer by the minute, and my nervous energy increased with each passing second.

Just deal with it, Bella, I chastised.

Stop thinking about the past and focus on the now.

SUDDENLY, A RAINSTORM burst through the blackened sky like a battleship cannon exploding at sea. In a burst of fury, a lightning bolt tore through the dark highway and collided with the metal piling, causing the street to light up so brightly that it felt like day.

As I crossed Cato's Bridge, rain poured from the sky like a giant waterfall, cascading its fury until the windshield wipers could no longer clear my view.

My eyesight was impeccable, yet in that instance, it failed me, making me feel disconnected from everything. I felt utterly stuck, like a massive rock and an unstoppable waterfall crept on me.

"I think it's best to slow down," CJ said. "We could slide off the road. So be cautious."

"Yes, I will. Trust me, I am going as carefully as possible along this road."

"Oh, my, would you look at this storm? We will look like drowned rats once we leave my car. So much for looking fabulous."

"True," I murmured, focusing on the flooded highway as I turned right onto Beach Road. I have a vivid memory of hydroplaning across three lanes of traffic one evening, and when my car finally stopped, a man pulled me from the wreckage and sat my drenched body on the side of the road. The experience was so awful that I have feared driving in the rain since that accident. "My head is pounding," I said, searching my handbag for a bottle of aspirin but coming up empty. My eyes burned as I searched each mailbox for a house number, but with so much rain, it was futile. So, I put the car in the park gear and turned off the engine. CJ sat upright. "Why have you stopped?" she asked." You're in the middle of the road, Bella, and this is not his home."

The sight of CJ's eyes, filled with cruelty and hostility, made me recoil in fear. "I stopped because I could not see the road ahead," I mumbled. "I also have a headache, and this storm is not helping at all."

"I have water on the back seat. Do you want a bottle?"

"Maybe," I said, exhausted. I sighed, aware that no client wants to see a tired escort, and right then, I would have paid a hundred dollars for one cup of hot coffee.

"Bella, are you okay?"

"Yes."

"Do you want to switch places?"

"In this downpour?"

"Do we have any choice?"

"No!"

"Okay, let's do this," she said. "I'm going to climb into the back of my car, and then you can move to the passenger seat. That way, we can maneuver without getting wet."

I glanced at my friend and sighed. "I'm so tired, CJ, and also worried the client will become angry because I am too drained to perform my routine. And..."

"Come on," she coerced. "Pull the car to the side of the road and let me drive. I can see you need a break. Besides, it will give you time to pull yourself together, and I'll give you a pill that will give you some pep." Delving into the Porsche glovebox, she retrieved a bottle. "Here, take one; you will start feeling better in minutes."

"What type of pills are they?"

"Caffeine. These tablets put the Perk in Percocet. Take half if you're worried, but please fix your makeup." Maddened, I wanted to punch my friend in the face. How dare CJ be so condescending to imply that I was the only one who needed to fix my makeup?

What about her?

I wondered if my coworker noticed her tired and drawn face or if the harrowing nature of these late-night excursions had taken on her looks. Anticipating each client's emotional state or sobriety was more aging than any daytime job I had held, and that freaked me out. In my anger, I wanted to inform CJ that I had a mother and did not need her maternal side to smother me, as I was not a child, but I said nothing because what was the point? She would reject my ideals in two seconds flat. So, to avoid a scene, I took the medication, gulped down a mouthful of water, and swallowed hard. "Thanks," I mustered and moved my head from side to side. "I just need a couple of minutes to feel alive," I added, watching as she prepared to climb into the driver's seat.

"If you maneuver yourself into the passenger seat, I will drive, but let's get busy as we're late, and this client is a clock watcher."

"Of course," I responded, unbuckling my seatbelt, and scrambling over the gearstick to rest in the passenger seat. I watched CJ ascend from the vehicle's rear, adjust the driver's seat, and start the engine. "Feel better?" she asked, without an ounce of compassion.

I nodded.

At once, I realized my partner in crime enjoyed the job theatrics, which was new to me as I had watched her function as two different people tonight.

A skilled communicator, CJ was born under the star sign Gemini, and like the twins, she was two personalities in one. The kind and loyal persona could switch to a shallow and competitive demeanor in seconds and throw in her explosive temper, and anyone in her path was well and truly fucked.

She was a true Gemini.

A bossy bitch.

Suddenly, she thrust a pad into my chest. "Don't forget, if the client asks what took us so long to get here, we cannot say we were on a previous date. We must tell him we were partying with friends and lost track of time. Got it?" CJ asked.

"Absolutely," I said, reading the note she ordered me to memorize. Then, I guffawed as CJ warbled to a song, sounding dreadful because she did not know the words and eerily reminded me of a stray cat in the night's heat.

In misery, I focused on the poorly lit road and wished for us to arrive soon to put this appointment behind us. I longed for a glimpse of Harry, his fiery anger burning in his eyes, feeling neglected and abandoned. Still, I felt that when he saw me, he would realize the error of his ways and forget and forgive, as the good Bible instructs. If not? Then my karma would doom me to spend eternity in hell. However, I felt condemned now as I watched the rain.

A drenched traffic lane flooded the road, and I could see a dark, glossy surface resembling an iced lake. The road's slickness forced the Porsche to hydroplane and swerve across Beach Road, missing a ditch by inches.

The worst thing about Florida was the weather. It was sunny and calm or dark and thunderous, creating havoc on the roads because the drainage could not manage the bucketloads of rainfall that fell from the sky. The most expensive neighborhoods, like Jupiter, did not differ from the poverty-stricken streets in Miami, as they all mirrored swimming pools when Mother Nature visited.

I felt tense in my seat, for it was an impossible drive, and I was thankful that I was now merely a passenger on this chaotic trip. A lightning streak illuminated the road ahead, and since I was not wearing a seatbelt, I lunged forward and screamed. CJ grappled my arm and pushed me back against the seat. In the distance, I saw a humongous black mist covering the car, and my foot slammed to the floor as CJ braked hard, which caused the Porsche to skid and swerve across the roadway, narrowly missing a large King Palm. Then CJ checked the rearview mirror, reversed, drove over the battered plants, and made a 360-degree turn to regain the correct direction. Through it all, she functioned as if nothing had happened, and I surmised CJ was, as Beatrice Ryder had told me, a woman with bigger balls than any man.

"Are you okay?" she asked again. I grew angry as she drove around a wrecked vehicle without stopping to check if the car held a person in distress. "Are you for real?" I spat. "There may be a driver inside that vehicle who could be hurt. Why didn't you check? What is wrong with you?" I yelled. "Stop the car. I'm going to make sure that nobody is injured." I unfastened my seatbelt and unlocked the door. "Oh, and another thing," I sobbed. "I'm leaving. I am not going on this date, and I do not care what you say to Lisa because I am quitting. You got it?"

"Calm down," CJ soothed. "Believe me, Bella. There were no injured people in that car. I was here last night, and I checked the car myself."

"Well, you could have mentioned that a minute ago," I snapped, becoming increasingly uncomfortable by the second. "I hate this job," I added and frowned.

CJ stopped the car and thumped my biceps. "Toughen up, girl. If you don't, you will never make it in this industry."

I inhaled deeply and exhaled. My anxiety was growing due to the unrelenting storm, but I was able to calm myself by taking a deep breath and looking for a way out of this nightmare if only to alleviate my suffering. Counting to one hundred helped, and I decidedly counted backward to one to ensure I would not have a panic attack. Still, I struggled to regain calmness as I watched everyone turn against me despite my fair treatment of others, which left me confused.

Why is everyone so quick to point out my flaws?

Why am I so quick to quit?

The companion job is all right, and the money is perfect. Instead of feeling sorry for myself and risking my boss firing me, I should get a grip and look at this situation more positively.

And I do try. I do. I swear I do.

But CJ?

She took patience, and I found her to be more obnoxious with each passing second, especially on late-night gigs like this. I noticed CJ stopped the car in front of a stately home, and as I spotted the house number on a fancy sign, I groaned. We had reached our destination, and our arrival only fueled more anxiety in my nervous mind.

Resolutely, I gave myself a harsh pep talk. You heard, CJ. I nagged. Toughen up, accept the good with the bad, and deal with it, Bella. And for the love of God, stop wallowing in the past and focus on the now, which was genius as the now was hard to avoid.

In the distance, I saw the outline of a man illuminated in the automobile's headlights. He was standing on the porch and soaked. But, worse, much worse than that, the ugly, fat pig of a man did not look happy.

LURCH

DOSTOEVSKY BELIEVED that the darker the night, the brighter the stars. The deeper the grief, the closer is God...

If you have watched The Adams Family, you will grasp the nuance behind this chapter's heading. On the show, Lurch was grotesque, but my second client that night, Clive Jenkins, was worse.

In contrast to the tall and lean Lurch, Clive Jenkins was a stout man who compensated for his lack of height with roundness, and I felt suffocated by his weight as he embraced me warmly. Though, admittedly, over the past two months, I have become accustomed to the daily hardships overweight people face, and while I have dated chubby men, my eyes can only oversee so much when confronted with their flabby skin. Still, in all fairness, it is...

Their life.

Their choice.

I have no issues sharing a dinner table with people who are obese. Regardless of appearance, I always seek out something appealing in the people I meet, often finding endearing quirks unrelated to physical attributes. Although, I do have zero tolerance for anyone, fat or thin, who dribbles like a Mastiff dog, as it turns my stomach. Therefore, try as I might with this client, there is nothing attractive about him, and I mean that... CJ's client, Jenkins, salivates worse than any animal I have met or seen, and he left me covered in saliva whenever he touched my arm. "I can't wait to see you intimately," he had said, pulling me close while standing on the doorstep of his stately home. The stench of his spit almost caused me to heave up vile. "Likewise," I lied, swallowing hard to mask my disgust. I used a napkin to dry my arms and stood at the front door, awaiting an invitation to enter.

"Go inside," Jenkins ordered.

"Yes, sir!" I saluted, annoyed by his demanding tone. Still, I nodded, pretending I was busy preening at a nearby planting pot, and waited for CJ and Jenkins to lead.

In the parlor, I stopped short behind them both because my sensitive nose had detected a foul odor, like a rotting corpse, and I sneezed until the offensive scent dissipated.

As I watched Jenkins hug CJ, I caught sight of his oversized stomach, which shocked me. It was clear the client was heavier than my first estimation of five hundred pounds. His weight is closer to one ton.

Ah! If I had a scale, I could put myself out of this questionable misery and fill in the missing blanks for you. The wobble in his step caused concern about his heaviness, but I cannot be sure.

What am I sure of?

I will tell you.

I am sure that his slovenly walk and dirty clothes made me nauseous, and you, too, would cry in disgust. Also, Clive's protruding stomach, lack of legs, and beady eyes resembling ping-pong balls reminded me of Jabba the Hutt, the slug-like creature from Star Wars. However, his slobbering mouth, causing fluids to fall onto his chin each time he smiled, was equally sickening.

Disgusted, I shivered in the chilly air, longing for a winter coat to comfort me as his home was ice cold due to his excessive sweating.

In this client's case, and knowing about copyright laws, I will rename Clive "Jabba the Hutt" Jenkins and refer to him as Tubby because I want to avoid a potential lawsuit. I hope you remember this reference point so that I can continue my story about Tubby.

The interior of his home was fashionable, with the usual Florida décor of soft pastels, green hues, and beige. An assortment of famous art paintings, antique statues, and soaring ceilings displayed the biggest and best merchandise money could buy. The furniture was oversized, and though it looked comfortable and inviting from afar, upon closer inspection, it reeked of body odor, and I almost vomited my guts out.

The worst, and I mean worse than anything, was the short-sleeved shirt Tubby wore since it exposed his hairy chest.

As if it could not get more revolting, let me add it does, and it did.

Clive's greasy hair was everywhere I looked, especially on his chest, arms, hands, and knuckles, making Tubby look dirtier than a homeless person who had not bathed in years. I squirmed, imagining how poor his hygiene would be if he smelled so foul. On top of his stench, dandruff covered the curly mop hanging from his crown, and though tucked behind his ears, it slid forward and mingled with a spotty chin that needed a shave eons ago.

I will also share with you that Jenkins sweats more than any other man I have met. Watching smelly droplets of body odor drip each time he moved made him resemble a rain-soaked gorilla.

No insult to monkeys.

As I share this encounter, I have added more descriptive because I want you to understand the filth I faced. However, I do not want you to vomit, so trust me when I tell you that Tubby's week-old beard grew sparsely and clung in clumps across his double chin, which was torture to look at while we were talking. Nonetheless, CJ treated Tubby like a king, and she did not raise a brow when the beastly man walked from the sofa and into the kitchen with a likeness like a hefty duck. He mortified me when his body bumped into expensive artifacts, leaving them yucky. Yet, dearest CJ smiled and continued chatting as if covering furnishings with grime was acceptable.

I tried vainly to focus on his impressive collection of paintings to distract myself from the smell of his armpits, which stunk each time his hand scratched his balding head.

If that distraction failed, I fidgeted with my grandma's watch and wished I were elsewhere. The date had just begun, yet I grew uneasy and yearned to leave. If my car had been nearby, say, next to his magnificent group of Bonsai plants, I might have walked out and driven off to somewhere I did not care, but Miami did spring to mind.

An enormous stainless-steel refrigerator dominated the kitchen and glistened against the whitewashed cabinets.

Unlike Clive, the sheen reminded me of cleanliness, as it was the only item I saw not covered in oily handprints.

Smiling, Clive opened the door and boasted about shelves filled with champagne, juice, and food. "Nothing but the best for my favorite girl," he said, smirking at CJ, who clung to his arm.

"Open a bottle, Clive," she urged. "You remember how much I enjoy mimosa? It always puts me in the right mood."

What is the right mood for sex? I wondered.

She kissed his cheek, and it became clear to me. CJ drank alcohol to make her date with this client tolerable, which made me wonder if that was the reason we had shared a ride. If she needed alcohol to deal with Tubby, she would need a driver, which is why she dragged me onto this awful date.

Ah! To learn, I was nothing more than a chauffeur, and even then, I was not particularly good at that, as CJ forever criticized my driving skills. Yet, here she was, reliant on me to get her out of this appointment once our time was up, thus far, a two-hour gig. It would be two hours of torture for me, as I could imagine doing nothing other than chatting with Jenkins because I had done nothing more. However, on that busy night, Lisa and CJ planned to break me in, which troubled me.

Nobody likes to feel like a fool, and right now, I feel more foolish than ever, and that hurts.

Suddenly, Jenkins handed me a glass of champagne and orange juice. I took the beverage and pretended to drink it, but I secretly poured the Mimosa into a nearby planter.

Watching CJ and Jenkins interact like old friends was difficult. Though relief swept over me because they knew each other, I feared what both Jenkins and CJ had in store for me.

She was my friend and supposed to protect me, but if CJ became blind, stinking drunk, what help would she be to me?

None whatsoever.

An idea appeared, and a wash of hesitation and relief enveloped me. I checked the time on a kitchen appliance clock—two hours to go. I began counting the minutes while thinking about how I would avoid a weird connection between Tubby and me. My only resolution was to play sick, which was easy since I always looked ill. Besides, I needed to get paid, as I had not messed up my night with Harry to end up without even minimum wage for effort.

CJ rested her arm on Tubby's shoulder, and I lingered behind as we strolled into the garden. Though I did not want to go outside in the pouring rain, I followed, hoping to stay dry, as getting soaked was not fun. Fortunately, Clive had a protective screened patio built atop a lavish pool, and the clear water glistened against the thunderous cloudy sky, which intrigued me because the water felt warm to the touch. Unlike the dirty house, the large pool was spotlessly clean and inviting.

Tubby flipped a switch, and the mosaic pattern on the bottom of the pool glowed in the downpour. The large pond resembled rough currents at sea and reminded me of movies about ships sinking as they crossed the Atlantic Ocean, which caused me to remember a trip I had taken with my boyfriend two months earlier.

While navigating the Atlantic on our boating adventure, Harry and I met a fierce storm that tilted his vessel with such force that we worried it might submerge. Thanks to Harry's ability as a captain, we could maneuver the small sailboat alongside the powerful current until the violent waters and the thunderous booms that pierced our eardrums gradually calmed, bringing peace to our minds.

Thank God Harry is an experienced sailor.

If not?

We would have perished that day.

After fifteen minutes of poolside chitchat between CJ and Tubby, we all headed back inside the house due to the high wind blowing foliage across the garden. Despite the wretched air conditioning blasting frigid air, I was content to be inside, even though I was freezing. However, I was fortunate to avoid getting wet in the rain even with the strong sideways wind, as the rain had drenched CJ, and seated on the same sofa as Tubby, she did not look happy.

I sat across from both and noticed a peculiar tension in their behavior, which concerned me as they were both best friends before entering the garden. I questioned the nature of their discussion that led to such anguish and prayed I would not endure the brunt of their hatred. "Is everything okay?" I asked nervously.

Tubby rose, crossed the room, and spoke to me. "It looks like you need a refill," he said. "Sit here," he gestured to a stained seat cushion. "You relax, and I will fetch you another drink."

I watched as he retreated into the kitchen. Though annoyed by his commanding tone, I thanked CJ for the borrowed dress because at least my possessions were safe from his stench. Yes, my clothing may be cheap and tacky. But, in my mind, even my affordable Walmart attire was too fancy to sit on Tubby's musty sofa. I turned to CJ and nudged her arm. "What's going on, and what do you want me to do?" I whispered, hoping she would see my nervousness. But drunk, she could only hiss, like Tubby, that I needed to relax.

The stereo system began to play disco songs, and dance tunes blasted from the speakers as Tubby returned carrying a round tray filled with fresh drinks, which he placed on the coffee table. I shuffled my feet away from the gorgeous handcrafted varnished table because the drinks at the top were unsteady and spilled onto the floor and my shoes, which I had hoped to return the next day. If they reeked of cocktails, the storekeeper would not accept them back, as it would be clear that I had worn them. Well, enough about my shoes. I want to continue writing about Tubby and CJ, who are far more interesting than I am or could ever be.

I sat up straight when I saw CJ suggest to Tubby that he take a shower, and though I agreed with her, in my mind, no amount of bathing would make me like him more. It was laughable to watch CJ struggle to raise his large posterior off the couch and coax him toward the primary bedroom with a flirtatious smile. I pretended not to notice and continued to drink and act giddy, as I could only imagine I should act in this situation. Still, I realized my seriousness was a turnoff to Tubby, who appeared irritated.

Two minutes later, bursting with joy, I am thrilled to announce Tubby's triumphant departure from his putrid seat as he trails behind CJ, who lectured about the advantages of a refreshing shower. I almost laughed when she promised to join him, as she described it with such vivid detail that it sounded more like an apocalyptic romance novel. Mind you, Tubby Tubs beamed ear to ear and admitted his senses were wide awake.

Thanks, CJ, I groaned.

Now, he is expecting quite the show.

Yuck.

CJ turned and instructed me to follow. Once inside the bathroom, she told me to change into a towel robe and sit beside the filthy tub.

"Come with me," CJ hissed, latching onto my hand, and dragging me into the closet. "What is wrong with you?" she asked, perplexed.

"Nothing," I stammered.

"Then change into the robe," she demanded. Without trying to hide my horrified expression, I gasped and said, "I can't. I have never done this before," I reasoned. "I'm scared, as this requirement is new. In the past, I have only had social dates, and now you want me to get naked and pretend it is, okay?"

"Listen to me, Bella," CJ warned. "You were lucky with your past clients and their dating requests, but tonight, you are here because Lisa insisted, I break you in. Do you understand?" She scolded me.

"There is no way I can be intimate with that man," I blurted out. "No way in hell. I'll throw up if you force me to be with him sexually, which in itself is already making me feel nauseous."

"Wise up, Bella, before you get fired from this agency. In this industry, we do not get to pick who or what we see or do. Do you get it?" I tried to reason, but CJ ignored my protests and threw the rule book at me. So, I stood, mortified, as she clawed at the straps of my dress and pulled it down to my ankles before throwing the smelly robe at me. "Change, now." She spoke roughly. "If not? Then, I'm going to fire you." She paused and eyed me with suspicion. "The point of this job is to make the client feel special. It is not about your happiness, Bella, because you are not paying; he is." She paused again. "And you do not get to choose what you do, nor do you choose with whom. This industry is about making money and helping the client think he is the most handsome man in the room. It is not about making a man feel ugly, which is what your actions are implying. You do not like or fall in love with a business associate. You are supposed to make him believe you could. Though we both know that will never happen, the client does not. Fulfill the illusion that is all I ask, and that is what the client is paying you for..." she said, hesitating. "My point is, Bella, He's paying! He deserves to get his money's worth, and he deserves fulfillment. Stop being selfish and just get with tonight's program. When you have changed and are ready to accept your assignment, I want you to return to the bathroom wearing a beautiful smile."

I snared CJ's arm, "but I can't," I told her. "I can't do it. Sex before marriage goes against everything I believe in. My mother did not raise me like that, and I cannot have sex for money. I just cannot. Why can't you understand that these dates are bothersome to the way my mother raised me, and this, having sex or being intimate, well, it is fawned upon in every Bible I have studied?"

"I truly don't give a fuck about your backward, hillbilly upbringing. You should have thought about God before you accepted a job as a whore."

"But I was told I am a social companion. I did not know that clients expected more. Had I known, I would have told you both that I cannot take assignments."

"Grow the hell up, will you?"

"I'm trying. But I do not remember you teaching me about this occupation's ins and outs. And why was that, CJ? Why didn't you tell me the job included sex with men, even ugly men, for money?"

"Oh, I see," CJ sneered. "If our clients were handsome, you would have sex with them, but because they are old and unattractive, you feel you are too good to satisfy their needs. Is that it?"

"Of course not," I blurted out. "It wouldn't differ how each client looked because I wouldn't go further than holding hands or kissing them on the cheek. Since you are asking, I will add that I would not be jumping into bed with any of my clients, so why are you forcing me to go to bed with yours?"

She threw her arms in the air and sighed.

I crossed the room and gnawed at my lower lip.

"Bella, I am sick of babysitting you. I want you to change your clothes. Please get your act together before you blow the date, leaving you owing Lisa's funds and me."

I watched as she exited the closet and slammed the door. Then, I crumbled to the floor and cried. What I was crying for or to who troubled me because, deep down, I knew I was alone because no one knew my location except Lisa, CJ, and Tubby. As I sat on the carpet, my tear-stained eyes wandered around the closet, and I wished I were dead. For, hanging before me were racks of women's clothing, which increasingly upset me, as, like my earlier client Mitch Carter, Tubby Jenkins was a married man.

Yuck! I thought. Who would marry such a pig?

Not I.

I ascended the floor and sniffled as I struggled to regain my composure. I fixed my swollen face in a mirror and then pinched my cheeks to add color. If the hanging clothes had not stunk so much, I would have wiped my face and blown my nose with the fabrication. Instead, I breathed deeply, realizing I needed an antihistamine to clear my blocked sinuses.

Get to it, Bella, I cursed. Do the least amount possible and end this crazy existence before it forces you to lose all sense of reality and become robotic, like CJ and Lisa.

Alas, easier said than done, but quitting in the middle of Jupiter, in a house that belonged to a stranger and without a car to drive, messed me up. So, reluctantly, I conceded I was at the mercy of my coworker and would do as told if I wanted to get out of this frightful ordeal in one piece.

Who would care if I lost all my dignity? I wondered. I considered this date the last price I had to pay to survive this meeting. Besides, I did not know Tubby, and my friends knew nothing about my middle-of-the-night adventures.

Granted, this dating scenario would burn me alive. Still, if managed correctly, I could get out unscathed. And though tempted to fall to my knees and beg the Lord above for death, I pulled myself together and faced the consequences before I lost all courage.

Later, in this hellish ordeal, I am going to confess to you, my reader, just what I experienced the day before I was born. You will not understand or believe me, but I swear it is true. Until then, let me continue explaining my experience with Tubby, the cigar-smoking drunkard who has yet to understand the importance of personal hygiene.

In a gallant effort, I appeared from the closet wearing only my underwear and the smelly robe, which I draped off my shoulders to expose my flesh as a subtle tease with hopes he would find me revolting and choose to devour CJ, his regular paid companion.

The first thing I noticed was the dim bathroom lights. Then, in all of Tubby's glory, I watched as he strode from the shower with a towel slung over his shoulder before descending into the sunken bathtub where CJ was waiting, champagne in hand. He basked with delight in the water and told me to come in, as the water felt refreshing.

Sickening. He looks evil, I thought. Mainly because he was expecting time spent with us both, which grossed me out; moreover, he was cooing like a dove about a much-needed visit to a spa earlier that day to release his excess energy. However, despite his newfound interest, he continued to pass gas with farts that stunk like moldy cheese. "Earlier today, I behaved like a beast," he said. "I also had a quick sex session at a massage parlor in Palm Beach, and unbeknownst to the people involved, I videotaped it to watch later. I have it if you want to see it?"

CJ rubbed his neck, and I crossed the room, filled a glass of champagne, and pretended to sip the acid-inducing grapes, trying desperately not to belch, vomit, or fart, as I noticed champagne appeared to cause all three symptoms in Tubby and I feared the same reaction.

"So," he asked as I sat aside the tub. "Do you want to join us?"

I shrugged. "I don't see any room for me," I answered and smiled.

"Hey, what is your name again?"

"Sarah," I lied.

"Do you know what I did today?"

I shook my head.

"I watched two men having sex, and I videotaped both. So, I will ask again. Do you girls want to watch the video?"

"But why?" CJ inquired.

"Because I'm a freak, that's why."

His words, not mine.

CJ laughed.

I felt sickened.

"Girls, let me tell you about my fetishes," Tubby said. He raised his foot, leaned forward, and picked at an overgrown toenail. "A friend of mine, Jimmy. Well, he likes to get what he wants, which is setting people up and then extorting them." he paused, and a sly smile etched his lips. "Anyway, I made ten thousand to watch two politicians go at it. I left after I had finished recording their meeting. Suffice it, Voila. That's why you're here."

"I don't understand?" CJ sounded perplexed and then asked, "What is the big deal with two same-sex people going at it? Being gay is not a big deal nowadays."

"I have to pee," Tubby announced. He rose from the murky bathwater as gray bubbles clung to his body. He turned to face me. "Do you get it?"

I nodded.

"Good," he said and smirked. "Now, get your skinny posterior in the tub."

I groaned, experiencing vulnerability and discomfort, I dropped the stinky robe to the ground and stood nervously in my underwear, afraid to move.

Suddenly, CJ stood, her nakedness covered by a sheer bodysuit and bath bubbles. "Clive, I don't want Bella. Er, I mean Sarah in the jacuzzi," she announced. "I've decided I want you all to myself."

Is this girl for real? I thought, and not knowing whether to enter the tub or stay put, I froze.

He roared with laughter and wrapped a towel around his middle. "Don't be jealous," Tubby teased, winking at CJ's reflection in a wall mirror. "You know, you're my number one whore, right?"

CJ nodded in agreement, which sickened me again. What woman would allow someone to call her a hoe? It has only been one hour since CJ and Lisa assured us that we were above street prostitution. Yet, here CJ sat, smug, just moments after Tubby called her a whore, which showed me that she was indeed a slut, hoe, or call it what you want, but regardless of interpretation, synonymous, it was the same.

Tubby chuckled and used his blow dryer to de-mist the mirror. "I look darn hot tonight," he said. "Maybe not like Brad Pitt, but I still look fantastic, considering my age."

I tried to hide a frown as I stared at his bald reflection, bulging stomach, and flabby arm.

"A workout with me at your fancy gym would help," CJ proposed, exiting the tub.

"I told you to go whenever you want."

"And I told you I would only go with you," she said, teasing his arm before brushing her hair. "I think I need a haircut and maybe a day at the spa. Are you interested in taking me to your salon later this week?"

I noticed Tubby's frown and wondered what part of CJ's last comment had irked him so much.

"Is everything alright?" I asked.

"Fine," he snapped. "I'm trying to lose weight, and seeing my mirrored reflection is daunting." He patted his stomach. "I was injured in an automobile accident two years ago, and since then, I've done nothing but eat and sleep. Hence the added weight," he rubbed his unshaven face. "Girls, I should never let myself go. It was foolish not to notice I am fat. I've never looked this bad and am fighting to regain my muscular frame."

I wanted to laugh, but I acted sympathetic because it was clear that Tubby's weight had not increased in the past few years. I reckoned he had been a fat person since childhood.

"You look perfect to me," CJ chirped. "You're not fat and will get fit again soon. Besides, most women adore a man with meat on their bones. The skinny look was over the minute modern women pushed the nineties waif models aside for a more voluptuous figure. All those guys who pump iron to become muscular look ridiculous, and their rock-hard stomachs are uncomfortable as the flesh is too hard to cuddle up with."

That is not true, I thought. My mind fell onto Harry's fit body and even how sexy Benny Boy would look shirtless.

Tubby grimaced and continued to clear the foggy mirror. If only to scrutinize his appearance. Again, he frowned as he stared at his humongous physique. "I'm calling my trainer, as I have to get back into a workout schedule," he spoke in a decided tone.

"I told you I would go with you. I'm always here to help you."

"But I have a trainer."

"Yes, I understand, but I will help motivate you and keep you in a workout program."

"Not right now, CJ. I need a man, not a woman. Besides, you live in the south, and I need people nearby."

"Well, I could stay here with you," she suggested.

"No!" Tubby snapped again. He posed sideways in the mirror and sucked his stomach in and out like a child. "I do not want a girlfriend. I like my freedom and the luxury of coming and going without questions. And you," he slapped CJ's bottom "You would be the ruin of me."

"Ouch!" CJ answered and slapped his bottom. "Why would you say that? I am happy to be your friend, Clive. I only want the best for you."

Tubby reached for his champagne glass and chugged the Mimosa. "I appreciate your concern, CJ. However, years of hard labor invested in nothing, but television and food have destroyed my physique. And I need to clean up my act if I do not want to look like an old man," he informed and then spoke to his reflection as if to assure himself he could succeed.

"Are you okay?" I asked, sensing the tension in the room.

"I am fine, though I must deliver a video recording sometime this morning. If you both want to watch it, you can. It's intimate, and the man who hired me to film it will be pleased with what I have gained on tape."

"Is that the political recording you mentioned earlier?" CJ asked, rubbing cream onto her legs, arms, and chest.

"Yes. It is all about sex, sex, and more sex. I'm getting hard just thinking about it." Tubby said. "Damn! The politicians were hot; the older one had hundreds of tricks up his sleeve," he added, feeling his hardness grow, which became plain to CJ and me.

"What is the purpose of the tape?" CJ asked.

"Don't worry your little mind about that," he said. "Though, I will tell you it is the bitch of all bitches, and one politician was thrashing orders around as if the male-bitch was mute. In fact," he glanced at us, "both of you can get dressed, as I have a friend stopping by in ten minutes."

"Seriously?" I asked, fearful the police officers were going to break down his front door since Tubby had boasted about filming potential politicians, which could put all our lives in danger.

"Why, yes," Tubby scoffed. "See, my dick is getting harder and harder, and if I weren't on to something brilliant, it would be limp because you girls do nothing for me."

"Oh, honey," CJ sighed. "You enjoy my company, and I adore yours. Why, we have been friends for over a year. That should count for something."

"It instilled in me I have no interest in girls. Now, dress and leave or hide in the closet. It is your call. I do not want my friends to see either of you. So, decide, and make it fast."

I pulled the robe tighter around my waist. "Let's go," I told CJ, but she ignored me. Why? I did not know, but it was stupid of CJ to sit frozen when Tubby said we could leave, particularly since he informed us both that he had no interest in girls. After hearing the good news, I wanted to go home, but my coworker had another agenda, which confused me more than Tubby's dislike of women. Dumbfounded, I wondered why he spent thousands of dollars for women to visit if he detested their company. However, CJ's client had no desire to answer my questions, and I surmised he liked the sound of his voice too much to listen to either CJ or me. In my resume, I concluded that Clive Jenkins, aka Tubby, was a strange man, and weirdos like him could be dangerous if not already a nut job. Either way, it was time for me to dress and leave.

Suddenly, Tubby started speaking again, and his voice chilled me. "I have to confess," he said, combing wet hair and slicking it behind his ears, exposing his balding. "The person who hired me to record the politicians wants to blackmail them, and he had due cause, for they were both rotten, lying sacks of shits. If elected, they would be no good to the public because they only cared about money and power, not Palm Beach County."

I wanted to escape to the quietness of the main closet again, if only to retrieve my dress, but Tubby had not finished ranting. So, I struggled to be calm and listened to more of his boisterous explanations. Bored out of my mind, I gnawed at my lower lip and waited for him to finish dressing. His floral shirt and black trousers made him look sharp, like a gentleman. His clothes were expensive, and it amazed me how two simple items could turn a slob into a human being. As quickly as I thought about the word gentleman, my mind wandered toward a man who was born one, a man who did not inherit the word, and there was a vast difference between both.

A man born with nobility would always be exemplary.

In contrast, a man who inherited wealth would always revert to his familiar upbringing. Please do not ask me why I thought of Benjamin Barrymore, as I did not know, and considering the sordid situation I engaged in, Benny Boy should be the last person on my mind. Still, I could not stop thinking about him and wondered if he had a secret life like Tubby, CJ, or me, which was insane for me to wonder as Ben was born with a silver spoon in his mouth. Ben's family had more money than God. Well, not entirely, but I am sure you understand what I mean.

Thinking about God, have I told you I have met him?

I have.

I have met him each time an angel summoned me to incarnate across one of my plentiful lives. No! I have not spoken with God while here on Earth, but we have conversed in a place far away from all the crazy chaos that dominates most people's lives. When I am ready to discuss my meeting with God, I will tell you in-depth how my soul renewed itself in peace, love, and security. But first, I do need time to decide if I want to share those meetings with you, as I understand not everyone is a believer, and I respect that. So, allow me to figure out if now is the right moment to expose the history of my soul's incarnations.

Okay, I just counted from one to thirty in my heart, and realizing that time is of the essence, I have decided to share a sacred part of my life with you.

The truth about my earlier existence became clear shortly after my brother's sudden crossover. One day, in the middle of a conversation with my mother, we discussed spirituality, and we agreed that humans rarely understood the fragility of death, let alone life. Then, I reminded Mom that she would eventually heal from her despair.

She never did.

I am sad to reveal.

In all fairness, though, I was far too young to understand the complexities that had repeated themselves throughout all the lives I have passed through while under God's guidance.

Allow me to explain... My older brother passed away several years ago. A freak accident happened during college football practice, and the intense Florida heat caused him to collapse, never to regain consciousness. On that fateful September afternoon, and following that tragic event, my mother passed away shortly after, as unfortunately, she never managed to overcome the grief of losing her child.

The loss of my brother crippled my mother mentally, physically, and spiritually, and while I saw my mother's pain and suffering, it was one of the most arduous periods of my life. Some years later, I still miss my brother, and I reminisce about the time spent with my mother, particularly on holidays, since she is no longer here to enjoy special days like birthdays and Mother's Day.

At the time of my brother's demise, I could only offer words of wisdom to my mother, as I was still a teenager and had no source of income to provide financial aid as my brother had done. A little later, I told my mother that it was awful when she fell pregnant out of wedlock and how rotten her parents were to force her out of their home because of embarrassment, which was the way in those days. Chatting away, I mentioned how sad she looked while stranded at a train station, with my brother at her side and another baby growing inside her womb. My beloved mother listened intently, absorbing all the details I described about that incident. I recalled the strangers walking the platform and garbage strewn along the railway to a man wandering up and down the train tracks with a cigarette in hand and gloom across his face. Then, and only then, did she interrupt me to ask how I could decipher so much about her life. I said I have a memory like an elephant and have seen it all since I was there.

My mother told me that, no, you were not there. I argued back. "Yes, I was sitting beside my brother, and you were pregnant with a new baby." On that dreary Tuesday, we quarreled for hours until my dear mother saw my reason and was eager to hear how I knew so much about that incident in her life. I rambled on about other issues which had happened at that station. After two or three minutes, my mother informed me that, yes, she was pregnant, but with me and not another child, as she had only been pregnant twice. Garbage, I declared, for I was positive I was already born since I had seen so much. Besides, how would I have known about this moment if I had not been there?

In angst, my mother's accusation that I had dreamed up the scenario annoyed my stubborn nature, and I refused to accept her explanation. It was impossible to remember such a robust and vivid memory as I, regardless of my mother's contradictions, recollected that I was present.

Two days later, I was still musing over this childhood recollection when I realized if mother was correct, then I had yet to be in her arms. My memory convinced me that I was born, but I was not. I was somewhere else. Now, I would be lying if I told you where since, to this day, I do not recall it myself.

I will do my best to describe the experience accurately.

Fingers crossed that it is logical and understandable.

A long time ago, I was alone when three friendly voices belonging to loved ones whose presence I adored approached me and cheerfully informed me that I was chosen to go on a journey and visit someone. The characters motioned for me to follow, and I did. As we walked down a long corridor, those familiar voices told me I was our master's choice to go on a mission. Still, he hesitated as he was concerned about my safety. On our walk, I noticed our shadows on the wall as we bobbled toward a room where I would wait for my interview.

I want to tell you something important. So, I will prepare you for what I am writing next, and I apologize if I offend someone. Trust me when I tell you I will only repeat what I saw. I hope you understand my recollection may vary as twenty-six years have passed.

Here goes... In our shadows, I did not see the human form of life as we see here on Earth, but the outline of who we were there.

Got it? I hope so.

Back to my recollection.

As, we entered a room where more friends stood gazing at a strange circular instrument, which was not high-tech but something unique. The beings motioned me to come closer so I could see where I was going, and feeling no fear, I obeyed their wishes. It brought me immense joy and happiness as I walked through the room filled with rocks and lights. Later, gazing into emptiness, a different extraordinary entity warned me that I might not receive permission to embark on this journey due to concerns about my safety. A rush of glee consumed me as I expressed my eagerness to go anywhere without any worries. I remember reassuringly saying, "You can relax. Knowing I have you, I will be fine. Trust me, I can manage all the adversity that comes my way." In that room, a profound feeling of security and comfort washed over me as I readied myself to leave, assured that I had protection with no sense of unease.

As I stared into the circular void, it seemed as if I was gazing through a telescopic lens, with the figures appearing both distant and discernible. What caught my attention was a woman sitting at a train station with a young boy beside her. "It is your responsibility to be with that woman, and you must help her," a voice said. The woman's expression of loneliness and sadness deeply affected me. I was highly intrigued by my willingness to sacrifice my joy to support the woman in her time of need. At that familiar location, I felt safety, contentment, and love, and I wanted to convey those feelings to the troubled lady at the train station.

I remember a different figure peered into the circle and communicated with me. "But our master is worried about you," the voice announced.

Since my incarnation as Bella Bloom, it is easy for me to explain this to you, being—neither a baby nor a child, but an adult now. So, I answered the worrisome question as I would address such concerns today... "I will be fine. There is no need to worry." Suddenly, a deeper voice boomed from a darkened corner behind me. "But I am worried." I swiftly turned, and I promise you, I saw the visage and heard the voice of God, growing more profound with each passing second. He appeared in the light, revealing his larger-than-life persona and his worry was obvious to me. Now, by reassuring him and expressing my purpose for my need to visit Earth, I alleviate his worries and persuade him that I am the ideal candidate for the job. And I was, as I cared for my mother until she returned home to her Lord, father, and master. In fact, throughout my brief life, I helped my mother and her son, and my brother grew to be a fine man.

Nonetheless, I have not seen him since he has not returned to visit me, except for a brief meeting shortly after his passing. In his life, my mother strained our relationship with her controlling nature, resulting in a deep-seated hatred that continues to sadden me each day. Still, even in pain, I find joy in the Lord and rely on his guidance for all that happens in my life, good or bad, because he is my savior.

In life, we must have faith.

In life, we must have trust.

In all my years, months, and days in this human life form, I have not lost sight of either, or will I ever, as constant reminders surround my aura. It is not unusual for me to experience goosebumps on my shoulders or feel a tickle in my ear. Still, and in a way, I know those experiences are my friends in other places, coming to my aid to tell me I am not alone.

Intuition is a powerful attribute; I listen to mine every waking moment. It leads me to success, shields me from danger, and awakens all my positivity, allowing me to ignore all that is detrimental.

Such as tonight... I am confident the heavens must tremble in fear as I plunge deeper into this treacherous get-rich-quick scheme against the promises I made to God, and desperation grips me as I beg for forgiveness, haunted by the sins I commit.

Yes, I know God listens to me, and I am calm and aware he is at my side. You are a witness that I have pleaded with him to ease my burdens and pain, and sometimes he does, but other times, not so much. I must learn more about life's hardships before I can understand the ways of our Lord.

As much as I believe in all life's goodness, I still see the horror that passes before me around every corner I turn. I noted that the key is to go through life believing no one can hurt me and remain faithful to God. I am not referring to my distress over my boyfriend breaking up with me or something equally less traumatizing, but the belief God will safeguard my body, mind, and soul from any harm inflicted by humans. Therefore, I have complete faith that my spiritual friends are protecting me despite the peculiarity of my current job.

In solitary moments, I have cried enough tears to flood a passing river, and though hurt and lost in life, I have once, and only once, fallen to my knees and begged for death.

I am still here, so the Lord has plans for me.

I will stay here until I had fulfilled God's requirements, which I thought were helping my dear mother until she returned home. But now, I realize he has more plans for me, so I will stay until I have learned and done all I can.

Admittedly, when my mother passed away, I thought I would die shortly after because in my mind I was sent to her to help her throughout her life, but no such luck, as I am not dead yet. I have implored the heavens during my utmost despair, begging them to listen to my plea. I am steadfast in my belief that there is a watchful presence through the lens of that distant telescope. And, though taught not to ask for me, sometimes I cannot do anything but ask, as I have become so lost and alone for such a long time that I perceive my existence as unbearable.

Yes, I have friends. But let me explain my thoughts to those individuals. It does not matter how close you are to this person or that person; we are all alone in this world. Whether we believe our dreams are too private to share or it is the eccentricities we hide from others to appear normal does not matter. Since birth, elders have instructed us to keep our mouths shut and only reveal what we want other people to know, which is why I understand the type of person who spends their life with animals; animals cannot hurt or judge them as people can.

I read we are all a moon.

We all have a dark side.

We share that dark side with no one.

I can relate.

There is darkness that hides within my soul, and I search for the light that will take me home. On the day or night, when I see that light, I will have no fear but will welcome its brightness with peace and happiness. Still, my only regret is not telling those nearest and dearest to me how I have cherished them and will miss them until I see them again. So, I wrote a brief note for my friends to read once my body gave up on me, which goes like the words below. I am trying to remember it; the original is in my attorney's hands for safekeeping.

Goodbye, for now, my dear friends on Earth. I must be moving on, but someday, in the not-too-distant future, we will meet again. If I do not see you or you do not see me, then one of us is in a hellish place where one of us deserves to be. I hope it is not me, and if it is, then know I will be relentless in finding my way out of the Devil's grasp. Let us approach others with logic and fairness as our guiding principles. We are here to enhance each other's lives and learn from the errors of our ways. So, do it in style and live without regrets. If you, like me, have regrets, then beg for forgiveness and move onwards.

Forget confessing, for God sees all.

Much love, Bella.

Thinking about my departure, I find it easier to admit wrongdoing. I promise to try harder next time I am here, which always works best for me. Although, I do have questions and observations to bring to your attention.

Have you ever met someone and felt you have known them for years?

You must have.

What about those strangers who show up at the most needed time and help you regain strength and disappear as quickly as they arrive? They are angels from heaven who come to your side to help you in your darkest hour. Since my teenage years, I have worn my grandmother's ring on my finger every day since I was eighteen. Yes, I am only twenty-six, but I kid you not. In the past nine years, that ring has caused me to receive strange visits from my grandma, and I am sure it is her way of letting me know she is watching over me.

Have you ever experienced the sensation of someone in the back seat of your car or doing similar activities? Yet, you were too afraid to turn around and see if anyone was there.

Yes, same here.

One day, I told my mother, and she told me the next time it happened, I should turn around and see who it was. I have thought about doing this, but it did not happen again. Then, one day, after I had forgotten about trying to glimpse a ghost, without a doubt, that eerie sensation entered my body and let me know that something magical was present. So, to this day, I never try to outsmart or trick angels, for they are wiser than all of us.

I enjoy the goosebumps and all the nervous energy that surges inside my body, reminding me I am alive. It is a beautiful welcome, allowing me to bask in the ambiance. I feel grateful to be in tune with our Lord's wonders.

Blessed is those who rejoice in the Lord.

Try believing.

You will be satisfied.

You might even experience that life suddenly improves, particularly if you are going through turmoil and strife.

I am no prophet. I am a girl who believes in the afterlife and that the soul lives forever. As peculiar as that world may seem, it is unquestionably the only one I know.

Just then, the doorbell's chime interrupted my thoughts, and I became fearful yet curious about who would visit at this time of the night. Though it was Sunday, it was still dark outside, and if I were home in my bed, I considered it, like most others, to still be Saturday night.

Out of the corner of my eye, I watched CJ as she rushed into the primary closet, and I pursued. As she pulled me inside, pushed me to the floor, and instructed me to be quiet, I glanced back and saw Tubby smooth his shirt before she slammed the door shut.

CJ raised a finger to her lips to remind me that silence was paramount. Then, she pulled a small notepad from her handbag and began scribbling words. Great! Another note filled with innocuous ramblings she would order me to remember, I thought. Aggravated, I crouched, leaned against a wall, and willed myself to disappear.

After two or three minutes, the room became isolated and creepy. The musty closet made me want to sneeze, and I pinched my nose to prevent an allergic reaction.

A kick on my shin from CJ alerted me to the sound of male voices, and my eyes bulged in terror as Tubby's visitors did not sound friendly at all. I shrugged and raised my hands as if to ask, 'What now?'

CJ's eyes widened in terror. She resembled a helpless lamb beside its mother, fearful of being next for a cut, and I could relate, for I, too, felt the terror.

Breathe deep, I told myself. The deeper, the better. Inhale. Exhale.

I continued my breathing exercises until the muffled voices became louder and more precise, forcing me to gulp and hold my breath. The tone in their voices expressed anger and perturbation, and I regretted my hiding place, wishing instead I had retreated to the garden because no one would think of searching amid the bushes, not while it was raining. Now, I was stuck, and that annoyed me. Suddenly, I grabbed a clothing rack of maxi dresses and used the fabric to camouflage my body. Then, I squatted against a wall and willed myself to become invisible. However, my jaw dropped in disbelief, and my eyes widened in amazement at the sight of CJ, who remained seated on the floor. I could not understand why she had not concealed herself behind the racks of clothes. I cursed myself for not helping her. Still, now it was too late, as Tubby's visitors were exchanging heated words, their anger was becoming more precise, and like CJ, I, too, became freaked.

Then silence filled the room.

Tubby spoke first. "Jimmy," he sounded exasperated. "I want more money for the tape. At the time, the ten thousand dollars you offered me to film the sex scene seemed like a fair price. Still, in retrospect, the tape is worth ten times as much. So, let us discuss a new price," he paused and belched. "That's if you want the video. I do not care either way. I want more cash. So, do we have a deal or not?"

Silence.

"Clive Jenkins, you dirty slob. If you think I am paying more, you are nuts." An Italian man, who I suspected to be Jimmy, replied. "Don't be a jerk, Clive. I have no patience with people who try to refute original deals. Give me the tape, and I will vacate your house faster than a speeding bullet. Got it?"

"Maybe so, but I am reconsidering. You see, the contents on that tape will destroy that politician's life and knowing that irks me to the bone."

"Do you see this?" he asked.

"I do," Tubby answered. And your gun does not scare me. I have an armory of weapons placed throughout my home. So, do yourself a favor and put your Glock away. If not, I will retrieve my AK-47, which will destroy our relationship," he hesitated. "Know one thing, my friend. I do not do business with bullies. Got that, Jim-Bob?"

Frozen with fear, I wondered why Tubby taunted the ill-tempered man. Why did he not hand over the tape and end this sordid business deal?

Why antagonize the mobsters?

It just made little sense to me because I am too chicken to force someone's hand, particularly the hand that held a gun.

In my mind, I willed CJ to hide.

"Business is business, Clive," a man reasoned in a familiar voice.

Alarmed by my sudden realization, I struggled to name the mystery man whose eloquent voice I was familiar with and who spoke candidly. How did I know that man? I racked my brain and thought hard, but no person came to mind.

"For Christ's sake, Pete," Tubby said. "We've known each other since childhood, and our families have been friends for generations. I was at your folk's home today. Do not tell me you became allies with this loser when I thought of you as a brother?"

"I am not your friend or your brother, Clive, and I never will be," Peter corrected. "And our family's friendship is of no concern to me. What is concerning, Clive, is that you are trying to double-cross Jimmy, which also messes with me. I do not appreciate your games. Do yourself a favor and hand over the recording."

A slap filled the room, then a thud, and I surmised Tubby had crashed to the ground. "Ouch!" he cried out. "Why did you do that?"

"The tape, Clive, give me the tape." Peter insisted. "Don't make me hurt you again because I can, and I will."

"Please, help me up. I cannot get up by myself. If you have not noticed, my weight prohibits a free range of motion. So, if you want the tape, get me off the darn floor."

"Lift the fat bastard." Ringleader Jimmy ordered.

"Let your goons raise his butt. I do not do manual work," Peter said. Then I heard footsteps, the door opening before he yelled. "Hey, losers, get in here and lift this whale off the floor."

The bathroom door burst open, and two unknown voices joined the conversation. I strained to listen to their chatter but could only hear them complain that whale rescue was not part of their job description.

Feeling downtrodden, I was at a disadvantage, and I wished I could see all four men because listening irritated me, mainly as I wanted to see all four faces. In frustration, I wondered why Tubby would associate with ruthless people and, better yet, be foolish enough not to recognize that he could not win. So, why force their hand?

"My head hurts," Tubby moaned. "There was no need to strike me."

"Roll him up!" The boss commanded.

"Hey, that's my shoulder. Go easy. I am not in the best of health and could die. You do not want me dead, do you?"

"Come on, fatso," a distinct voice urged. "Grab my hand and help me pull you up."

"I can't," Tubby said and sighed. "My legs are too weak. Help me out, Pete."

Heavy footsteps crossed the room and halted. "You two grab Clive's arms while I push his shoulders, and we don't stop until he stands," Peter ordered. "We don't want to kill Dumbo."

Oh really, I thought. The brutes did not want to kill Tubby, yet they threatened worse unless they got the tape. As for Peter, I concluded that the man with the familiar voice was younger than the others. Still, I could not place his face, and that bothered me.

Another wild idea entered my mind.

My foolish imagination believed there were cracks between walls and doors in every house built because there were plenty in all the homes I lived in. If I find one, I could spy on the men and describe them all should they kill Tubby for holding out. Of course, I would need to exit my sacred hideout, crawl towards the door, and risk exposure. Just do it, I urged. At the very least, you can coax CJ into moving into your hiding place. Before starting my adventure, I took off my bracelet and grandmother's watch, mainly as I worried the rattling might alert one of the men threatening Tubby. Then, I lay on my stomach and prepared to cross the room. I used my shoulders and upper body strength to pull me over the itchy carpet, ignoring the bristles that tore into my elbows. The pain was unbearable, but I kept moving until I reached CJ. I encouraged her to hide against the wall where I had built a cave-like dungeon, as there was room for both of us, but she stayed frozen. So, I signaled to her to stay silent and crawled until I reached the entryway.

Once there, I rolled on my side and searched for a break in the door frame until I found a gap. It was not a big hole, but at least my eye could focus on the men threatening Tubby. I was presumptuous in surmising that Jimmy was the well-dressed criminal, but I could not be sure since there were two flashy males. Then, a middle-aged man stepped forward, his attire styled as if he had just finished a photo shoot for a famous men's fashion magazine. He resembled double agent James Bond.

"Jimmy," Tubby said. "You don't have to explain to me you're not a man to mess with, and I know that because I have seen you in action. In that dark alley on Ft. Lauderdale docklands when you beat two men for messing up your plans. It was on another scorcher of the night, and I was sweating like a baked pig. Yet, you stood as if every air-conditioned unit in South Florida was blasting right at you. Do you know what I call that friend? I will tell you. I call it ice because you are an ice machine, a heavy hitter who gets what he wants. And I admire you but understand that I am not a lost cause you recruited. I am a man with a famous name in this godforsaken town, and messing with me could cause you more harm than good."

To his credit, Tubby defended his theories, I thought. However, I wondered who had shoved him hard and hit him, as he was in obvious pain. Still, I did not ponder about it for long, as Tubby was back to yapping. Yes! His brows quirked, and his face wildly flashed as he realized his last announcement sounded challenging, yet he expressed amusement. "The shiner on my eye will show tomorrow. But..."

"Shut up!" Another well-dressed man said.

He was the man whose voice I recognized earlier, and it drove me crazy that I still could not see his face.

"No, I will not shut up," Tubby Jenkins said in defiance.

The well-dressed man looked at Tubby. Though he looked tough, I suspected this leader was a coward who was no challenge without his money or hitmen. "Let him be," he said. "I can manage Jenkins, and it will bring me joy to tackle him myself."

At once, relief swept over me as the Italian mobster reconsidered and, instead of hurting Tubby, had chosen to protect the man he had known for years. I prayed I would not see a murder because I doubted, I would be silent if a horrendous crime took place.

"If you don't mind, boss. I will manage Jenkins."

"Didn't I tell you I will do it?" the older man snapped.

"Okay, boss."

Tension filled the room, and then the older man calmed. "Is something wrong?" he asked.

Yes, it would help if you corrected things, I wanted to call out, but I stayed quiet, imagining that the worst of the worst had just begun. I saw Tubby stare at the mob leader, and my lower lip trembled. Please do not make him angry, I pled, noticing my heartbeat, as my breath was more rapid than called for, considering it was not my life at stake. When I noticed Tubby's eyes widened, I gasped as it shocked me that Jimmy's nearness affected Tubby's emotions. Then, their eyes locked, and I trembled because both men resembled two wild creatures meeting in a forest clearing late one night who could not decide whether to retreat or defend their territory. I cringed when the Italian lothario hovered over Tubby, for his eyes held a smoldering wretchedness.

To do what?

I did not know. However, the smooth-talking man overlooked the blood on Tub's injured face, and that bothered me. I feared their showdown would turn evil when I watched Tubby turn to face Jimmy and inhale his scent without fear, rhyme, or reason. "You smell musky tonight," he teased. "I have a strange sensation I'm dissolving and flowing into your body. Such is my attraction," he smiled. "The emotions we share are alive, and the luminous glow on your face is tempting, but I cannot enjoy you tonight. Not with all your goons around."

The Italian nodded. "I want to complete this deal and nothing more," he said and sighed. "You may think I want you, but you are mistaken. Now, hand over the tape, and let's end this charade."

"Giving you the recording will be my demise," CJ's client mumbled. He patted his hips to show he had no weapon. "I swear I am not armed."

The ringleader, Jimmy, clenched his hand, pushed past Tubby, and shoved him aside before ordering his men to search the cupboards, drawers, and linen closet.

The room became chaotic, and I saw the client eye his mobster friend. Both men appeared encased in a cocoon of mutual greed as if their only escape was death. I predicted a wrestling match to start at a moment's notice.

A man walked toward the closet where I hid, and I almost swallowed my tongue, but to my relief, Jimmy ordered his men to vacate the room. I thanked the angels protecting me and panted. However, that joy dissipated when I saw the Italian lover-boy pull Tubby close as if his arms carried a magical force like he owned enormous powers, in which strength was top of the list.

I experienced only despair when Jimmy held Tubby. My nerves became insufferable, my lungs constricted, and my anxiety soared.

As the minutes wore on, mob boss Jimmy's robust features softened. But Tubby mocked his femininity, and

I thought World War 3 would erupt. Though, I became mortified watching the Italian man's lips descend onto Tubby's. Their lips moved in a togetherness I had not seen in real life. I will be the first to admit I did not want to watch two men kiss. So, I retreated to my hiding place, especially when Tubby murmured, and the lustfulness in his voice caused my skin to crawl. "Don't stop," he begged. "My body is on fire, and my heart is beating like a drum at a rock concert. Do you know, I believe my desire for you will be the death of me," he moaned. "I surrender. I'll give you everything you want, including the tape."

The Italian paused and grinned at Tubby. "You were always an easy target," he spat, laughing.

"I am melting," Tubby moaned. "I'm so hungry and horny for you, my dream lover."

Now, I am not prudish but watching two men become sexual was not my idea of fun unless the man in question was someone like Tom Hardy or Bradley Cooper. However, seeing Jimmy tease and mock Tubby after noticing his desire, almost palpable in intensity, appeared to be a power trip for the wealthy Italian.

The unfairness of the situation was clear to me.

Worse, Jimmy managed Tubby with pure hatred. It was pathetic to watch the mobster jump and crash downward on Tubby's plump bosom, and I had such strong sympathy for my client because he held a profound sense of sadness as he sought love in all the wrong places.

I listened as Tubby groaned. "Jimmy, I sense something flowing between us and will not resist it." Then the Italian man's face hardened, and he thrust Tubby aside. "You've had too much excitement for one night," he scoffed.

"You are so cruel," Tubby said. "I feel like a part of me has died, and it feels like you ripped me from limb to limb."

I thought I saw remorse on the mobster's face, but I was dreaming. His eyes held only hatred and madness.

I shivered.

I inched closer, and my vision darted to my client, who mocked the contempt in the Italian man's aloof exterior. "When I see you, I sense a newly discovered life force in a distant world, only to be abruptly brought back to Earth with no defense."

The Italian walked to the basin. "I'm sorry I kissed you," he muttered. "The next time my groin aches, I'll ignore it."

My date sat dormant, wounded but not broken. If anything, Tubby appeared fascinated. For the second time that night, I experienced sorrow for this client, as his lustful gaze was visible to all. "Jimmy, I want to protect you. I would like you to quit your job and live with me. I will take care of you, I promise. Better yet, you'll never have to worry about money, as I have enough for ten lifetimes."

The mobster taunted, flashing a sly smile. "Not interested." He spoke with bias.

"But you cannot deny your feelings," Tubby argued. "I can't, as my body is surging from the waves of your heat, and If I feel like this, then you do, too?"

"I am not interested in your emotions or attracted to you. I have a gorgeous man in Palm Beach, and I am the envy of gay men across three counties."

"How can you say that? If others want him, why aren't you with him now? Oh, I know why. You realize beauty is skin deep, and superficial people are boring. Besides, the lefties keep the best of company and will never associate with a criminal who is working his way up from the streets. Political people want old-time money and have no interest in rags to rich stories."

"You talk too much."

"Not really. I'm trying to help, that's all."

"Save it for another day."

"Come on, Jimmy, be nice to me."

"No chance. Not tonight, not while my men are here," he answered, then paused. "So, was the kiss another form of extortion? Are you secretly recording me, too? If only to make a laughingstock of my reputation?"

Tubby smirked and raised his hand. "I plead the fifth," he said, joking. Instantly, a series of popping noises echoed throughout the room, and Tubby screamed as if the Lord Almighty himself had whipped his ass for being a fruit cake. "Oh my God," he sobbed. "What did you do that for?"

Jimmy dropped to the floor. "You've served your purpose, you faggot. Now, get the tape," he demanded, slobbering another kiss on Tubby's lips.

"It's outside," Tubby said, pointing to a glass door leading to his garden.

"Get up, you fat bastard."

Shaken, I watched Tubby roll onto his stomach and struggle to rise. Sadly, he resembled a turtle as he flapped his arms and legs, and I could not help but pity the man who, earlier that night, had grossed me out. Then, the mobster tugged his curly mane and hoisted him to his feet. "Lead the way."

Suddenly aware that if they ventured outdoors, I would need to be clueless about the events unfolding and unable to eavesdrop on their conversation, so I strategized my next step. I needed to shimmy outside the closet and peep through an open window.

But which one?

And how safe was that?

Only God knows, I surmised and waited for both men to vacate the bathroom. After one minute, I sneaked into the room and hid inside the massive shower. I chose that area because the window was large enough to see outside but small enough to hide behind.

"Jimmy, I think I'm dying because I am finding it hard to breathe, and the soggy ground will be my grave."

"How do you turn these blasted sprinklers off?"

"I'm struggling to remember as my gardener set them up. They go on every morning at six. That's all I know."

I gazed into the darkness, aware that dawn would signal a new day in minutes, and people dressing for Christ would attend church. As I did with my mother, we trudged in the hustle and bustle of families attending Services every Sunday morning. I should have been going, too, but I dared not leave. Besides, my fixation on Tubby was enormous.

"Why did you kiss me?"

"Well, certainly not because you're attractive. Listen, Clive, I like you, but you know I came here for one thing. So, let's not pretend there's more to us than business."

Garbage, I surmised. Something had happened, but it was not crucial to the Italian, who would decide it was a trick of fate, a betrayal of the senses brought about by the lateness of the hour and the opportunity to try something with a new partner. But to my client, who had drunk too much, becoming intimate with a man whose money could buy an extortion tape was excitement personified. Still, the Italian man's desire to extort a politician was a mystery to me. However, I was sure the mobster was a cautious man who covered his back in every shady deal he planned.

"Can we go back inside? I am wet, and you grazed my arm when you fired your gun," Tubby asked. He raised his arm and showed his injury.

"Let's go," Jimmy agreed. "But I want the tape, and I want it now. The man in that recording is the man I love."

"I suspected as much. Still, I am confused about why you moved on me, but it will remain one of life's greatest secrets."

Poor Tubby trembled, and I felt sorry for him. Still, my misguided sympathy caused me to forget he was returning to the bathroom, and I was stuck in the shower and needed to get out fast. But seeing the mobster's giant strides, I resolved to stay put. The shower had depth to hide. If Italian Stallion Jimmy did not want to shower, that was.

The outside door swung open, and both men crossed the floor, the mobster first and CJ's client trailing behind. "I was thinking," he said.

"You mean you think?" Jimmy scoffed.

"Don't be a dick."

"Okay, tell me what you were thinking?"

Tubby trembled. "I have to make you forget your obsession with that politician. If I do not? Then, we will have no business, friendship, or potential love story. Now, if I were to throw myself at you, I may doubt what might take place, and though I want to, I do not want to come across as a total jerk. I also do not want my pride beaten again, so I find it difficult to contemplate doing such a thing. Does that make sense?"

Goodness gracious, Tubby. Why are you tormenting this goon? Give him the tape and tell him to leave. Have you forgotten that you have two women hidden in your bathroom? The questions whirled inside my mind at ninety miles per hour. Though I sympathized with Tubby, he must face the reality that the Italian Stallion did not love him. I wanted Tubby to hand over the tape and end this charade but to no avail. In the past, patience was not a virtue with me, and I doubted it would be in the future. I have always been too impetuous and strong-willed in my convictions to have time for others who do not share the same ideals. I mention this because it is pathetic for Lisa's client to ask the mobster for companionship or romance, and I prayed he would receive a sign from our Lord and stop this cat-and-mouse charade. Still, instead of hearing from God, Tubby continued pursuing the Italian mobster, who strode to a vanity mirror and smiled. "So," he chirped. "You want me, a ruthless bastard, to be the man who will make love to you?"

Tubby nodded. "You may find me inexperienced, and I may impress you less with my body than my mind, but I love you."

Oh no! Why did Tubby confess that?

I wanted to die of shame.

Tubby and his idealism.

A friend or an escort might have told this client that men are not only dogs, but they will also leave you brokenhearted. But, listening to love-struck Tubby, no woman, CJ included, had bothered to offer advice, which made me wonder why she had not told the delusional client the truth.

Why would she?

CJ was only interested in money.

There was nothing wrong with that, but since she had never indulged in sex with Tubby, she could have guided him through his turbulent relationships, as CJ was a professional in that department.

"Clive, it is never going to happen," Jimmy said. "Why not come clean, and I will leave your home?"

"Will you please reconsider?" Tubby begged. "I can help you forget that man-whore politician and teach you to love and trust again."

At that moment, the Italian man pushed Tubby to the ground. "Never call him a whore because he is not one. Cash may be king in your flab-ridden world, but not mine."

I glanced at Tubby and his injured hand as he struggled to rise, and I pitied the man who I had until recently despised. Life was strange that way for me, as I always held empathy for people I initially detested. Tubby was no exception, for my heart ached for him. Then, he squealed. "What the heck!" he exclaimed. "What did you do that for? I am bleeding bad, you pig. How could you? Get the hell out of my house."

I steadied my feet on the cold shower floor and etched toward the shower door, desperate to see why our client screamed. Shocked, I saw Jimmy standing like a cowboy with a gun. Then my eyes rested on Tubby, and seeing his bloody shirt, it was plain that the Italian mobster had shot him. "Bang, bang," he said, laughing as he fired two more shots.

The client pressed his hand against the chest wound. "That silencer may stop people from hearing gunfire, but the smell of gunpowder will drift across this neighborhood, and someone will investigate."

"Nobody cares about you. Not even those whores you pay. They visit because you have money. You dumb bitch."

"Get out. The tape is my security; you will never see it unless I live. Oh, if I die and you ransack my home, it will take a rocket scientist to figure out where I hid the tape."

What? I gasped. Jesus Christ, Tubby, do not die. You cannot let the Italian lothario, and his trashy men search your house. For if they do, they will uncover CJ and me and kill us, too. I urged him to give the mobster what he wanted and let him leave. I frowned, worried about CJ, suffering from shock in the closet. I had hoped she had concealed herself amidst the caftans, which I assumed belonged to the client's wife, until I learned about his preference for dressing in women's clothes.

"Jimmy, I'm in sad shape. My eyes have become glazed. For the love of God, help. At least call emergency services and ask for an ambulance. Can you do that?"

"Where's the tape?" Jimmy yelled, rifling through cupboards. "Get me the tape, and you live."

"I already told you," Tubby muttered, coughing, and spitting blood. "If I die? You will never find the tape. Never!"

Tears stung my eyes when I heard the client sob. He so loved the brute who had turned his world upside down.

"I am dying. Help me."

"Why would I help you? You'll rat me out, first chance you get."

"I won't, I promise."

"You could have avoided this scenario. All you had to do was cooperate and look at the mess you created. Loser."

"I am a winner!" Tubby yelled triumphantly. "You are not only worthless without me, but useless too. Years ago, you promised we would be together. If our outcome ends, what would I lose? Nothing. Because, from day one, there was nothing."

Huddled on the marbled shower floor, I listened as Tubby's final breath escaped his mouth, and I prayed for the man who enjoyed the company of women but preferred the love of a man.

I wondered if my client had died. Then, Jimmy's voice interrupted my thoughts. "Give me the tape, and I'll phone a doctor," he offered. Tubby's voice gave me hope, but not for long. "No, I cannot trust you. I want to close my eyes and hope they never reopen. I want to meet my creator, a bigger man than you. And do you know what? It is a pleasant sensation to know that I triumphed over you, an individual with mafia-like characteristics who believes he is impeccable. I would venture to say that your shit stinks worse than mine. More importantly, I conclude I should have respected the two whores who were here earlier because, like me, they did what they had to do for the love of a dollar bill. Now, I can only pray they are well on their way back to Miami and not lurking around my home to fall prey to you. Screw you, Jimmy. I am dying. Thank you, and goodnight."

I sat, cowering against the cold shower wall, and shoved my entire fist inside my mouth to bottle any sound escaping my lips. However, I wobbled from the tension in my legs and the pain in my feet. Still, I stayed silent, counting each breath I took. If I told you I cursed to all damnation for my stupidity in not retreating to the closet, I would not be lying. In that agonizing moment, I heard Jimmy cross the floor, and the sheer knowledge that he might discover me terrorized me. Suddenly, the bathroom door swung open, and footsteps entered the room. "What the hell did you kill him for?" Peter, the man whose voice sounded familiar, asked.

"He was holding out on me, and I don't like cheaters," Jimmy said. "Besides, hopefully, I put the bastard out of his misery."

"That's a murder charge. I did not sign up for that. I am leaving."

"Relax. Nobody knows we're here."

"You cannot be serious?" Pete said and hesitated. "Didn't Clive mention two chicks were here earlier? Has anyone checked if they left the house, or are they still here?"

"Get real. We would know if there were women here."

"Maybe so, but a handbag is on the sofa, and ladies need necessities. So, for sure, one girl is lurking around this house."

"There's nobody else in this house. Clive may have had company earlier, but not anymore. If anything, the woman forgot her handbag. However, when she returns, she will alert authorities if she sees him dead. That is why we need to hide the fat bastard."

"Wrong, Jimmy. That is why we should leave. Screw the tape. You can look for it later after the cops finish investigating."

"Don't tell me what to do. I want to inspect the closet. If you want out, go. But I am not going anywhere without my tape."

"I will search inside the closet. But you need to tell your men, who are watching television, they need to search the house."

"Right!"

"I'm serious. Do you think you are clever, poking fun at me with your childish salutes? Well, you are not. Besides, you need to keep track of your workforce. If not? They will be your demise."

"Give me two minutes, and I will summon them."

"I'll check the closet, and then I'll be going," Peter said.

My eyes almost popped out of my head when I heard his footsteps walking to where CJ was hiding. At that moment, I prayed she had taken refuge in the den I had created from all the hanging dresses. If she was still sitting in the middle of the room, I dreaded the outcome once discovered.

As I pondered my next move, I felt more pathetic than ever, and though desperate to see Peter's face, I feared exposure. Still, unless I glimpse the man whose voice tormented me, I would never be able to rest easy. I debated whether to crawl on my stomach against the rough gravel or move like a baby learning to walk.

I chose the latter.

This slippery stone had a steep incline toward the drain because of overuse or old age, and I slipped and ended up in the middle of the shower, visible to all. I scrambled on all floors back to the wall just as all hell broke loose.

CJ's voice filled the room.

And what did I do?

Nothing.

I wanted to lend a helping hand, but fear paralyzed me. It was sad to think about CJ's current situation. In my mind's eye, I longed for her well-being, although I knew if Peter had not taken her life, Jimmy would.

Oh, please let us get out of here in one piece. I prayed as I squatted on the shower floor. I shook my head and willed myself to find a solution to end this torment.

I think this may surprise you, but I did not want to die that night, particularly as I could only imagine the tasteless gossip the local television news stations would broadcast across South Florida. The blonde news anchor would speak in a condescending tone when announcing that local Police found two women and one man brutally murdered in Jupiter. Then, without batting her lashes, she would say that the Police suspected the women were prostitutes and the man who owned the house was a client.

Imagine that scenario.

Can you?

I could not and still cannot.

So, I did what anyone else in a comparable situation would do. I stayed quiet and prayed. But the sheer terror in CJ's voice caused her screams to louden, which in turn brought Jimmy and his goons crashing into the bathroom.

Despite feeling disloyal to my coworker, I did nothing to help. Instead, I sat silent, wishing I were invisible.

Selfish, right?

Like you would have acted differently.

Please put a sock in it because we all know you would have done the same as I did, which was nothing.

Back to the mess at Tubby's house.

I took a deep breath, peered around the shower door, and heard CJ sobbing; I breathed an enormous sigh of relief. I was thankful that she was still alive because I honestly thought she was dead. Now, what was going to happen? Leaning against the shower wall, I calmed my breathing and pondered my next move.

A shiver racked my body, and fearful, I plunked beside a bamboo shelving system holding an assortment of scrubs and beauty products and waited for whatever was coming next. Holy mother of God. I cried, realizing this entire evening was going to end badly.

Holy bloody shit, now what? I frowned.

It will be a miracle if I leave this client's home alive.

Suddenly, I wondered if God was worried because he foresaw this mess before he allowed me to incarnate into this world, my current life. Remember, I shared earlier that I met him before Bella Bloom was born?

Do try to keep up.

I gripped the bamboo shelf, and in my distress, I hoped with all my heart that God did not regret his decision as I did not want to go back to his den, for I was not yet ready to die. I still had lots more things I wanted to do, and at my age, I was just too young.

Would you not agree?

Fingers crossed you do.

I stared down at my hands. What to do now? I want to scratch my head and smooth my matted hair away from the wet stone shower wall, but I am scared to lessen my grip on this bathing cubicle's only piece of furniture. I do not want to fall, slip, or make any noise that can attract attention, and though strained in my crouched position, I clung to a handrail and swallowed hard.

At that moment, I had an overwhelming urge to break free.

But how?

I did not know. I was hoping that one of my irresponsible friends would realize I never returned home last night, considering we usually meet for breakfast on Sunday mornings. Stupidly, I expected Harry might try to search for me, but I knew he was in a drunken stupor. Then, I thought of Benny Boy, but no such luck. I had not given him my cell phone number, and I did not have his digits.

I swear, my unfortunate situation and all the added drama had caused me to chew savagery against the inside of my mouth, which felt red raw. And aside from the burning sensation, my tongue felt thick, making swallowing painful.

I sighed heavily. My thoughts returned to CJ and the carnage hell she was experiencing at the mercy of Jimmy, Pete, and the rest of his sick goons.

"We cannot leave her," Peter said. "She can identify us."

"I'm not killing her. I have already taken one life tonight, and I'm not taking another."

"Can we lock her in the garage?"

I listened as the other men laughed.

"What is wrong with my idea?" Peter asked.

"She will escape and alert the cops." Jimmy spat.

"So, what do you suggest?"

"To hell with her," Peter said flatly. A muffled pop echoed throughout the bathroom, and I surmised it to be another gunshot. All four men were silent until Jimmy yelled. "Man, you are ruthless. Why kill her? She did not do any harm to anyone. I'm leaving."

I listened as heavy footsteps crossed the room. Then, I winced as I heard the bathroom door creak open, and slam shut. Knowing someone had left the bathroom, I wondered if they were going to the house or lingering in the hallway. It was sheer torment, besieged in sweat; I shivered against the stone-cold shower wall.

While staring at the moldy floor, I ran my fingers across a small pool of water and began to pray the first moment I heard Jimmy's voice. "Toss them both in the shower," he ordered his hoodlums.

I cried, listening as the goons dragged CJ and Tubby in my direction, figuring it was only a matter of time before they uncovered my hiding place and I, too, would die.

This catastrophe could not have happened to me.

Holy Mother of God, I prayed. Please help!

"Wait a minute," Peter said. "Toss the bodies in the closet. If the housekeeper comes today, she may not look inside that room but will look inside the shower. Better yet," he paused and coughed. "Lock the closet door so the maid thinks it's off limits. Come on, guys, hurry. Time is money, and we have got to jet."

I tried to be calm as I struggled to hold my horror. Poor CJ, I thought. I could not imagine the pain she suffered at the hands of those brutal men, and I prayed she died right away as I did not want her to suffer like Tubby had, which was savage. My bra strap had slipped down my arm, and I pulled it up, remembering a lecture from my father, who told me nothing good happens once the sun goes down, and right then, I could not agree with him more. There were inherent risks and dangers in this realm of living after dark. Saturday night events emphasized the destructive consequences of pursuing fast money and greed, highlighting the need to stay away.

I looked down at my feet, shriveled and blue, trying to figure out how much longer I should stay hidden. One minute later, I acknowledged the bathroom was eerily quiet, and aside from my lonesome self, the sterile painted room was empty. Still, I was too afraid to change my position, let alone exit the frigid cubicle that held me captive and turned my pale skin blue, pink, and purple. The hue was grayish, reminiscent of a distressed bottlenose dolphin near the Florida coast. Like the stranded mammal, I longed to immerse myself in the warm waters and bask in the blazing sun.

If I could wish for anything, I would want to sleep safely in my bed, away from all the drama of this crime-ridden evening. Saturday nights are dangerous and too corrupt for partaking in a companionship date.

Remembering that brutal night, I frowned.

A shiver ran down my spine, for I cannot count how long I sat in that shower, as I was numb with shock and emotionally battered.

Today, the time is still a mystery, as I still cannot remember if it was hours, minutes, or seconds because fear made me push that night's events to the back of my mind. Nonetheless, I discovered the inner strength to tackle my dilemma, and my first move was to stand and face an open window.

Outside, the brilliant Florida sun was high in the sky, and I squinted at the glowing ball of light as I rested my head against a pane of glass. Then, I studied the garden before noticing the sprinkler-soaked plants drying in the heat from the stunning yellow flames cascading across the sky. I exited the shower and searched anxiously for my dress, but in my panic, I could not find it. Then, I recalled I undressed in the closet, and that memory chilled my bones as Jimmy had locked the door to the room where two bodies lay dead.

The flimsy robe, two sizes too big, was all I had.

For now, anyway.

I am not writing because I was out of luck, but honestly, if Tubby's home were not so cold, I would not have cared if I wore only my bra and panties as I searched throughout his home, but quite frankly, the house was freezing. And while I did enjoy the sun's warmth that basked against the cold window, I was still shivering in this icy home that ominously resembled a morgue.

Let me be clear and inform you of one crucial detail: I have not visited one of those dreadful places. Though I have seen morgues on television shows, they differ from places a person longs to go. Per say, I may wish to go to the beach this weekend, but I would not yearn to visit a morgue.

Nobody would blame me.

Death scared most people.

Not me, but others?

Yes.

As I opened the cubicle door and fled the shower, I replayed the night's incidents and loathed how cowardly I behaved. Indeed, there must have been something I could have done to help.

No! I decided. Since I am not Jesus Christ or our almighty God, I am powerless and unable to fight the evil that had encompassed not only Tubby's life but also CJ's and my own.

I headed out the door and into the hallway.

The sound of muffled voices filled my ears, causing me to become instantly alarmed. However, two minutes later, I realized it was a TV special, not someone still at home.

I snaked the long corridor, not stopping until I held the remote and silenced the religious show featuring Sunday morning church services with Pastor Edward Graves.

The virtuous man was unaware of someone as wretched as me, nor did he realize his sermon had me mesmerized for almost ten minutes. I would continue to watch whether I needed to find clothing to cover my near-naked body. So, I resigned myself to the tedious task of searching each room for an outfit to fit my frame.

In my quest to cover up, I strode toward a closed door beside the kitchen and peered inside. The obvious guest room featured a closet, bathroom, a king-size bed, and various beauty products atop a dressing table. Bravely, I trudged toward a room next to an en-suite bathroom to rummage for clothes. All the while, I mused why single people needed to have homes filled with guest bedrooms and bathrooms since few people voluntarily stayed.

It seemed ridiculous to me that someone who lived alone needed such a large home when it was clear they did not use but three or four rooms. Despite its small size, my cozy apartment had a comfortable atmosphere. I would get lost living in such a monstrous home that Tubby owned, not forgetting that I would fear not hearing if an intruder broke in. Of course, the house featured an elaborate alarm system to protect valuables and human life. Still, burglars can disarm even the most ornate of security systems. I even knew robberies were inside jobs contracted by maintenance specialists onsite to fix faulty wiring or a pool company servicing the pool as they become familiar with homeowners' schedules. Therefore, knowing when the house was most vulnerable was important. Unlike an expensive fortress, most property developers constructed homes cheaply. God bless any homeowner who foresees the dangers of having wealth, as having money can be hazardous to one's life.

Oh, the perils of being rich were not something I could attest to, as I have zero dollars saved.

Feeling lucky, I opened a closet door. My eyes surveyed women's clothing, and I smiled when I saw a pair of jeans and a simple white tee. In haste, I dressed in casual attire, and then I stooped to the floor, scooped up a pair of sneakers, and shoved my chilly feet inside their warmth. Since the shoes were one size too big, I needed a pair of socks to fill in the gaps, I noted, and with widened curiosity, I spied a basket in the corner with multiple socks, and I ransacked the container for a matching pair of the thickest socks I could find.

Then I took a deep breath and stared at my reflection in a dresser mirror. "Well, now you don't look so rumpled, do you?" I told my pathetic self and finger-combed my mousy blonde hair before securing it with an elastic band.

Despite the obvious signs of suffering on my face and my eyes reflecting profound trauma, my once bright blue eyes are now as dark as coal. I held my gaze for five plus seconds, then, in despair, I ran from the room. My thoughts focused on finding a computer with a Google search or a local phone book so that I could summon help.

There had to be one.

A PC is a survival tool today, but it could take me a minute or two to find one, since I needed to find out where the home office was.

I first stumbled into the kitchen and noticed a secretarial station built into the tall oak cabinets; I checked the countertop to no avail as I saw no laptop beneath the mounds of brochures or bill payment receipts. Quickly, I pulled out the top drawer and found a phone book, but it was an ancient Yellow Pages, which proved useless as only business and residential listings filled the pages.

"Drat!" I cursed and shook my head. "Where in God's name would Tubby keep a White Pages?" My eyes darted around the room. "In his home office," I decided. I fled the kitchen and rushed along the art-lined hallway, searching for a room that would offer a techno gadget to save my life.

Several rooms later, I opened a door and stumbled into one room at the pinnacle of my mind. It was a stylish office with a broad mahogany desk and shelving lined the soaring walls with books. Since I loved to read, I spotted familiar titles and made a mental note to borrow various books on my way out. Not wasting any time, I sat on Tubby's leather chair, gripped the keyboard, and willed the computer to wake up. Unsure if a password protected the Sony PC, I pressed the mouse to awaken the screen, and as I caught sight of the search engine Google, I calmed down and began my search.

I cannot express my euphoria as I searched for a familiar name and saw only two listings. These confirmed my hunch that few people carry the Barrymore name, as it is such a unique surname in a small town like Jupiter, Florida. However, my work began when I had to figure out which listing held the correct contact, as I could not unquestioningly contact anyone during the morning.

I stared at the clock; it was seven-thirty. It was not too early to contact someone on a weekday, but the untimely hour could be a nuance for somebody sleeping on a Sunday. Aware that the fragile nature of my disturbance could rouse the entire house and might cause the homeowner to perceive my call as intrusive, I nervously gnawed my lips and swallowed hard.

It was one minute later when I realized I would have to use the house phone because my cell phone was in my handbag, and Jimmy had locked both inside the closet with

Tubby and CJ. Now, I would have no choice but to admit where I was calling from, and stressed, I spun on the chair and thought about whether to break the lock on the closet door or use Tubby's location as my point of reference.

Could I enter that closet?

Of course not.

Dummy.

Determined to make the call, I lifted the phone and dialed the three-digit phone number area code first. On the third ring, a woman's recorded voice announced that no one was home; since I needed help, I left a brief message and hung up. My heart was pounding, my breathing was shallow, and worse, I could not move. The nervous energy made me shake as if I had drunk ten cups of coffee or twenty cans of energy drink, and each second spun faster than the speed of sound. Desperate to calm my growing anxiety, I rose from the chair, crossed the room, and read book titles. All the while, I wondered how many cans of worms I had just opened and how many calamities would come my way after doing so.

What did you do? I questioned.

What if you left your ridiculous, frantic message on the wrong person's phone?

What if the woman calls the Police, and they trace the phone number back to Tubby's home?

What if the Police surround his house?

What if the Police uncovered two dead bodies within the closet walls?

Dear Lord, now what? I longed to ask because I was so close to erupting into molten lava and risked destroying everything in my path as I could not stay tranquil for much longer. Still, I reminded myself to be silent, and instead of crying into the void, I methodically questioned my actions in behaving like a kept woman, which is so unlike myself.

Why did you leave a voice message for a man? What independent girl would cave in and ask a man for help?

None, I quipped. Yet there I sat, a woman once proud of a Miss Independence reputation, and yet, that day, I had flung that name tag out the window and behaved like all the other needy women in the world, which was pathetic to me and to you, too, my reader.

Yes! I am aware of your disdain. And I, too, would roll my eyes and groan. But before you do, please read on... I reached out to this man because he was no ordinary man. This man had proved himself repeatedly by triumphing over the same adversity that had devastated others, and just like a firecracker, he had blasted all adversity into outer space.

Nonetheless, I worried he might become defensive. Still, I believed in his courage and prayed he would accept the challenge.

Would today find him weak? I wondered.

Not likely, I argued.

I was confident he would help and solve my dilemma.

If not, I would face the rest of my life in ruin.

My worry intensified as minutes passed, and negativity prevailed. However, I refused to accept defeat and forced myself to be upbeat. My yearning for this man dominated my thoughts because I knew I needed a man like him who would see my situation without lecturing me about my blatant disregard for self-respect.

On a positive note, I had unwavering faith that he would grasp the depths of my love for money, even though countless scriptures declare it the root of all evil.

Filled with hope that he would refrain from revealing my scandalous existence to my friends, I gripped the phone tightly. Then, I walked into the kitchen, poured a glass of chilled water, and swallowed the liquid in three gulps.

I sat atop a stool and fought obsessing over the man I had rang. In my will to erase his memory, I slumped forward, allowed my head to fall onto the countertop, and willed myself not to think anymore. However, my patience was short-lived, and noticing I was waiting longer than expected for a return phone call, I worried that my decision to reach out was a huge mistake.

What if he ignored my call?

What if he told me to leave him alone?

What if he visited and chose not to help?

What if he then threw me to the wolves?

Time will tell... I rationalized, burying my face deep in my arms as the first tears of defeat fell down my cheeks.

LOVE

SOCRATES BELIEVED THAT one word frees us of all the weight and pain in life. That word is love...

In the year 1665, in London, England, a renowned horse whisperer named Nicholas Browning, who today is known to me as Benjamin Barrymore, lived a meagre life as a stableman. His unique love of horses brought him work, and his notoriety spread from his deep affection for animals and his ability to keep stables in meticulous conditions.

The townspeople praised Nicholas and voted him to become the top caretaker of the city's prized stallions. Throughout his life, in both past and present, Benjamin Barrymore was equally charming and handsome. Well, to me, at least, but I am biased because I love this man more than life. I have always found Ben to be the most attractive man I have ever met, mainly because of his robust features and strong, athletic body, and let me tell you, my eyes have spent hours gazing up and down the length of his spine.

I am confident enough to admit that I have fantasized about his strong arms pulling me close, holding me near, and kissing the softness of my lips with such ferocious passion that I could so easily fall with dizziness. If not in love, then most certainly to the ground, but let me not focus on my clumsiness, as I have explained in earlier parts of my story, how easy it is for me to tumble.

The length of his fingers always intrigued me, as did the size of his strong hands, which are large and strapping, and regardless of which lifetime we meet, I have dreamed of his touch caressing my body, even when acutely aware that such dreams could propel me into another orbit or heaven itself. For, whether I have met this proud, masculine man as Benny, Nicholas, or whomever, the electricity I felt pulsating from his broad chest sent me into a dreamlike trance. The magnetism in his smile and eyes, and even how he sauntered, caused my heart to soar. One of my favorite moments with Benny Boy was on one of our strolls around Hyde Park, as we would spend hours admiring the lakes, trees, and picnic areas. In that lifetime, he was Nicholas, and I was Cassandra. Since we held hands as we walked, it felt so good to feel my icy fingers safe and protected, not to mention warm while encased in his strength.

Phew! Let me calm down, as I am getting hot flashes just thinking about a meeting when our lips innocently touched one sunny day in London. Though long ago and far away, the memories stayed throughout the test of time and never faded, not even the bad ones, and we both had plenty of those. In unity, we forgot the problematic images that have taunted us over the years. Since Benny Boy has lived as many lives as I, and we have sought each other out throughout the centuries, we have learned to grow accustomed to each other's achievements and failures. So, in 1675, we agreed never to focus on negative energy. Subsequently, we also chose not to fall head over heels in love with each other ever again, and yet, each time I recognized his aura, I felt myself sinking faster than Titanic. For, in my heart, I adore only one man and seeing that man throughout generations is another reason I pled with the Lord to allow me to visit, fulfill obligations, and fall in love with my soulmate once again.

I may be selfish, but I am who I am, and I will not sugarcoat any instances within my existence here on Earth to make myself look better to you, my reader, and my friend.

One glorious summer day in 1664, when Ben Barrymore was Nicholas Browning and I was Cassandra Downing, we stole time away from our family's judgmental eyes and went swimming. We frolicked throughout city parks across London Town in those heated summer months. In all fairness, we had no choice but to enjoy the city discreetly because I had a reputation for purity to protect, and the upper-class Lords and Ladies would not only scorn me but inform my father should they see my associating with a pauper such as Nicholas or Nicky News as I liked to call him. I will admit it broke my heart when I recognized Benny Boy's reincarnation as pauper Nicky News, as he was always gracing earth as a noble person, and worse, his job tending to horses ravaged my emotional soul. However, in an upbeat mood, I dreamt one day he would arrive gallantly on a white stallion and whisk me away to his castle in the countryside, away from the judgmental eyes of London's high society.

No such luck.

Nicholas Downing did not have two shillings when we first met. Later in that body, he amassed a fortune, but my knight in shining armor was initially far from perfect to the outside world. Though to me, he was everything I had hoped for and more. Still, my family raised me to be a lady, and

Ben was a stableman with no means to provide a home or food, particularly to my father's expectations. Besides, other townsfolk scorned a lady spotted in the company of a gentleman out of wedlock, let alone holding secret meetings with a man encased in poverty.

In those days, Benny Boy, living as a young Nicky News, was excruciatingly poor and not the gentleman he is today, and the Lords mocked his assertiveness to conquer my heart. Despite my father watching over me twenty-four hours a day, I still refuted his will to keep me away from the man whose heart I longed to win. My father and his friends believed Nicolas to be rogue, not good enough for any daughter born to them. Though, to me, the local stable helper had always been a first-class man. Still, he was nothing but a street laborer in London's society. Sometimes, I find it hard to remember the man I know as Ben in this life form or that he had no wealth when living as Nicholas. I have always found this robust and statuesque man to have incredible courage, character, and handsome good looks, which must count for something as I have yearned for his touch for over two thousand years. Despite our difficulties, we fell into each other's life path and eventually came together, even if we stubbornly fought it tooth and nail. We are as one and destined for togetherness, whether we like it, want it, or need it. We are, as the stars above might agree, soul mates.

The lack of money in the Downing family was daunting, as his family had yet to venture into medicine and health. However, shortly after the plague killed so many people in London in 1665, Nicholas's father, Hector Browning, married a wealthy widow, Lady Elizabeth Berry, who gave him the status of Lordship. In turn, he began the long and tedious task of educating himself in scientific studies and medicine. Through countless trials and errors, his research uncovered various cures for the people of England. However, the feat took work, particularly his ranking into Lordship, which the uppermost royalty of London oppressed, creating delays in his ambitious journey into nobleness. Still, through five years of dedication and perseverance, Lord Browning became a famous physicist who, along with other scientists, helped to create a cure that abolished the plague, which killed hundreds of thousands of people across England and Europe.

The elder Browning stopped Nicholas from working for pennies and financed an educational program to enable his son to become respectable. Within the walls of an elite university, with one year left of studies, Nicky News joined his father's medical practice and enjoyed a long, fruitful career as a top scientist, standing alongside his father and physicians across England. Knowing Nicholas had turned his life around satisfied me, as I desperately wanted to wed. Still, knowing my father would abolish the idea unless my hero was born a gentleman, I had no choice but to wait because marrying into poverty was off-limits in my family's quest for riches.

There, I said it. Ben Barrymore was poor.

He was poorer than me in my present life.

The difference between our social status in 1664 was that I was born into a noble family known throughout the city as one of the most profoundly respected names in town. My father's righteousness, values, and notoriety spread faster across London than the deadly plague. Still, after the Great Fire of London in 1666, my family's home, Downing Manor, burned to the ground, along with their money. However, the gold bars my father had hidden in his country estate meant I could continue to live an elegant lifestyle. My family dreamed I would wed a man of extravagant means, as my forecast was to live in riches. In that time, I was a lady with a wealthy family. While my mother was a talented tailor who crafted beautiful gowns, she only worked on her daughters' dresses, namely my sister Jane and myself. So, now you know I have lived a wealthy and poor existence. Fortunately, during my existence as Cassandra and the London fire, my family had funds to enable us to escape. If not, we would have perished. Still, I was happy to escape the sickness that spread across England's capital city. However, I missed and mourned Nicholas so much that my heart ached for his soul to visit me in my times of need. Yet, he never came.

True. Nicholas left me alone for seven long, lonely years, much to my father's frustration, who canceled each arranged marriage that was to be my future. I stubbornly refused to spend my life as a companion to a wealthy Baron who only needed me to bear his children.

Yuck!

Who wants to live like that?

I certainly did not.

The endless charade of suitors at my family's manor made me nervous. To avoid the glaring look in one Duke's salivating eyes, I would feign nauseousness and purposely vomit on my mother's best rug, if only to deter any man who fancied himself a suitable partner.

I despised life at my family's Norfolk Manor and spent endless days daydreaming about Nicholas until I could only cry, as I missed him so much and thought only of him. The summer days lasted the longest, but the nights worsened in July and August and became unbearable since the burning heat tore through our home, and though I had fans, my heavy-draped dresses drenched my slender body in sweat.

Still, the long days allowed me to engage in early evening walks with my mother, and we would stroll along the cliffs and gaze fondly at the North Sea, watching ships sail to shore and admire the abundant wildlife that fed on angler's fish. Mother and I enjoyed the farming that grazed our grounds, particularly horses, cows, and sheep. Although I am an animal lover and have tended to the birth of calves, I could not milk a dam and settled on feeding her offspring, as that was a well-suited position for my squeamish mannerisms. My favorite moments were watching kittens feast on cod fish that men generously threw their way on vessels that sailed close to nearby cliffs in their sailing luggers. The gaps in those ragged cliffs allowed access to the ocean that harbored Cod and Haddock and the huts where they kept their fishing kits in one of the structures.

The small town we lived in, Siringham, today known as Sheringham, dates to the Domesday Book of 1086. Though of Scandinavian origin, my family and I were English Blue Bloods in every sense of the word. While blessed in wealth more significantly than others, I could only worry about how Nicholas was coping with sicknesses that spread throughout London, mainly because he was not born into a family with ample means.

As months turned to years, I continued to miss Nicky News and yearned to converse with the man who held my heart, and while I lived, dreamed, and fretted over this man, I worried that he had moved on and found another love. Each time the postal service arrived at my family's home; I checked for a letter delivery. Still, none came, and that tore into my heart with such savagery I suffered from extreme nervousness, and I found it difficult to eat or sleep. Then, almost ten years later, I learned of his father's good luck. I also read that Nicholas was attending classes at Cambridge University, which excited me, as Cambridgeshire was only a day's ride from the sleepy village where I lived.

In my mind, I had mapped a plan to visit with the man I love, even if that meant risking embarrassment if he scoffed at my adoration and presented a more mature woman as his companion. I argued back and forth that he would not do such a thing. Still, I was also acutely aware of the trickery a woman can play to capture a man's heart, especially a woman with the intellectual ability to match his own. I feared my life would see me unmarried with nothing but farm animals for company, which spurned me to act on a plan of action. After receiving the news that the Browning family had a respectable place in London society, I was sure my father would accept his former stable hand as a man for me to marry. I only needed Nicholas to visit and ask my father's permission, and each day, I waited and waited, yet he never arrived at my family's countryside manor. So, aside from not writing and not visiting, he did not even send a courier to assure me I was in his thoughts. The lack of communication made me rationalize that my darling Nicholas perhaps had no interest in seeing me again, and that caused my health to suffer as I was lovelorn and desperate to reconcile, even if I was not on his mind or he had replaced me with a mature woman who could attend balls across the city of London, regardless, I would not give up.

Yes, I was inwardly happy for Nicholas Browning. But I continually obsessed that he had forgotten about me and our promises and moved on with a woman better suited to be his bride. The sheer torture that he may marry another burned inside my soul, and not being the type of woman to accept his loss of words as disinterest, I could no longer stand my anguish or his lack of correspondence.

One October day, over a breezy fall weekend, I ran from the house across green fields fueled by high winds spurning me onward before settling on a bench in the center of our seaside town. I decidedly boarded a fast coach to Norfolk with plans to travel onward to Cambridgeshire until eventually arriving in London. In my mind's eye, if Nicholas would not come to me, so be it, for I would go to him if only to stand before him to prove his absence wrong. I may be frail and young in his eyes, but over the years, I have grown, and I am now a confident young woman. I was determined to make him aware of my femininity. Though the plague outbreak happened ten years earlier, I could easily escape the village and bypass the chain put across the river to keep out the infected people who swarmed into town.

Since officials placed protective precautions around the village, only those with health certificates could pass into Siringham, which interested me, as I was desperate to leave and return to London. My health was good, as the plague had not infected my body, though I feared becoming contaminated with the black death and falling into sickness myself. Yet, regardless of the risks I was taking, I banished all my fears as I was determined to see my handsome Nicky News. Besides, I was desperate to stare wistfully into his sparkling blue eyes and see his beautiful smile again.

Within two days, the smooth, thoroughbred stallions that pulled my stagecoach had me comfortably seated and parked in front of Browning House, a structure similar in size to Somerset House but built in Covent Garden. Tired from my trip, I persuaded my coachman, Carmen, to allow me time to refresh my appearance at a local Inn, and though sinful in those days, I felt it necessary to groom before seeing Nicholas and his family. Later that day, I arrived at Browning House and found out that Nicholas had saddled a horse and traveled across the roving countryside on horseback to seek my father's approval for us to get married. It startled me because his appearance at my family's manor alerted all that I was missing, and for me to write my father's anger echoed across the lush valleys and down every street in London was an understatement.

The knowledge of my travels infuriated my family. Still, with gratitude, I appreciated the thoughtfulness of Lord Browning as he graciously explained to my papa that his willful daughter was a woman in love before assuring my family that his invitation to attend his home in Covent Garden extended to all. However, my alarmed sister Jane, who fell ill from my escapades, refused to take part.

Some days later, I sat in the parlor beside all our relatives, and to date, it was one of the finest gatherings I have experienced. After our family members endured an arduous introduction, respectable Nicholas approached my father to request my hand in marriage. The proposal filled me with immense happiness, and I cried joyfully. My papa blessed us, and our simple wedding occurred in early November, coinciding with Guy Fawkes Day. We celebrated through a fiery Bonfire Night, which delighted me as the weather was chilly, yet I was warm with Nicky by my side.

In that lifetime, Nicholas and I lived happily together for fifty-plus years.

Present day...

As I sat in Tubby's office, I playfully pushed the chair with my foot and spun around the room. I inhaled and exhaled loudly, fully aware of the daring and hazardous nature of the risks I had taken in that era. In overwhelming frustration, I mocked the fragility of my emotions in those worrisome days, particularly my overactive mind, which had exaggerated the drama surrounding a man who favored studies instead of champagne parties on campus. However, I was unaware of Benny Boy's interests or motivation to improve himself as we had not communicated for over a decade.

Gazing outside the small office window, I raised the phone receiver to check that it was still working. It was. I could hear the dial tone echo in my ears, and that saddened me because my knight in shining armor had not responded to my telephone call or voice message, which made me more anxious than ever. I summoned all my psychic energy and willed him to call. Then, I called out to all the gods in heaven and begged for their pity in helping me in this explosive situation. With each passing minute, I felt completely and utterly neglected by the man I had depended on for over two thousand years.

In the garden, I saw and admired select orchids in full bloom. I thought about swimming in the Olympic-sized pool but chose not to in case a visitor unexpectedly arrived and asked me who I was, let alone what I was doing on the property of Clive Jenkins. I could have easily explained that I was not trespassing and was a guest, but the thought of that scenario freaked me out beyond my wildest dreams. Resolutely, I stayed inside the home, choosing to admire Tubby's oceanic views via the safety of the tall windows that lined one side of his house.

The bathroom was still off-limits in my mind, mainly because I could not stand facing the deathly eyes of Tubby or CJ, as I feared their facial expressions would haunt me for the rest of my life. I had enough horrifying moments to contend with without allowing further terrors to derail my mind. Sadly, I refused to return to the left wing of the house and focused my energies on the glorious Sunday morning and rows of books on a shelf in Tubby's office. However, after twenty or thirty minutes of pacing the floor, I became impatient and contemplated calling the phone number I had dialed earlier again. However, worrying that an angry person may answer the phone and curse at me for disturbing their tranquil Sunday morning chilled me. I sat atop a stool and stared into space, thinking about nothing but the Atlantic Ocean bashing against the Florida shoreline.

A loud beeping sound alerted my mind to a telephone ringing, and I hurried from the office and back into the kitchen. Standing short of the wall-mounted phone whose ring volume erupted throughout the first-floor level of Tubby's mansion like a steam train pulling into a station, I willed myself to take a deep breath while deliberating whether to silence the annoying tone.

If the caller were not who I was expecting it to be, would I be strong enough to pretend to be the house cleaner? These concerns manipulated my thoughts. Unfortunately, I stalled for too long. The person hung up after nine rings, which frustrated me as the caller could have been my friend.

And if so? I surmised the caller would ring back, and struggling to support an upbeat composure, I walked to the refrigerator and opened the door. I scavenged among the fruits and cheeses that Tubby had proudly displayed hours earlier.

The fruit tasted juicy against the dryness of my mouth, and I gobbled down grapes, kiwi, strawberries, cheese crackers, and a large glass of orange juice until my hunger subsided and my stomach felt full. I filled a coffee pot with fresh coffee and reminisced about a high school job I held in 1977 when I was fifteen and worked in a restaurant serving breakfast, lunch, and coffee.

It was a part-time job I held during summer months while on school break, and though I enjoyed the free food, the work was hard, as were the customers, who did nothing but grumble and complain about undercooked meat and stale-tasting buns. I worked at Lilly's Diner one evening a week and on weekends, but not long after I started my night shift, my career as a server unexpectedly ended. It was no fault of mine but the ill-doing of someone else, a monster whose evil eyes had sought me out and watched me week after week before decidedly choosing to take my life.

The maniac who killed me cared nothing for my life or my family's grief. If he had? He would have never coaxed me into his vehicle with the sole intent of abducting me, torturing me, and killing me. He would also not have driven my battered body miles away from my home and buried me under apple trees that filled an orchard, which made it almost impossible to find me, as most people were looking closer to town. The scheming monster escaped charges, and in that life form, my darling parents never recovered from their grief. I had visited my mother five or ten times shortly after my death, and though I longed to comfort her, I could not, as she did not believe in Christ, goodness, or spiritual well-being from one soul to another. Both my parents were narrow-minded and atheist, which hurt as I walked the grounds of their small home every day for fourteen days, howling with hopes they would hear my cries. Still, they could not hear my anguish, and shortly after that, I begged God to accept my failure and allow my return so that my weary soul could finally rest, and the healing process could begin.

Upon my return to our Lord, other life forms told me that on my sixteenth birthday, it was destined for Benny Boy and me to reconnect at a local baseball game, and though the Gods had planned for us to live out our lives together in harmony, my sudden demise had ruined the structure of another future for Benjamin and me together. I was sad to learn that shortly after my death, Benny Boy, too, returned to heaven so that we could both heal together and reincarnate later. The knowledge hurt me as I did not want Ben deprived of enjoying a fruitful life, and I feared he would detest me until the end of time, even blaming his short life on my being too trusting to accept a ride from a man with ulterior motives. But Ben recovered well in heaven, and the injuries he sustained after his motorbike accident healed at record speed, indeed fast enough for him to rejoin Earth only nine years later.

As I told you earlier in Lust, Benjamin Barrymore was fortunate to be reborn on July 1, 1986, and I followed his triumphant arrival almost twelve years later, on March 6, 1998, to be exact. I am ecstatic to know we are, once again, unionized under the Chinese Year of The Tiger, as we have been throughout all our encounters. I like to think the Lord above has a wicked sense of humor in that he purposefully enjoys watching the feistiness that Ben and I have fought with over the years and that others in the heavens also chuckle at our blatant forthrightness, as I know Ben and I have had our moments when we either love each other or act in angst. Still, it is never malice that returns us to our rightful place at each other's side. Nowadays, to write I am joyous is an understatement, for I am thrilled to live as Bella Bloom, even if I am poor and in trouble for all the wrong reasons. Still, I have enjoyed life up till twenty-six, and hopefully, I will live well into my eighties or nineties if I am lucky, for aging is a gift and not a guarantee.

I am aware my server life, living like Sally Peters, ended abruptly and conscious that I am risking life and limb in my current occupation as a companion; trust me when I assure you, I am not taking great chances. Well, other than last night's unsightly massacre, which happened less than six feet away, and the bloodbath hidden within the primary closet walls is terrorizing me and my will for life.

I thought about how I needed my friend at that moment. I long for his embrace, hoping it will ease the chaos that engulfs me.

Where are you, darling Ben?

Do you no longer care for me?

I pray you do.

I hope you also understand the extent of my thoughts and need for you, particularly after last night's intense events and the early morning rampage on this peaceful Sunday.

In bravery, I thought to break down the closet door where CJ and Tubby lay, and though fearful, I surmised I must find out if CJ was alive or killed instantly or if she suffered, for she deserved that much from me after all the help she had shared in helping me catch up on my finances.

I rose from a stool against the central island and strolled toward the sink to wash my empty glass. Though there was a dishwasher, I scrubbed the glass repeatedly. I have watched police shows where criminals left fingerprints at crime scenes, leading to their eventual capture and arrest by the police. So, in good keeping, I wore bright yellow dish gloves and wiped down all kitchen surfaces and the living room furniture. Finally, standing inside the primary bathroom, I choked from a putrid smell that irritated my nostrils.

Oh no!

Can you tell me if it is too early for rigor mortise to settle into a deceased person's body? I am not an idiot, and I know you cannot answer, but I did not think it was too much to ask.

Or is it?

Please tell me, and please know that I will read your opinion and treasure it until the end of eternity.

Suddenly, my mind wandered into the past again, and remembering my short life as Sally Peters and Ben as Jake Thatcher, I recollected that we never kissed while incarnated in those willful bodies. As in the seventies' lifetime, we were too busy fighting, especially in our teenage years. Though, I hope as we are today that we will kiss as we have historically throughout the times we have met through the various stages of life on Earth. Besides, I yearn to feel the warmth of his embrace around my body, as the strength in his arms makes me feel safe and secure, and despite my acting like a working girl, I need his love to help me reflect on all the bad choices I have made in the past couple of months.

Ben, being himself, will naturally be more flirtatious. I, being myself, will always slap him down. Mainly because Ben believes that since he has kissed me hundreds of times, he can repeat the passion without the slightest effort, which is ludicrous as I want romance as much as the next woman. Still, I will never give up without a fight, as the dullness of a subservient woman would never hold Ben's attention for long, and I intend to keep my man coming back for more for an extraordinarily long time. Thus, I may pretend to despise the gallant man who becomes confused by my wickedness, or I may function as if I have no interest in a romantic encounter. But secretly, I adore Benny Boy, and I yearn to feel the touch of his gentle fingers caress the nape of my neck.

On this glorious Sunday morning, I glanced across the horizon and admired the sun's warming as she helped dry the flooded roads from last night's rainstorm. It is chilly inside Clive Jenkins's home, and I am happy to see the bright morning sunshine helping to dry rain-soaked gardens and flowerbeds, for there is something magical in seeing how plants stand tall and proud when drenched in the rainwater from our Heavenly Father. Praise the Lord, for he will nurture, and his gentle breeze will return the soil to the flowerbeds. Then, he will water and dry if each bud needs his help to grow into beautiful plants across our wonderful planet.

The bright sunshine blinded me as I stared at the Atlantic Ocean and watched beachgoers walking the seashore, dogs running freely, and men kite surfing. Though not eight thirty, it is pleasing to my tired eyes to see people enjoying the simpler things in life.

At the end of Tubby's driveway, I see the roadway strewn with bushes, as are his impressive collection of Bonsai plants. Seeing the drenched floral display saddens me as I love gardening and nurturing plants. The feel of the soil between my fingers always gives me hope while keeping me grounded.

I strode toward a larger window and looked outside to see how much the wind had damaged his manicured lawns and abundant flowering plants. It was then I noticed CJ's Porsche was gone, which shocked me, for I knew of no one who could have driven the vehicle from Tubby's home, mainly because Tubby and CJ were dead, or so I thought.

The plot thickens.

The time for bravery had arrived, and I realized I must investigate the bloodbath inside the closet, a room I feared would haunt me forever. Since CJ's vehicle was missing, it seemed the only logical thing for me to do was enter the gloomy bedroom and en-suite, if only to ensure that CJ was, in fact, still inside Tubby's house.

A highly polished antique wooden grandfather clock in the hallway signaled nine that morning. I am surprised that thirty long minutes had passed at a rapid speed. To affirm I was alive and not deceased, I grasped a cutting knife and grappled the nerve to stab my right arm to see blood, if only to signal that I am well and truly part of the living, for deceased people no longer bleed once they have left their body.

Am I alive, or am I dead?

I rushed along the corridor, threw myself atop a stool inside the kitchen, and gnawed at my lower lip just as I slashed the sharp knife across my right forearm.

Ouch! I wanted to scream in pain, and I could have, so quickly, but I was afraid of the sound my painful cries could create. I feared a visit from a nosy neighbor, so I bit heavily on napkins that I had shoved between my jaw and shuddered at the sight of the blood that poured from my wound.

The paper napkin trick was something I had mastered years earlier whenever I was afraid the sound of my breath might alert a dangerous entity to my hiding place. To hide my terror, I piled a one-inch thickness of paper towel and chewed down heavily to muffle any whimpering noise that might escape my lips. However, now I must contend with finding a bandage to wrap around my wound if only to stop the onslaught of blood that flowed easily from the cut that was deeper than I intended. Moments earlier, my left hand had crashed and stabbed my flesh harder than I could ever have expected.

You are foolish. I cursed as I wrapped ice cubes in a dish towel, placed it on my arm, and searched the pantry for a medical box to protect my injury from infection. The wonders within Tubby's food hall were incredible to me, as I had never seen such a large assortment of items to eat, drink, or smoke, and forgetting my search for a medical box, I read labels. I marveled at the imported foods that lined the floor-to-ceiling shelving and noted the countries Tubby imported the most food from, which surprisingly was Russia, in particular, caviar, vodka, and crackers.

Suddenly, the sound of a cell phone echoed along a hallway and into the kitchen, and I jumped, afraid. Though I recognized the ringer tone on my phone, I grew nervous about who would call early this Sunday morning. However, I was more anxious about why my phone was outside the main closet when I was sure I had left it with the rest of my belongings.

I thought it might be Harry. I wondered if he had awoken and felt remorseful over his behavior last night. Though I was no longer inclined to or wanted to explain my predicament, I cringed at the prospect of satisfying his egotistical needs, which may inspire him to lecture me about my absence again.

I adored Harry in my innocent way, and while he had charm and charisma and could make me laugh wildly and louder than most other men I have met, somehow, Harry did not make my heart soar the way Ben effortlessly could, and that troubled me. If a man could ever take Benny Boy's place, it would be Harry. However, first, Harry would have to quit drinking or, at the very least, curb his alcoholic outbursts, as I despised being his punching bag on occasions when he burst into a furious rant.

My phone rang louder with each new chime, and I retreated from the pantry, ran along the corridor, and spotted my mobile on the living room coffee table, which annoyed me as I would have used my phone instead of Tubby's house phone when reaching out to call a friend earlier that morning. I grabbed the beeping technology that always held me captive and glanced at the screen.

To my relief, it was not Harry but my new friend Beatrice Ryder, the Georgia Southern Belle I had enjoyed conversing with last night at the ball to honor my client, Mitch Carter. My index finger pressed the screen, and I silenced the call.

"Good morning, my dear friend," I chirped. "I hope this Sunday finds you rested and joyous. It is lovely to see your name on my phone screen. How are you?"

"Darling Bella," Beatrice spoke softly. How wonderful to know that you, like me, are an early riser. I'm thrilled to hear your sweet voice and to make your acquaintance, and I trust you, too, are enjoying this wonderful Sunday."

"My, yes, my dear friend. It is good to hear from you."

"So, tell me, what are your plans for today?"

I could hardly admit that I was in a strange man's house, and that I had two dead bodies locked inside a closet, or that

I had slashed my arm to investigate if I were dead or alive, so to appease Beatrice, I stayed silent while struggling to think of something interesting to say. All the while, I wished for a return phone call from the man who could help me swiftly flee this rotten situation, but he still had not contacted me, and the feeling of abandonment crippled me with fear.

"Hello, are you still there?" Beatrice inquired.

Against my better judgment, I should confess my current dilemma. If only to seek much-needed help. However, the startling reality of the double homicide I had seen scared me more than anything, and I decided I would force myself to give an Oscar-worthy performance. If only to convince Beatrice, all was well. "Yes, I'm here," I said and paused. "I'm sorry for my delay, but I was cutting oranges; I had picked fresh from a tree and sliced my hand," I lied and nibbled on a piece of tape to secure a dressing around my injured arm. I flexed my wrist to ensure the bandage was tight and reclaimed my seat atop a kitchen stool. "But" I paused again. "I have cleansed my hand, wrapped it in gauze, and secured the cut. So, please don't worry, as no infection will grow, and first thing tomorrow, I will visit my doctor's office."

"Do you remember Emily Parker?" she inquired as I glanced outside a large window after noticing a figure in the back garden. The figure's presence caused me alarm as it referenced a man, I knew but did not want to see.

"Yes! Of course, I remember her, as she attended the ball last night as your guest. Correct?"

"Absolutely. Emily is a former nurse, and should you need help, she will gladly dress your wound. If you want to visit, you are most welcome, and I would love your company as you are an intriguing woman. Plus, Emily could help you or be of aid if that makes sense."

"Oh, that is so kind of you, but I will be fine as it's only a small cut," I lied again and leaned closer toward the window to search for the figure of a man I had spotted moments earlier, but he had disappeared. No longer seeing the outline of his body, I focused on Beatrice and her insistence on helping. "Besides, I am not exactly close by, as I am a Miami girl these days and no longer a Palm Beach resident. So, driving to your house, particularly with Sunday drivers, will take me forever."

"Bless your heart, Bella. You are so thoughtful, and ordinarily, I may agree with you, but since today is Sunday, I think it could be a beautiful day for a drive. If it would please you more, let us meet at the halfway point. How does Fort Lauderdale Beach sound?"

I winced and strummed my fingers on the countertop, struggling to find a valid reason not to visit today, but I came up empty, mostly because I was too tired to dream up any more lies.

Suddenly, a tap on the back door's window startled me, and I quickly turned toward the frosted glass to figure out who was outside. But I could only see the outline of a tall figure. I feared it was Peter or, worse, Jimmy, and afraid, I shrank to the floor and hid between the dishwasher and the island.

"Bella, are you there?" Beatrice asked, concerned.

"I'm sorry, but I thought I saw someone at the door," I whispered.

"Why are you talking low?"

"I don't know. Though, I need more time. Last night was fabulous, but I'm tired and ready to return to bed."

"Rubbish! You are far too young to sleep. You will have plenty of time to do that when you are as old and weary as I am."

"You're not old, Beatrice," I argued, and I meant it since she was such a gregarious, mature lady. I enjoyed her company more than ever. I wish I could level with her, but I feared she would not understand my life and disown our friendship as quickly as it had begun. Thus, I continued with my flimsy excuse that the long drive would be too exhausting.

"Come on, Bella. We will have a lovely day out. Emily is looking forward to visiting you, and I am, too. So, what do you say? Are you in or out?"

"Er! I do not know," I said, wondering if I could sneak down to Broward County, have lunch with Beatrice and Emily, and still have time to return to the house of death. "It sounds tempting, but I think it would be best to drive up to Palm Beach as Fort Lauderdale is busy on the weekends, and it's almost impossible to find a parking space."

"Now, that is terrific news. What time shall I expect you to arrive?"

A slight smile crossed my lips since hearing the chirp in her voice eased my concerns. And besides, I liked Beatrice, and until Tubby's demise, I had planned to visit with her today. So, it was only natural that I should continue with my first plan, even if that meant leaving two dead bodies alone in a house that a cleaner may or may not see.

The only issue that genuinely bothered me was what to tell Harry and what to do about the voice message I had left on a particular answering machine less than two hours earlier.

To be utterly truthful to you, that was not my only problem, as I also worried that Emily Parker would notice that my injured arm was a self-inflicted wound. She was bound to, I thought. She was a former nurse and would not take my excuse of slicing fruit lightly. She may question such a deep puncture wound, which troubled me as I did not know how many more lies, I could get away with before someone caught, trapped, or even exposed my tales. For each lie, I told created a hundred more, around one straightforward piece of bullshit.

Drat, I cursed. You are well and truly screwed, Bella. It might be best to wave a white shirt, surrender to the world and pay the piper before you are well and truly fucked.

Easier said than done, I surmised. Mainly because I did not find it extremely hard to admit to Beatrice that I am an ordinary girl with nothing worth bringing to the table, so to speak, other than gossip about dirty pigs of men and the revelation that I am trash, and both options freaked me out, for I didn't want my new friends to think badly of me.

Not just yet anyway.

In the not-too-distant future, I am confident they will find out, but as of right now? I am enjoying my anonymity and discretion. Plus, it is none of their business what I do privately or what I do to make money. My day job comforted me because I could chat about my work obligations and not tell tales. So, on that affirmation, I thought there might be a possibility of my visiting with Beatrice and Emily. At the very least, I can converse with ordinary people compared to the nutty clients I have spent time with this past week.

"Did I lose you, Bella?" Beatrice said, interrupting my thoughts.

"No!" I answered. "I am here. I was merely thinking of a good time to meet and what restaurant to eat lunch at."

"Rubbish. If you are going to drive up here, you can visit my home, and I will have my cook, Maria, prepare stone crabs and a seafood salad. Do you eat fish?"

"Only on days when I can afford to," I replied. "My awful job doesn't allow me to eat seafood as often as I would like. So, it will be lovely to sample fish. Thank you, Beatrice."

"Then, it's settled. You are coming here. I will send my assistant to the store and ask Maria to prepare a seafood medley feast, with all the fresh fish available from the local market. What time do you plan to arrive?"

"I am not sure, but I plan to leave Miami in one hour, as I need to shower and freshen up," I said and grimaced, noticing my lack of lunchtime clothing. Yes, the jeans and tee fit, but each piece of cloth faded and differed from what I would like to wear for brunch with Beatrice. Right now, I had no choice, as I could not return to Miami to change my outfit. "Is it okay if I don't dress up, as I'm more comfortable in casual clothing?"

"Oh, sweetheart, wear whatever you want. Neither I nor Emily will care if you dress in a paper bag."

"Thank you so much. I will be on my way in less than one hour. What is your address?"

"Fabulous news," Beatrice said gregariously. "Do you have a pen?"

"I do."

"You are such an organized young woman, Bella. My address is 2240 Ocean Drive, Jupiter, Florida."

"Jupiter? But I thought you lived in Palm Beach?" I asked, confused.

"I did, but I recently moved to Jupiter Inlet, as there is less traffic here. Also, my nephew Clive lives next door, and I'm in a better position to check up on him if I'm living nearby."

"No worries," I said, perplexed. If I had family, I would want to live nearby, too. So, I understand your reasoning."

"Well, dear, if you know Clive like I know Clive, you'd completely understand my reasoning for living right next door, as he's still a baby and immature in his ways. I cannot fathom why my sister spoiled him so much, but she did, and sadly, he's beyond saving, I'm sad to announce."

"Well, if he's just a baby, there's always hope."

"Oh, dear, Clive hasn't seen childhood in almost forty-five years. I am ashamed to tell you that my nephew is a mature man whose sole interests lie in drugs, women, and criminal activities. Suffice it, I am living here to keep a watchful eye on him and all his shady business dealings. I am sure you understand?"

"Absolutely," I said and glanced outside at the sunlight that basked throughout the eastern side of Tubby's house, reflecting a warm hue onto my pale skin, making me feel warm and cozy in such a chilly kitchen.

"Will your nephew be joining us?" I asked, dreading her reply. Yet, I was curious about who else might attend Sunday brunch.

"I'm doubtful, as I have yet to see him today, which is strange as Clive visits each morning," Beatrice said, pausing. "Still, I presume he's hungover and sleeping off a massive headache. So, no worries, dearest Bella. Unless my sister's troubled son discovers a bottle of Tylenol attached to a massive joint, I doubt I will see him in the unforeseen future. Of course, he may surprise me, but I doubt it."

"It's okay with me if he shows up." I stammered. "It will not bother me as long as you're happy; that matters most to me."

"Thank you, sweet child," Beatrice said.

"I expect to arrive in a couple of hours, and I will call you along the way to update you on my trip's progress."

"Thank you. I look forward to seeing you soon."

"Of course."

"Be careful driving."

"Most certainly, I always watch the roads as one can never be too careful with the lunatics driving drunk and so forth. Do not worry. I will be fine."

"Good girl. I knew there was something responsible I admire in you, and now, I wish that..."

"What?" I interrupted.

"Well, to be honest," Beatrice sighed, long and hard. "I may invite my nephew, as I think it will cheer him up to meet someone stable like you, but of course, I don't want to pressure you. Still, I only need to pop next door, persuade him to clean himself up, and invite him to join us. It is your call. Just let me know?"

"I am fine if he wants to join us, but I do not want you to feel you must go on a mission to gather his attention or feel you need to please me, as I am happy to see you regardless of company."

"You're such a good girl, Bella. I'm so happy to have met you."

"Likewise," I said and smiled. "It is so hard to meet kind people today and even harder to make friends with someone thoughtful, as most good people are too weary of getting attached to evil hidden beneath goodness."

"I wholeheartedly agree."

"Thank you, Beatrice. I cannot wait to see you today. We will have a wonderful time, as will Emily, and should your nephew decide to grace us with his presence, then he, too. What was his name again? I'm sorry to ask, but I have forgotten."

I listened as Beatrice laughed heartily. As she chuckled, I imagined the fine lines around her soft skin had crinkled as her blue eyes sparkled from a soul-searching reason to giggle. "His name is Clive," she told me. "I am crossing my garden as we speak and walking toward his home, so I hope I can keep the phone signal while chatting with you. I know I should have waited, but I became so excited to introduce you both that I acted hastily instead of gathering your permission first. I trust my actions will not spur you to come."

I laughed. "Of course not," I said and gasped. But honestly, I did not want to meet Clive, the drug-addicted nephew, nor did I want to hear any more about his pathetic existence, for he was fortunate to live a life of luxury, yet he chose to throw it away, which disgusted me.

Why did people with every richness available to man always live in complete and utter chaos?

Why the need to abuse a luxury life by falling into drugs and alcohol?

I was sure the easy life bored most people and was confident that Beatrice's nephew, Clive, whatshisname, was precisely the same as all the other rich pricks I had met throughout high school. Clive was the last person I wanted to spend my Sunday afternoon with; he was dull and superficial.

Yuck!

Double yuck.

Clive sounded like a real pig, and I had had enough of oinking men for the rest of my life, particularly after spending part of the early morning hours with Tubby Clive Jenkins, who I found to be the biggest loser known to men, women too, as he was insufferable, narcissistic, and selfish. Though wealthy beyond his means, his money was the least of his problems, as no amount of money could make him attractive to others, not with such a rotten egotistical attitude.

Sitting alone in Tubby's home, I was glad that Clive was no longer in my world. I did not want him dead because it hurt me after seeing his performance with Jimmy. Still, Tubby was a whiner and blamed others for his downfalls in life, and I was sure this type of rich brat was similar in ways to the nephew Beatrice was complaining about. If not exactly alike, then Siamese Twin-like in mannerisms, and

I am grateful that the nephew, like Tubby, was also incommunicado.

I mean that in the nephew being hungover and not dead.

I would not want Beatrice to suffer from a loss, as I saw firsthand the anguish my mother suffered after the death of my brother. I would not wish that torment on anyone, least of all Beatrice, who has unselfishly welcomed me into her life, and soon I would sit inside her home, which must count for something, right?

Yes!

It shows me that my new friend is wise enough to see the goodness in people and intelligent enough to see various forms of evil lurking in so many others. It flattered my heart that she chose to befriend me, but I was not surprised since she has a keen mind. However, I did not doubt that Beatrice could lash out should she feel threatened or violated. The Southern Belle's helpless routine was merely a public display, and I believe deep down, Beatrice Ryder could kick her heels up with the best of them. She was in phenomenal shape and had an unusual, sculpted body that convinced me she spent long days engaged in Pilates or Yoga. If not, another form of exercise, such as swimming, kept her fitter than most.

Suddenly, secure that I was safe, I rose from the floor and peered outside an uncovered window to see if I could still spot the figure of a man I had heard knocking on the back door moments earlier, and though I saw no one walking the grounds beside the pool, I still feared who the trespasser could be. Then, out of the corner of my eye, I focused on a man's tall, slender figure as he strolled across an uncovered window, which grabbed my attention full throttle.

Who is that? I gasped and returned to my squat position beside the stainless-steel dishwasher.

I wondered if it was a gardener, a pool company, or the cleaner's relative. However, the likelihood of a service company performing work on a Sunday morning did not sit right with me, and all my reasoning appeared futile.

Again, I crouched upward, peered outside the window, searched for the man tapping the pane of glass on a French door, and scoured the garden for a sign of an intruder but found nothing.

Double drat! I cursed loudly. Then, I urged myself to check the front of the house for a clue as to who was walking on the property. I exited the kitchen, crossed the hallway, crawled on all fours toward a large door designed in lead-patterned glass, and spied outside into the front of the house and the city street. Seeing no one, I became concerned and rested against an entryway table as I studied my next move. It was then that I noticed the figure of a woman chatting with the man, and may God strike me down dead, but the woman was none other than Beatrice Ryder.

Goodness, gracious. NO!

She was the aunt of Tubby, and now he was dead, and much worse, she lived next door. What was I going to do? And how would I get out of this situation?

I have no idea.

If I had told you I had almost fainted, I would not have been lying—not this time. I know you have heard several of my tales but trust me when I tell you I almost passed out from the shock.

Soon after that, my earlier conversation with Beatrice taunted my memories as I remembered our chat, and the reality that Beatrice lived next door caused me anxiety. The knowledge that her nephew Clive was Clive Tubby Jenkins shocked me because the recovering addict was dead, and worse, Beatrice did not know her nephew's fate, not yet anyway. Despite feeling an overwhelming need to confront the mature woman and confess all my sins, I could not let her know I was nearby, as I had already lied and told her I was in Miami, which put me in an embarrassing position should she discover I was in her nephew's house, and because of my location, I feared she'd hate me indefinitely.

Slowly, I moved from the entryway, and on all fours, I crawled across the kitchen floor to find solace within the pantry walls. It seemed the only place to hide from Beatrice and the mystery man's figure I had spotted outside.

Inside the small room that stored food and dishes, I tugged in my jeans pocket for my cell phone, only to discover I did not have it. Then I recalled leaving it on the island next to the dishwasher, and inwardly, I cursed my stupidity as I peered across the kitchen until I laid eyes on my phone.

You fool, I snapped.

Now, what are you going to do?

I shrugged, leaned back against the shelf packed with canned goods, and struggled to accept my situation, which was more challenging than I imagined. And if Beatrice had a set of keys to Tubby's home, I was well and truly screwed, which sucked as I had not received even a partial fee for my time.

The pantry walls felt like they were closing in on me, and feeling claustrophobic, I pushed open the door and welcomed cool air from the ceiling air conditioning unit that swirled from a vent at the base of the floor.

Inhaling and exhaling deeply, I wiped away beads of sweat from my forehead and relaxed for a couple of seconds before I heard tapping on the exterior door again.

Who would visit Tubby early Sunday morning?

I struggled to understand if it were a friend, foe, or family member, or worse, the police performing a welfare check on Clive Jenkins, as he certainly knew enough people who would worry should he disappear for an extended period. Namely, his aunt, a housecleaning lady, and a friend who cared about him. Aside from his trainer, I imagined he had lots of acquaintances who competed to be on his favorite list of people as they amalgamated to climb to the top of his list, and though I did not know any of them, I surmised they were all scroungers who were out for what they could get.

A couple of minutes later, I exited the food cupboard, leaned against the wall, crossed my legs, and folded my arms. I closed my eyes and rested my weary head on my palms while basking in the ambiance of solitude. However, my relief was short-lived because shortly after that, I heard a thud on the glass windowpane, followed by a pounding on the wooden frame as persistent as a police officer's battering ram, which they used to lever a door open, and the sheer force of the knock encased me in fear. I jumped upward and crossed the room. "Hey! Open the door!" a man screamed through the keyhole.

I could hear the man's exasperation, and I recognized his voice. I halted my exit and turned toward the door.

"Well, will you stand looking at me or unlock this wretched entryway?"

In an instant, I stood beside the door, positioned the key, and unlocked the lock, but not before I bawled as a wave of relief swept across my trembling body.

The backyard door swung open, and standing before me, with rage in his eyes, stood the only man I knew who cared enough to risk all to rescue the girl who landed in one problematic situation after another.

"Dear God, Ben," I said and gasped. "How did you...? How did you find me?"

"Are you okay?" he asked as his eyes searched mine. "Bella, what the hell are you doing in this house, and why are you here?" He paused, glanced around the room, and stopped face-to-face before he held me close against his body. "Have you been here all night?"

I imagined I looked like a caged animal trapped by hunters after pilfering through supplies, and facing this reality caused my legs to weaken and shake vigorously within his arms.

Suddenly, Ben's hand smoothed my unbrushed hair, and his calm words eased my pain. Still, I fought between giving a truthful reply or making up yet another elaborate lie about why I was inside Tubby's home.

I exhaled. "Ben, you won't believe this, but I..." I spoke in a rambling tone. Initially, I tried to lie, but there was no explanation for my current predicament, and my voice failed. Then, as I processed the seriousness of my predicament, I wept until I could cry no more tears. After what felt like hours, I finally stopped expressing my emotions as I faced the reality that I could not lie to Benjamin Barrymore. This consciousness caused me shame, and though I longed to fabricate a fictitious story to satisfy Ben's questions, I could not do it. Therefore, for the first time in months, I accepted that my lying days were over and finished.

Just like that, and in all fairness, I could not be happier.

I told Ben the whole sordid details of my life as a companion, my date with Tubby, and everything else in between. When I finished, I prepared myself for the unforeseen, which would be Ben turning around and leaving. Yet by my side, he stayed, and despite feeling saddened by my cheap existence as an escort, he assured me that if I quit, he would stand by me, as we were and are, friends until the end.

Slowly, I exhaled, dried my eyes, accepted a tissue from Ben, and blew my nose.

"Calm, Bella," he soothed.

"I'm trying," I assured myself, checking my cell phone atop the kitchen island. I wondered if Beatrice had tried to ring, but I had no missed calls.

"Are you expecting a phone call?" Ben asked, fists by his side, a pensive look etched on his face.

"No," I lied, and after seeing the knowing look on his face, I quickly corrected my tale and shrugged. "Old habits die hard," I teased and crossed the room to where he stood and rested against his massive chest. "I have a new friend, Beatrice, and she's expecting me for lunch, but I told her I was in Miami, as I didn't realize she lived next door or that she was Tubby's aunt."

"Tubby?"

"Clive Jenkins."

"Oh, I see. Yes, that is quite a situation to be in the middle of. It is no wonder you are an emotional wreck. I suppose we could," Ben said and paused.

"We could what?" I queried.

"Well, we could sneak across the back garden, go to the beach, and pretend we've engaged in a sandy stroll. Then we can hightail it along the seashore toward the Marina and return to this house or Beatrice's home in a pretentious stroll, if you catch my drift?"

I smiled. "Ben, you have quite the imagination. Don't you?" I said and nuzzled against his chest. "Your stories are as bad as my own."

Ben squeezed me tightly. "I believe it's catching," he said and guffawed. "Perhaps your love of fairytales is rubbing off on me?"

"Oh no! I hope not. But I love that you have such a fun sense of humor."

"I'm serious, Bella.

"I get that, Ben. I'm just surprised you will go along with such an elaborate tale to save my reputation."

"What other reason would I have if not to help you?"

I sighed deeply. "Benjamin Barrymore, you are a man to love," I said, kissing his cheek. "However, I don't believe we will make it to the beach, as I fear Beatrice Ryder is combing the gardens, looking for her nephew."

"Do not underestimate my smarts, Bella Bloom," Ben instructed, placing a large straw hat atop my head. "Tuck your hair underneath; Voila, you are incognito, undetectable to all others except me."

The sizable floppy sun hat hid my face, and I shoved it back and gazed up at Ben. "Do you think this will hide my identity?" I asked, securing my long hair underneath the material.

"Absolutely."

"But what about you? How will you hide?"

"Nobody will question me, not even Beatrice Ryder. She's a friend of my mother and has feasted on dinners at our formal table for years, and she is familiar with my appearance at nephew Clive's home."

"Are you certain?"

"Yes! Now, relax and heed my lead."

I nodded and prepared to follow Ben into the garden when he drew me close, locked his arm around my waist, and hurried toward the banyan trees, which hid a pathway to one of the most beautiful beaches I had seen in South Florida.

"Wow! I did not know Tubby had access to the beach," I said as I gazed longingly toward the Atlantic Ocean and relaxed as the late morning sun caressed my shoulders. "This is an incredible view, Ben. And I love the coconut palms swinging on that trail. Who knew? I certainly did not."

"I know about this area," Ben said smugly and smiled.

"Oh, come on, Ben. You are seriously not going to gloat, are you?"

"Maybe," he said and chuckled.

I thumped his chest hard, and he faked an injury.

"Okay, okay, okay!" Ben said, laughing. "I promise not to act like a jerk. Scout's honor."

I giggled as I watched Ben raise his right hand upward to the arch of his eyebrow and palm down; he signaled the three-finger sign and salute. "I'm guessing you spent many years in the Boy Scouts?"

"My best childhood years were in that company."

"And all these years later, you still remember all the codes, which are commendable, Ben."

"I believe I paid more attention to Boy Scouts than school studies, much to the annoyance of my parents."

"It shows," I told him. "For you are a master of your craft."

"Thank you, darling Bella."

As we strolled the beach, I relaxed. The saltwater and wet sand squished between my toes and kicked up to my calves as I hurriedly walked next to Ben. Today, I was having fun spending time with Benny Boy more than ever, and it was since I could finally talk honestly to the man I loved so much. Of course, it helped that my hero did not judge or put me down, which still was a massive shock as I was worried, he would find me unfit to be a friend, let alone the woman he loved and yearned to hold.

The ocean breeze cooled and warmed my tense muscles, and strolling northbound toward Jupiter Yacht Club, I basked in Ben's strong arm as he stabilized my walk. On that sunny Sunday, I held Ben's hand as we admired Jupiter's unique paradise. As we strolled along the shoreline, it felt good to feel the warm waves splashing against our legs.

"Don't forget, Bella, we must perfect our alibi?" Ben cautioned as we neared Beach Road.

I nodded.

"Do you want to walk to the lighthouse?" he asked as we crossed the street and stopped at the Marina.

"It's your call, Ben," I said, sounding more casual than I felt inside. "How far away is the lighthouse?"

"If you have to ask, then you won't make the walk, which is fine. We'll take it easy today and take a more strenuous stroll tomorrow morning."

"Tomorrow?"

"Sure," Ben said and smiled. "You are going to spend the night, right?"

I shrugged again and sighed. "I don't know, Ben, as I am worried about what your parents may think if they discover you're involved with me."

"Rubbish. My parents adore you. Why, my parents look upon you as a second daughter. So, do not worry; please do not behave like a silly adolescent, Bella. My parents love you."

"Now, that sounds strange, doesn't it?"

"Why?"

"If I'm like a daughter to your mother and father, then I'm basically a sister of yours, which may be incestuous."

"Ha!" Ben laughed. "You really know how to take the wind out of a man's sail, right?"

My left leg kicked his thigh harder than intended, and I grimaced. "Oops! So sorry. I did not mean to hit you that hard. I hope I did not hurt you."

Ben pulled me close and whispered. "Your words have wounded me more," he kissed my cheek. "Oh no! I did not mean to be so cruel. I was afraid that you were playing games, and I was also worried because of my secrets. Do I need to explain more?"

Two kisses later, Ben smiled. "No, Bella. I understand you, and I know you better than anyone else. So, it is fair to say you do not need to add further details. Besides, I love how you care so much about keeping things under wraps."

"That's a polite way of calling me a liar, right?"

"We all lie, Bella. We all hold secrets and reveal what we want others to know. If we want to keep our emotions private, that's our prerogative, particularly if questions become too intrusive."

"Since when did you become so philosophical?"

"I have my moments."

I laughed.

Ben laughed.

Then, we laughed together, which was magical.

As we approached the Marina by Catos Bridge, I could see the tall red lighthouse across the bay. It looked like the tower could touch the darkened sky, which had changed from blue to black as a storm cloud had blown ashore.

"It's going to be bad rainfall," I told Ben while we crossed the parking lot and walked toward his car.

"Don't worry, Bella. My vehicle is close by. So, we'll make it inside before we get drenched." He gripped my hand, squeezed gently, and dug into his trouser pocket for his automobile's remote control. Two clicks unlocked the doors, and we climbed inside just as the first drops of rain fell.

"Phew! That was close. I was certain we'd get wet."

"Well, we could have run for cover sooner, but best I remember, you don't like to run."

I pinched his stomach. "Ouch! That was mean," I told him, wiping water droplets from my legs.

"But it's true."

"Yes," I agreed and removed the large straw hat that had protected my skin from the burning sun and masked my identity.

"So, Ben," I said and sighed. How can you afford such a fancy truck?" I asked as I realized I was sitting inside a blue Mercedes G Wagon, packed with all the latest technology, and designed to know when it was swimming. "Is this the model that can go up to thirty inches deep in water? If so? That's pretty impressive."

I watched Ben blush. "Yes," he admitted. "A sensor closes the intake channel behind the radiator, allowing the engine to draw air from a higher, alternate intake behind the headlights," he said and paused. "It's my baby, and I love driving this vehicle as it keeps me safe, particularly when coastal streets flood."

"It puts my old, battered Toyota to shame. Ha! I'm embarrassed for you to see my dilapidated car."

"Do not put yourself down, Bella."

"It's true!"

"Listen to me, Bella. Do you want a vehicle like this? I will buy you one if you do, mainly because I want you to be safe."

I secured the seatbelt and leaned back against my seat. "Don't be ridiculous, Ben. You do not need to buy me an SUV like this. Besides, I would be nervous about driving such an expensive vehicle. What if I crashed it? You would be mad at me, and I do not want to make you angry.

However, I love the navy paint job, which is perfect for the South Florida blue skies. Well, aside from grey skies now, that is."

"It's not navy. The color is Lunar Blue Metallic."

"Well, excuse me, Mister Fancy Pants." I teased as my finger swept across the expensive leather passenger seat. "This leather is even fancier than the couch in my apartment. No wonder women are trying to land you, Benny Boy. They're after all your money."

"And I thought it was my dashing good looks."

"Oh, come on, Ben. You know more about girls than I do. What other reason would they want to date you other than to marry into your fabulously wealthy family?"

"Bella, I insist you take that back," Ben demanded.

Seeing the hurt on his face made me shudder, and I grimaced, knowing it was me who caused him to become upset. "I'm sorry, Ben. I didn't mean for my words to sound as awful as they did."

"I'll forgive you this time but be careful when insinuating that those girls only want money. I have more to offer a woman than a large bank account. Besides, it's primarily my family's wealth; I was just lucky to be born into it."

"Agreed. Okay, a change of subject is coming up. Will you answer truthfully?"

Ben nodded, a sly smile curving his luscious lips.

"Don't tease," I said and rolled my eyes. So, tell me, Ben, how did you know where to find me?"

"You're asking this question now? Why not earlier when you opened Clive Jenkins's door?"

"I feared your answer, but now I'm comfortable and more secure to inquire."

"If you must know, Bella," Ben sighed and paused again. I watched him gaze outside toward the lighthouse, and then his eyes crossed over the sailboats docked at the Marina. Growing impatient, I tapped my fingers on my knees and let out a deep sigh so he would know I was still awaiting an answer. "If you must know... I saw the caller ID containing the phone number you rang from, and then I used the internet to find the reverse phone number's owner and address."

I blushed again. "It figures. I should have known you would snoop. I should have never used Tubby's house phone."

"Tubby?"

"Clive Jenkins."

"But why do you call him Tubby?"

"He reminds me of Jabba the Hutt from Star Wars."

"Yet, you changed the name?"

"I am afraid of being sued, Ben. So, yes. I changed his blasted name. If I could have used Jabba throughout this episode, I would have, but I don't have enough money to afford backlash or a lawsuit."

"I have to tell you something, Bella, but I don't want you to take my words as a lecture, and I certainly don't want you to become angry."

"Just say what you want to say, Ben. I will not get mad. I said and scowled.

"That sounds like another lie is ready to slip from your tongue."

"No, it's not. I promise." Okay, I had lied. Of course, I would become upset, especially if Benny Boy ripped me to pieces, particularly when I had become comfortable in his company and trusted words. Besides, what girl would not be upset if someone criticized her? I would be, as cruel words can wound deep within anyone's soul.

Ben sighed again and shrugged. "Here goes, Bella," he said and inhaled deeply. "You must understand the most prominent battles we face are within ourselves. You are facing your inner demons, whose words are more complex to ignore. All I want is for you to call upon your strength and ask for guidance. That's all."

I listened until he had finished exhaling before I replied. "That's it?"

"Yes. Well, other than..."

"Other than what?"

"Well, I want you to know that you're never alone and do not have to face trouble alone. Never be afraid or ashamed to ask for help, Bella, or even share what you are going through with me," Ben said and paused again for what seemed like the hundredth time.

I was acutely aware that he was choosing his words wisely, and I was grateful.

"Would you think less of me if I were going through a similar fate? Of course, you would not. So, please show yourself the same compassion. Do you understand what I am trying to tell you, Bella?"

My turn to pause.

"Earth to Bella."

I nodded hastily and groaned. "I want to tell you everything, Ben. I'm still unsure how to get all the words out, as I don't want you to hate me, nor do I want you to ask me to get out of your lovely vehicle." I murmured.

"All I'd like to know, Bella, is why you used Clive's house phone and not your cell phone?"

"Ben," I said and hesitated.

"Go on," he coaxed.

"Goodness, Ben, last night some thugs came by Tubby's home and killed him and my friend CJ, and they're still dead inside his bathroom closet, or I think they are, but now I'm unsure as CJ's black Porsche is missing and I don't know who drove it away because I was hiding in the shower fearful of being killed." I blurted out, shaking my head in terror as I recalled the incidents from early morning when Jimmy shot Tubby in cold blood before CJ's shilling screams haunted my tiredness. "So, do you understand my predicament? Not forgetting my reluctance to chat about my evening at Tubby's? For God's sake, Ben, I'm stressed beyond my years and about to lose my mind over all that happened at 2250 Ocean Drive." I glanced out the window and watched a family dock a boat. After disembarking, they made a mad dash for cover from the pounding rain. Staring at the mother and children, I struggled to control the anxiousness in the pit of my stomach, and suddenly, my body shook in uncontrollable spasms. "I'm sorry, Ben. I truly am, but I did not expect to be at Clive's house. I was supposed to attend the ball at the Carlisle Hotel and Resort. Then, my boss would relieve me of my duties, which, in my estimation, would give me enough time to attend Harry's party without him noticing my overdue arrival. Still, I got suckered into taking a second date at Jabba Clive's home, and..." I froze and conjured up more courage to finish my sentence. "And if you're angry? That's fine because everyone else is furious with my actions, Harry included."

"Say what?" Ben asked incredulously, a look of dismay upon his face.

"Harry, Ben. Have you forgotten I have a boyfriend?"

He cursed profusely and shook his head. "Of course not, Bella. I have been trying to understand all the drama in the past twelve hours."

"So, what do I do?"

Ben shook his head again. "Well, first, we must check the closet to ensure your friend DJ is still there. The shooter could have fired at a wall if only to pretend to kill her, and that could explain why her vehicle was missing. Perhaps she abandoned ship, so to speak?"

"CJ! Her name is CJ, not DJ."

"Got it, Bella," Ben said and winced.

Have I mentioned throughout this saga how I enjoy the way Benny Boy always uses my name when he speaks to me?

I do, and I have never heard my name spoken with such affection in my entire life. My darling Ben has a way of pronouncing Bella that makes his words sing, particularly when he calls me Bella Bloom, and I love him so much more for making sure I am aware he is talking to me. Even if he is saying words I do not want to hear, it makes no difference, as it is endearing to hear my name spoken softly without conviction or malice.

Suddenly, a lightning bolt shot across the cloudy sky and lit up the neighborhood like a firecracker blasting into space on the Fourth of July, causing us both to jump and huddle together.

"Are you okay?" Benny Boy asked gently.

"I'm fine," I lied again and buried my face against his chest.

"No, you're not."

"Honest, I am."

"Stop lying, Bella."

"I'm not lying, Ben." I hissed. "I've never been more truthful since the day I was born."

"I know you well enough to know when you are lying. So, please do not tell me tales, not today, never."

I shrank back against the passenger seat and stared outside at the black clouds as they blocked the sun. As lightning strikes ripped through the sky, a burning orange hue simmered as the last rays of sunshine peaked out of the darkness, creating a hostile environment both on the horizon and within Ben's fancy car. A burst of flashing lights lit up the sky like a fireworks display and echoed throughout the midday cloudiness, with thunder roaring furiously across the turbulent sky. The sound tore through the neighborhood like a fiery cannonball blasting at an enemy ship. The intensity of the thunderstorm and its vivid electrical surges tore across the sky and into the Earth's atmosphere with the loudest acoustic I have heard in years. When the thunder roared onto the shoreline, I worried about the safety of Ben's G Wagon as a puddle of ocean water inched higher on his wheels, and I feared we might sizzle to death from the electrifying storm.

"I'm scared, Ben," I said and groaned. "I didn't survive last night to die here, and though I'm happy with you, I still do not want to die. Not today, anyway."

"You promise to stop telling me ridiculous tales?"

I nodded solemnly.

"Come closer, Bella. I will protect you, as I have always done when trouble is near."

"But Ben, what am I going to do?"

"Nothing."

"What?"

"Who can prove you were ever there?"

I shrugged. "Lisa, CJ, and maybe Clive Jenkins, but he's dead."

"And you drove up in CJ's car?"

"Yes!"

"So, if your vehicle was never at Clive's home, neither were you."

"But what about my fingerprints all over the interior?"

"You've visited there before, with me. Don't worry, Bella, there are parties at Clive's every day of the week, and fingerprints are a topic of conversation in his home, especially the greasy ones, whether from friends or foes."

"So, it's settled. You spent the night with me, and we drank at least two bottles of champagne and enjoyed a wild night of sex."

"You have got to be joking?"

Ben smirked. "Why? Who is to say my explanation is not believable? Besides, Bella, my family knows everyone in this town, and if I say you spent the night with me, then that is what you did. Nobody will argue with my statement."

"But what about my fingerprints all over Tubby's house? Not forgetting my clothes inside the closet and my handbag?"

"Calm down, Bella. I know Clive Jenkins and can easily enter his home and retrieve your possessions. As for fingerprints? Well, that's easy to explain to the law enforcement officers, as we will say that last week, you attended a barbecue with me, and we visited for four hours, at least."

"You'd lie to the police to save me?"

"Abso-fucking-lutely."

I watched his hands reach to cup my face, and this time, when he pulled me near, I did not fight against his grip. Instead, I welcomed his arms and the sweet taste of his lips as he kissed my mouth so intensely and dearly.

"I love you, Bella," he whispered as his lips caressed my neck, decolletage, and shoulders. "I have always loved you, and I always will."

"But, Ben," I repeated, feeling the warmth of his kisses on my lips. Though thrilled, I wondered how we would pull this new tale off because, unlike Ben, I did not believe we could convince or fool anyone else, let alone the local police department. "My darling Bella, you worry way too much," Ben said sympathetically. "I wish you'd trust my instincts and learn to rely on someone else instead of yourself. You do not have to be so strong, Bella, not anymore, and certainly not now that I have your back."

"I wish I could believe you," I sighed wistfully. "I'm so used to dealing with my crap that I have forgotten what it's like to share the brunt with another person."

"Wow! Bella Bloom," Ben exclaimed. "We have known each other for centuries, and just because one lifetime has been shitty is no reason for you to lose faith, particularly in me. Will you allow me to erase your problem? If your answer is, yes? Trust me when I tell you, I will fix it, and it will magically disappear?"

"Okay, Benny Boy," I sighed. "I will give you a chance to prove that you have once again the answer to one of my many problems."

I watched Ben's concern disappear, and suddenly, his face lit up as if he had recently visited Father Christmas, and that made me smile as Benny Boy was so easy to please.

Since the dawn of time, we have had each other's backs, and throughout our lives, we have built a solid foundation through hundreds of years of trust, love, and respect. I did not doubt that Benny Boy could guide me out of another one of my impetuous calamities, and I was not concerned about his ability to see it through. What scared me more than anything was whether the knowledge of my companionship dates would destroy his love for me once the harsh reality of my escapades hit him like a ton of bricks after the first shock wore off. Right now, I surmised our reunion had overwhelmed Ben, and soon, the first connection would wear off, and that was when I feared he would look down on me and decide I was not good enough to be his friend, let alone girlfriend.

"So, do you want to see the lighthouse or go to Clive's?"

"To be honest, Ben, I've had a conversation with Beatrice Ryder this morning, and she's expecting me for Sunday Brunch," I exhaled deeply. "The story is that I told her I was in Miami as I needed to stall for time and guess what?"

I grinned at the look on Benny Boy's face. If looks could kill, I would have died at that moment. I thumped him hard in his stomach and scoffed when he pretended to wince in pain. "Well, let me continue," I said as he pretended my punch had caused him injury. "I don't know how to explain to Beatrice why I lied, and how do I tell the old dear that I was at her nephew's house the entire time, particularly as we're now in agreement that I spent the night with you?"

"Ah!" Ben chuckled. "So, now you see my version of events is best?"

"It appears so," I sighed and grinned at the handsome man sitting close to my side.

"Bella, it is simple, and since I know Beatrice Ryder," he said and paused. "Well, my parents know her," he corrected, turning on the window wipers as the beating rain made it impossible to see outside. "Anyway, I think it best if we just come clean and tell her the truth."

"The truth?"

"Yes."

"Ben, you cannot be serious. It is wild to suggest we tell Beatrice that her nephew is dead. There's no way I can confess to all last night's drama, no way at all, and I won't." I told him defiantly. I turned away from Ben and stared at the lighthouse that stood contiguously at Cato's Bridge. I yearned to climb the spiral staircase, walk around the watch room or gallery dock, and marvel at the magnificent views I had read about on every search engine I had used to study its history. Sadly, I could not today because the lighthouse was not open on Sundays. "In better times," I said haphazardly.

"Say what?"

I blushed. "I considered visiting the lighthouse, but it's not open. So, I was making a mental note to go during the week, that's all."

"I'll go with you, Bella. I'd love to stand at the top and enjoy a view as beautiful as you."

"Flattery will get you everywhere."

"I hope so. Let us plan on what we are telling Beatrice. Okay?"

"We can do that later, as it will give us time to think of something."

"We don't have time, Bella."

"Why do you say that?"

"Do you see what I see?" Ben asked, pointing to the lone figure of a woman bundled in rain gear, resembling the Michelin man, as she fought high winds to cross the Marina.

"Oh my," I exclaimed. "It's Beatrice. She is looking for her nephew. What are we going to do?"

"Leave it to me," Benny Boy said, unfastening his safety belt and exiting the vehicle.

I watched as he crossed the parking lot and waved as he strolled to Beatrice, who, despite wearing massive rain gear, looked drenched, as was Ben in his flimsy button-down linen shirt and khaki dress pants. His wet loafers looked black instead of light brown, as did his hair, which clung in long waves to his face as the rain poured overhead. Somehow, I was relieved to be sitting inside his car, as I was dry and warm, considering the cotton tee I wore was damp, as were the jeans I had stolen from Tubby's house.

In angst, I tried to listen to Ben and Beatrice's conversation. Still, as hard as my ears strained, I could hear nothing but the rain falling against the Mercedes rooftop, and as the heavy thunder roared across the sky with such ferocity, I feared they would both get electrocuted should lightning strike a nearby tree.

I urged Ben, trying frantically to keep Beatrice dry and steady on her feet while high winds blew inward from the turbulent coastline to hurry.

To tell you I was nervous watching them talking is an understatement. At any second, I suspected a strong gust of wind would blow onshore and knock them off their feet and into Sea Oat and Cocoplum plants growing on nearby dunes. The pounding waves forced the foliage underwater, and though temporarily submerged, such plants can survive submersion for prolonged periods and are perfect in high tides and floods. However, just because dune grasses can withstand almost drowning, I did not like that grass could entangle Ben and cause him to become unconscious. I prayed he had coaxed Beatrice away from the seashore and continued their conversation at the Yacht Club as the Marina was solid and structurally sound. At the very least, the marina had tiki huts to dry off and shield against the savage winds. Remembering the pouring rain, I thought, spotting a pavilion, a pool, and a captain lounge among the vessels.

A quick internet search assured me showers and toilets were also onsite, which was a relief as I longed to freshen up or, at the very least, wash away the sand that clung to my ankles and rolled-up jeans. Plus, food would be an excellent choice as I am hungry, and though the marina closed on Sundays, I noticed a row of select restaurants across Cato's Bridge, less than a mile from where Ben parked.

Suddenly, a tap on the automobile's window alerted me I had company, and looking up, I saw Beatrice standing next to Ben, a giddy smile etched her mouth. I supposed Ben had already informed the Southern Belle that we had spent an enthusiastic night of drinking and sex beneath the crisp cotton sheets of a king-size bed, and I flushed with color, knowing the older woman was gloating after hearing the gossip of our torrid affair.

I pressed a button, rolled down the passenger window, and smiled, a slightly forced smile her way, as I patted her hand, which rested on the car door. "Hello, Beatrice," I said in my cheeriest voice. "Is everything alright? I told Ben how surprising it was to see you in this awful weather. Are you okay?"

Beatrice smiled and nodded yes. However, I could see her worried look, which bothered me. I gnawed at my lower lip and glanced at Ben, who was busy ushering Beatrice into the back seat of his Mercedes.

"Well, Bella, I must admit that I am shocked to learn of your relationship with Ben, but I could not be happier as I have been friends with his family for many years, and I can attest that they are one of the better families in Palm Beach."

"As you are," Ben said, climbing into the driver's seat. "It's always a pleasure to see you, Beatrice, and I trust that you and Emily are doing well. Before I forget, did Emily get a library job last month? I hope she did, as she has the patience of Job and would serve the community well."

"You are such a sweetheart to remember such details, Benjamin. Yes, Emily took the administrative position at the library, and as soon as she finishes book auditing, she will join us for brunch. I hope you are hungry, Ben, because we are having a seafood feast. You too, Bella. It's going to be a wonderful Sunday."

"Thank you, Beatrice. I love seafood, and I know I can speak for both Bella and me when I tell you how thrilled we are to join you for lunch, as you are the first person we've told of our ongoing and private romance."

I smiled as I listened to Benny Boy. For he was a far better bullshitter than I ever was, his clear confidence gave him an advantage, as did his conviction of words that rang so true in our past. However, today, we are still in the beginning stages of our partnership, but I was confident that we would take our relationship to every level humanly possible.

"Is it true?" Beatrice turned and asked.

I smiled broader this time and nodded.

"You're both going to make beautiful babies," she fussed. "Oh," she paused. "Ben, you too, Bella, will have to let me plan your wedding because I will invite the best from Palm Beach society and all the trimmings from far and beyond. Your wedding will be the event of the year. It will be an extraordinary day filled with royalty, movie stars, and a choice of savory food, the best that money can buy. I will import specialized cheeses and caviar from across the globe, and Emily will create a menu that will make even your Royal guest's mouths water. The wedding will be so exciting. I can hardly wait to host them all."

"Let's not jump the gun," Ben said shyly.

"Oh?" I asked challengingly, standing with my hands resting on my hips in a pretentious stance, which was funny considering I was sitting in his SUV.

I noticed Ben driving faster than a speeding bullet and arriving at Beatrice's house in rapid succession, and I wondered if the thought of my bearing children scared him. "You do want kids, don't you?" I asked nervously.

Of course. I was only joking, my sweetheart," he said, stopping the Mercedes on the curved driveway. I watched him shift the gear stick into the park gear and turn off the engine. "However, now that we're exiting the safety of my truck, I'm worried my beautiful tigress is ready to pounce and hold me to my recent proposal, to which I'm aware I need to follow up with a certain piece of jewelry, such as an engagement ring."

"Well, you'd best ensure it is large enough to keep your wonderful fiancé, Bella, at your side." Beatrice cajoled him.

"Oh, I don't want fancy, Beatrice. Ben, I do not need a ring, as I am secure in our friendship and trust that our Father in Heaven will pave our way. Besides, I'm not really into jewelry."

"Rubbish!" she said as she descended from Ben's truck. "It's every woman's dream to have a unique ring, and if I know the Barrymore family, they will insist that your ring be an original or a family heirloom from an ancestor who wore it when jewelry was incredible: a rarity and a truly remarkable sight. So, Bella, get ready for the ride of your life because when Margaret Barrymore gets wind of Ben's intentions, she will be delighted to insist on taking over every detail. So, please do not forget I offered to help plan your wedding first."

At that moment, my face turned five shades of red. Though I had prepared myself for the happiness the news of our engagement had brought to my dear friend Beatrice, I secretly dreaded the reaction I would receive from Margaret Barrymore because, inside my tired mind, all I could think was that Ben's mother would detest him marrying a commoner like me. In the future, if I were expecting a welcoming toast, which I did not, as it would never happen, for even I knew hell would freeze over before Margaret Barrymore accepted me as a daughter-in-law.

"Of course, Bella will not forget," Ben quipped as we walked along the gravel pathway toward the front door.

"Ben is correct," I reassured Beatrice and followed her inside her home. "My, this is stunning. I love your decor. It's so earthy and bright." I added and turned to face the older woman. "I love your decorations and feel so tranquil inside your home. Bravo, your interior designer has done a fabulous job."

"Thank you, Bella. I'm so happy you like my home."

"I do!"

"Good, now sit, and let's enjoy a cocktail. Emily should arrive shortly, and we will eat soon."

"So, Beatrice," Ben said casually. How long have you and Emily been a couple? My mother has told me for over forty years, but I do not believe Mom, as neither you nor Emily looks old enough to have enjoyed a forty-year union. So, how long has it really been?"

Suddenly, I felt faint and was thankful a sofa was nearby since I almost fell to the ground. Leaning back against the fresh-smelling linen fabric, I inhaled deeply. I slowly exhaled as the news of Beatrice and Emily's romantic relationship reeled inside my mind. I had not suspected or seen any intimacy between either woman. They both acted more like sisters than lovers. Though, how would I know? I only met them last night, and it is common knowledge that Ben is the sharpest tool in the shed, particularly in our relationship. Besides, who am I to judge?

Nobody, that is who.

Only last night, I was frolicking around town as a companion, and compared to Beatrice and Emily's secret, my sleazy occupation was the cause of scrutiny and disdain.

Both Ben and I stared at Beatrice, awaiting her answer. Though others may have flushed with color or hurried away, she stood tall and proud, and held her head high. "Darling Ben," she said affectionately. "Emily and I came together with mutual respect and love, and like you and Bella, we care deeply for each other. My wish is that both of you can share as long a union as Emily and I have enjoyed, as we have been together for hundreds of years and undoubtedly across the past two centuries. I'm certain of this because, like ships that pass at night, we recognized each other from afar and fought long and hard to secure a union of mutual respect and friendship."

Intrigued by her last statement, I could not help but ask an intimate question that was burning in the pit of my stomach. "Do you believe in life after death, Beatrice?" I asked without judgment and noticed the faraway look in her deep-set eyes.

"Of course I do; as God's children, we are from the same bone that created Eve. The Book of Genesis - Genesis 2:21-22 - tells us that Adam was lonely, and while in a deep sleep, God created a woman called Eve from one of Adam's ribs. Though both naked, their innocence prevented them from experiencing shame or knowing good and evil. Soon, however, a serpent came slithering onto the scene. He slyly revealed why God did not want Adam and Eve to partake from the forbidden tree. Eve succumbed to the serpent's temptation. She ate from the tree and made sure that Adam did as well. "And then," says Genesis, "the eyes of both of them were opened, and they knew that they were naked" (Genesis 3:7). For this transgression, God evicted them from Paradise. Devoid of their earlier childlike innocence, Adam and Eve became aware of their nakedness. Then they became spouses. At the proper time, Eve gave birth to her first son, Cain." She said, pausing to drink from a water glass. "The Eden story underscores that human existence is merely an exile from a primordial state of divine perfection. Indeed, the fall of man, the expulsion from the Garden, marks the loss of innocence only redeemed by God's later covenant with Abraham and Moses."

Alarmed, I listened intently, and though I found her biblical knowledge impressive, I still did not understand the lecture behind the scripture.

What exactly did Beatrice mean?

Turning to Ben, I saw that he, too, was confused, and that made me anxious because I wondered if Beatrice was hinting that she was aware that Ben and I had done as Adam and Eve and eaten from The Tree of the Knowledge of Good and Evil, which would signify that Beatrice was very much aware of our involvement with the death of her nephew, particularly mine, and that caused butterflies to circle within my stomach.

Ben broke the silence first. "So, what are you trying to say, Beatrice," he asked confidently.

"I wanted to express to you that it was the disobedience of Adam and Eve, who God had told not to eat from the tree, which caused disorder in the creation and explain that we humans inherited sin and guilt from Adam and Eve's sin. It is all available to read in The Book of Genesis. The point is that..." she said, glancing toward a photo of herself and Emily atop a fireplace before returning her attention to me.

Ben and I sat silently, awaiting Beatrice's point. While seated, I felt each second lasted a lifetime and impatiently awaited her continued lecture.

"In Genesis, God curses all three and banishes them from the garden, lest they eat the fruit of a second tree, the Tree of Life, and live forever."

"How does the Book of Genesis apply to us?" Ben asked forcefully, and while I admired his demanding tone, I shuddered as he lost his grip or his urge to protect me from something Beatrice knew but hastened to tell.

"The story in Genesis 3 with the expulsion from Eden narrative applies to all humans, mainly as the story can be characterized as a tale of wisdom, meaning to have faith. In the Bible, we share the most famous examples of wisdom literature, such as Psalms, Job, and Song of Songs, but not all Psalms belong to the wisdom tradition. Others, such as the Epistle of Aristeas, are also considered sapiential." Beatrice muttered, stopping to refill a glass of wine. She sipped a small mouthful and raised the glass to Ben. "The point I'm trying to express is that regardless of lifestyle, living a good and fulfilling life is crucial in preparing our souls for the afterlife."

"Tell me, Beatrice, do you believe in reincarnation?" I asked, delighted to finally find a living soul who could understand that Ben and I have been friends since the beginning of time.

"Yes, Bella. I do. As I have studied different theories about our existence, and after reading challenging articles, I am inclined to seek Ancient Egyptian religious doctrines, including their three afterlife ideologies: belief in an underworld, eternal life, and rebirth of the soul. For instance, the Egyptian gods played roles in guiding the souls of the dead through the afterlife. So, to answer your question, I will admit that we live through different lifetimes throughout time and that our fears in our current life are from painful occurrences in a past life."

I sat mesmerized and watched Beatrice take another sip of wine before I decided to speak, as I did not want to disrupt her thoughts. "Ben and I have lived throughout time, and we can prove it," I said hastily, afraid of hearing my words as they spilled from my mouth.

"I believe we, too, have met before this life," Beatrice said and smiled. "In life, we meet strangers who are closer than our best friends, and immediately after meeting you last night, Bella, I told Emily that I had met you before. In which century, I do not know, but I am sure we are united in time, as I am confident there is a God. What is creation if it is not to learn? In this life, I am an Aquarius. In my future life, I will be born under the sign of Pisces, and living as a Pisces, if I learn all life's lessons, my soul will rest. If not? Then, the cycle will begin again, starting at Aries, mainly because we start a twelve-step process. After each death, we are destined to rebirth under the following sign until the lectures and lessons we're born with are complete, which is the only form of reincarnation I relate to as it's the only one that makes sense to me."

"But what does reincarnation have to do with Adam and Eve?" Ben asked, pouring everyone a fresh glass of wine. "I'm curious, that's all."

"The reference to Adam and Eve is in wisdom. We must do what is correct and, above all, maintain faith in the Lord." She said and paused. "Take a look at my life, Ben. I am an eighty-four-year-old woman who has been involved in a same-sex relationship since I was twenty-two years old, which adds up to sixty-two years, most of which I hid from public opinion because it was culturally unacceptable and taboo. However, my point is that I do not fear that God will punish me as he did Adam and Eve but welcome me as I have always lived without malice, and I hold our Father and his wise words within my heart. Do you understand?"

Ben nodded, as I did. "So, Beatrice, if we have known each other for hundreds of years, do you believe we shall meet in the future?"

The older woman bobbed her head, and I quickly joined in, nodding profusely at Benny Boy with all my heart, for I know our friendship started when time began. I could contain myself no more, and placing my wine glass atop the crystal table, I rose and asked Ben and Beatrice to heed my words.

"Let's make a pact," I said excitedly. "If one of us should die, then we will promise to visit those we leave behind. If only we could solidify our union and tell such people we were all right, then instruct them that they must continue living without remorse or regret."

"But we have done that before," Ben argued.

Perturbed, I stared at Benny Boy. It was so typical of him to question my motives. "I know, Ben," I said and shrugged. "But that was before we discovered Beatrice shares the same alliance. Therefore, I think it would be an incredible gesture for us to visit Beatrice, or vice versa, to enforce our beliefs that we are all reincarnations of God's greatest gift, life."

Ben's face twitched, and Beatrice smiled, but I could not fathom their hesitation. Still, I was grateful to see Ben's enthusiasm in our discussion and finally have him back at my side.

As usual, Beatrice was philosophical, curious, and wise. It was a treasure to learn she had faith in thousands of people as a true disciple of God should, and I relished the upcoming days when we would share so much more in our quest for eternal life.

Suddenly, Beatrice rose and refilled her glass. "Who's to say who will die first," she asked. "It could be me, or it could be one of you. If you return home before me, will either of you visit to let me know you are well? I ask because I am getting too old to be strife with excess worry."

After she spoke, I nestled with the idea that she had a point, but I stayed quiet and did not answer her question, mainly because I knew who was returning home to our father first and who was I to spoil the fun.

LOSS

GITA BELIEVED THAT death is certain for one who has been born, and rebirth is inevitable for one who has died...

As I sat in the kitchen, pretending to eavesdrop on the conversation between Ben and Beatrice, I was really focusing on Emily and the medical attention she gave to my slashed arm. I had no idea she was such a talented nurse, and the seventeen stitches she sewed into my wound looked as professionally dealt with as any nurse at the local hospital. However, I doubted it would heal without leaving a scar, though I did not express my concern to Emily, mainly because I did not want to sound like a nag or an ungrateful patient.

I was not looking forward to joining Beatrice and Ben in the dining room because I dreaded their ongoing questions about my injury. However, whether I liked it or not, I had to be sociable, and besides, I was starving, and the food smelled delicious. Of course, there were the cutting my arm inquiries, and Beatrice seemed doubtful that I caused so much damage while cutting an orange. Ben remained tight-lipped, mainly because he knew the truth about the horrific events late last night. He did appear to get a slight chuckle from my story, making my face turn beetroot red.

The worst thing about last night, other than my actual presence at Tubby's home, was knowing I would have to return there sometime today. Worse, I could not stop looking over the garden hedge, half expecting to see a swarm of police cars parked in the driveway. The anxiety that swept through my body, often causing me to twitch, was maddening for Emily as she stitched my arm with precision.

At the dinner table, I rose from my chair and excused myself with a need to visit the bathroom, which did not go over well with Beatrice, who insisted Emily join me just in case I felt dizzy and fell to the floor. Ben pretended to ignore the situation, but I knew he was planning a new strategy to save my reputation should something arise. I hope it did not, as I could not take any more of last night's capers, and though worried about the deceased next door, I ordered myself to forget about it and focus on the moment.

I could hear Beatrice muttering to Ben about my accident, and his explanation was overwhelming. I never realized how calm Ben's voice sounded when under pressure, and the more stories he told, the softer it became. I was surprised at how detailed his lies were, considering he was absent, which made me wonder how he could know so much. Do not be ridiculous," I cursed while washing my hands. "There is no way Benny Boy was at Tubby's last night." But still, I was intrigued by how he got so much knowledge when I had merely skimmed the surface of events when I confessed my sins hours earlier.

"Don't let their inquiries upset you," Emily whispered as I dried my hands. "Just be careful not to get your new bandage wet. If you do? I will have to change the gauze." I smiled to express what I understood and carefully lowered the sleeve on a thick lavender cardigan Beatrice had offered me to wear when she noticed the air conditioning made me shiver.

After lunch, Beatrice and Emily sang show tunes and played melodies on a grand piano. They both were talented, just as good as entertainers who made a living performing in front of crowded music halls.

We played games, my favorite being charades, and afterward, we drank more wine and exchanged stories of our lives. I listened to all the tales haphazardly, but when Ben rose to take center stage in front of the fireplace, my full attention was on every word he spoke.

He stood tall, and though flustered from the obvious signs of drunkenness, he did not miss a beat in recollecting events in our earlier lives. As he began to speak about our time in London, I looked at Beatrice and Emily to make sure they were paying attention. They were smiling and holding hands, which made me feel blessed to see the love they had shrouded from so many others throughout their life. Their open display of affection made me believe I fit into their small circle of friends, as did Ben, but of course, Ben did; he was rich. I, on the other hand, was an outcast. Still, it was refreshing that they treated me like a human being, not a freak show, as others had often behaved when in my presence. Suddenly, my thoughts centered on Ben. His description of our date in London in 1937 was beginning, and from the lustful grin on his face, it proved to be a scorcher of a tale. Though I remembered the evening with a photographic memory, I did not want to miss his story as this was the first time I had ever heard him recite any tale about our night spent watching famous opera singer Laci

Devereux. I needed to pay attention to his words to remind him of the facts when he recalled something inaccurate.

To keep my attention focused on Ben, I relaxed in a comfortable armchair and tipped my wine glass to signal I was ready to hear what he had to say. However, I told Ben that recollections may vary, and my version could be more exciting. He flashed a grin and sipped a mouthful of wine before using his hands to signal he was about to begin his walk down memory lane. Beatrice, Emily, and I sat penchant on our seats and clapped, urging Ben to start talking. He grinned again. "Ladies, please allow me a few seconds to remember all the details necessary to make this tale, if not the best you have heard, perhaps the most interesting," he said, beaming a wide smile.

I coughed repeatedly. It was my subtle sign to encourage Ben to continue his version of events, which he did.

"Born in 1905 to an English mother and father, I met your highness," he paused and bowed my way. I grimaced and rolled my eyes. Still, deep inside, I was ecstatic that my hero was recounting a memory with nothing to do with crime, murder, or death. "Continue," I said, blowing a kiss.

Ben feigned an exaggerated enthusiasm and patted his chest. "Thank you, my love," he answered, leaning against the fireplace. "As I was saying," he said heartily and exaggeratedly, rolling his eyes. "In those glorious days in London, I met innocent Bella, and on our first date, I took her to an opera with famous French singer Laci Devereux, who was starring in a west London show with her daughters and sons. Also in attendance was her grandmother, Lolly, a retired but still incredibly gifted soprano. Of course, we were not alone, as

Bella's family had insisted a guardian go with us to watch my every move," he hesitated. I jeered him on. "Keep going," I said, giggling. "You are doing a fabulous job in your storytelling. Just don't forget the juicy details."

"May I proceed?" he asked without awaiting an answer. "I took Bella, named Lexi, in that life. Though, as much as I wanted, we did not hold hands throughout the concert." He paused. "I believe your governess was a battle axe of a woman, who, if I remember correctly, was of German descent? If not? Well, she functioned as such with her rolled-up stockings and frumpy shoes, and let me not forget her uniform, which emphasized a figure that any linebacker in the NFL would admire."

"You are terrible," I called across the room. "Where is the romance of the music or the meeting we shared with soprano Laci and her children Lulu, London, Lyam, and Lync? Thus far, you have only mentioned the grandmother and family matriarch, Lolly. Have their names forsaken you?" Ben winked. "I have not forgotten anything, but you must realize, my darling woman, that I could not focus on anything but you. So, forgive me if my recollection is far from perfect. Now, ladies," Ben turned to Beatrice and Emily. "I am confident you will agree that Bella is a striking woman, and I hope you understand that my mindfulness may have floundered while in her company. But I am sure you would agree that it would be impossible to focus on anything else, least of all a famous soprano, when in the company of the one girl who holds my heart."

I rose from my chair, crossed the room, hugged Benny Boy, and turned to face the others. "He forgot the details,"

I announced and rolled my eyes again. "I know he has forgotten, as he hardly paid attention to the show, mainly because Ben was so focused on holding my hand without my governor seeing that he did not even look at the stage, which was a shame as Laci Devereux was immensely talented. Why, Ben, did she not have a fantastic voice?" Not waiting for him to answer, I continued speaking. "In particular," I explained. "Aside from being spellbound in Ben's charming company. I was also overly emotional. I became mesmerized by Lulu Devereux's singing as she hit the high notes. Right, Benny Boy?" He wrapped his arm around my waist and kissed my neck. "She is such a romantic soul," he said lovingly. I nudged his side and squeezed his arm. "Should I continue?" I asked and patted his flat stomach. Ben's face flushed with color, and I winked. Since Beatrice had understood that we had spent a blissful night together last night, I thought it was best to pretend that we were close enough to touch each other's bodies, even though we had yet to kiss. Still, it was fun to play around with Benny Boy, as he was such a playful lover, and despite my not agreeing with his alcohol consumption, today was allowable, considering we were under so much stress. I told Beatrice and Emily I had an enjoyable evening; the artists' performances were incredible, and how blessed Laci Devereux was to bear children with equal musical talent—not to forget her voice, which was a melody, mainly because it was clear to her audience that Laci loved to sing. The white-haired widow with piercing black eyes knew what her talents were, and she captivated her audience with a finely tuned voice that held no limits. She was also raising five children, which was quite an accomplishment in those days, and as Ben reminded her, Laci's sons and daughters bestowed the same talent as their mother and grandmother. The show was quite the affair as soprano Laci encouraged her offspring to sing along, even allowing Lulu and London to take the lead in various tunes, a bonus to all her fans.

Ben interrupted and expressed his admiration for the children, particularly Lulu, who, it became clear, had captured his heart that night. I elbowed his ribs, and in an instant, his hands were around my waist, pulling me close. "We have had some amazing dates," he said, kissing my neck again. "Not forgetting how wonderful our past lives together have been. Right?"

I leaned into his chest and relaxed, listening to the beat of his heart and the rhythmic pounding that brought joy to my senses. "We are blessed to find each other in every incarnation," I answered. "Though, I think we have had a lot of help along the way."

Ben's eyes soared upward, and mine followed his gaze. We stayed in our world until Beatrice announced the midday news was airing shortly. Though I usually enjoyed the local news, it held no interest to me then, but I nodded yes if only to appear complacent with the day's planning. Ignoring Beatrice, Ben began to ramble. "Laci Devereux and family were a star-studded evening out," he said, taking my arm and sitting us down on the couch as Beatrice searched amongst the coffee table papers for the television remote. "I thoroughly enjoyed my evening out that night, as I always do when in such fine company."

"Yes, I agree with you, my darling," I said, falling against his arm's powerful muscles and resting my head.

Clean, articulate, and educated, Emily leaned forward and handed the remote to Beatrice, who was still aimlessly looking. "Here," she said and turned to face us. "So, it sounds like you both just had a wonderful evening. Did you escape the roving eyes of your governess, Bella?" she asked with a slight chuckle.

We both shook our heads, no. "Emily," I began to speak, but Ben's lips brushed against my own suddenly, and I fell silent. Though reluctant to do so, I did push him away, but not because I wanted him to stop. Far from it, I wanted all that he offered, just not now and just not with an audience.

I noticed Beatrice catch sight of our kiss, and I blushed. "Don't be embarrassed, Bella," she soothed. "Life is short. It would help if you learned to grasp every moment bestowed your way. We do, right Emily?"

It was Emily's turn to flush with color, and she did, which made me happy, as now I did not feel so alone in expressing my emotional side. "The children of Laci Devereux were spectacular that night, as I am sure they were every night of their performances. The entire evening was magical as we were attending the Royal Opera House in Covent Garden, and the venue was just as beautiful in those days as it is today. And I know that because on my last trip to London, I went there to see The Royal Ballet two years ago, which was majestic, as was the orchestra. Still, it might have been better if I had attended the ballet with Ben instead of a rowdy group of girls who could not stop talking throughout the night, which angered people sitting nearby. Still, the ballet was an incredible show, and..." I froze mid-sentence after seeing the television light up. My focus drifted from London and toward the screen as I read in bold letters that earlier that morning, police had arrested a woman named Lisa Goodman on charges of running a house of prostitution. I felt my stomach knot inside out, and noticing that Ben experienced my discomfort, I lowered my gaze and excused myself under the pretense of needing to use the bathroom again.

"Dearest Bella, are you feeling alright?" Beatrice asked incredulously before sitting down next to Emily.

"Yes," I lied automatically, as if on autopilot. I have a stomach bug," I explained and crossed the room.

"She gets lightheaded from seafood," Ben quickly cut in, glancing at me from the television. He descended his seat and followed me into the bathroom. "The woman on the news, is that the woman you know?" he asked as soon as he closed the door. "Yes!" I exclaimed. Though relatively calm, I spasmed, and in an instant, my body trembled with fear. "What will I do?" I turned to Ben and sighed. "Do you think they can access her records? Will they discover my name on one of her lists of clients and girls? Please help, Ben. I'm scared to death." I began to sob when suddenly his arms encased my shaking body and pulled me near; he assured me that even if they found my name on a notepad or computer file, he would tell all that I did not know the Madam. Ben went as far as he could to explain to me that he would answer all inquiries with the same response, which was the wretched woman was in the habit of harassing girls to join her agency.

Stressed, I moved away from him. "Do you think they will believe you?" I asked, naiver than ever. In this situation, I was very much a child, not as worldly as I was pretending, and I was grateful that Ben knew me inside out.

"Why, yes," Ben answered. "Of course, they will believe me. Why would they doubt my word?"

I shrugged. "I don't know, Ben. I'm guessing that maybe they will not believe me and harass you until you tell the truth."

"Nobody will question me, Bella. If reporters or even the police ask me anything, I will request my attorney's services and instruct him to manage the predicament until the fuss dies."

"But what if it doesn't?"

"Meaning what?"

"Think about it, Ben. What if the media blows the entire story out of proportion and hounds us until eternity?"

Ben wrapped his arms around my shivering shoulders and pulled me near his protective body. "No one is going to subject you to a media frenzy. I love you, you crazy woman, and I will not allow anyone to say anything bad about you. You may have to stay at my house until this investigation goes away, mainly so my lawyer can help me protect you."

"But Ben, what about Harry? What will he think? And what if the police uncover my documents in Lisa's files?"

"Do not worry about Harry. I told you last night that Harry and I are not friends. Now, what documents are you referring to?"

My eyes glanced at the floor, and I groaned wearily. "Ben, to work for Lisa, I had to show my driver's license, and she made a copy. Lisa told me it was her policy to know the identity of her girls. That way, they would never cross her or cheat because she would know how and where to find them." I dreaded his reply, and I could barely stomach this revelation myself, and in my brokenness, I cried so hard that my tears flowed faster than the rapids atop Niagara Falls. "I'm screwed, Ben. I truly am, and just when we started to... Never mind," I said, exasperated.

"We started to what?" Benny Boy asked.

"Get along," I snapped. "Do you see us? Ben, this is the first time in this life that we have come together with honesty. Can you not see that you own my heart and that I have not stopped needing you, nor loving you since day one," I explained in a tone that was not my own, for I would never admit such dribble, not in a million years. It had always been Ben who spoke first of love. Still, now, I was the withering idiot who stood foolishly admitting my lustful yearnings toward a man who saw no worry in my predicament or haste in mending my tarnished reputation.

What was I thinking, confessing my emotional turmoil to Ben Barrymore?

Ah! I wanted to scream. I was so relieved when a knock on the door returned me to my senses. It was Emily who spoke hurriedly, explaining that officers from the Jupiter Police Department had surrounded a house on Beach Road. In her excitement, she mentioned that most neighbors, Beatrice included, had rushed to the home to discover what was happening to create such an uproar.

We rushed into the garden, Emily leading the way.

Ben and I hovered behind, mainly because we were nervous. Then, in the bright, blinding sun, we gasped in astonishment as our eyes focused on Tubby's bricked patio, which was swarming with police officers and news crews. In the center of it all, Beatrice stood stoically amidst the chaos.

My bare feet burned on the hot concrete pathway, and my heartbeat raced at ninety miles per hour. My mind swirled with hundreds of questions, and my legs buckled from all the commotion. Suddenly, Ben's hand slid around my waist, and I leaned against his chest for strength while surveying the influx of people. He urged me to move forward, and I dragged my feet as I walked over a bridge built above a stream that, under normal circumstances, I would have enjoyed admiring as it was an unusual water feature.

Plodding, I traversed the wooden archway, inhaling the aroma of the salt water and savoring the mist that splashed against my face upon hitting the moss-covered rocks. I stopped at Beatrice's side, sighed at the mayhem, and inhaled deeply. Then I faced the older woman, offered a commiserative smile, and hugged her softly before reaching for Ben. Naturally, he was busy poking around, questioning neighbors and police officers alike. I crouched down and rested my head in the palms of my hands, aware the police would soon discover the body of Tubby, CJ too, and a full-on investigation would begin.

I groaned, knowing that an officer would secure the house with yellow crime scene tape, prohibiting me from retrieving my items inside the main closet. Eventually, Ben and I would make our way inside, but not anytime soon, at least not while anyone was watching.

To the East, a strong wind blew into the cliffs alongside the Atlantic Ocean, harsh and damp, and despite the hot afternoon sun, I shivered. To avoid interacting with the police units, I focused on a flock of Seagulls and a fleet of Pelicans hovering above the waves, their keen eyes looking for a fish supper. Noticing the beach had emptied, I turned my attention to the sunburned tourists fleeing to their vehicles to avoid an upcoming rainstorm. I frowned as storm clouds blew inland and hovered along the coastline, threatening to soak this sweltering Sunday, but for the time being, they stayed offshore.

To the West, broadcasters stood with microphones and camera operators ready as they memorized and practiced their news bulletins. I spotted multiple police agencies dressed in plain clothes; some were local, and others were FBI agents. One officer stood five feet away, and despite not recognizing him, I had the distinct feeling I knew the middle-aged man, yet I could not fathom how that was possible. I am not in the habit of having law enforcement officers as friends, not because I engage in an illegal job but because they made me feel guilty, even when I had done nothing wrong. In my assessment, law officers created a shared experience among people without implying any criminal activity.

Searching for Ben, I spotted him chatting to a sharp-dressed man in an orange shirt and khaki suit, Miami Vice style. The robust gentleman flapped his arms as if discussing this sudden turn of events. I wanted to talk to

Ben, but I pushed my needs aside and stayed shaded on a seat inside the screened porch, hidden from the intense sun rays.

I mused a cigarette would be nice, looking around to see if anyone else smoked, but noticing nobody did, I resorted to picking at my chewed fingernail polish. "Are you Bella Bloom," a petite female officer asked. She dressed in a black Palm Beach County Sheriff uniform, which suited her blonde hair and blue eyes, but the Glock peering out of a gun holder attached to her belted pants was intimidating. However, her smile remained kind, causing me to suspect that she was privy to information she did not divulge, yet I had no alternative but to function as if I knew nothing about the events that unfolded. I wanted Ben to hurry to my side, and I nodded yes to signal that I was indeed Bella Bloom. Just as she was about to ask another question, I heard a voice that caused all color to drain from my face. Suddenly, my stomach churned, my windpipe blocked, and I swallowed hard, which caused a faintness that triggered a panic attack and forced me to the ground.

I awoke hearing Ben's soothing voice urging me to have faith. My head rested atop his knees, and his hand tapped my cheeks. He lowered his head and kissed my lips. If folktales were authentic, I would awaken like Sleeping Beauty. However, Ben was not a prince, and I was not a princess cursed by a witch for one hundred years. My wounds were self-inflicted, and not even sweet Ben could save me from the hellacious karma that was due unto me.

The reality of my conviction encompassed my troubled conscience, and I rose quickly from the ground. With Ben's aid, I sat atop a lounge chair, drank a glass of ice water, and complained it was too hot a day to sit outside, which was the only excuse I could muster to explain my fall. I groaned and shared my discomfort with the determined female officer about the oppressive humidity of South Florida. Then, I enlisted Benny Boy's help to return to the house where the air-conditioned environment would offer a welcome respite from the oppressive heat.

Naturally, she followed.

Of course, she did.

Why would she not?

The pretty blonde officer had questions that demanded answers, and, to her, I held the key to solving the violent mystery inside Tubby's home, which incurred in me that, once again, unlike Sleeping Beauty, my problems would not dissipate after I woke.

Ben made me an iced tea, which I drank slowly, carefully sipping each mouthful. I rinsed the cup and put it in the dishwasher when I finished. My body ached as I retreated to a stool beside the kitchen counter.

"Do you feel better?" he asked, massaging my shoulders, and wiping my brow with a damp cloth rinsed in chilly water. I nodded slowly and yawned. "I think I drank too much wine at lunch," I admitted, rubbing my temples. "I have a massive headache. Do you think Beatrice has Tylenol?"

He shook his head and shrugged. "I will ask Emily. She will know where they are. Do you want me to find her or wait here with you until she returns?"

I fidgeted on my seat and groaned. "I want you to stay. I cannot sit here. Not with the neighborhood surrounded by police. Please stay with me, Ben. I am so afraid."

He nodded and refilled my glass. "Of course, Bella. I will not leave you in times of trouble," he paused. "Hey!" he hesitated. "You have done nothing to warrant feeling guilty or even responsible for what happened next door. Do not beat yourself up. Okay?"

I was about to argue when all hell broke loose.

"Bella Bloom!" I heard a stranger call, and it was not the female police officer but a man. Not just any man. No. This man owned the voice that had become familiar to me, the same voice that had caused me to faint only minutes earlier.

Under duress, I could only eyeball Ben and grimace with no time to think. "She is in here," he yelled, grasping a glass of juice, and rushing to my side.

Fearful, I looked around to see the stranger, the voice that haunted my mind, leaning against a wall in the entryway. I wondered how long he had been standing there and how much of my conversation with Ben he had listened to. He wore a grey suit, white shirt, and black tie, though in civilian clothes, it was clear he was a police officer. Undercover, I surmised, but an officer of the law, all the same. I recalled how the police had that authoritative aura in their presence regardless of attire. Whether standing in line at a bank or at a local mall, the sickening feeling of someone watching me, alerting me that security was nearby.

Ben grasped my hand, and we listened to the assertive detective while the female police officer stood against the sink. She strode toward me and introduced herself as Officer

Caroline Carter and my heart sank. The knowledge that this meeting would not be a lighthearted conversation scared me. I leaned against Ben and tried to groan again, but no sound left my mouth. Instead, I sat pensively and willed the ground to swallow me whole for the second time in twenty-four hours.

"You visited Clive Jenkins early this morning, correct?" The male detective told more than asked.

Standing before the man, Ben blocked my view. "And you are?" He inquired, more forceful than I had ever given him credit for.

"Detective Edward Shaw. I am working on the case next door, and it came to my attention that the young lady seated next to you was indeed inside the deceased man's home late last night, early morning."

Ben shrugged and raised an arm to dismiss the claims as gossipy garbage. "She was with me," he said. "We spent the night together. First, we attended a ball at The Carlisle Resort in downtown Palm Beach, and then at sunrise, we walked Jupiter Beach, admired the sunrise, and basked in the peacefulness of Sunday until we saw Beatrice Ryder. After chatting for several minutes, we accompanied Ms. Ryder to her home, where we ate and, as you can see, are still here." I pulled on Ben's belted pants and slid my thumb between the leather and the fabrication. Then, I pricked his back with my thumbnail to warn him to be careful. He twitched, but he continued to recount an alibi for me, which made me wince since the mature detective already had the answers to the questions he was asking. Coughing loudly to interrupt Benny Boy before the police officer arrested him for obstructing justice, I rose. I faced the inquisitive female officer and the older, determined detective.

"Ben," I spoke softly so as not to attract too much attention. "I was at Tubby's, I mean, Clive's home. But it was in the middle of the night, and you were sleeping when I visited. Therefore," I hesitated, noticing the keen eyes of both officers, who listened with interest to my admittance of guilt. "My boyfriend, Ben, did not know I was there," I admitted. "Honestly, I was tired, yet I could not sleep, and my friend was there. Thus, she invited me over, so I came, but I did not stay long. I left because other people arrived, and despite my hope for a quiet night, it was as if the party was beginning there. And I was not in the mood to socialize since I had done that earlier at Hotel Carlisle."

"We have evidence of an intimate moment between you and Mr. Jenkins," PD Ruth Boyd said.

"No!" I gasped, ashamed of what Ben might think. "I was never intimate with Clive." I felt Ben distance himself and feared he would turn State Evidence if he believed I had behaved in a manner that was not ladylike at Tubby's.

"So, you admit you were at the house last night? And in being inside his home, you must have knowledge of at least one or two events, correct?"

"Yes!" I answered. I watched him reading his notepad and I wondered what he had written inside his private pad, while I predicted what he might say next.

He ignored my obvious curiosity, and slammed his pad shut. "Okay, tell us everything that occurred while you were there?"

Officer Ruth Boyd interrupted. "Should I bring in Agent Davenport?" she asked a confident Detective Shaw. "He just arrived, and it is his case." I glimpsed him, nodding cautiously, and then she left the kitchen.

"I honestly have not done anything wrong," I said. "I would never hurt another soul, let alone shoot someone in cold blood."

The burly detective eyed me suspiciously, "Really?" He questioned. "But for someone who simply paid a quick visit, you certainly left with much knowledge. So that you know, we have not released to anyone the cause of Clive Jenkins's death. Yet, you know exactly how he died. How is that?"

"I did not know," I stammered, twitching nervously; I sighed, unhooked my thumb from Ben's pants, and refilled my glass. Walking back to face both men, I began to speak. "Though I will tell you that some men did visit, and since I was scared, I hid in the bathroom closet. However, I did not see the events unfold because I was out of sight but heard the violence. As for evidence? I did not kill Clive."

"We have an eyewitness who placed you at last night's fundraiser, and the same person also saw you at Clive's hours later. It was clear to our witness that you took part in more than a casual visit. An insider informed me that your visit was more than a close encounter. Our eyewitness revealed it was not social but a business meeting, with the source also saying that you were in an intimate bathtub session with Jenkins. Are you implying our dependable informer is lying?"

"Just a minute," Ben said sternly. "Do I need to call my lawyer? If you plan to charge her with a crime, don't you have to read her legal rights?"

"Nobody is charging Ms. Bloom with a crime. Not yet anyway. Though, she does need to cooperate. She can do that here or downtown."

I coughed to alert both men, who were busy discussing my life that I was still in the room and asked them to quiet down. Then, I scoffed at their theories and groaned aloud: "Gentlemen, I want you both to listen because I will only tell you this once. You were confused about my whereabouts last night. Yes, I was there. But while there, Clive was alive and well. It was towards the end when they shot Tubby." I paused and flushed. "Sorry, I meant Clive's. A mob of men arrived, demanding a recording of a politician involved in an escapade yesterday afternoon. Since I was hiding, I wondered if they had found the tape. Moreover, I did not see the men's faces but listened to their voices—heavy Italian."

Ben approached me. His arms encased my shoulders, and despite wanting to slump into his chest, I stayed staunched, determined to deal with the accusations my way.

"All I am saying is that a witness told me you seemed obsessed with Clive. This bystander also informed me you looked relaxed and that you changed from a sexy black dress into a seductive robe. My insider said you wore a white tee shirt tied off to show midriff and jeans. You showed up some hours later dressed as you are."

I grimaced. "I have not left here. Initially, I was in Clive's home, but then I was with Ben. Beatrice will account for my whereabouts."

"I will oversee this now, Shaw." Another familiar voice echoed across the room, and I spun around, determined to match the face to the voice that had tormented me since last night. Upon seeing the robust man, I gasped. "Agent Peter Davenport," he said, extending an arm. "I believe we have met?"

I gnawed at my lower lip and exasperated, moaned, "I do not recall meeting you, but I know the sound of your voice and Detective Shaw's tone. I have struggled to remember how I know you, which has transfixed me for many hours."

"Last night's ball at Carlisle," the agent announced. "I saw you when you were exiting. You stood atop the stairway if I remember correctly. Then you," he pointed to Ben. "You tried to accompany Ms. Bloom down, but she refused.

Puzzled, I shook my head. "But when and where were you last night?" I asked. "I am still confused since I did not know that police officers attend balls for rich people."

Agent Davenport smiled. "We poorly paid agents double up as bodyguards when off duty, and we protect many financiers, celebrities, and royalty. Last night, though, while undercover, I complimented you on your dress to engage you in conversation. Although he distracted you," he pointed at Ben. "Therefore, I did not want to cast my suspicions last night since I knew I would talk with you eventually."

"Suspicions about what?" Benny Boy asked. He adjusted his crumpled shirt and pants and chewed his inner cheek.

"Yes!" I interrupted, recalling the man who had accosted me by the stairs—initially a weird man who I thought was fresh with his flattery. Still, I did not know he was an FBI agent. "Were you also at Clive's house last night?" I asked curiously. "I am certain I heard your voice talking with Jimmy and his mobsters."

The agent nodded yes. "I was there with Agent Clarke. We were working undercover, and my partner almost died in the mayhem."

"I hope your partner is alright?" I sympathized. "One can never be too careful. Those men at Tubby's were despicable criminals who wanted him dead."

He nodded yes. "Tubby?"

"Sorry, I meant Clive Jenkins."

I watched him check his watch, then he walked to the window and peered outside. "Agent Clarke is returning. She will be inside momentarily."

Overcome with shock and intrigue, I rushed to the glass door and stared at the rundown Honda Accord parked beside the back door. I stood pensive and waited for the mysterious driver to exit the vehicle. Then I stared incredulously at the slender frame as she ascended the car. Instantly, I rushed outside and confronted the articulately styled female wearing a printed summer suit, subtle heels, and incredible gold jewelry. "My God," I gasped. "What the hell is going on? And why are you driving this awful car?" I spewed the words before I had time to correct myself. She grinned and flaunted her hand to signal me to relax. "So," I persisted. "Who exactly are you, and where is your Porsche?"

CJ Clarke smiled ruefully, threw up her hands, and laughed. "Well, if you haven't already heard, or if you haven't already noticed, I'm not dead, and I am not who I claimed to be. The bank job was part of a money laundering operation, as was that beautiful black Porsche. Since I can now shred my undercover persona, you might as well know I have been an FBI agent for over ten years. Unfortunately, to get inside Lisa Goodman's organization, I had to pose as a working girl."

"Listen to me, CJ. I am happy to see you alive, as I have worried about you for hours. However, I was curious as to how your Porsche disappeared from Tubby's home. Now that I know nobody killed you, I feel better. However, I wonder what will happen to your apartment and fancy clothes. Who will use them, or were you like Ben, born rich?" I asked in bewilderment.

Again, CJ smiled. "Like Ben, I am ashamed to admit that I, too, was born into a rich family," she hesitated. "Though I have not touched one cent of their money, hence my beaten and old Honda," she grinned. "Honest."

"You are rich, too?" I gasped.

"Bella, I never meant to deceive you. I merely needed an inside view of that agency's practices and recruited you for better jobs at Miami's Delight. We've been trying to bust Lisa for years, and when I met you, I knew you would be a perfect match for me to get into Jimmy Cavill's organization, which you were." She hesitated, reached out for my hands, and held me dearly. "I am sorry I lied to you. I truly am. However, we needed that tape before the media exposed Politician Pickering's sins and sold them to the highest bidder, and I was too nervous about taking the date alone. So, please forgive me for using you as harshly as I did, and please do not take it personally because I like you, Bella. Honest."

If there is a reason to complain, now is the time and date. "I cannot believe this," I snapped. "I cannot fathom for the life of me why you did not tell me nor why you put me in harm's way. Why would you do that? Do you not have pretty girls at the academy?"

"Bella, Bella, Bella," CJ practically sang my name again. "I chose you to take the date with me to protect you. Knowing Lisa was determined to break you in, I had to get you away from the client she wanted you to see. Lisa was in Palm Beach last night because she wanted you to take a date with her, and she intended to have a threesome with you?"

"What?"

"It is true," CJ said. "Which is the only reason I insisted you go with me. I did not want that industry to damage you anymore. I knew that lifestyle was messing you up. I had to keep you away from Lisa Goodman and her perverted clients. Clive, included." CJ rumpled my hair. "Bella, I swear I had your best interests at heart. Why do you think I told Clive Jenkins that I did not want you in his bathtub? I did not tell him to leave you alone because I was jealous. I told him I wanted him to myself because I wanted to save you from that awful ordeal."

"Jimmy Cavill has run his crime-ridden operation from Ft. Lauderdale to New Jersey. It was time to take him down. Unfortunately, Clive was involved, but thankfully, he needed a date, and I was the first choice. Mainly because we had reliable information that Jimmy was going to kill Clive, and I wanted to keep Clive alive. Sadly, I failed, which angered me, but it is what it is," she said, waving at the officers and Ben to come over.

"I am so shocked. I cannot believe I was involved with a woman who sent me on dates for money. I regret it so much. I will never recover from any of this."

"Be happy you were able to keep your dignity. Well, what little Lisa allowed you to have."

"I cannot believe this..." I began to speak but became speechless as I genuinely did not know what to say. My eyes rose toward the house, and I saw Ben with Agent Davenport, Detective Shaw, and Police Officer Caroline Carter. They were all chatting like old friends, and fighting back tears, I lowered my head and chewed my lower lip. Shaking my head, I frowned. "She wasn't so awful," I said. "Though she was pushy, she would tell me so many tales about the industry. Still, I was shocked as she told me not to bed her clients, yet you told me she wanted me to accompany her on a date last night."

"She did. Goodman was a professional manipulator. She used reverse psychology to get girls to do what she wanted. Be happy. Lisa spared you from the horrors to which she exposes most girls."

The situation had calmed down, and I inhaled deeply. "So, CJ. Tell me the truth, please."

"Of course," she interrupted.

"All the days and nights you mocked my Toyota, you were driving this battered red Honda?"

She laughed, and her face radiated a warmth as bright as the morning sun. "The Porsche automobile was a cover. And yes, putting down your Toyota was cruel, but I needed to act out my role perfectly. If not? You would have suspected me, and then I would have been taken off the case."

"The whole time?" I asked, surprised. She nodded. "But your vehicle is in worse shape than mine."

She laughed again. "I know. I admit the best part of that undercover operation was driving that beast of a car. I cannot tell you how much I enjoyed sitting behind the wheel of that Porsche. The pickup was incredible."

"But what about Harry? The things you said about him were so mean."

CJ raised her hand. "Look at yourself, Bella. You are a beautiful, refined young woman, and you should have a man like that hottie over there," she pointed to Ben. "After all you have told me, I am confident Harry is an outstanding man, but come on, Bella. Do you want to live your life with a drunk whose sole purpose in this life is wearing flip-flops, surfer shorts, and supping Bud Light? Ben is a better match. If given the choice? I'd choose the devilish Ben Barrymore."

In my mind, I pictured Harry and tried to picture our lives together, but I could not. In a strange sense, though, Harry helped to bring Ben and me together, and for that feat alone, Harry deserves my respect. I rubbed my palms together and glanced across the garden to Tubby's house, still overrun with media and police. "Harry is a good man. He was not exactly my soulmate, but he had moments where kindness and compassion overtook all bad feelings. Though he was a terror last night, I still care about him, even if he upset me. As for Ben. How did you find out his name? Last I remember, you became enthralled with the mysterious stranger, and the only emotion you showed was obsession."

CJ smiled sheepishly. "Last night, I was teasing you on Worth Avenue. I knew of Benjamin Barrymore and all your other friends from day one of this investigation. Bella, in my profession, I must know who everyone is, regardless of involvement. It is a safety measure that comes with training. However, I admit Ben is one of the hottest men I have ever met. Well, aside from my husband," she added, pointing to the tall, dark, and handsome FBI agent, Peter Davenport.

"He's your husband?" I gasped, staring at the man wearing the orange shirt and khaki suit. "I like his style. He dresses like a movie star, particularly his outfit, reminiscent of..." I struggled to remember... "the television show Miami Vice. Still, you know last night, we were on Hibiscus Avenue and not Worth, right?"

She grinned, turned, and high-fived me. "Of course I did. I was playing dumb. I wanted to believe you know yourself better than me, and if I behaved as I normally do, then you would have suspected I was not some dumb bank manager, which you almost did last night."

I squinted in the bright sunlight and shrugged. "When?"

CJ ushered me closer to her vehicle. "Well, if you must know, I thought I had blown my cover when I recounted my fictional story of life working for Lisa. Initially, I pretended she had snared me into slave labor for over seven years, but then I realized how pathetic that lie sounded, considering I worked in a bank. You are brilliant, Bella, and good fun too."

I shrugged again. Then I glanced at Ben and sighed. "I cannot believe your husband resembles Ben," I said, almost dreamlike. "He even dresses the same," I added, rubbing my forehead.

"Peter has always been a sharp dresser," she informed.

Both men dressed similarly in their attire, and though one bought from a high-end shop versus the other buying from an affordable marketplace, looking at them both, it was not that obvious. "He is a good-looking man. No wonder you liked Ben," I said guardedly. "They could pass for brothers." My eyes wandered up and down both men's bodies. Aside from the difference in their builds, Ben being taller and fitter, both men resembled each other and could fool most strangers into believing they were indeed related. I watched Ben and Peter chatting as they stood beside the magnificent waterfall I had crossed earlier and noticed they shared similar mannerisms. It became clear why CJ was fond of Ben because Peter and Ben shared such a strong resemblance that most would mistake them as being born from the same mother, which made me wonder if they were indeed related. Since nothing made sense in this scenario, I began to doubt Ben.

For what did I know about his life?

Other than the obvious, nothing.

Yes, Ben was born into a wealthy family. I know Ben had a sister who lived in New York or New Jersey, but I did not know if he had a brother. Did he, and if so? Was his brother living a secret life due to extenuating circumstances out of his control, such as being a secret agent?

I did not know. However, these were questions I wanted him to answer quickly. As much as I loved Benny Boy, I must tread carefully.

Ben and Peter crossed the garden, looking at CJ and me. Their look confirmed what CJ, and I had said about them looking like brothers rather than acquaintances who had just met. Both shared similar strides, expressive faces, and piercing blue eyes. If not related, then a hospital nurse had mistakenly separated both men at birth, allowing one man to flourish in opulent wealth. At the same time, the other man lived an average upbringing, as in most homes across America.

Ben stood at my side, and though I desperately wanted to lean against his robust body, I stood my ground, still confused about his identity in this game of love.

"I love you so much," he murmured.

I said nothing back, which shocked Ben. Still, I ignored his needs as I was unsure of everyone around me.

We were both silent then. I watched the interaction between CJ and Peter. They embraced with so much emotion that it did not seem real. It looked forced, like I had seen on Lifetime Movie Network, in one of those cheesy romance films that played all day and every day of the week. I was aware of CJ looking at Ben first and then me, like all the other agents and detectives around us. I was afraid I would never walk freely from this scenario, not after my admittance to CJ and not today. Their eyes hinted it was the end of the line for me, and I wanted to disappear magically. I could not allow myself to flounder, nor could I allow CJ, Peter, or even Ben to trick me into a government agency scheme. I had to break free and could not waste one more second.

"Can we go now?" I asked desperately, not caring about his involvement, just wanting to escape from this brutal crime scene. "I am tired and want to leave."

He looked at me swiftly, more intensely than before, freaked by the nervousness in my voice. "Where do you want to go?"

"Home, Ben. I want to go home."

"To my place?" He suggested.

"No, Ben. To my apartment." I replied.

"But I thought you were staying at my house until this investigation ends?"

"I am so tired from all the drama. I want to sleep for one hundred years." I murmured. I want to rest like nothing ever happened, least of all a murder. Please, Ben, can I go to my place? At least let me get clothes and toiletries?"

He exhaled. "Of course, I will take you to get stuff from your flat, but then we come back here, right? But bear in mind, Bella, we cannot leave right now," he reasoned. "Not until the police finish questioning us about the death of Clive Jenkins."

"But I have told them all that I know. What more do they expect me to say? Please, Ben, can we go?" I begged.

"Yes! I have told you that I will take you. I want to make sure we are allowed, nothing more."

"I am confident we can leave. Why would we not be able to go to my house?" I asked in a faint voice.

"They asked us to stick around, Bella. It could be that they are unsatisfied with your alibi or do not believe you. Let me get an update."

"You are going to ask CJ's husband, Peter?" I questioned, astonished.

"Why yes," Ben replied. "What is the big deal in talking with him?"

"Because he creeps me out, that's why."

"Don't be ridiculous, Bella. Davenport is a respectable man who earns an honest living. He is not the enemy."

"Tell me why you think these officers will not believe me when you told me earlier today that I had nothing to worry about. You also told me you would stand by me no matter the outcome of this investigation?" I demanded. I realized my voice shook, my eyes wet with tears, and I fought against the damming truth that was trying to deceive me.

"I will always stand by you, Bella." His voice was low.

"But you are acting like I am guilty, Ben. Why do this to me? Do you not think I have been through enough these past twelve hours?"

He shrugged. "I love you more than life itself, and I will stand by you, regardless of what happens. As I told you earlier, I am a man of my word. But know this, Bella. Regardless of rank, I will not allow anyone to take you away from me. Either they arrest us together, or we leave this mess in unity. Regardless of their choice, you will not be escorted away from this residence by anyone other than me."

"It could prove difficult," I mumbled.

"Not to me."

"Are you in contact with an attorney?"

He sighed. "Since early morning, since before I arrived by your side."

"So, you are worried about my freedom?"

"Why would you doubt my concerns?"

"The way you stood when talking to the FBI agent. I saw you laughing, and it shocked me as I thought you did not know people in law enforcement. But the way you were joking around, you know certain officers very well, true?"

He smiled. "You are such an anxious young lady, aren't you?"

I did not answer right away. I thought about Ben's comment for all thirty seconds and then laughed, knowing I was behaving like a lunatic to have doubted he had anything but his best interest in saving me.

"Is he your brother?" I asked when I saw FBI agent Peter Davenport heading in our direction. "Never mind, you do not need to answer. My instinct is telling me he is your sibling. At the very least, a distant relative, right? Why else would you spend so much time chatting to him?"

He grew serious. "Bella, I make it my point to know as much as possible about the people managing situations that are important to me, yours included. He is not my brother, nor is he related to me. I met him with you today, and that is the truth. Yes, I met your friend last night, but I did not suspect she was an FBI agent, and I am still as surprised by that revelation as you are... Bella, I would never lie to you or let you down. You are my world; I only live in this body to safeguard you. Once free from this life, we will live on and travel to another continent where we may flourish. Do you understand?"

"Why do I not believe you?"

"Since I have always been honest with you, I do not know." I saw his eyes bright and blue, and they dissipated all my fears, even those I felt were true. "I adore you, Bella. I have loved you for hundreds... thousands of years. I worry about you throughout all my different lifetimes. Last night, I did not sleep because I thought of you. I was consumed with worry, wondering if you would arrive back in Miami safely or if I would need to ring Harry with some feeble excuse, if only to make sure you arrived home okay." He shook his head as if remembering something. "When you left Palm Beach, you consumed my thoughts, my wants, and my needs; only God knows for how many hours I lay tormented alone in my bed."

I stood, mesmerized by his words, but still, I did not reply, I wanted to hear everything his enamored mind wanted to confess.

"I do not have to tell you how dangerous highway traffic is, particularly with drunk drivers driving on the weekends, do I? Why would you doubt whether my heart is pure, my feelings are honest, or if my mind fixates on you when I have reassured you for over two thousand years that my love is true?"

"I am sorry." I sighed.

"As you should be." His eyes twinkled as his lips curved. "I expect such insecurities from the countless other women I have met but not from you. You, of all people, should know my word is my honor and to whom my heart belongs, particularly after I just described the six feverish hours I spent tossing and turning throughout the night. You have no idea how jealous I was, imagining you in Harry's arms." He smiled ruefully at me, and though tempted to argue back, I basked in the ambiance of his love. Several minutes passed before Ben could no longer stand the silence. "What are you thinking?" he asked, his voice still forceful. I did not reply but kept my eyes forward, staring at the police as they conducted their investigation. "Are you smiling?" He sounded frustrated. In my world of thoughts, I had not realized the curves of my lips had risen. I quickly ran my hand across my mouth to check, and sure enough, a beaming smile was there for all to see.

"I did not realize I was," I told him. "I was daydreaming about our earlier walk on the beach and became reminiscent, remembering how sweet you behaved in rinsing the sand off my feet. Stupid thoughts always trip me up," I said, slightly flustered by my admittance. I felt him reach his hand around my waist, kiss my head, and raise a hand to tickle my ear, all the while I stood gnawing on my lips. If I did not stop, soon, they would be too sore to kiss, I surmised, feeling a soreness in my mouth while I fantasized about Ben's lips.

The lazy Sunday afternoon promised to pass at a snail's pace, and since each minute appeared to pass in slow motion, I grew weary of extreme boredom. "So, where do you suppose Beatrice and Emily are?" I asked minutes later.

"I believe both women are trying to gain access to Clive's house." I followed his gaze across the garden toward a jacuzzi tub and spotted CJ and Peter Davenport chatting to Detective Shaw and Caroline Carter. I stiffened when I noticed Shaw staring my way, glaring like Bruce Willis with a wicked glint in his eye, which irked me as I felt like a deer caught in a vehicle's headlights. I shuffled my feet. Suddenly aware, I was still wearing the oversized sneakers I had stolen from Tubby's guest room. I cried, afraid their rightful owner may return and shame me in front of all bystanders.

"There they are," I said excitedly, pointing toward two parked police vehicles. "Sadly, I do not think they will be allowed access to the home, do you?"

Ben shook his head. "Probably not," he said. His voice echoed the emotions of a man suffering deep within. "Let's hope officials can put an end to this show. The sooner, the better if you ask me."

I nodded in agreement. "Hopefully, we can leave and head to Miami soon."

"For what reason?"

"Ben, I need to see Harry. At the very least, speak with him to explain all that has happened."

"For what?" He sounded alarmed. "I already told you Harry will not care that we are friends or lovers. You are wasting your time if you think he will beg you to come back. Not after all this mess becomes public knowledge."

I sighed. "Are you serious?" I demanded. "Why would you say such a horrid thing? Harry may not want me, but I still owe him an explanation."

He shook his head again. "You owe him nothing. Listen to me, Bella..."

"How can you say such horrible words to me after all I have gone through?"

"Calm down, Tiger. I did not mean what I said. I am under duress and stress, and the words came out wrong. My screw up, not yours."

I sighed again, louder this time. "I understand. I want you to realize that I need to speak to Harry. Not for long, but I do need to explain something to him, and if it helps me deal with my inner demons if only to free up my bad karma, then so be it, Ben. Let me clear my conscience."

"Don't go to Harry's."

I stared at him in disbelief. "Why ever not?"

He frowned deeply. His eyes resembled sliced black coal, cold and dark as if awaiting a flame to light his fire. "I feel dreadful things will happen if we go to Harry's home. Something inside me is warning me not to go. A similar feeling to your women's intuition. Only this is a man thing that I cannot explain." He said as he eyed me with concern.

I shivered at the despairing misery in his voice, but I was happy. The clarity of his message enforced in me that true to his word, Benny Boy feared losing me, and as he had told me earlier, he honestly had tossed and turned all night. "I only want to say goodbye to him, that is all. I am not interested in seeing Harry for anything else, and certainly not because I still feel for him. Okay?

"We will drive to Miami after supper," he sighed, and I knew he wanted to delay the meeting as long as possible.

"Then, after dinner, it is." I released his arm around my waist and waved to Beatrice and Emily, who strolled toward where we stood.

"Bella," he said, reaching for my shoulders. I turned, and he leaned into me, his handsome face inches from mine. Suddenly, he kissed my lips. My heartbeat soared, fluttering twice as fast as his tongue caressed my mouth, prodding gently and deeply. I felt ablaze on the ride of a lifetime, and a warm fuzzy feeling sank from the top of my head to my lower torso. Feeling heat surge upward between my legs, I shuddered as the taste of his saliva engulfed my senses. One moment, I floated on a wooden raft across a calm ocean; the next, I raced through turbulent currents or on a trampoline, bouncing so high I could reach the sky.

Was I dreaming?

I could not be sure.

Diffident, I struggled to escape his grip. Fearful, I might fly away and never return to the girl whose body I have occupied for twenty-six years. Once free, I exhaled. "My god, Ben," I gasped. "Are you trying to kill me?"

"I have powerful feelings for you, Bella," he said. I could feel his breath against my face, and the aroma of his mouth lingered. It was the same smell as the taste of his kisses, and just like that, I was adrift. A burning desire surged through me as a new passion took hold, radiating between my inner thighs. My legs gave way as his intense passion consumed me, making me feel weightless. Almost succumbing to my rigidity, I desperately sought an escape.

Just give in, Bella, I urged. Experience the pleasure Ben wants you to enjoy. Embrace it, do not resist. Relax and release all emotions, and let all feelings flow as you drift away into blissful ecstasy. Under the shelter of the Florida room's screened roof, I shuddered and pulled away from Ben. Over his shoulder stood Beatrice, Emily by her side. "Beatrice!" I gasped when we were two feet away. "I am so sorry about your nephew, Clive. I know this must be a shock. If there is anything I can do to help, please let me know, Ben, too." She did not reply but merely waited for Emily to catch up.

"Good to see you again, Beatrice. You too, Emily," Ben said softly, slipping his hands into his pants pocket.

"Beatrice is devastated," Emily sighed. She glanced from Ben to me, trying to hide her wet eyes. "I have to take her back inside the house. She is beyond upset. Are you staying to watch the show or returning to the house with us?"

Ben pulled his hands from his pockets and extended them to Beatrice to aid the older woman. "We are following you," he soothed. "You are more important to us than this tragic turn of events."

We walked back to the house. We paused once to glance over our shoulders to ensure we were distancing ourselves from the busy crime scene.

"What are we going to do, Ben?" I murmured.

"Just go with the flow." He advised.

"I am worried," I paused, looked back toward Detective Shaw, noticed he was still watching me, and grasped Ben's hand. "I have an awful feeling that the police are going to detain me. I honestly do."

"No, the police will not. But Beatrice may want to ask a heap of questions." I groaned, wiped fallen strands of hair from my face, and shoved them behind my ears. He smoothed my tethered brows and smiled.

"Do not worry," he smiled and kissed my forehead. It will all be okay. You will see," he promised.

"So, what do you think Beatrice wants to know?" I hesitated to ask but decidedly chose to inquire. He shook his head, smiling ruefully. "Hey! That's not fair to ask me that, particularly since I do not know."

"Oh, come on, Ben. You not helping is not fair." I moaned for a moment as we walked through the door.

"I'm guessing she wants to know if I was at her nephew's home last night. And if I saw Clive's murder," he finally explained.

"What are you going to admit to?" The smell of coffee brewing in the kitchen wafted throughout the hallway. I was not a coffee drinker. Even so, the aroma of Jamaica Blue Mountain beans aroused my yearnings and hypnotized my senses. "Smells good," I said and inhaled deeply.

"Not as good as you," he said, securing a stray lock of hair hanging over my eyes. "Why do you grow your fringe so long? Why not cut it?" he asked inquisitively.

"I am trying to grow it out, Ben," I admitted. "I made the mistake of cutting my hair and making an awful mess; I had two options. I could have a stylist cut my hair and blend in the travesty, or keep my bangs clipped to the side until they grow out..." He smiled, thoughtfully. "There is no need to tell me which choice you made," he grinned. I watched his eyes twinkle as he eyed me suspiciously. "Ouch! Benny Boy, you are surely not teasing me, are you?" I gasped.

"Not right now, but later?" He chuckled, hungrily. "Be prepared to have the time of your life. I will heighten your senses until you squeal with delight and beg me to stop, and even then, I will not quit".

"Do you promise?" I joked, licking my lips.

"Yes," he nodded and led me into the living room, where Beatrice sat, holding a coffee cup, and looking distressed.

Emily Parker entered the room just when Ben and I decided where to sit. "Would you like a mug of fresh coffee? Even a scone or a biscuit?" she asked as I worried about explaining the previous night's drama to Beatrice. How would she manage our friendship once she uncovered the truth about my secret life and all the escapades my job took me to while working for Lisa Goodman?

Suddenly, a voice spoke to me... 'You do not have to explain that disturbing lifestyle to me. I know that a lack of funds enables others to victimize and take advantage of you. I do not want you ever to feel that you must explain that sleazy existence to me, Bella. As I told you last night, I am your friend. Let us put this comeuppance behind us and focus on the future.'

Startled by the voices in my mind, I jumped from my seat and strode to the window, looking at the late afternoon skyline. The sun was beginning to set in the west, and though cloudy, I could still see the burning orange ball of flames. I squinted up at the sky and smiled. How very convenient for Beatrice that she can read minds, even mine. Like most law enforcement officers, she already had answers before asking one question, which could be annoying for anyone who tried to fool the old dear.

Turning to face Beatrice, I slumped back in my chair and shrugged. 'Okay, so what do you know?' I asked without uttering one word.

'Everything you see,' she replied. Then, I coiled at the harsh reality that she knew all my secrets. I surmised every truth I had hidden from countless strangers, all for nothing. If the truth is known, Beatrice had me well and truly trapped. In shame, I reminded myself never again to tell the white-haired debutant from Georgia one more tale.

'Quite right,' she advised, telepathically. She sat in her seat and smiled devilishly, almost challenging me to continue our private conversation.

Despite my curiosity, I refrained from thinking of anything that might entice her mind to interact with me. Still, I could not wait to share my findings with Benny Boy. Outwardly, I was cool as a cucumber, but inwardly, my emotions raged more violently than an F5 Tornado. Intense winds blew wildly, fueling my nervous energy. Then, fearful I may dissipate, I counted to one hundred and prayed for Ben to rescue me again.

'Ben will not save you,' Beatrice teased. 'Not after he is reminded of your past behavior.'

I groaned and forced my feet into the plush carpet to stop my knees from shaking. I did not want Ben to notice my discomfort. Yet, feeling his hand next to my thigh, I sensed he already knew distress was destroying me.

'Why are you trying to ruin my life with tidbits from my past?' I demanded as I stared the older woman down.

Beatrice sat upright. 'I am not trying to expose sordid secrets. I want to ensure that you take accountability for past mistakes that hindered your growth and eventually prevented you from transitioning into a new life.'

'Ben knows I have been sincere in all I have said. Unlike you, he does not doubt my words. We will fulfill our duties here, and when our Lord wants us back, we shall go together, as he transcribed long before our birth.'

'The sun and the moon at your times of birth contradict each other, and unless Ben can free his soul from a discerning situation that you forced his way, he will not return after this life has passed.'

I rose from my seat, pretended I needed a glass of water, and fled the room. In the kitchen, I strode around the central island, filled with pastries and picnicking gear, and wondered if we were going out. But seeing the housekeeper Maria placing table mats, I realized Emily had requested the woman to prepare a feast to satisfy our hunger. I rinsed a glass, filled it to the brim, and sat atop a stool, thinking about outsmarting Beatrice Ryder. The wretched woman who once pretended friendship now seemed determined to destroy my life with Ben.

Suddenly, Beatrice's hoarse voice echoed throughout the colonial house, commanding everyone to return to the living room and sit, and I did. A recount of the weekend's turbulent activities ensued. The conversations though lengthy did not mention the death of Tubby, and while I fretted for what seemed like an eternity, the resolution was short and brief. According to the older woman, her nephew Clive had chosen to surround himself with criminals and decided the outcome of his fate. And nothing and no one could have saved Tubby from the resolution that he was fated.

It was getting dark in the house; no light had come on with the turn of the switch, and I could barely see the older woman's face in the glow of the faux flames burning in the fire pit. The blue and purple colors flickered against the cold metal stand, moving upwards toward a chimney that held no smoke. I stared directly into the rainbow colors as we sat silently and willed the lights to turn on.

"A fuse must have blown," Emily said, and I realized I was clutching my knees, willing them to stop shaking. She reached for a flashlight and ascended her seat. "It happens every time it storms," she explained, leaving the room.

"Do you need my assistance?" Ben asked, his voice assertive and helpful.

"No," she said sharply, and her tone was curt.

I sat silently, watching his face contort as he struggled to discern what bothered him. I looked toward Beatrice, but it was too dark to see the woman's face, which I was sure was full of gratification. The minutes passed slowly, and despite feeling uncomfortable, I stayed seated to keep my trembling nerves under control.

"Bella," Ben asked, his voice nervous and weary.

"Yes?" My tone was fearful, too, but I tried desperately to conceal all worries.

"Why did you not remember how I fought to secure my place in your heart?"

"What?" I asked, startled and afraid of the direction our talk was heading.

"In one lifetime, you did not help me. Why?"

"Why would you say that?"

A full moon high in the sky shone through a large window, and I watched his eyes burning brightly against shadows that danced across the room. "I just remembered it, that is why," he sounded sad.

"What is wrong with you?" My voice whispered.

"I do not know." He whispered back, his eyes staring across the room as if he struggled to remember. "For some strange reason, some force is prompting me to recall a moment when you rejected me, which bewilders me considering we have always protected each other, or so I thought," he paused, his face twisted. Suddenly, I knew the precise moment Ben was referring to. "At least help me out," he snapped, and this time, do not let me down."

"I did not forsake you, Ben," my words seemed weak, but I could not force myself to relive through that saga again.

In the room's darkness, I could feel eyes peering deep within my soul. I need not guess who they belonged to as images of Beatrice and Ben flashed through my mind. "I love you, Ben," I murmured. "I have always loved you and always will. And you know that is the truth. Why are you questioning my loyalty now?"

He turned away from me, leaned back against his seat, and did not say another word. We were silent again, which ordinarily would not irk me, but this time, I shuddered, knowing Beatrice could read my every thought. He closed his eyes, lowered his head, and breathed deeply as if sleeping. Then, he stirred and spoke harrowing words of suffering he had gone through all because of me.

I ordered Beatrice to stop it. 'You are hurting Ben, and I will not allow you to injure his aura, even if it means we may never speak again. Do you understand me?'

'Bella. I wish I could take credit for what Ben is going through, but his pain is not my doing, as I cannot cause unbearable pain to others. I am sorry, but Ben is recoiling alone, and you and I can do nothing about it.'

'Then, could you help me?' I begged. 'Please, I cannot bear to see him suffering. I am confident, between us both, that we can pull him back from whichever memory has transfixed him and end this horror before it is too late. Do you not agree?'

'Yes! I agree with you. I will try my best to bring Ben back. Sit beside me and let us all channel our energy to aid him in battling the negative spirit that has attached to his aura in its attempts to smother his soul. Hurry, Bella. You too, Emily. Quick to it, ladies. Time is of the essence.'

I crossed the room in silence and plopped myself down beside Beatrice. Just then, Emily appeared at the entryway, flushed and nervous. I noticed Beatrice squirming against her cushion. "Is everything alright?" she asked anxiously.

"I was trying to fix the lights," she smiled slightly, but her eyes were more complex than a block of Alaskan ice. "I checked the fuse box to see if anything had tripped a switch, but they were all on. I am afraid to say it, but here goes... The electrical outage only affects this room. Initially, I thought an incoming storm was the cause, but after investigating, I realized that the incoming storm had nothing to do with the lack of electricity in this room." She hurried to our side and sat adjacent. "Are we ready to bring Ben back?" she asked. I fumbled with my hair and exhaled deeply, aware that both women knew more about Ben's urgent situation than I would know in a million Sundays.

'Do not fidget, Bella. Beatrice cautioned. Now, let us hold hands, and then repeat after me...'

'Are you seriously going to perform a séance?'

'Absolutely. So, instead of questioning my abilities, relax, believe, and allow me to help both of your souls before it is too late.'

'But why are you helping? Not fifteen minutes ago, you threatened to send me to hell, knowing I could burn for a thousand years. Why the sudden change of heart?' I sobbed.

'Bella. Relax and watch the magic unfold,' another voice instructed.

'Emily, is that you? I muttered, surprised and shocked to hear her voice. Are you both witches, and were you born with the ability to read minds?'

Neither Emily nor Beatrice answered my question. Intrigued, I decided to spy on both women to see what they were doing. I stiffened, seeing them sitting in a circle while in a hypnotic state, arms outstretched and eyes glowing like flames atop an erupting volcano. After thinking it through, I figured out I was in the company of witches. Though alarmed, I stayed quiet and did not express my nervousness vocally or mentally. At this moment, I decided to shelve my opinions, ideas, and grievances. If they helped Ben, I promised never to share or discuss them with anyone outside this room. In agony, I waited for their cantillate to end so that I could check Ben's health. However, their chants reverberated in the emptiness, growing more potent with each repeated verse until the room fell silent. Out of nowhere, a faint voice pierced my chest and gripped my heart.

It was Ben.

'Please help me, Cassandra. I am descending in the dark, filthy sewers beneath London's streets, and without your aid, I fear for my life. If the plague does not kill me, I will perish among the filth, and my body will be a feast for the rats.'

Suddenly, Beatrice and Emily stirred in their seats. Their eyes bulged from their sockets, expressing pain I had never seen in any living creature. "Are you going to save him or leave him to perish?" They asked in a tone I no longer recognized.

I shivered at the urgency in their words. "I will save Ben," I said vehemently. "But first, I must grasp why he is suffering today for a crime centuries ago."

"In that era, a person broke his heart, and the wounds have not healed," Emily breathed. "You were there, as were we, but neither Beatrice nor I could help. Only you can,

Bella. So, think long and hard and fix this tragedy before it is too late for you and Ben to transgress."

I looked at the floor, frustrated. I rested my hand against Ben's fevered brow and sat down beside him. I linked my hand to his left arm while muttering words I hoped would remind him that I was not the enemy. I spoke slowly at first, still staring at the floor, and then my words tumbled from my mouth at a rapid speed. The light in Ben's eyes, though dim, did shine brighter, and while holding his hand, I kissed his neck before looking up to face Beatrice and Emily. "I am ready," I murmured, slowly caressing his hand. "Ladies, I need your guidance. If we are to save him, I need every ounce of power you have. The stronger the bond, the greater the result."

The housekeeper, Maria, entered the room, bringing fresh coffee. Despite my dislike for the bitter drink, I gulped down an entire mug, figuring the caffeine would help me stay alert. Maria refilled my cup without speaking and turned to leave the room.

"Maria, we need you to stay," Emily ordered. I drank more coffee and sighed. The Latin housekeeper looked from Beatrice to Ben, pulled a string of beads from her pocket, and sat cross-legged on the floor before Beatrice and Emily. Now, three sets of eyes locked with mine, and they were deciding right then whether to include me in the covenant or let the sinister spirit destroy me to save Ben.

"Are you going to help me to save Ben?" I murmured. I rose, walked to the circle, and reached forward to retrieve the Pentagon, but the other women pulled it away swiftly, and I pulled back. In fury, I stood tall, looking down at the women who no longer resembled themselves.

"Do not doubt us, Bella," Emily said. "We are focusing our thoughts on helping you rescue Ben. Right now, we are fusing our energies to intensify our powers, which we will use to kill the demon attacking his soul."

I straddled Ben and leaned onto his back. I pushed my hands upward from the base of his spine to his shoulder blades, summoning the evil entity to remove itself from his body. "Fight Ben, fight," I yelled. "Do not forsake me, and do not allow this evil to control your soul." The room turned from dark to grey, and objects flew with ferocity. I gasped in fear and wanted to collapse, but knowing Ben needed me, I willed all the gods in heaven to aid me. Then, half dazed, I turned to Beatrice, Emily, and Maria and demanded they focus all their powers and force evil from Ben's body. Suddenly, a cry escaped Ben's lips, and he withered in pain as a massive discharge exited his mouth at frightening speed. Though tempted to hold him, I recoiled and rushed to Beatrice. I shook the fragile woman and deliberately broke her trance. "You have to help him. I cannot do this alone. I need you; truly, I do." I begged, and, hesitating, I glanced at Ben, and seeing him shake vigorously, I pushed Beatrice aside, sank to my knees, and begged the evil presence to take me instead. I received unpleasant stares from Emily and Maria, but I did not care. Neither woman was aware of how crucial Ben was to my immortality, and at this moment, I was not about to explain.

"Spirit of the unknown world," I heard Beatrice speak clearly and concisely. "I command you to leave the body in which you have possessed. You are inhabiting a body belonging to another host and are not welcome to stay in such skin and bone. With all my powers bestowed upon me from this universe and beyond, I order you to leave. Get out. Get out before you cause irreparable suffering to someone who does not deserve punishment." She paused to let Maria and Emily wipe her brows before she grabbed a crucifix and held it before her heart. "In the name of the Father, the Son, and the Holy Ghost, and as God is my witness, I order you to leave. My strength, given to me by our Father in Heaven, who has invested in me the courage to face you, will ensure the merciless penalties you will face should you not obey the wishes of our Lord."

"A day of reckoning is coming to you," Emily chorused. She prayed the rosary prayer, holding a cross and a rosary, and while moving the beads, she prayed to Saint Michael. In my awe and with respect, I adhered to the words that filled my heart with longing, and I willed myself to learn biblical passages to protect Ben.

Michael the Archangel, defend us in battle.

*Be our defense against the
wickedness and snares of the devil.
May God rebuke him, we humbly pray,
and do thou, O prince of the heavenly host,
by the power of God, thrust into hell Satan and
all the other evil spirits who prowl about the world
seeking the ruin of souls.
Amen.*

AFTER PRAYING, EMILY clutched three rosary beads, made the cross sign again, and quietly returned to the sofa.

In a dark corner of the room, a flame grew. Maria ambled, mumbling words that made no sense. The Cuban woman held her cross and gripped it with her St Benedict medal. "The incubus is feeding on his negativity and has feasted on a memory that causes him extreme despair. Today, the memory returned, as has the brute, who is determined to take over. We must eradicate the demon to ease Ben's torment and destroy the monster who is feeding from his body. If not? Death will come unto your boyfriend. The supernatural aura will not stop until he wins. Do you understand?" she urged. I nodded and groaned. "Good, now believe everything I tell you. The demon that has entered Ben is enjoying his visit. He will play nonstop games to create as much suffering as possible, as causing suffering feeds the demon and gives him pleasure."

"Are you telling me Ben enjoys hosting this presence and does not want to break free?"

"No. The beast is trying to break Ben's life. To take over by plunging Ben into negativity, which is the root of all other energies, like pain and hate. We must surround Ben, confront the animal, and tell him we are not leaving. In doing this, the evil spirit will give up and search for another host. Beasts, demons, and ogres want an isolated body. A body protected by friends and family is nearly impossible for a demon to take ownership."

"Ben and I have been partners for thousands of years," I paused. "Ben has been alone long enough for any entity to enter his body. I would know if he had, and I can assure you he has not, not today, not ever."

"The spirit world is complicated. I know Ben is suffering at the mercy of a fallen angel, and something is troubling his soul. What part? I do not know. Your spirit is not physical, but it is part of your character and your feelings. Looking at Ben, it is clear that he is a victim of emotions."

The room began to spin, lights flickered, and items moved without help. Though I did not incline what Maria meant, I had no choice but to trust her instincts. "I will do whatever is necessary to have Ben back."

"Let me speak to the demon again. No matter what I do, do not interfere or interrupt my séance."

I watched Emily rush towards Ben. She unfolded a white cloth, creating an altar. Then she placed candles in a circle and instructed Maria to light them. Though filled with questions, I stood quietly against a wall, allowing Emily and Maria the necessary space.

In a dream state, Beatrice moaned as she sat focused so profoundly that external distractions were ineffective against the size of people or feelings. It was also clear that the older woman was unable to function voluntarily. I shivered as I watched Beatrice, who looked dazed and bewildered and in a state of complete mental absorption while deeply musing in an unconscious hypnotic condition.

Suddenly, Maria encircled and spoke loudly, challenging the beast who occupied his body to show its evil face. I cringed at the terror controlling Ben, and while I prayed for bravery, my weakness was clear to all.

A scream echoed around the room. Windows blew open, winds howled, and objects crashed to the floor. Throughout it all, Maria did not stop reciting words in Spanish.

A prayer

A magical trick?

A biblical passage to conjure evil?

I did not know. I only recognized one word in the sermon. The word 'Dios' means God. A word I had learned in high school when I befriended a girl from Honduras who had emigrated to America with her family of six. My school friend, Emilia, had tried to teach me Spanish. Still, sadly, I was not a good student of languages, and, I only remembered the naughty words, particularly profanity. However, it was clear Maria was using Santeria to heal Benny Boy, as I have seen a Latin psychic in Miami performing a ritual on a boy who believed a girl had taken his photo and put a spell on him so that he would fall in love with only her. Still, it seemed like utter garbage at the time. However, now, as I watched Maria, the purification process felt authentic and that caused me to respect the witchcraft that originated in Africa. Still, without faith, psychics are opening themselves up to spiritual attacks that could create a worse predicament than the person they are struggling to help.

Interesting theory, Bella. Beatrice corrected. *But sadly, your theory is wrong. Maria is not exorcising anything; she is asking God to do it for her and using Ben as a conduit. All Maria said was the Lord's Prayer, but she delivered the prayer with faith, her most significant weapon in asking the spirit to leave Ben's body.*

Emily contacted me next, telling me Maria was healing Ben just by saying something simple, such as The Lord's Prayer. Still, Emily quickly added that Maria could demand the intruder leave because she had stronger faith than most other people. Of course, if that does not work right away, Maria will recall when the apostles could not cast a demon out, and Jesus had to do it himself, to which Jesus told all that evil will only leave with prayer and fasting.

As God is my witness,

I command you, by the power of the Holy Spirit

and in the name of our Lord Jesus Christ,

to come out of Ben and go back to the Abyss.

Amen.

BRAVO, EMILY CLAPPED. We appreciate your prayers and support for Ben. Thank you...

"In all honesty," Beatrice said carefully. "If I had to choose a prayer to cast out a demon, I am confident that The Lord's Prayer, a prayer our lord Jesus Christ verbalized for his followers to use, would be equally effective. Still, knowing Maria likes to add prayer to everything she does, I suspect she will recite something personal to ensure Ben will never suffer again, at least in this lifetime, and at least with not this evil spirit that has tried to own his body."

As Maria prepared to speak again, Emily rose and lit a larger candle, blown out by the negative energy swirling through the room, before settling next to Beatrice on the sofa. She folded her arms and waited pensively before expressing herself that she wanted to share something meaningful that would comfort and shock us.

And it did.

Despite our grief

Maria did not say her second prayer to Ben. Instead, she sang the words, and her voice was as beautiful as some of the most popular female singers worldwide.

Guardalo, O Señor, de manos de los impios; Protégelo de los hombres violentos que planean hacerle tropezar. O Señor, te decimos: "Tú eres mi Dios".

Escucha, O Señor, su clamor de misericordia.

Que el espíritu de quienes están dentro de él se cubra del problema que su maldad ha causado.

AFTER SHE FINISHED her performance, we all gathered in a circle and clapped appreciatively. "Thank you so much for your generous applause," Maria chirped. "It amazes me that you listened." She looked stunned.

"I enjoyed the song," I said, forcing a smile. "I liked the tune, though I did not understand the words."

"It was not a song," she contradicted.

"I know. Emily told me it was a prayer. Since I did not know how to describe it, I just said song, as that was how it sounded to me." She stared at me, confused. "Did I say something wrong?" I asked.

"No." Beatrice coughed. I took her subtle interruption as a cue that it was not wise of me to question Maria, mainly since she looked tired from saving Ben. "I will guide you," she informed.

"I would appreciate your help. I haven't been able to do anything right lately."

"Do not be so hard on yourself, Bella," she muttered. "All good things happen when least expected."

"Fingers crossed you are right, Beatrice. Lord knows I cannot manage any more drama today. Here's hoping this evening goes smoothly."

The worst is over." While she spoke, she smiled and nodded appreciatively at Maria, who was picking up cushions, straightening blankets, and checking that Ben was in better health. I wanted to believe her. "I hope so."

"We girls are meeting in the kitchen for coffee," her eyes flickered to Ben. Concern etched her face, and despite Ben resting, she was worried.

"I will join you in a few minutes. I just want to make sure Ben is okay." I promised.

"See you in a few then," Beatrice said, moving towards the door. "You bet," I answered. She looked at me again, her face flushed with concern, and as she left the room, she sighed heavily. Guilt welled up inside me. I had a sense of dread about seeing her exhausted face again in the kitchen while she drank a coffee.

Seeing Ben stir, I unfolded my hands and sat by his side. I signaled Beatrice and Emily to hush because I did not want him to hear our conversation about ghouls, angels, or entities. Though we spoke telepathically, I still did not know if Benny Boy could read minds, so I thought it was best not to assess his telepathy right now. Both women agreed and exited the living room, following Maria into the kitchen. My free hand smoothed his hair, the curly mop that clung to his neck, and even after a new cut, I reckoned there was still enough length to pull should sweet Ben need reprimanding.

I am joking, of course.

I would never intentionally hurt my mate.

A tap on a pane of glass startled me, and imagining the entity had returned to torment Ben again, I rose quickly to my feet, fists by my side, ready to fight. I charged toward the thick, heavy blanket Maria had used to cover a bay window and pulled it to the floor.

I looked outside and smiled at the sky, marveling at the glorious full moon shining brightly into the room, casting shadows across Ben and various pieces of furniture. Seeing no one, I sat momentarily in a built-in seating area, admiring the panoramic views and staring wistfully at Ben's reflection. He appeared utterly serene, and I could not recall the last time I had seen him so carefree. Seeing him finally unburdened made my heart melt. For so long, I ached with the guilt I held for hurting him, and knowing Ben was peaceful gave me relief as it had been ages since I had seen him looking so free of worry.

"Hi, how are you doing?" Startled, my eyes stared at a figure outside. Recognizing the female, I smiled. "Sleepy," I said, mimicking a tiredness with my palms together at the side of my cheek. I motioned a door into the garden and watched CJ walk along the pathway.

Once I opened the door, she hugged me hard. "You look worn out," she commented. "I have had better days," I groaned, inviting her in.

She glanced at Ben, resting nearby. "And how is he?" she asked inquisitively. I noticed her eyes rise and down as they followed the length of his body. "He is doing better now that..." I began to speak.

"Ah!" She conferred. "I noticed earlier that he seemed agitated, somewhat troubled," she hesitated. "His persona differed throughout the afternoon, and I wondered if he was struggling with schizophrenia or something similar. Is he okay?"

I shrugged. "Ben is fine, just tired," I whispered, nodding. He had a rough night and an equally challenging day, hence his sleeping."

She seemed unconvinced, swaying from side to side. Her eyes bore into mine, and I surmised she was thinking about approaching me with her suspicions.

"He is fine!" I almost shrieked. I leaned forward to grab her arm, but she pulled away, and I retracted my hand.

"Earlier today, he was not as confident," she judged, glancing at Ben. "Well, not as confident as last night, if you understand what I mean?" she murmured and paused. "I told you my job teaches me to notice certain characteristics and not to be rude, but surely you must have realized that Ben appears under extreme pressure?"

"I did not notice anything different at all," I lied. "Still, about one hour ago, Ben did start to overreact to stress, but I thought today's summer heat most likely took a toll on him, particularly since he was outside in the burning rays most of the afternoon."

"Whatever," CJ groaned.

I inhaled deeply and exhaled loudly.

"You can trust me, you know," CJ's voice was low.

"I know that." I gnawed at my lip and stalled for time, wishing Beatrice or Emily to return from the kitchen. "In the kitchen, there is fresh coffee brewing. Do you want a cup?"

CJ shrugged and walked toward where Ben lay resting. "Are you sure he is, okay?"

I rushed to her side. "Absolutely," I whispered. "Ben needs rest, which is all, and then he will be good as new."

"Is he drugged?"

"Ben has no health issues and does not take drugs."

"Er, I am not talking about prescription medications; I am referring to recreational drugs, such as LSD, marijuana, cocaine, or molly," her voice trailed as she studied Ben's face. "I am curious because he looks wasted to me."

"Are you serious?" I asked indignantly. "How do you suppose a family member, such as one from the Barrymore family, would know where to buy illicit drugs, never mind partake in them as well? That is absurd."

"It can happen to the best of us," she shrugged again. "Clive, is a perfect example of what can happen to kids who get everything life offers too easily to adjust to adulthood. The poor bastard. I felt sorry for him."

"Maybe so, but drugs are not the cause of Ben's problems. Besides, he is sleeping and not coming off a drug-fueled bender or whatever law enforcement calls it. You police people always think the worst." I fell silent.

"What are you thinking?" she asked, her voice raw from smoking too many cigarettes. I stared at Ben, unsure if I should answer the question or any of her inquiries, which were becoming borderline intrusive.

Suddenly, Ben stirred. My eyes caressed his body as he turned onto his side, facing the room. "Ben is so cute," CJ muttered. He looks like a little boy. If you both get married, you will have beautiful babies." I groaned. "That will not be for years if it happens," I sighed. First, he has to ask, then comes the house, and then the kids."

CJ eyed me suspiciously.

"What?" I demanded.

"It never occurred to me that you were such an old-fashioned girl," she said, folding her arms.

"And what if I am?"

"Oh, nothing, it was just an observation, considering... Well, you know?"

"You mean, considering I was working for Lisa?"

"Sort of... No disrespect."

"It is okay. I get it."

"Maybe later, if your honey wakes up, we can all go to dinner. My treat?"

I turned to face Ben, who was mumbling in his sleep and shook my head. "Unfortunately, Ben is supposed to take me to my apartment in Miami tonight. If he ever wakes up," I rolled my eyes. "I hope he does because I am desperate to shower and change my clothes."

CJ laughed. "I remember you do not travel with extra outfits. However, you look great in those jeans and that summery tee-style top. The motif is cool."

Knowing I had stolen my outfit, I flushed with color. "I appreciate the compliment," I smiled.

"Let's have dinner tomorrow if you and Ben are up for it. It is Monday, but Mondays are often better nights as most restaurants are less busy. What do you think?"

"It sounds like a plan."

Suddenly, Ben stirred again. This time, he spoke. Though his words were primarily ineligible, other sentences upset me. Surprised by his bold voice, I coughed loudly to prevent CJ from hearing his words. But CJ was no fool, and she quickly learned that our relationship was not going well. "Hey, your man seems to be struggling in his dream," she mentioned, moving closer to where Ben lay. "Are you sure you don't want a paramedic to check him out?" I coughed again, louder this time, and ignored CJ's questions. I willed Beatrice to hear my cries for help and urged the older woman to rush to my side.

In the meantime, Ben took a turn for the worse, and before I could stop him, he was talking rapidly about someone who had deeply hurt him, namely me. "Wake up, Ben." I coaxed. "You are talking in your sleep."

"Let him continue," CJ teased. "Are you not ever curious as to what he dreams about?"

"Not really."

"Oh, come on, Bella. It will be fun to listen to his wants and needs."

"Not tonight," I said and nudged Ben. Despite my size, I turned him to face the back of the couch. I shoved a couple of cushions around his head to ensure his eyes were not visible. Then, I prayed that CJ would leave him alone.

'I need you, Beatrice. Please help me now. The FBI Agent is snooping around, and Ben is beginning to remember something from our past. Please hurry.'

'Bella, come to the kitchen. Maria told Emily that Ben would be fine and not remember much about today's traumatic cleansing. I will help you, but we cannot speak openly with that FBI Agent lingering.'

'I am on my way.'

I headed to the door, watching CJ sit beside Ben. "Are you leaving?" she asked.

"I was going to get some juice from the kitchen. Are you thirsty?"

"I would love a cup of coffee. If it is fresh?"

"Of course," I hesitated in the doorway, wondering if I should ask her to leave Ben alone. Realizing she would not listen, I said nothing. "Cream and Sugar?"

"Two and two."

"Consider it done."

"Thanks, I can hardly wait." She sounded perked already.

"You are most welcome," I smiled, happy that she was calmer than before. She looked at me with curious eyes, just like she had before I met her at the bank when she was concerned about my financial status. I held my half-smiled gaze, and she pressed her lips together in a hard line.

The women were chatty and friendly in the kitchen—everyone except Maria was busy preparing snacks. In contrast to the living room, the kitchen glowed against the crystal chandelier, and the smell of blueberry muffins filled the room.

"Here, I think you should eat something," Emily said firmly, telling me she would not take no for an answer. She looked at Beatrice and smirked. "I know you told me Bella would not likely eat, but I am determined to get her to taste at least one muffin before she tells me no."

I leaned against the oven, welcoming the heat on my frigid legs. Rubbing my hands together, I noticed the unfriendly looks Maria glared in my direction. Though I understood she was upset that I mistook her prayer for a song, I still found her actions immature and petty. However, she seriously needed to grow up. I did not mean any ill intent; I genuinely did not grasp the size of her words.

Whatever, I mused.

It is what it is. Such is life and all the other idiocies that follow along those lines.

I yawned profoundly and exhaled. "By the way, may I get a coffee for CJ? She takes it with two creams, two sugars, and piping hot." I watched Maria reach for an oversized mug and fill it. Then she picked up the cup and walked toward the living room. "Oh, I can take it," I called, but she ignored me and left the room.

Astute, Beatrice smiled coyly and shook her head. "Let her be," she groaned. "Maria will come around eventually. Just give her time to work out what is bothering her.

"Agreed," Emily chimed in. "Maria has a notorious temper and mood swings. Over the years, I have been on the receiving end of many of Maria's tantrums."

I smiled, happy to hear that the moody Maria was known for being problematic. I did not feel like she had a personal vendetta against me.

As I sat on the stool, trying to focus on what Harry would say about my absence, I was mindful that CJ and Maria were in the same room as Ben. Despite knowing he was safe, something was wrong. My intuition was working overdrive, I noted and rose from my seat. "I am going to check on Ben," I explained to Beatrice and Emily, who also rose. "I can hear chatter from the living room, which is unusual considering when I left, Ben was sleeping."

Beatrice raised a hand to caution me to wait. "We will go with you," she smiled. "That is if I can get off this stool. Why Emily chose such tall chairs since we are both short is beyond me. I suspect it was to appease some of our taller houseguests."

I smiled again. "Do you want me to assist you?" I started to cross the floor, but Emily quickly moved to her side, and as both women linked arms, I stood my ground.

The lights were back on in the living room, and a New England charm I had not noticed before filled the room. On the ceiling, crafted whitewashed beams paneled upwardly added height. At the same time, the checkered upholstery glowed against the gold fabrication on the sofa where Benny Boy sat upright, talking about one of our first meetings. The wall along one side of the room was primarily bookshelves, holding more manuscripts than I had ever seen in any home I had visited.

Seated opposite the couch, CJ and Maria relaxed on a loveseat and appeared entertained while listening to his romantic tale. Of course, he did not mention that our date occurred over four hundred years ago, but I had a sinking feeling they knew Ben was a unique soul with more wisdom than most men. Proudly, I stared as everyone gathered around and lingered on his memory. It was also inspiring that he remembered so much detail in his account of living in London. However, I wish Ben had not mentioned that one day, while suffering severe hunger pains, he ate leftover pigeons from a feisty cat he had befriended named Ollie.

I rolled my eyes and shook my head.

He sighed and looked into my eyes, seeming to forget his thoughts on the cat who had graciously allowed him to eat his scraps. Then he looked around the room and shivered before moving closer to the warmth of the fire. I noticed the flames illuminated his golden suntan, and the windows to his soul shone brightly against the flickering light. I stood guarded, unsure if Ben had fully recovered.

He winked.

I groaned.

He was back.

Though grateful that Benny Boy was feeling better, more himself than earlier, I rolled my eyes and shook my head, but inside, I rejoiced in the Lord.

"You didn't like that story?" Ben asked, confused. "I was sure it was one of your favorites."

"Of course, I love that tale," I lied. "It's just that I want you to rest, that's all."

He winked again. "After my nap, I'm wide awake." he paused and glanced at me from the corner of his eyes. My head shook again, cautioning him not to speak. He smiled coyly and continued. "The London plague was killing people in droves, and while fearing for my safety, I struggled to find a solution to avoid the death that crept along every street in Londonderry town."

He paused momentarily, hearing the other women gasp, but determined to tell his story, he would not allow anyone to disrupt the memory he desperately wanted to share. "At age twenty-three, I was not ready to succumb to the unknown virus that had killed my mother, siblings, and closest friends, nor was I willing to die without a fight, even if that meant hiding among the horses at Downing House, whose stables I cleaned daily. Since the early morning hours, I have had my plan mapped out, and throughout the days passing, I yearned for food and shelter, a place to sleep from the misery that etched across the streets of London."

I watched Ben rise and cross the room to refill his glass of juice. He gulped down two mouthfuls and coughed. "By the way, Beatrice, this is the best orange juice I have ever tasted. If I forget, kindly remind me to ask where you bought it." He returned to his seat, and deep in thought, he visibly struggled to remember where he left off. Suddenly, he remembered and began to speak. "In the darkness of night, I, an athletic man, climbed a wall that led to riches that could save me, risking all for my life. In awe, I sat on the lavish lawn, ate blades of freshly cut grass, and while staring up at a tall white Georgian structure, I groaned as hunger pained my stomach. Sometime later, my chin rose, and I rubbed my aching belly as the smell of cooked pheasant spread across the garden foliage, making me hungrier than ever. One evening, my chin rose, and I rubbed my aching belly as the smell of cooked pheasant spread across the garden foliage, making me hungrier than ever. Searching, I ascended the ground, crossed the garden, and ducked behind a cart pulled by a horse I knew named Jasper. "It is I," I soothed, patting the horse's chest, and rubbing the tired mare's ears. "Have no fear, for I am with thee, my dear friend."

"Hey! You are not telling them why we did not speak for almost ten years, are you?" I jumped so fast my head was spinning. "Ben, women want to hear stories of love and romance," I paused. "Not sad tales about a relationship we shared in which we did not speak for over ten years. Please don't talk about that night." I begged, knowing I would look cold and selfish in everyone's eyes.

His tranquil voice swept the room and pulled everyone in like a vacuum that sucked up dust and dirt. "Wrong, Bella." They chimed. "We all want to hear Ben's tale."

I silenced and sulked in my seat.

"Relax, Bella, I'm not going to tell your friends that you ate a rotten pigeon," he murmured. I looked away, hiding the fury in my eyes, and said nothing.

"Ah, where was I?" Ben asked. "Oh, yes, I remember," he smiled. "The sixteen-year-old horse snorted and shook his head, causing his hooves to tap atop the cobblestone as he struggled to rid himself of the cumbersome cart strapped to his body. Thrusting my hand into a basket, I searched for a ragged sack and grasped three carrots, handing two to Jasper and keeping one for myself. Finally, Jasper calmed down, and I rubbed the horse's nose as he finished the only food, he had eaten that day. A noise in the distance startled us both, and I stiffened my stance. Fearful of exposure, I reminded myself of what was at stake and swiftly hid behind a bush, out of view of the onlooker."

"You seriously cannot tell these people that my family did not feed our horse, surely?" I gasped, furious that Ben would imply such a rotten deed. He looked up at my strained expression as I tried to absorb his bitter memories of living in poverty in London. Still, his blue eyes scared me more than the lights on every police car I had seen that afternoon, and I grimaced.

"You can't deny the horse was hungry, can you?"

I struggled to calm down. "Of course, I can because it is the truth. Jasper lived on a healthy diet, and I cared for him every night after I had finished my homework," I argued. "Why do I remember that night myself? I know what I said when I visited my horse."

"Oh really," his eyes mocked.

"Yes!" I protested. "When I saw my horse, I rushed to his side, and after rubbing him, I spoke softly, asking if he was ready to go to the stables."

Ben eyed me with suspicion. "Actually, you said it was..." he frowned at me and then returned his gaze to the others, sitting pensively awaiting an outcome to our bickering. "My darling Jasper, what concerns you tonight?" Ben smiled. "Those were the first words I heard you speak as Cassandra when you were the youngest daughter of Lady Elizabeth Downing," This time, he smiled at me, and relief halted my temper. I watched as he faced the others and winked. "In those days, Bella was Cassandra, and despite having a love for that horse, she kept him on rations. Not every day, but most," he winked as if his joke was funny.

Beatrice and Emily faked a yawn, but CJ expressed a colossal groan. "Why are you putting your girlfriend down," she asked, annoyed. Ben grinned. "I would never," he expressed earnestly. "I merely want to recount the tale as accurately as possible. If it were up to Bella, she would recall herself as fragile as Florence Nightingale, which is far from the truth."

"Thank you," I snapped. "Please continue your version of events. If necessary? I will fill in facts from fiction when you're not around."

"You're welcome," Ben rose from his seat, and reaching for my arm, he pulled me close. "Sit on my lap," he suggested. "You know I love you; I was only teasing." He kissed the nape of my neck and, swinging me over his shoulder, carried me back to his seat. I nestled across his legs and fell back against his chest, smelling the sweet scent of his cologne. While I faked annoyance, I was thrilled to be in his arms again.

He told another joke and continued. "I watched Cassie's eyes survey her horse lovingly," he smiled. "I saw her caress the stallion and felt jealous."

"That is not true," I blurted out before I could stop myself. Then I felt Ben's fingers caressing on my own and relaxed. "She is correct," he said. "Though, she did ask if Jasper was ready to retire for the evening. She was even calling the thoroughbred a faithful friend. Still, In the darkness, fearful of discovery, and since Cassie did not know me, nor did I know her, I feared she would scream if she saw me lurking between the trees. So, recognizing the youngest daughter of Earl Thomas Downing, I sank deeper into the Earth. Though fit and robust, I could not outrun the young woman's guards should her watchful gaze stumble on me and force a scream to escape her luscious lips. Longingly,

I watched as she stroked the masterful horse's body and tenderly kissed the mule's nose. She is, I thought. The loveliest girl I have ever seen," he paused again.

I smiled. "You are too kind," I said, feeling my cheeks flush with color.

To my surprise, he kissed me before everyone, making me turn red beetroot. I looked at him, and he looked a little embarrassed, particularly as the others in the room started whistling. "I can't help myself," he explained. "I love Bella and am utterly useless while in her company."

"So not true," I grinned. "I don't have that much power over you," I added suddenly.

"Ah, but you do," he smoothed my hair, straightening an unruly strand that refused to stay put and kissed my head. "I truly am weak when around you."

"You know I feel the same," I finally said. "If not for you, I could not cope with a fraction of the drama that lands on my lap," I muttered. "I'm such a mess."

"Yes, you are, but luckily for you, I love messy chicks," he agreed, laughing. Our eyes met, and we laughed at all the idiocies we had survived together. Suddenly, he stiffened. "I forgot the ending to my story," he said, slapping his forehead jokingly. "Are you ladies ready for the point of this tale?" They nodded yes. "Okay, here goes..." His face grew serious. "The other stable hands had said Cassie was pretty, even gossiping about her youthfulness and kindness, and I saw why at that moment. She was petite, slim, feminine, and possessed an angelic and lithe figure from the top of her head down to her exposed ankles, and not even the homemade dress, styled with a perfectly set hairstyle, adorned with ribbons, could hide that she was indeed a beauty. Her pale white skin glowed against the candlelit entryway, and her smile warmed the coldest that grew across the evening sky. Her eyes were a soft light color, changing between the morning sky's blue and the succulent meadows' green. They shone then, as they are now, curious, and fearful, like a force of reckoning every time she spied on my presence. I rose from the Earth and bowed, nervously aware that danger was mere seconds away. Still, instead of screaming, I watched Cassie march toward me, and though I was afraid, I extended my hand and introduced myself."

Listening to Ben, I squirmed. "I told you, hello," I smiled, recounting my version of that night. "And you told me you are Nicholas Downing, working in the stables. And then, you mentioned that you were not supposed to be there but were worried about Jasper and hungry."

Ben patted my knees. "So, do you remember?"

"Of course I do. I may play dumb, but trust me, there is a smart brunette underneath this bleach-blond hairstyle. "If I recall my words, I told you I would bring you some food, right?"

"Close," he critiqued. "Not exactly my words, but I am impressed. What you said was..." He paused as if struggling to remember himself. "Ah! I forgot." He raised his hand and slapped the side of his head, trying to knock sense into his fuzzy memory.

"No way!" I exclaimed. I placed my hand across his forehead, acting as if I were checking his temperature. "This is not like you forgetting anything, let alone an important event like our first meeting."

He laughed loudly and squeezed my sides until I laughed, and then we laughed together. "I was teasing. Your blue eyes smiled, and you told me I should eat. You also insisted on waiting in the garden while you went to fetch some leftovers from the dinner table."

"So, I was generous with the food after all," I laughed.

"Yes, your sweet, cheerful tone mesmerized me, and the intangible aura you had sent a flurry of shivers up and down my spine. I knew I should be careful that I was in danger should she tell her family they had a visitor. Still, I felt safe enough to trust you and relished the anticipation of eating food better suited for my growing physique than rotten carrots. While I waited for you to return, I spent the entire time straightening my shirt and tucking it into my pants. But you took longer than I predicted, which made me nervous. So, I trod gently away from the bushes and toward the horse, moving sideways to ensure no one could see me. Then, I lurked along the rough gravel that encased the house and crouched beside the entryway, leaning out enough for you to see me without becoming alarmed."

"I brought you a feast, best I can recall."

"It was delicious, and like a pig, I ate everything on my plate," he joked.

"That night was the beginning for us," I remembered.

"Absolutely. We met as often as possible, careful not to let anyone suspect our friendship."

The dimming of the living room lights startled me. Seeing agent Peter Davenport standing at the entryway, I jumped off Ben's lap, crossed my palms behind my back, and prepared myself for arrest. Something, like a nightmare from a restless night's sleep, haunted all my thoughts. In my terror, I moaned and glanced at Ben, who rose quickly from his seat and rushed to my side. And then, he challenged the agent so forcefully that I cried until CJ burst out laughing. "Peter, do not torment Bella," she said sternly. "You are rotten, especially after Bella and Ben shared a romantic account of their first meeting, and you just ruined the melancholy."

Agent Davenport eyed the floor and shrugged. "I didn't mean to cause anyone distress," he said thoughtfully. "I just arrived and was standing here, minding my business, unaware anyone was telling a love story. You could have dimmed the lights to add some ambiance to their story."

"Pete, you're here," CJ rejoiced and swiftly threw herself into his awaiting arms. They hugged in silence. After one or two seconds, CJ spoke. "Any news on capturing Jimmy Cavill?" I noticed Agent Davenport shake his head and look sternly at Ben and me. "Not yet," he sighed. "However, neither Jimmy nor his gang will get far, particularly if they are still in Southeast Florida. We alerted Florida Highway Patrol and airport personnel to be on the lookout," he informed, rubbing his face. "I am so itchy. I have not stopped scratching since I entered Jenkins's home. I swear I am allergic to carpets or drapes, as I have a wicked rash. Look at my arms," he exclaimed, removing his jacket, and revealing a hard stomach underneath his fitted orange tee. "Ouch! I feel like a dog with fleas."

CJ smoothed her hand across his upper body and kissed his cheek. "I hardly think you know how a dog with fleas feels," she said, patting his buttocks. "And I doubt Clive's home is causing you any health issues. If anything, you could be reacting to last night's stormy weather. Ben had issues earlier, but we women have had no problems. You men are such babies."

Ben flung out his hands, rolled up his sleeves, and pointed to bite marks running up and down his arms. "I don't know why my skin reacted this way," he sounded puzzled. But my skin was so irritated and was becoming red from scratching until Bella gave me an antihistamine," he paused, examining his skin, and smiled. It has done the trick. My skin is not as inflamed as it was some hours ago."

"Good to know," Peter Davenport said. "So," he turned to me. "Do you have an Allegra or Zyrtec to spare? I could use some relief."

"Yes, but I wonder which will work best," I grimaced. "The Zyrtec is better for skin issues. Of course, if you prefer Allegra, I will ask Emily for the bottle. It's your call."

"So," Ben stared at the officer. "I wonder if you are finished with the investigation," his eyes shifting to mine. "I know Bella needs to return to Miami, and I did offer to drive down with her. Just so you know, she will be staying at my place for a couple of weeks, hence our trip, because she needs to get her personal stuff. You know," he hesitated, raising his arms. "How do girls live without clothing, cosmetics, and skincare? Silly analogy. They don't."

I nudge Ben. I glanced at Davenport and CJ and rolled my eyes. "I am no different than other women concerning my need for fresh clothes and toiletries. Right, CJ?" She nodded and smiled. "I wholeheartedly agree."

Peter Davenport shifted. "How long are you both planning to stay in Miami?" he asked seriously.

"Oh, we're not planning on staying down there, just the quick errand, and then we'll be back in Jupiter." Ben swiftly added. He adjusted his belt buckle and straightened his shirt.

The blue hues in his eyes softened as he turned to face me, and reaching for his hand, he pulled me close. "We will be back late tonight or first thing tomorrow morning. If you have no plans for Monday evening, let's go for dinner, my treat."

I am not saying I was surprised by Benny Boy's invitation because he loves to visit the finest restaurants and eat out. However, I was shocked that he would want to spend time with two investigators working on a case involving me. As much as I liked and admired CJ, I was no longer comfortable in her company, and I could not imagine eating dinner with her husband, Peter, either. Intuition told me both FBI agents would supply us with drinks if only to question me endlessly about Lisa Goodman. In my mind, CJ would no longer be a person I would talk to daily, mainly because I worried that she knew too much about me. I feared her telling Ben secrets about my life, which I had fought long and hard to keep secret. I yawned, stretched my arms above my head, and signaled Ben that we must go. Then, I turned to Beatrice and Emily, thanked them for a memorable day, and hugged both ladies before CJ rushed to my side. "You can't leave without this," she mumbled, handing me my handbag.

I stepped back. Afraid and ashamed, knowing everyone could see my guilt-ridden face. "Nice timing," I muttered, checking my purse's contents, ensuring my private property was intact. Satisfied that all the items were there, I eyed Ben and signaled that we should leave.

Peter and CJ shook Ben's hand and mentioned ringing him tomorrow to discuss our dinner date. I thanked them both for their help and followed Ben towards the door.

My head spun as I reached for Ben's hand and walked to his vehicle. Sitting inside his SUV, I leaned back against the seat and exhaled deeply. Then I turned to him and grinned. "I didn't think we would ever get away from here," I sighed. "I have never in my life felt so cornered, and I do not mean it was all bad; I simply mean that at times, I was scared. Do not get me wrong, I adore Beatrice and Emily, too, but I honestly felt like I was sinking into quicksand. Does that make sense?"

He waited to answer, fastening his seatbelt, and even when he started the car's engine, I knew that though he acted distracted, his thoughts focused on me. I looked across at the space between us, leaned over, and kissed his cheek. "Thanks for saving me, Ben," I whispered, resting my head against his shoulder.

"Bella," he murmured. He held the steering wheel and played with my hair with his free hand. "I have known and loved you for hundreds of years. I could never let anything happen to you, as it would kill me. If we reversed the roles, you would do the same for me. All that matters now is that we stick together and do not let anyone ruffle our feathers because I plan to lie until I die for you and can only hope you reciprocate my feelings. It is, right?" He lifted his beautiful blue eyes to mine. "You are the most important person in my life. You are more important than my mother and knowing how much I love and care about you has made me realize how fragile our time together can be. So, let us promise to share our thoughts and feelings, even our innermost concerns. That way, we will always remain one step ahead of any evil that comes our way."

The late Sunday afternoon sun was disappearing behind a muted yellow full moon. The round mystery ball glowed against the darkening clouds, lighting the street ahead as Benny Boy drove down Beach Road. Crossing Catos Bridge, I was thrilled that the Super Moon hung so low that I imagined that I could reach through the Mercedes sunroof and touch it.

"It's magical, isn't it?" Ben said, sensing my awe at the incredible brightness that lit our way.

"I can hardly believe how beautiful and bright it looks," I murmured. "I don't think I've ever seen the moon so low. It is breathtaking to see such beauty. I almost feel like I can touch it."

"The Super Moon will be visible all week. We should camp on the beach one night and watch as it moves across the sky."

"Ben, I believe the earth moves, but the moon, to my knowledge, stays where it is."

Ben remained silent. His face seemed confused as if he were trying to figure out whether it was the earth that moved, or the moon. "I'll have to Google that, Bella. I was sure the moon moved across the sky, East to West."

I quickly opened Google on my cellphone and checked. "Ben, you're correct. The moon orbits the Earth. According to the search engine, the Moon orbits the Earth at a speed of 2,288 miles (about twice the distance from Florida to

New York City) per hour and rotates on its axis once every twenty-seven days, called a lunar day." I told him, reading the information I had found on Google. "Oh, and listen to this... The Moon locks with the Earth, which means it spins on its axis exactly once each time it orbits the Earth. It is Interesting, isn't it?"

"Google is amazing," Ben said excitedly. "I don't know what we did before computers became part of our lives."

"Don't forget the internet."

He yawned. "No kidding!"

"Ben, if you're too tired to drive, we can pull over and..."

"And what?"

"I can drive." Noticing his demeanor change, I regretted my words. "What's wrong?"

"I was hoping you were going to say we could return to Jupiter," he whispered, eyes focused on the highway.

"Ben, I must see Harry. I truly do."

He nodded. "I understand. Though I will tell you again, I had a horrible suspicion about driving to Miami tonight."

"I know. You mentioned it earlier."

"Just know that regardless of tonight's outcome. Harry may need help with changes as they are difficult to accept. But irrespective of how he resists, the change was due to come. If you see flaws in your relationship looming in the distance, this is your chance to deal with them now. Doing so may prevent more significant problems later. When you keep quiet because you think an issue is not worth arguing over. Well, those small problems become significant issues that can uproot an otherwise happy relationship. Sometimes, leaving a relationship that is not working is all right. Do you understand all I am trying to explain?"

I nodded, and then, seeing two vehicles ahead sway out of their traffic lanes, I screamed. I slammed my feet to the vehicle's floor as if I could break faster than Ben, which was insane considering the Mercedes did not have foot pedals on the passenger side. "OMG, watch out for that Porsche. It is racing with a Mercedes, and the driver is all over the road," I cautioned, afraid of crashing. I felt Ben's car swerve aggressively across the road, and deciding I no longer wanted to watch the hazard, I closed my eyes.

On the dimly lit road, I sat quietly. Then feeling that Ben's auto slowed down, I reopened my eyes and stared at the stopped vehicles along the highway. The road ahead had become a traffic jam, with automobiles stopping in every lane. "The freeway never just flows, does it?" I moaned and shifted in my seat.

Adjusting the air conditioning, Ben kept his eyes on the road. "I had a feeling tonight would be awful," he sighed. "Weekend traffic is always chaotic and slow."

"Should we get off the next exit and take Ocean Drive south?"

"Bella, you cannot be serious?" He sounded exasperated. "Taking route A1A will take hours with all the traffic lights. We're much better to stay put and wait out this accident."

I glanced out the window and saw an SUV that had flipped on its side and crashed into the emergency lane. The roof and windows looked severely damaged, and I shuddered, wondering if the passengers had made it out of the car alive. "Do you think the fire rescue crews had to smash the windows on that wrecked Mercedes, or did the accident itself cause the damage?" I asked Ben, as the SUV was identical to his, and he was familiar with Mercedes's safety features.

He shrugged. "Hopefully, they didn't perish in their vehicle."

"But, why would you say that? I thought Mercedes was the safest car in the world?"

"It is, but it's obvious to me that rescue crews had to use the jaws of life to cut the couple from the car."

I looked at him, puzzled. "Why would you presume it's a couple?" I asked. "It could be a lone driver who fell asleep at the wheel, such as an old man or woman, or someone our age, driving drunk."

He eyed me mysteriously. "True," he admitted. "It was wrong of me to judge."

"No kidding." I snapped. "Imagine if it were us in that wrecked vehicle and passersby were thoughtless to assume we were drunk, when in fact we could have been pushed off the road by a selfish driver who thought they owned every passing lane."

He did not reply, and I did not add to my point. We sat muted for at least twenty miles and did not engage in idle chatter for at least forty minutes. Only when I could stand the silence no longer did I speak. "Are you mad at me?"

Ben's fingers strummed around the steering wheel, and he exhaled. "Not at all. I am tired, more so than I care to admit. That's all."

"If you want, we can stay at my apartment tonight," I suggested, my voice provocative. Benny Boy and I smiled.

"Well, what do you think? Are you up for a night of uncomfortableness at my place, or are you deciding whether to retreat to your luxurious beachfront villa?"

"If I'm with you, I can take the good with the bad."

I grinned, excitedly. "Good to know."

"Meaning?"

"Just that... After I see Harry, we will stay at my flat. Then, tomorrow, we will go back to Jupiter."

I felt his hand reach for my hand, and he squeezed it tight and kissed my fingers while exiting the freeway. "We're almost there," he said joyfully.

I noticed the Coconut Grove hospital sign on Grove Road, and I grew nervous, knowing I would see Harry in less than ten minutes. Stopped at a red traffic light, I imagined my speech to Harry, and though worried, I trusted Ben that Harry would not be too upset since Harry would be happy that we were now an item.

The wind gusts grew strong along Bayside Road, and despite the shimmering view of Miami Bay, I longed to be inland and away from the turbulence. Turning right onto Rising Lane, we drove through a mound of fallen leaves, and they scattered over the windshield, blocking our view.

"Be careful, Ben," I moaned. "We don't need an accident."

He ignored me. I considered him to be angry or upset or both. I surmised he was jealous because I had put so much emphasis on seeing Harry tonight and had not wanted to wait till the next day. I wondered if I should have listened to Ben and driven to Miami on Monday morning instead of late Sunday night.

It was too late now, I thought. Besides, I was too exhausted to admit that Ben was right. I rubbed my elbows, which hurt, and I did not know why. I surmised I had placed them awkwardly against the car door, as that was the only explanation I could muster as to why my body ached.

Ben drove into a driveway, parked under one of three oak trees, and turned off the engine.

"Are you ready to face him?" he asked. "Bella, do you want me to go with you inside? If you want me to, I will, but I think I should stay in my car so you can both talk."

I gnawed at my lower lip and stared at the modest home where Harry lived. The massive Sea Grape plants growing in the garden added shade from the intense Florida sunshine and, at night, provided a privacy fence. Though the house looked creepy, the smell of Bougainvillea wafted across the manicured lawn, and I inhaled the succulent scent. Bamboo lined the driveway as tall as the eye could see, and familiar with the hanging spider webs, I carefully strolled toward the front patio.

Nervously, I pressed the bell and waited for Harry to open the door, but he did not answer. I thought him out for the evening, but I could hear music and chatter inside the home. Not deterred, I walked a pathway toward the back of the house, and unlocking the gate, I soldiered along the path toward the pool area. It was the only area of the home with light and peering inside the French door windows. I saw Harry sitting with friends conversing in idle chatter as a football game played on the television. I debated whether to bang hard on the glass or tap lightly, but knowing no one would hear me, I did neither. Instead, I checked if anyone had locked the door. Nobody had. I opened it quickly and walked inside, calling out as I entered the house. To my surprise and to add insult to injury, not one person acknowledged my presence. Upset, I stood in the kitchen, and calmed down, recognizing that Harry and his friends needed time to adjust to my being there without my creating a scene. Besides, I wanted them to continue to enjoy the televised sporting event without feeling uncomfortable. In the kitchen, I cleared away umpteen empty bottles, cans of beer, and empty pizza boxes. Then I loaded the dishwasher with silverware and dishes, nauseous by the smell of alcohol that stained drinking glasses, leaving them coated in a brown sticky substance. Aware Ben was waiting outside, I grappled with the garbage and went to the bins at the side of the house. The concrete path, littered with old cardboard beer cases, stretched the entire length of the walkway, and stepping over large piles of boxes, I spied bugs scurrying underneath mulching that accentuated soil around Hibiscus blooms.

Suddenly, a hand grabbed my arm, and I shrieked. I spun around, ready to fight. Though, I calmed down when I saw Benny Boy standing in front of me. "What's wrong?" I asked, surprised. "I thought you were going to wait in the car?"

He looked annoyed. "I have been waiting for almost one hour, Bella," he hissed. His eyes were hard and cold. "How much longer is this going to take?"

I groaned. "Ben, I have not spoken to Harry. There is a football game on the television, so I decided to make myself useful and clean up the kitchen."

"All this time has passed, and you are cleaning his house?" His voice was harsh.

I nodded.

"But why?"

"I don't know," I muttered. "It's a habit of mine to pick up other people's messes, and I have always cleaned Harry's home. Well, whenever I can, that is," I sighed. "I shouldn't have done it, right?" I asked, perplexed but understanding Ben's annoyance. "I'm sorry, Ben. I screwed up. I'm just accustomed to cleaning up his mess and forgot that I no longer need to do it."

"No shit," he folded his arms. "Harry needs to clear out his own garbage, and I'm not just referring to empty bottles of alcohol. He needs to get the people who use him for a place to party, and let us remember, they go to his home for free drinks. Harry needs to get a grip on his life. If not? He will become a lonely old man with only beer for company."

I gnawed my lip and eyed him suspiciously. "Have you spoken to CJ about Harry?" He looked surprised. "Not about Harry," he moaned. "Why would you ask such a ridiculous question?"

"Because she said the same words last night," I paused. "Or it was this afternoon," I said, shaking my head before I threw the garbage in the bin. "I honestly cannot remember, but help me, god, she said the same thing as you did."

His brows rose. "Good to know," he said. "Knowing two people who care about you are telling you the same thing should help you realize that it's wrong for you to feel that you must still babysit Harry."

"Goodness, Ben," I moaned. "I merely straightened up the kitchen. It wasn't as if I cleaned the entire house." I stepped away from his arms and faced the back garden. "I'm going back inside," I said, walking away.

"But why? When you just told me, Harry ignored you."

Slowly, I turned to Ben and groaned. "I want Harry to know that we are through and no longer a couple, and that is not something I can say in a text message or over the phone, right?"

Ben's blue eyes turned dark. "Why not?" he yelled. He hesitated, "He would not take the same care if your feelings were involved. "Well, at least that's what CJ told me."

"Ah! So, you did chat to CJ about Harry," I spat. "Yet less than two seconds ago, you told me you hadn't, which, in my estimation, makes you a liar, Ben Barrymore."

Instantly, Benny Boy rushed to my side. "Bella," he grabbed my arms and forced me to look at his face. "We seriously need to talk," he hissed. "Things have happened that affect us, and the sooner you understand the magnitude of our current situation, the better off you'll be."

I shoved Ben away. "I'm talking to Harry," I told him. "If I have to force the situation, I will. Harry Higgins will acknowledge my visit, regardless of whether his mood is upset, happy, or angry. Do you understand?"

He nodded, leaned against the trunk of a Royal Palm, and waved. "Go see Harry and speak to him, although..." his eyes softened. "I doubt he will speak to you regardless of how much you demand his attention as he will not be able to..."

"To what?" I snapped.

He shook his head and walked toward me. "Nothing, Bella," he said and grimaced. "Go see Harry, and when you're ready to return, I will be here waiting for you."

As I have emphasized throughout this journey, I am not one to lose my temper or blow off steam for amusement. I always try to control my emotions, especially my significant mood swings. Unfortunately, I know how crazy I am when I lose my temper. That night, though, as I made my way down Harry's path, my rage escalated to the point where I vented my frustration by kicking wet leaves off the concrete and cursing Benny Boy with all my might. I plucked broken twigs from their stems and crumpled delicate petals. Ignoring the pain from the thorns piercing my skin, I crushed them in my palms and haphazardly tossed them aside. I turned the corner and halted behind Harry's house. I saw him embracing another woman, and I felt disgusted as they clung to each other.

"You deceitful jerk," I exclaimed, feeling defeated. "So, she's the reason why you treated me poorly last night?" Despite my presence, he ignored my words and continued, comforting the curvy blonde woman, which intensified my contempt tenfold. I stared at my straight up and down frame and wondered, jealous, where all these women with mega curves had suddenly come from. In the past, most women envied tall, slim, and slender figures like mine.

Not anymore, I thought wistfully. Now, teenagers and most fashion-savvy women, in particular, social media influencers, resembled Kim Kardashian, or Jennifer Lopez, and the bigger the butt, the better.

Ahh! I could scream.

In seconds, my anger skyrocketed. I grabbed a patio chair and hurled it towards Harry, but he was unfazed.

I watched Harry's hugging partner glance around the patio. I was sure she sensed my presence because she quickly retreated inside the house, leaving Harry alone beside the jacuzzi hot tub.

After she left, I charged Harry with as much strength as I could muster, and forcefully, I punched his stomach with all my fury. Finally, he acknowledged me, and though he looked fearful, the shock in his green eyes upset me, as it was clear he had not expected to see me.

"Who is she, and why didn't you tell me you were involved with someone else?" I demanded heartlessly. Still, considering I was under extreme betrayal, I ignored my conscience and engaged in tortuous bickering, lashing out at Harry at every chance. My eyes filled with rage, but mostly I hurt. Just then, my hands fell to my sides, and before I could stop myself, I began to cry.

Wind gusts battered against the west side of the house, causing a whistling sound to skim over the aluminum pergola canopy. The hardtop gazebo rattled in the breeze, and though securely fastened, I shivered, unsure if the structure would fail under such high winds.

I looked at Harry. He stood transfixed, staring into nothingness. "Bella," he murmured, pain in his voice. "Are you here?"

I nodded. "Yes, I am here. And I am angry at you for cheating on me with that woman."

Harry still sounded shocked, like he could not allow his eyes to believe what his ears heard. "I am not cheating on you. Still, I cannot believe you came back. I thought I would never see you again. My god, Bella, it feels so long ago, yet the stabbing in my heart reminds me that you left only tonight." He smiled.

"Last night. I left last night," I corrected and smiled. I sniffled and watched the twinkling fairy lights lining his bay windows flicker on and off as if dancing across the wooden garden deck. Then we smiled together, and peace prevailed.

Momentarily anyway... Then, I was back to being a curious witch.

"No, Bella, you went away tonight." Harry insisted. "I know it was tonight because the police came to notify me of the accident," he hesitated. Seeing my confusion, he threw his hands in the air. "I swear, Bella. The cops were here, and they just left."

I folded my arms and stood intrigued. "Why would the police visit you?" I asked, bewildered. However, I did wonder if it was due to Tubby's demise. Of course it was, I surmised. There was no other reason for them to visit. The police were obviously snooping to check if Harry took part in the death of Clive Jenkins, and that was okay because Harry had no idea who Tubby was. "Harry," I said and gnawed at my lip. "Tell me exactly what the police told you."

"Good God, Bella!" he exclaimed. "I will tell you everything. But first, you must remember that you kept my business card in your wallet. You had written on the back of it that in case of an emergency, officials could contact me."

"Okay," I said. "So, the police officers visited you, and you told them nothing. I understand that. Still, I want to know who that girl was and why you were all over each other."

I noticed the twang of bitterness in my voice but focused on retrieving information; I ignored my emotional distress. Harry appeared to fluster. "It was Helena Roberts. She works for my company, and despite being my secretary, she is also a friend of mine."

"How long have you and Helena been going at it like rabbits?" I asked, tormented by envy.

"Helena and I have done nothing like what you are thinking. My goodness, since hanging out with Ben, your mind is in the gutter," he sighed, sadness in his eyes. "Hear this, Bella Bloom," he paused. "Your tempestuous rant is hypocritical, considering you were running around with Ben Barrymore late last night. Now that is what I call irony," he turned away and shrugged.

I watched the pain sweep across his face, and if that did not make me feel lousy enough, a stream of tears falling from his eyes crushed my insides raw. "I am sorry, Harry," I said truthfully. "I never meant to hurt you."

"It's okay. I am getting over it." His voice was low, and I strained to catch his words. "How are you feeling?" He asked.

"I'm hanging in there," I assured him. And though I sighed loudly in relief, he must have seen the frustration in my eyes.

He smiled. "I am so happy you visited tonight. Now, I think I can move onward in life," he hesitated. "That is if you don't mind. Of course, I will think of you and remember our friendship. And despite your relationship with Ben, I know he will care for you, which hurts like hell, but it is what it is."

"We will always be friends."

His smile widened. Then he started to walk away from the side entrance of his house, pulling me along by the hand. "Come on, Bella," he encouraged. "Ben is waiting, and he needs you now much more than I ever did."

Harry led me back to Ben. He paused beside the Royal Palm tree where Ben stood patiently awaiting my return.

"Thank god you are back," Ben's voice echoed in my ears. "I was worried you might disappear, and I would never find you, and if I did, I worried you might feel differently about me."

Harry extended a hand to signal a truce with Ben, and after both men shook, Harry turned to leave. "You're cool with us together, right?" Ben asked pleasantly, moving from the tree.

"Yes. I walked Bella back to you because I wanted to make sure she did not get lost," Harry said. "And as much as I'm heartbroken, at this moment, I want nothing but the best for her, even if that means being with you, Ben."

"I think Harry now accepts us as a couple," I added sheepishly. But Ben needed more convincing. "You were always a good sport, Harry, particularly with me. Hopefully, we shall meet again somewhere in the future."

I watched Harry shrug, "You never know," he admitted. "But in all fairness, I'm not a big believer in life after death."

"One would think seeing us might change your mind?" Ben said optimistically.

"I doubt it," Harry added standing two feet away. "God does not exist in my world."

I winced. I had not expected to hear his unholy words and felt faint hearing how little faith Harry held in his heart towards our Heavenly Father.

Ben reached forward and held me up. "Do not get dizzy now," he cautioned. "Hey, Harry, would you please explain to Bella the truth about the night's events. I ask because I am worried as she is having a tough time accepting our demise?" he asked.

I shivered nervously, predicting another mind-blowing lecture as Harry faced my flushed awkwardness.

"I would," he replied. But to be honest, I am still suffering from shock at the news. Due to my skepticism, I fear my version might ruin an unbelievable story. Still, Bella needs to understand and accept the size of this daunting evening. Therefore, I will oblige, and then, you can take her with you."

It was a strange conversation for me to absorb. Ben and Harry agreed to let me know of something that had happened that was out of my control. It was even more confusing that they were back to being friends when Ben insisted, they had only been business associates.

Looking at the ground, I fidgeted on my feet, then I glanced up at Harry, and turned to Ben, who, surprisingly, had faded into oblivion. "What is going on?" I asked Harry while searching among the garden foliage. "Where did Ben go?"

Harry nodded to a row of potted plants, and I looked to see what was so interesting about Hibiscus blooms. Yes, they were beautiful, and the red flowers matched the house's front door, but seriously, it was not that magnificent to distract me from Benny Boy's disappearance.

Suddenly, Harry grabbed my hand and whispered. "Ben knows what he has become. He fought it as long as he could to stay here with you, and he will continue to struggle to leave until you accept your fate."

"Harry, are you drunk?" I asked indignantly. Though I did not intend to sound so panicky, the fear of losing Ben caused enormous pain.

His brows arched, then lowered together as he fought to say the words that he doubted even himself. "You are dead, Bella, and so is Ben. A drunk driver cut you off in traffic and the automobile you were traveling in rolled over, killing you instantly. The police told me the high rate of speed was the determining factor and that you did not stand a chance of survival. I am sorry, but whether you accept my words or not, you both died in the car. It happened on I-95 near the Pompano Beach exit." His eyes turned dark. "I am sorry, Bella. I do not know how to say it respectfully, and I am still puzzled about why or how you both ended up at my home."

I scowled to hide my nervousness. "You are wrong, Harry. Ben and I did not die in a car accident. Not tonight, and not ever." I argued.

Harry looked amazed at what he was seeing, and then his face expressed fear. "This is not funny," I yelled. "Where is Ben? Stop playing games. You are truly making me madder than a caged animal."

He struggled to compose himself. "I agree this is not funny, Bella, but I do not know how else to explain this situation. You must understand I am not a religious man, and until tonight, I knew nothing about life after death, but after seeing you and Ben, I am going to rethink my values.

So, thanks for that insight, but I swear to you, you are dead, and so is Ben. Accept it and move forward. This is your only chance to be with him."

"Fuck you, Harry," I yelled. "You are a liar. There is no way I have died, and neither did Ben. Stop playing games."

He sighed deeply. "But I am not lying, and I am not playing games with you. I would never do that, never."

I saw the pain in his eyes again and gnawed at my lower lip.

"This is the end of the road for you. Please accept it and go where you must go," he muttered. "For there was no coming back from that accident. It was a hellacious crash, and not even that expensive Mercedes Ben drove could protect you from that head on collision, not forgetting the mangled mess on the side of that road," he stuffed his hands inside his shorts pocket, slumped his shoulders, and exhaled. "Bella. I am so sorry, but you and Ben perished on that highway, and this truly is the end."

"Wrong, Harry," I argued. "A freak auto accident is not the end for Ben and me. It is the beginning. We will triumph through this transition as we have done in the past, and do you know what else we will do?" But I could not explain because it suddenly became clear to me that Harry could no longer see me as a person, least of all a ghost, and the reality shook me to my core.

I watched him step backwards, distancing himself from where I stood. "Did you leave?" He asked, walking blindly between the bushes with his arms outstretched. Then, he stopped, turned around and decidedly walked back to where he remembered me standing. I stood silently until he stopped midway, and I sighed wearily. My thoughts became erratic, and I feared for my safety. I wondered where Ben had gone, and since being alone scared me, I listened as Harry started to speak again. However, I did not have to strain to listen as his voice was louder this time. "Bella, I cannot hear you anymore. So, just let me say one thing."

I nodded before I realized he could not see me. Then, I folded my arms and looked around the garden, determined to find Ben. If only to send Harry and his lies to hell because it was cruel of him to imply, I was deceased when I knew I was well and truly alive.

Just then, Harry spoke again. "I know you are probably still here. But it would be best if you left before, it becomes too late for you to catch up with Ben. Gosh darn it, Bella. Just get yourself together and stop lingering at my house. Please find Ben and follow him before you lose your way. I hate myself for being mean to you, and I regret the nastiness I expressed last night, but you must go, and you must do it now. Can you hear me? Go find Ben, and get out of here, now." He frowned, remembering my stubbornness.

Accepting that I was not winning any popularity points with Harry, I agreed it was finally time to leave. Exhausted and anxious about facing my creator, my knees began to shake, and I was afraid I was going to fall to the ground, amongst the bugs, to sit and rot while waiting for the devil himself to drag my ungrateful soul to hell.

Suddenly, a rain cloud burst over my head, and I huddled for shelter beside the massive palm tree where Ben had stood moments earlier. From the corner of my eye, I could see

Harry entering the house where I had once eased his pain, only now would he find comfort in Helena's arms.

The reality was worse than any reckoning I would face later that night. Still, I ignored the burning heartache and sought solace in a passage my mother had recited since childhood.

Whoever sows to please their flesh, from the flesh will reap destruction; whoever sows to please the Spirit, from the Spirit will reap eternal life... Galatians 6:8.

Saddened, I accepted that I, the deceitful companion, was now companionless, and the irony was daunting. My mother was right, in lecturing, that I was unworthy of a pig and that reality hurt more than any slap I had ever experienced. Still, I was not going to linger on the negative, as I was also generous in kindness and blessings, and if our Lord should take mercy on my soul, I am sure he will grant me eternal life, with or without Benny Boy. However, I yearned to continue my journey with Ben, even though my battered heart told me he was no longer waiting.

In shame, I stood solemnly and let the rain drench my body, willing the water to wash away my sins. My feet sank into the thick, sticky mud, and my arms stung against the furrowing bark. In the rage-filled cyclone of that ominous thunderstorm, I gasped for air and fought against the anguish that tormented me, determined to reclaim my place in God's good graces. Because worse, much worse than God, I feared an evil spirit would condemn me to roam the planet in turmoil, and I knew I needed to claw my way back from the wickedness that threatened to engulf me.

If only I could soothe my mistakes and banish my remorse indefinitely, then, and only then, would I find salvation. A lightning strike struck the tree before me, and I fell to the ground. At that moment, I vowed to redeem myself, giving respect first to God. I prayed to the Lord to repent every trespass I had committed against him and my brothers and sisters. Then I beseeched Jesus Christ, the Lamb of God, to take away the wrongdoing of my world and, through the grace of the Holy Spirit, restore me to friendship with his Father.

As the storm raged on, my despair intensified, and each bolt of lightning and each boom of thunder illuminated a painfully clear path into my future. Alas, the Heavens were ferociously loud. The continuance of their fury whipped my anxiety into a frenzy, for I knew their wrath would not halt until they had chartered a map to my terminus.

Afraid of hell but not of death, I kicked away clumps of soil and freed my feet from dirt that had stiffened against my skin. In my quest to flee, I stumbled on uprooted trees and injured my foot, leaving me unable to walk. I yelped in pain and fell to the ground of God's great earth and cried enough tears to fill a million rivers. In angst, I rose to my knees atop the battered branches, and though I was unfit for reverence, I raised my hands to the holy skies and begged for mercy.

Suddenly, the ground split, and I started to descend. I glanced upward one last time and was surprised to see a vibrant blue sky extending across the horizon, dispelling the darkness surrounding my aura. And I smiled, joyous for forgiveness and thankful to start anew. Nevertheless, what truly lifted my spirits was seeing Benny Boy's hand bursting through a large, fluffy cloud as he reached down to save me once again.

SOMETIME LATER...

I watched clouds cross the sky, some so high I could not reach and others so low I could almost disappear. Benny Boy, gifted with height, remained visible in all his glory, and I marveled at his muscular physique.

Sitting atop an Egyptian pyramid, I nestled closer to his firm body and sighed. The height of the Great Pyramid of Giza was daunting as I leaned against the stone structure. While I struggled to breathe in the elements, particularly the desert air, Ben was well at home, which was easy for him as he had no allergies and no fear of heights.

"So," he teased. "Do you want to play a game?"

Confused, I clasped his hand and inched closer to his body. "I don't know. I am afraid, Ben," I admitted, looking past his welcoming smile and toward the dunes that carpeted the earth for miles. His face lit with intrigue. "Oh, come on, Bella," he teased. "We're both due some fun, especially now that we're dead." Clutching his hand, I stiffened, mainly because, unlike Ben, I had yet to accept that we were no longer part of the living. Still, as he wrapped his arms around my waist and pulled me near to kiss my neck, I relaxed since, at the very least, we were together, side by side in this waiting game.

For what are we waiting?

I was still trying to figure it out.

Still, I hoped whatever it was, we would always be in each other's universe, as going it alone, without Ben, would be hellacious to me, and since I had almost floundered once already, I honestly wanted only to spend my days with the man who I loved.

I exhaled. "What do you have in mind?" I asked perplexedly. However, seeing his mischievous smile alerted me to a dangerous activity that Benny Boy had held for eons. "Oh no, please don't tell me you want us to do that?" I begged indifferently. Still, knowing he would ignore my pleas, I resorted to dealing with the crazy and thrilling adventure that had become a ritual to Ben. It was a habit of a hobby he sought every time our lives ended and would continue until we embarked on a new life.

He walked toward the edge of the great pyramid, faced me, and smiled. "You're not chicken. Are you?" he teased again.

I shook my head.

"Come on, Bella. We are visiting this monumental spot because you wanted to come here. Yes, I am also enjoying it, as it is one of the best views in the world. But let's have some fun and enjoy this moment."

"Oh, I don't know if I'm up for it," I sighed, knowing my words would disappoint him. At the same time, I was still reeling from the reality that I still had much to do in life like Bella Bloom. Troubled, I watched his hands fall to his sides, and a look of dismay etched his face. "Are you for real? It is not every day we get to play on the oldest of the Seven Wonders of the Ancient World," he coaxed. "Think of the fun we'll have. Why, we may even see King Khufu while we're here."

"I understand your reason, but more than anything, I want to visit the temples and the cemeteries. I would also like to go down there," I said, pointing to the ground. I want to see the pyramid's faces because their curvature matches the radius of the Earth, which is far more interesting to me."

"We can do that later," Ben moaned. He stood on his tiptoes and raised his arms as if to take flight. "Come on, Bella. Can we go? If you fly down for me, I will show you the Southern shaft in the King's Chamber, which points to the star al Nitak in the constellation Orion. So, what do you say?"

I rolled my eyes. "You cannot tempt me, Benny Boy. I want to go down my way, and while descending, I want to explore the passage pointing to the pole star Alpha Draconis. You do want me to be happy, don't you?"

"I'll take you to all three chambers if you do this with me," Ben promised.

"There are three?" I asked, grinning. "Now you have my attention."

"Do this with me, and I'll show you some cemeteries next to the pyramid that people couldn't excavate in the 20th century."

"Why ever not?" I asked, my hands resting on my hips as I surveyed the depth from the tallest point of Giza down to the ground below. I almost became crippled with fear. "How high up do you think we are?"

Ben shrugged. "At one time, it was almost five hundred feet tall, but since it's nearly five thousand years old, it's shrunk," he said, becoming more solemn than ever. "As years passed, people and the elements removed most of the limestone casing, making it shorter in height now."

I frowned when I thought locals and archaeologists had scavenged this magnificent structure. "You know what I think?" I spoke in a low tone, a whisper, as I did not want the gods to hear what I was about to say. Benny Boy eyed me with interest. "Tell me so that no one besides us can hear," he encouraged, reaching out a hand to aid me as I stumbled against loose stones while crossing the tallest peak.

I sat atop the tallest peak closest to God and rubbed limestone from my hands. I glanced past Ben and stared into the distance. "Well, I, for one, think that many people have no respect for history. And..."

Knowing exactly where my sentence was going, Ben swiftly interrupted my words. "Be careful," he hushed. "We don't want to cause any trouble with the spirits allowing us to enjoy this magnificent view."

I silenced myself. Then I rubbed my dry eyes, brittle from the elements, and sighed. Sneezing, I quickly rose and walked to Ben. "Okay," I whispered. I'll be quiet, mainly because you know what I would say."

He laughed. "Yes! And the answer is no."

"Nothing at all?" I questioned.

"Bella, the pyramid chambers are mostly empty. Though filled with gold, ornaments, and jewels, most locals looted it at one time." He paused, wistfully. "If I thought for one moment that there were treasures here, I'd search through each chamber for something overlooked and give it to you, if only to make your smile the brightest I'd ever seen. But, alas," he shrugged. "There's nothing left. Nothing that would interest you, anyway."

"I'm more grateful to the masons who built this structure than intrigued about what's inside," I corrected. "The craftsmanship in putting this temple together must have been tremendously demanding work. I cannot imagine the number of stones it took to build this stunning piece of architecture. And do you know what, Ben?" I asked.

He turned to face me and grabbed my hand. "Tell me." He demanded. His blue eyes shone in the midday sun.

"I'll bet you all the jewels in the world that this pyramid holds many souls, as I'm sure many masons died in their orders to construct this pyramid."

Ben nodded. "I agree with you. It took close to thirty years to prepare the rocks and cut them. Imagine all that work to satisfy the orders of King Khufu. Which reminds me," he paused, glancing across the desert before sitting down and guiding me atop his lap. I wrapped my arms around his neck and kissed his cheek softly. "Pray tell," I whispered, nuzzling his neck.

"Well, Bella. If historians are correct in their theories, artisans built this using over two million stones, weighing up to fifty tons each. Can you imagine the ingenious minds that figured out how to lift such heavy weights?"

I nodded again. "I get it, Ben, and I respect the work involved. Though, I'm still trying to figure out why and how we arrived here in the first place." I noticed his eyes still searching the desert below, and following his gaze, I spotted a reflective light shining from the ground. "What in the world do you suppose that is?" I asked incredulously. But he did not answer.

Shortly after, I watched as the light moved toward us, and I stiffened on his lap and held my breath. "Ben," I exclaimed fearfully. "What is that beam heading our way, and how would it know we are here?" I pointed across the desert toward a beam that seemed reluctant to fade. Then, his arms wrapped around my shoulder as he pulled me closer. "It's an illusion, Bella. It's not coming our way."

"But it is," I argued. "Look!"

Ben ran his fingers through my hair, and, rising upward, he hoisted me with him. "The light may look like it is coming to us, but it's not. However," he said, agitated, before turning to face me.

In my mind, I questioned his knowledge and gnawed at my lower lip. "Dearest Ben. Please explain."

"Okay, but I do not want you to become upset or transfixed on issues we cannot control. Understood?" He cautioned.

I nodded for the umpteenth time.

Aware that a group of Hooded Crows was about to fly by, I ducked. I love birds and admire their ability to fly across the sky from one destination to another. However, knowing they could not see me did not comfort me, as I worried spirits could hurt me even if I were invisible. Feeling parched from the hot midday sun, I wiped my brow and tugged at my clothes, which stuck to my body, causing me to sweat.

"Are you okay?"

"I am roasting in this intense sunlight," I answered, wafting my face. "The temperature in Egypt is hotter than any of the hottest days I've experienced in Florida. Plus, it doesn't help that I am wearing these heavy denim jeans."

He laughed. "Take them off," he suggested. His eyes hungered with lust.

I ignored his request. "Can we leave now?" I fussed with my hair, searching pockets for something to keep it from falling into my eyes. "I'm hot and tired, Ben. Let's do something else or find somewhere else to hang out."

"But you wanted to come here."

"I did not."

"Yes, you did. On the steps at the Carlisle in Palm Beach, I overheard you ranting about that giant staircase reminding you of this great pyramid, so naturally, I wanted to bring you here."

"My reference to Giza was the height of that stone staircase, which was ridiculously high. As you know, I am terrified of heights. Which should make you wonder why I would want to sit up here?"

"Oh, but Bella. We are here now. So, let us enjoy our visit and our time together. If you like, we could visit The Sphinx. Last, I remember, you like cats, right?"

"I love cats, but I'm more concerned about how we're getting down from here as I don't want to travel the way you always do, and..."

"Goodness, Bella. How can you say that?" He moaned. His eyes squinting in the bright sunlight. "Why, I watched you sprinting down that huge staircase at The Carlisle with as much gusto as an Olympian Athlete." He paused, chewed his inner cheek, and sighed. "You do remember Bruce Jenner. Don't you?"

I nodded. "Yes. He is the father of Kylie and Kendall Jenner."

"Who?"

"Never mind," I shrugged.

"Well, Bella. He may be their dad, but just so you know, before becoming a father, Bruce Jenner was a world champion track star who broke the world record in decathlon. But had you been in that Olympic race, you may have won because I watched you run down Carlisle's steps two at a time and the speed of sound. So, please do not pretend to be fragile like a lamb or an easily faint-hearted woman because I know you better than that."

"He's now their mother. Bruce Jenner is no Caitlyn, and she kicked Bruce to the curb years ago. And just so you know, I ran down those stairs that fast because I could not face you or admit my reason for being at the ball," I argued, determined to solidify my defense.

"Whatever," he said. He raised his brows, gazed across the desert, eyed the pyramid from top to bottom, and shook his head. "Surely you're not suggesting we descend this pyramid one stone at a time?"

I scratched my head and wondered. "It was a thought, Ben, just a thought."

"But I was to jump off the highest peak and soar like an eagle hunting its prey on the ground below."

"You fly down, Ben. I am taking the easy way, and if that means clambering down the side of this pyramid, one stone at a time, then that's what I shall do."

Ben folded his arms and sat. "I know why you want to descend slowly," he smiled, a knowing look across his face. I shrugged. "You want to listen to Songbirds singing as they fly inside."

I rolled my eyes and laughed. "Why not?" I rose and moved closer to his body. "Ben," I soothed. "The birds who fly inside sing, and their chirps signal sexual intentions to potential mates. Imagine how romantic that will sound as we listen to their calls to the heart."

"Bella Bloom, are you insinuating that we shall, like the Songbirds, solidify our relationship?"

My smile widened, and I breathed more profoundly than ever as my heartbeat pounded. "Benjamin Barrymore, as if I would ever suggest something as provocative as us consummating our friendship. However, I would like to drink a cup of water and walk with you inside the stone masses along the passageways leading to the burial chambers underneath each pyramid. Can we do that?"

Ben swooped down to where I sat, wrapped his arms around me, and hoisted me. "I'm all for making you happy. We can do whatever you want if we fool around while admiring this architecture."

Suddenly, breathless again, I closed my eyes and felt myself falling. Although, according to Ben, we were flying. It still felt too fast a drop for flight, and I stiffened until we touched the ground. Once my feet landed on solid ground, I punched him jokingly in his stomach and watched as he pretended to keel over in pain. "I have no sympathy for you, Benny Boy," I said, walking away to search for an entrance. I remember when officials discovered a long corridor above the main hall. They had found the passage behind a chevron-shaped stone structure and explored it using an endoscope. Its purpose is unknown, but officials believed its function was to redistribute the pyramid's weight. However, regardless of reasons or mythical fantasies, I wanted to explore the depth of this pyramid's size, and fearing nothing, I strolled, stepped aside from the stone structure, and walked inside.

"Hey! Wait for me," Ben called. I ignored his bickering and continued my journey. Then, feeling his hand grasping my arm, I felt him pull me backward. "You cannot go wandering off, Bella. Not here, not anywhere, and certainly not without me. Do you understand?"

"Ben, I simply want to look," I explained. "Besides, you promised not to take me with you when we jumped off this structure, yet you forced me to fly with you." Noticing the concern on his face, I stopped speaking. "What now?" I asked in exasperation.

He softened. "I was worried about you, that's all. I don't want you to get lost, so please don't disappear."

My eyes closed, and I groaned. "Surely you're not worried a ghost may kidnap me," I said jokingly. Then, seeing the torment on his face, I latched onto his hand and convinced him to follow.

Walking along the newly discovered corridor, I sniffled and listened as Benny Boy sneezed. The old ruins emitted a distasteful limestone scent into our lungs. "It stinks in here," I complained. "And my eyes are burning," I added, ducking to avoid fallen rocks that were becoming dislodged from the ceiling.

"This place creeps me out," Ben complained, stopping suddenly to signal he had no desire to walk deeper into the darkness. "There are bodies buried here and many unnamed people who will remain anonymous. I find it blasphemous. Let's leave."

My dry throat caused me to cough, and I craved an icy cold drink in my mind. However, still troubled to see the distant light flashing in my peripheral vision, I became confused, and despite my temptation, I ignored the light. Determined to search for lost treasures, I trudged deeper into the pyramid; I also ignored Ben's concerns about disturbing the dead spirits, as I had my mind set on finding gold.

At the end of the corridor, I spotted Ben and watched as he tucked in his shirt, adjusted his belt, and kicked clay off his shoes. "How'd you get here so fast?" I asked, surprised yet not interested in how, why, or when. He shuffled across the way. "Bella!" he yelled. "We need to leave this place now."

I stopped walking and looked at him. I saw his face aggravated, and his stance was argumentative. So, to stifle his sudden moodiness, I grasped his hand and dragged him back outdoors. "Okay," I snapped once, standing in the hot sunshine. "What's going on? And why are you so troubled?" I looked at my watch, checked the time, and stood with my hands resting on my hips, ready to fight. Not waiting for him to reply, I continued to question his concerns. "Not long ago, Ben, you were nagging me to be adventurous and begging me to have fun while we're here. Yet, when I decided to enjoy our visit, you became madder than hell, which is unfair, considering I jumped off the top of the pyramid to appease you. So, I will ask again: what is bothering you?"

Suddenly, Ben's hand covered my mouth, and before I could argue or fight, he wrapped a scarf around my neck and secured it over my nose and lips. "What the..." I muttered, frantically struggling to catch my breath. Then, Ben swung me around to face the impending disaster. The approaching sandstorm was thick and heavy, which was tolerable when standing high atop the pyramid. But on the ground, it was heavier and thicker in density, and the coarse granules of stones scratched at my eyes. I rubbed my eyes to focus on my whereabouts and fought to see where Ben was, which was impossible, considering I could not see past two feet in front of my face. The thick, swirling brown clouds of dust and sand stretched for miles, making breathing harder than ever as the storm played havoc on my respiratory system. As the wind speed increased, sand particles vibrated and then dislodged, engulfing me with so much dust that I feared my throat would dry. I panicked. My hands flew out wildly as I reached for Ben, who was not nearby. With the storm's fury, I started spinning across the desert, rolling along in the wind with tumbleweed that had broken away from their roots, scattering seeds as they did, leaving me sightless from all the debris. The dust became unbearable, and I began coughing so hard that I thought my eyes might pop out of my head. It was then that I sensed I was falling, and just like earlier, I panicked and started asking for guidance from the gods watching over me before I fell unconscious.

I woke next to Ben, sleeping with the wind against his back and an arm holding onto his scarf. The massive sandstorm was fading, and light streams filtered through the lingering dust particles rolling over his naked chest. I smiled.

My fingers were mere inches from his stomach, and I wondered if I should wake him. A gash on his forehead looked painful, and the dry blood and sand would be hell to clean, as would the other one across his neck, which looked slightly more profound than the first cut. I dabbed my finger in saliva to touch it, and his body stiffened. Thinking that Ben was as fragile as a lamb, something I had never noticed until now, I left him to sleep despite wanting to nurse his wounds.

The light was shining from afar again, and I froze. I did not know what it was trying to say, whether it was some kind of Morse code or simply someone lost in the desert desperate to call for help. While tempted to stay with Ben, I was also intrigued to walk to the light, even if Ben had told me not to. Seriously, how dangerous could a light flickering from afar be?

I pondered that very question for what seemed like eons, at least until I could no longer bear to focus, and despite Benny Boy's instructions, I chose to behave in my usual stubborn, pigheaded way and ignore his orders.

Besides, as much as I trusted his judgment, I could not help but become captivated, almost spellbound, with a deep desire to investigate. So, throwing caution to the wind, I rose from the ground, and though huffing and puffing, I decided to walk the distance and see what that light's purpose was. The air was clearing, and my breathing had calmed down, so I removed the face scarf Ben had insisted I wear, let it drop to the sand beneath my feet, and continued my stroll across a dune.

I hesitated in front of the brightest light I had ever seen. A sense of calm engulfed me and eased all my anxieties, even the phobias I had suffered from since childhood. Feeling euphoric, I walked toward the light, hands tucked into my jeans' pockets. Around the light, I noticed the dust had settled, and though cautious, I sensed I was moving towards peacefulness. I looked at the sky, pointed at a fresh clump of clouds, and smiled. Then, I stepped forward, full of hope and relief. A positive outlook enveloped my being, and despite all the trauma I had experienced, somehow, I found clarity and love. But more than that, I felt as if I could move forward and not only leave the past behind but also negativity, which was something I yearned to do.

I grew confused between my thoughts, dreams, and reality at that moment. However, I knew that the answers to all my questions were within the light. Just like I knew I needed to accept that the light would give me growth in holiness and maturity in faith, I also knew both gifts would enable me to follow Jesus. And right now, I wanted the protection that Jesus offered. I also wanted eternal life and fellowship with others, but more than anything, I wanted to heal my relationship with God. I could only get that by entering the light. Yet, my fear crippled me as thoughts of Ben willed my mind not to go.

I sighed, torn between light and darkness, with darkness standing for confusion and deception, while light is God's way to joyfulness, and I paused.

Yes, I wanted to live according to God's truth and the life that he gives, but at this moment, I was not ready to give myself to all things good. Somehow, my mind was holding me back, cautioning me against entering the pathway set forth by the spiritual world, and in worry, I turned away from its brightness and returned to Ben's side.

For as long as I can remember, Ben has been sensible. He achieved everything I had hoped to do, such as attending university, getting a high-paying job, and never worrying about what others would think. Ben was never without a backup or a plan, which he told me he had learned from professors at school. All the clever things he did drove me insane. Still, I loved him more than anything else, and as much as I wanted to venture into that lighted pathway, I was not living without Benny Boy.

I was sitting on the edge of a rock when he awoke. My knees bent, ankles crossed, staring at his toned body, even more reason he was causing my anxiety to soar. "You went to the light, didn't you?" Ben's eyes opened as he spoke. I folded my arms and rested my chin on my hands, eyeing him with desire. Then, lazily, I admired his flat stomach and how his muscles strengthened when he stretched to rise to his feet. "Come closer to me," he sighed, reaching out and coaxing me to join. Now, this was one order I was not going to disobey. I jumped and let him pull me close to his hardness, his intoxicating smell, and his luscious lips that began to tease my neck. "I need you," I muttered, enjoying the magic of his kisses moving downward to my breasts. "Please don't stop."

"What was it like?" he asked, his body stiffening as I wrapped my arms around his neck. I ignored his question, preferring to tug at the collar of his sports shirt and sink my fingers deeper down his back. I focused on nothing but the softness of his skin, the smell of his hair, and the roundness of his buttocks. It was not until he shoved me away and walked toward the light that I remembered his question. "It was like nothing I have experienced in a while, Ben. And I know you are upset because I went to the light, and do you know what? It was incredible, beautiful, like something in a fairytale," I admitted, sad that at that moment, he did not want to take our romance more seriously, at least to a more intimate place. But he was furious. And I understood his moods and respected his decision, even if his distancing himself was making me crazy with hunger, lust, and desire.

Suddenly, my emotions felt as vulnerable as the day I was born, and not in a safe way and for no good reason, which frustrated me. Why had I offered my body to Ben in such a sensual manner, only for him to rebuff me?

The rejection hurt my fragile ego and made me feel like a love-hungry brat, desperate for attention, which I was not. I had initially thought we were on the same side in our quest for peace, love, and harmony, but now I realized we were not. If I did as Ben instructed, he would be comfortable, but the minute I wandered off to do something that made him cringe, it was as if all bets were off in our friendship, or so it seemed to me. However, watching Ben begin to walk toward the light, glancing back only to smile, I began to doubt his commitment to me, which caused me anxiety, not forgetting an uneasiness I had not experienced since the end of our earlier life together.

As I told you in Livelihood, Ben was Jake Thatcher in that incarnation, and I, Sally Peters, a teenager working part-time as a server at Lilly's Diner during school break.

Even then, I had always felt Ben's love, especially when he became angry at my determination to do things my way. But that was long ago, and right before anyone knew, a madman's interest in stalking me. The crazy man eventually hunted, murdered, and dumped my body far from town so that nobody would discover my remains. Still, it was not my fault that a lunatic had taken me hostage, and nowadays, it frustrates me that Ben still held me accountable for that psychotic man's fanciful whims.

After Ben left, I took a minute to cool off and calm down. The best thing I remember was we still existed on this windy Sunday night, and I was sure it might be midnight, the witching hour, or at least that is what I told myself to try to fathom Ben's sudden desire to distance himself from me. Thinking about witches and the evil they cast upon people who do not believe them made me skittish, and I rushed to his side without thinking of anything but the safety of Ben's arms.

Sitting in front of the pathway to Heaven, I felt my nails digging into the palms of my hands, not because of my fury but because Ben had chosen to investigate the gateway to God without me since it was unusual for him to leave me alone in a place where his watchful eye could not protect me from all that was evil.

My gut told me he wanted to leave our partnership, but something held him back. I pondered the notion that giving up what we have built was difficult for Ben. The time and energy we invested in each other was long and arduous. But indeed, he was wise enough to know that staying in a partnership that was not working out would be complete and utter madness. I decided to give him time to work out if our togetherness was worth fighting for or if he believed we had, as one, run our course. Moving away from the light, I thought it was best to give him space to clear his head about what he wanted to do, particularly with me. However, I hated myself for being weak and for allowing him to feel that he was the only one who may be unfulfilled.

It could be that I was, too.

What if I was not as obvious to read as Ben often teased, and what if I was in limbo and stuck between two critical decisions, just like him? It gave me something to think about. Nevertheless, believing my theory was complete and utter rubbish, I calmed my anxieties. Still, leaving the security of what we have both built filled me with fear, primarily because we are both scared of change and losing something that has brought us comfort.

Rattled, I stomped my foot. There was no chance Ben wanted out. None whatsoever. I was just being foolish. I cursed myself with such harshness that I suddenly felt faint, and the worry of existing without Benny Boy made my blood boil, as there was no way I could survive. Realizing I needed to fix the problem before it escalated beyond my control, I put my big girl boots on and swiftly returned to Ben with an urgent need to recapture what I feared we had lost. I ran my fingers seductively through his sandy brown hair, ruffling longer layers behind his ears as I admired and complimented his new cut. Then, I grabbed his arms and placed them around my waist to rekindle our bond. "I need you," I murmured, kissing his neck, cheeks, and lips lightly.

Ben looked at me, puzzled. "As much as I enjoy what you're doing, we have unfinished business to tend to," he said. Then he looked away, embarrassed that he would ruin our magical moment.

"No problem," I said, feeling more embarrassed than he looked. "What is it that you need to do?"

"We need to do it together. Do you not remember that we promised to quell all questions about life after death?"

I frowned. "I'm completely lost."

"But it was your idea, and you agreed. How could you forget?"

"I don't know," I said. "But can you give me a hint to help me remember?"

Ben was marching toward a lone tree in the distance. His footprints led the way across the sand, and I trailed haphazardly behind, wondering what I had done wrong this time. He stopped aside a fallen branch, focused on the emptiness around, and inhaled deeply. "Come closer," he demanded. He turned to face tumbleweed, and then his eyes emptied as if he were suddenly soulless.

"I'm confused..." And then I stopped. Seeing Beatrice and Emily in distress broke my heart; my stomach churned from their obvious pain, and saddened, I began to cry.

The sight of Beatrice clutching Emily as they wept together on the same sofa where Ben and I had sat together created emotional distress to surge through my body and shaken, I stiffened in fright. "Oh God, no," I sobbed. "I had completely forgotten my promise." I grabbed Ben's shirt, and, sliding down his tall frame, I dropped to the ground.

"Ready," he asked.

"Ready," I answered.

I reached for his hand, but he did not respond. Instead, he strolled by my side, his arm occasionally brushing against mine. And though I wanted to cling to him and feel the magic we had shared moments ago; I stayed mute as we walked into a gigantic beam that filled me with nothing but remorse. Then, the overwhelming smell of salt filled my nostrils, and I sneezed successively. I did not stop sniffling until we were standing in Beatrice's home. Along the hallway, I could see her sobbing with so much pain and anguish that Emily appeared at a loss as to what to do. I wanted to rush to her to offer comfort, but Ben promptly stopped me.

"We have to wait for a sign," he said cautiously.

I raised my brow. "Then why are you whispering?" I asked, bewildered. "Indeed, if we are here, can we make ourselves known?"

I gnawed at my lower lip. He chewed his inner cheek. We were both deep in thought. "It does not work that way, Bella. We must wait for..." he said before his voice trailed.

"Wait for what? A hall pass?" I jeered, more annoyed than ever. I adored Beatrice and would have rushed to her side by myself.

"If we don't wait, she will never be able to see, hear, or even know we're here."

"Why ever not?"

"Because we are dead, that's why."

I inhaled deeply, and feeling my throat dry up, I winced. I coughed heavily before Ben patted my back to help ease up my swollen chest.

The seconds ticked by at a snail's pace, and just as I had resigned myself to comforting Beatrice with or without authority, Ben finally told me we could make our presence known. Without waiting for him to speak, I unhooked his arm around my waist and fled from the hallway where we both had stood.

I moved swiftly into the middle of the room, Ben following close behind, and we both stopped side by side under a brass chandelier lit with clandestine bulbs that flickered above our heads.

In union, we recited a verse from Matthew 5:4 in hopes it would soften our hearts and bring solace to our friend, who appeared bestowed with grief that we had left her behind in torment and pain without so much as a farewell from neither Ben nor myself.

We had no other choice, as our departure was not conducive to Ben's or my desires. Unfortunately for our friends, a higher-up had requested us to return to our Father's spiritual home in heaven, and whether we wanted to go, or stay was not a decision we could make. In my resume, I thought about my friends, and while my family was in God's home, I knew I would miss the people I met while living as Bella Bloom. And as much as FBI Agent CJ Clarke had annoyed me, I will always remember her with fondness, though I wondered what she would think and feel once she received the news of my death. Despite my bitterness toward her falsehood, I had forgiven her misgivings and wished her an extended life filled with love and happiness. Our holy Father arrived in spirit and entrusted us with a passage from his royal order through his grace and power.

Blessed are they that mourn, for they shall be comforted...
Mathew 5:4

Holding hands, Ben and I stood vehemently, grateful for our contact with the other world as our voices repeatedly spoke to our Father in Heaven's heartfelt verse. We continued our sermon until I could stand the silence no more, and though wrong, I ignored Ben and rushed to hold Beatrice in my arms. In my haste, I tripped and fell to the floor. Still undeterred, I crawled toward the blue couch with a bright yellow sunflower pattern and kneeled beside my dear friend. Eager to make my spiritual being known, I caressed and gently rubbed her shaking legs. Then, I let my hands move upwards, and I did not stop until they rested upon her frail shoulders, which shook in sorrow.

The light in the room shimmered, and as Ben quickly joined me, we unitedly sat down next to the darling mature woman and prayed. Together, we spoke words of comfort in the hope that our presence would ease her pain. Suddenly, I noticed the mature woman looking toward my face in our prayer. Though she had yet to acknowledge my presence, she beamed a million smiles, and at that moment, she no longer cried.

"The hand of the Lord is upon you. God has approved of you. Know that we are using you to achieve God's purpose for your life. Praying together can help unite believers, as Jesus prayed for in John 17:22–23. Let us pray to ease your troubled soul and bring you peace." I said in a voice I almost did not recognize because my confidence was never as profound as in that moment.

I felt Ben's arm touch my shoulder, and instantly, we were walking backward, away from Beatrice. While my eyes were still watching, the pain I experienced through her was fading into darkness until only light remained. In that light, I stood, caring, concerned, and hopeful that now Beatrice had felt our presence, she may begin to heal. In my heart, I prayed she might rest peacefully, knowing that both Ben and I stayed committed to our earlier promise of visiting those we had left behind. The image of her weeping was fading fast, replaced by a look of hope upon her tear-stained face, and seeing her appear stronger than before brought comfort to my tethered soul.

Standing alongside Ben, I felt his hand grasp my own, and he squeezed it tightly. "Now we can go," he told me calmly, leading me into a brilliant beam of light that blinded my vision. As we stood together, I glanced at his face as his eyes caressed my being, and I found my answers in the blue hues of his eyes. The love we shared in its purest form brought me joy as we both faded away and though I did not know where we would go, if I am with Ben, I did not care, for I was safe in the arms of the man I love, a man who also loved me and always would.

The Eyes of the Lord were upon us when suddenly we transferred to another place, and in that place, we became unified, perfectly molded back to our earlier selves, filled with innocence. "So, what now?" I asked, slightly weary of all the rays that had cleaned my soul. I spied on Ben, adjusting his shirt; a slight smile crossed his lips before he kissed my cheek. "Well," he said affectionately. "We have time left for one more adventure. So, where do you want to go next?"

I tapped my heels together and flapped my arms. "To the sky, Ben. Take me to the sky. I want to dance on Mount Kilimanjaro and slide down the most significant ski slope possible. I grinned and playfully tried to strike a sporty pose.

He wowed me with a huge grin and laughed. "But you detest the cold," he teased. "And you always have. You complain you are cold even on the chilliest days in Miami, which are not that often. Yet, here you stand, announcing that you want to visit one of the coldest places on earth. I am so confused," he said jokingly.

I shrugged. "I don't know," I lied. "Though I'm not fond of frigid climates, the cold does not dishearten me or my moods, and I doubt it ever will."

"Bella Bloom, I do believe you're telling tales again."

"Think what you may, but I want to go."

"But..."

"No buts, Ben. Let's go."

I glided upward and hovered above, not knowing how to get there, as Benny Boy usually led our adventures. Mainly because he had a keener sense of direction than I did, and I often and lazily relied on his guidance.

"To the mountains in Tanzania and back," Ben teased, raising both arms as he flew by at unprecedented speed.

"Wait for me," I called and soared toward the sky.

Suddenly, I shivered. I shoved my arm around Ben's waist and huddled against his shoulder, welcoming the warmth his body omitted. "It's a beautiful view," I sighed lustfully. "Look at all that snow. Isn't this view magical? I forgot how it feels inside when in the company of such beauty."

We sat silently at the top of a large crater, flattened after a volcano erupted and the peak collapsed and admired Africa's tallest peak, the tallest free-standing mountain in the world. The wondrous snow-capped volcano was a popular hiking spot. Though the climb was dangerous, altitude sickness was worse. Fortunately, neither concern applied to us, and we basked in the ambiance of all its splendor. Embossed on the Tanzanian landscape, we marveled at the glittering beacon of African beauty.

Intelligently, Ben spoke first. "When explorers first reported seeing glaciers, people didn't believe them, as they thought it impossible for ice to form near the equatorial sun."

I shook my head and moved closer. "You're freezing," he said, rubbing my shivering body. "Well," I sighed. "I hate to admit it, but you were right when you told me earlier that I would freeze to death atop this peak."

He unbuttoned his shirt and partially covered my chilly arms. "The sun will rise shortly, and you will forget about being cold when you see dawn. However, I don't want you to suddenly forget to cuddle with me." Then, his arms pulled me even closer to his warm body. Snuggling against the softness of his skin, I swallowed hard and exhaled. "I would never cuddle with anyone but you," I said confidently. "You were right in presumption that I'd be cold here because I am freezing to death."

"You're not telling another of your magnificent stories, are you?"

I rolled my eyes and frowned. "Don't be a smartass, Ben," I moaned. "I lied when I said I wouldn't be cold, but that was because I wanted to come here more than anywhere else. I have had an affinity for these peaks since childhood, and the fascination has only strengthened. So, if I had to lie to get us here? I'm sorry." I explained, kissing his cheek.

"It's okay, my darling."

"Good. Now, let's enjoy this view."

Ben's elbow nudged my back, and my eyes followed the length of his finger, pointing to the sky. Overwhelmed by immense beauty, we sat in awe as we watched the sun rise above the horizon, and we cuddled, mesmerized by the beauty of this succulent morning. Then, we felt the cold that penetrated every inch of our bodies disappear as the sun's warmth climbed high into the sky.

The bright, yellow rays illuminated the crater, making the icy glaciers shimmer like fairy lights atop a tree in the dead of winter. "Wow!" I gasped, enthralled by all the beauty bestowed before my eyes. "Try as I might, I cannot find one word to describe the gloriousness this brutal landscape holds."

"Me neither, Bella. Though happy to be here, I am cold, just as you are. However, visiting Africa is a dream come true. Who cares if it is freezing? This view alone is worth all the chattering our teeth are making. Besides, the harsh climate is not a dealbreaker, particularly when sitting next to someone as beautiful as you."

My heart soared, and I almost cried as I listened to his revelation. I pondered what to say to assure him I felt the same way, but as I struggled to think of comforting words, my chance to express myself passed as Ben began to speak again. "Listen, Bella. The scenery is incredible, and I am happy to admire the pink hue of the sky as it turns the ground into a million different colored crystals. However, I am tired," he said earnestly. "But... And trust me, Bella, this is a big but...," he yawned. "Despite my tiredness, I am thrilled to be a part of your world, and sitting here with you makes my empty life a million times better." He paused momentarily, and I focused on the seriousness of his words: "I love you, Bella. I truly do."

I held his hand and kissed his cheek again. "I love you too, Ben. Honest, I do," I said with sincere conviction just as the sun disappeared behind the blackened sky. We sat watching Thunderheads building to the north and the east and prepared ourselves for a heavenly cleanse. When the season's first monsoon came pouring down, we scrambled for cover, even though we were soaking wet. We cried in pain as the chilly air and large chunks of hail stung our bodies while the wind blew against our skin. Still, we did not let the arduous weather disrupt our need to satisfy a lustful hunger that pummeled our longing to a feverish pitch. In silence, at Africa's magnificent summit, we explored and caressed each other's bodies, and we did not stop until we reached eternity.

Ben grabbed my arm and stared into my eyes. "Promise me, you'll find me the next time we come here," he said. I rubbed his back and smiled. "Always," I replied, pinching his buttocks to make him smile. Then we smiled together.

A part of me wanted to see whether I could become aroused again, Whether I could see the lust in his eyes once more, to be sure that it was real.

I knew Ben would say it was silly to doubt his love, but I had to be sure. As our hands intertwined, I leaned forward and kissed him long and hard.

Now, I am not one to fret, but for one obscure reason, my uncertainty escalated, causing my hungry stomach to roar louder than a savage lion in the African Plains. And amused, we burst into laughter.

Suddenly aware, our boisterous chuckles echoed throughout the halls of heaven, alerting all spirits that we were home; we covered our mouths and flushed with color.

Still, I am hopeful to kiss just one more time…

Until we meet again...

Be kind, believe, and be good.
Have faith, always.
Love and blessings,
Bella
XOXO

My Thanks To...

GOD
My Father who art in Heaven, without YOU
I would not be able to do any of this.
I am forever your servant!
YOU
I hope you enjoy reading this book,
as much as I enjoyed writing it.
YOU ROCK!
GOOGLE
You recognize my search queries on days when my mind
works faster than my finger's ability to type,
And for that...I love YOU!
TOOLS
Wikipedia, National Geographic, Discovery Channel
Smithsonian Institution, MS WORD, Amazon Publishing.
You make my life so much easier!
Stay Cool
☺ ☺ ☺

Keep reading for sneak peek at
NO NIGHT SO LONG
The next exciting novel by Sam Smith

NO NIGHT SO LONG
SAM SMITH

Preface

LIFE IN A NEW TOWN was exhilarating for Kelly Evans, as was driving her new car. The air smelled fresh, and the automobile's interior intoxicated her senses. But better than both, was her newfound freedom and the number of cute boys she had seen this semester at school in Gainesville, Florida.

At age nineteen, this was Kelly's first year in university, her first year away from home, and her first year living as an adult.

Growing up in Miami, the heat and humidity were stifling. The calm blue skies changed hourly from tranquil and serene to cloudy and grey, making the weather potentially dangerous to boaters and outdoor thrill seekers.

The temperature in Gainesville felt brisk and invigorating to Kelly, who welcomed the change. The open sky was perfect for viewing space, especially Venus, the planet of love, and stars like Sirius, the closest star to Earth after the sun.

Kelly spent endless nights passionately photographing Sirius, the rainbow star that flickered with colors. She was an avid stargazer who spent her spare time fixated on the constellation Orion, and thanks to Grandma Evans, she had a professional telescope to fulfill her hobby.

Late last night, twinkling stars filled the atmosphere, and a full moon made the world so bright that Kelly excitedly swore to roommate and best friend Stevie Fox that she could see for miles while peering over the fence in the densely lit garden surrounding their rental home.

Still sleepy, she rolled out of bed early in the morning and reluctantly studied for a university exam later that week. After two or three cups of coffee, at ten o'clock, she showered, dressed, and chose to explore Gainesville, especially the parks and recreational areas that interested her the most.

Following a visit to Paynes Prairie State Park in the nearby town of Micanopy, Kelly floored the gas pedal on the blue convertible and raced along bustling city streets. She sped through mounds of fallen leaves in shades of red, amber, and brown, thrilled as they blew over the windshield.

Thinking about the park's large wetland, scattered shrubs, and pines where wild horses and bison roam the prairie, she was excited to see new species of birds and plants. She also looked forward to seeing stars and planets and hoped to see rocket launches on a clear night.

Driving along, listening to the radio, a lonesome man sang country music, and though she had never heard the song before, Kelly quickly learned the lyrics and sang along to a tune about whisky and women.

At noon, she drove along Newberry Road, passing stores and restaurants like a supersonic jet in flight, and just when she felt she could fly, she saw something that would alter her destiny forever.

It was ironic that on that Wednesday afternoon, fate would present itself, neatly wrapped in a vibrant red bow, a gift she could not refuse even if she had wanted to.

Kelly was born on a Wednesday, her parents died on a Wednesday, and it was a Wednesday when she spotted a disheveled man sitting with a dog by the side of the road.

Stopped at a red light on a busy intersection, she watched them feast on hamburgers from a nearby restaurant, and after spotting a pet store, she decided to help the man by gifting his dog a bag of nutritious kibble.

Quickly, she counted twenty dollars in cash, more than enough for food and any leftover change she would give the man. If he bought beer? So be it; she was nobody to judge.

Kelly drove into a parking spot, turned off the car engine, and exited the vehicle. On her way to the animal supply store, she greeted the older man, complimented his dog, and asked him not to leave because she was buying dog food.

Incredulously, he objected, arguing that he did not need charity. Still, Kelly stubbornly ignored his wishes and repeated her intention while caressing the dog's head.

The man then smiled, revealing perfect white teeth.

He dressed in casual clothes and looked well-groomed with a handsome face and twinkling eyes. He was tall, six three, six four, with brownish blonde hair, deep green eyes, and a dark suntan accentuating a weathered face and white bushy brows.

Kelly noticed his manicured hands. She thought about how nicely he dressed for a homeless person, mainly because she had not seen a street urchin in designer clothes, and that left her wondering if he had stolen his entire attire.

Kelly smiled back, feeling the small dog's wet nose against her leg, then looking at the fawn and white female, she spoke softly while gently stroking a hand across her glossy coat.

"Robert Vaughn." The man said, extending a hand to signal a truce.

Startled, Kelly accepted and shook hands. "Kelly, Kelly Evans," she said, sitting on the sidewalk. "I'm still buying your dog some food, but don't worry, I won't saddle you with a humongous bag. I will buy a smaller size and attach a couple of gift cards so you can buy more supplies. What's your pup's name?"

"Her name is Bella, and despite knowing plenty of people, she is my only friend. I rescued her five years ago, or perhaps it is correct to say she rescued me. Either way, Bella has been my favorite companion ever since."

"She certainly is a beautiful female. She seems to like her ears rubbed, and I think she likes me too."

"I believe Bella likes you," he said. "Take it as a compliment because Bella doesn't ordinarily take to new folk, especially when stubborn young ladies like yourself start telling me what to do."

Kelly gritted her teeth and swallowed hard. She began to object but chose not to. Robert spoke correctly in seeing her stubbornness. It was a trait she inherited from her father, who, according to her mother, was a willful soul, determined to stand up for his beliefs, even if wrong.

For a moment, Kelly felt dispirited, remembering her parents, but quickly cheered when Bella plopped down on her feet.

She spied the older man, grinning as Bella nuzzled her ankles. The sweet pup yearned for more caresses, particularly belly rubs, and Kelly obliged with soothing words and soft scratches on the dog's pink stomach.

Robert Vaughn smiled again and rolled his eyes with amusement, not taking his attention away from Bella. "She enjoys stomach rubs, but her favorite pastime is begging for food." He spoke softly.

Kelly nodded, and then asked. "Do you think she's still hungry? I saw her eat a burger, but maybe she wants more food." She glanced at her watch. "I should go inside the pet shop and get the dog's food now; in case they close for lunch."

She stopped petting Bella, rose to her feet, and politely glared at Robert, silently instructing him not to argue.

Robert waited for a minute and then spoke quietly. "I'm so sorry. I drifted off for a moment." He was about to say more, but suddenly, his tanned face paled, and he fell unconscious at Kelly's feet.

Alarmed, Kelly descended beside Robert and shook him hard, but he did not wake; he lay on the ground as passing cars sped by, none stopping to help.

At that moment, Kelly grabbed the leash attached to Bella's collar and coaxed the scared dog into her vehicle while dialing emergency services and pleading for help, citing an older man had collapsed.

Five minutes later, two police cars and one ambulance stopped next to Kelly, who was performing CPR.

Seven minutes after his fall, a medic strapped Robert Vaughn onto a gurney and whisked toward the nearest hospital. Kelly followed behind, driving at the speed of sound to keep up with the speeding ambulance.

Twelve minutes onward, she found Robert Vaughn in one of the better rooms at the private hospital. He lay sleeping on a bed, and his arm strapped to machines as a doctor and nurse swiftly checked his progress.

It was the fastest rescue she had ever seen.

Satisfied her new friend was in capable hands and would survive, Kelly drummed her long fingers on the arm of a chair outside the room where Robert Vaughn lay and debated her next move.

She needed to tend to Bella; she had locked the frightened dog in her car, and though the engine was running, Kelly feared it might turn off after a certain amount of time.

She also needed to call Grandma Ella and ask her to come to Gainesville because as much as she felt mature enough to oversee most things life threw her way; this incident was out of her league.

She clutched her cell phone, quickly dialed her grandmother's phone number, then explained the horrible situation and asked that she please come to Gainesville.

"Don't worry, Kelly, I'm heading there shortly. In the meantime, I will ask my friend Beverly Simon in Ocala to help you. I'll also contact the doctor in charge, and we'll meet up later today."

Kelly thanked her grandmother and ended the call.

Then she explained to a nurse that Robert's dog, Bella, was in her custody and wrote her phone number on a pad. She also informed the nurse that she would be back later that afternoon.

Leaving the hospital, she received a phone call from Ella's friend Beverly, and she asked Beverly if she could help her find Robert a bed at the local homeless shelter, explaining that once discharged, the streets were no place for a sick man.

She stood on the steps outside the hospital for one or two minutes, warmed up in the early afternoon sun, and then strode to her car.

She had parked far away to avoid gawkers, the meddling souls who would assume she neglectfully left Bella in a hot car.

Kelly did not own a pet and had not grown up with animals, but she had read enough news alerts about forgotten pets in vehicles and later dying. Though people smashed windows to rescue animals, she hoped if someone spotted Bella, they would at least notice the car engine was running.

When she reached her parking space, she glanced across the pathway at a hotdog stand, and while greeting Bella, she teased how lovely a juicy hamburger would taste right now.

Searching inside the console of her car, she rifled through documents for her credit card as Bella licked her face and scratched her arms.

"Do you want to walk with me and breathe fresh air?" She asked the excited pup. The pretty canine jumped from the passenger seat, landed on Kelly's lap, and slathered her face with appreciative kisses.

Kelly quickly attached the dog's leash, checked it was secure, and then they exited the vehicle and strolled toward the mobile food stand, both hungry.

She ordered two hamburgers, one with cheese and one without. Then, she walked Bella onto a small field of grass surrounded by flowering plants and oak trees. In the center was a fountain, and she watched as the dog drank, noting that she, too, was thirsty.

"I am buying soda for me, but I will buy bottled water for you because you cannot drink soda," she said teasingly, looking while the canine gulped mouthfuls of water, still chilly from the early morning freeze.

An ambulance passed with lights flashing and sirens wailing, pulling to a stop in front of the emergency room entrance.

Troubled, Kelly watched two men pull out a gurney with an older woman lying atop. As they pushed the gurney through sliding doors, she wondered how it felt to arrive at a hospital in such a life-threatening and critical condition. That worry made her think about Robert Vaughn and whether he had been lucid enough to feel scared when wheeled through the hospital doors. Though she knew little about the man, she surmised he would be more concerned about his dog, Bella, than himself.

Kelly noticed the hot dog vendor waving, then tugged at Bella's leash. "Our food is ready," she announced, gently pulling the extendable leash to signal the dog to follow.

Walking back, she heard the frantic cries of a female passenger and stopped to let a distraught driver pass.

A few moments later, they sat in the warm midday sun and feasted on burgers and fries, and while watching Bella drink water from a disposable bowl, Kelly sipped her soda and smiled.

She glanced at her watch.

Knowing Gran would arrive shortly, she debated whether to stay at the hospital or take Bella to a park to enjoy a leisurely walk.

After eating, Kelly thanked the vendor, strolled across the road with Bella to a pet store, and bought much-needed supplies before leaving the hospital grounds.

Two miles away lay Forest Park. It was one of the largest urban parks in the Gainesville area at twenty-two acres, and the newly renovated park boasted basketball, volleyball, and pickleball courts. Kelly suspected Bella would happily wander over rolling hills and pathways, investigating all she saw and met.

She could meet other doggies in one of two fenced dog parks if she grew tired and play tug of war or fetch, a more leisurely pastime than climbing hills. Regardless of activity choice, restless Bella would certainly tire after a couple of hours spent running, walking, and playing.

At the park, people stopped and chatted with Kelly, and others offered pleasantries as they shuffled in and out of the gated dog park. Kelly thought the park was a safe place to meet new people, make friends, and share jokes and local gossip.

"Can you take our photo?" A couple asked.

Kelly shrugged and grimaced. Though she enjoyed photography and considered herself quite good, shooting people was much different than glancing at the cosmos through a telescope, but rather than say no, she took their cell phone and snapped a picture.

"Thank you." A girl with brown hair and ringlets gushed with a smile. The blonde male looked up from the photo and beamed at Kelly. "This is good, really good," he said excitedly. "Thank you so much. Look!" He showed the picture to his companion, and she gushed silly critiques such as she looked fat, her hair was a mess, and she was not smiling correctly.

"I can take another photo if you like?" Kelly interrupted.

"Please, do you mind?" The girl asked.

"Not at all. This time, before I click, I will count to one, two, three, and on the third count, I will snap a picture. That way, you'll know when to perfect your pose." She took the phone from the girl and directed her where to stand against the sun's rays. "One, two, three," she called and took a photo. She glanced at the screen before handing back the phone and smiled. "I think you'll like this picture better," she said and grinned when she saw the look of joy on the girl's face.

"Oh wow! Yes. Thank you so much. By the way, I'm Sarah, and that's Matt, my boyfriend."

"I'm Kelly." she said, waving to Matt and smiling at Sarah. "I think you look great, so don't worry so much about casual snapshots," Kelly told her before returning to the bench she had been sitting on.

She glanced at her watch again.

It was getting late.

Gran was arriving at five, and it was almost four now. Kelly excused herself to other pet owners, coaxed Bella away from their dogs, and swiftly returned to her car.

Her phone rang just as she began programming the address to the airport into the car's GPS.

It was Grandma Ella.

"Hi, Gran, you must be psychic. For, I was just thinking about you. Oh, so you know, I am setting my car's GPS to the airport's address, and once done, I will be on my way. Did the plane land yet?"

"Oh, honey." Gran began. "It was faster to fly into Orlando, so I did, and then Beverly met me, and we drove up. I will be there in fifteen minutes, tops. Are you still at the hospital?"

"I left because I took the man's dog to the park, but I'm only five minutes away and driving back to the hospital now."

"Dog?" Ella gasped.

"Yes, Gran. A dog. You heard me correctly. Robert Vaughn had his dog with him when he subsided. I could hardly leave her, so I have been babysitting. She's adorable, her name is Bella."

Ella Evans let out a soft sigh. "Kelly, you sound so grown up, and you've matured so much since being in Gainesville. I'm so proud of you for acting like a responsible adult, and I'm certain Mister Vaughn will be equally happy that you've taken his beloved pet into your hands and are taking such good care of her."

"You're a good girl, Kelly." Beverly Simon added. "Obviously, Ella has raised you well. And I am happy to hear that you know how important animals are to their owners.

I have three dogs myself, and if stricken with an illness, I'd worry more about them than myself, especially about their welfare."

"Let's hope you never find out." Blonde hair, blue-eyed Ella murmured. She pulled a floral scarf around her slender neck and glanced into the vanity mirror to apply fresh lipstick and face powder as Beverly drove the car into the hospital parking garage.

"I agree with Gran." Kelly cheered. "By the way, according to my GPS, I'm two minutes away."

"Good girl." Beverly and Ella said together. "We just arrived ourselves. We are entering the garage. We will meet you out front. See you soon." They chorused and ended the call.

"She's grown up so much.," Beverly said, turning the car around a corner in the garage. "She was just a kid when I saw her last."

"They do grow up fast these days," Ella told her. She smiled. Her granddaughter was now a young woman, and now more than ever, Ella realized Kelly needed someone to watch over her and protect her from every male with ulterior motives. In high school, Ella's daughter Sandra had fallen in love with Gerald, a fellow student with alluring charm and good looks. After three months of dating, Sandra became pregnant, and at fifteen, she gave birth to a baby girl named Kelly. Though Ella knuckled down and protected her daughter and newborn from the nosy neighbors who scorned the baby news, deep inside, it enraged her that Sandra fell prey to lust. Surprisingly to Ella, Sandra and Gerald remained loyal to each other, and once they graduated high school, they married, and both parents doted on Kelly until their dying day. The loss of Sandra at age twenty-five crippled Ella with fear, and she prayed every morning, pleading for hindsight as to what she had done to deserve such torment as the loss of a child. However, the answers never came, and Ella struggled daily with remorse and guilt, believing herself to blame.

So, throughout Kelly's high school years, Ella did whatever it took to ensure her granddaughter found other interests besides boys. She spared no expenses, keeping Kelly so busy that the teenage dating scene seemed dull.

For the past ten years, and mainly because Sandra was a shining example of a child having too much freedom, Ella realized that youth is too precious for a youngster to live with grownup responsibilities because those duties will come later in adulthood.

Ella fiddled with a ring on her middle finger that her daughter wore daily, and after noticing a green band on her skin, she pulled the ring off and put it in her pocketbook. The cheaply made jewelry had little monetary value; it was only sentimental and priceless to Ella.

She directed Beverly to a parking space next to the elevator. After her friend turned off the engine, Ella unfastened her seat belt, ascended the vehicle, adjusted a belted skirt, buttoned a checked Chanel jacket, and clutched a handbag by her side. 'Ready.' She announced and patiently waited for Beverly to finish any last-minute primping. "We're here, Kelly." She texted into her cell phone, then placed the gadget inside her handbag.

Petite Beverly Simon smoothed her sleek brown hairstyle behind her ears, applied a fresh coat of mascara above her deep brown eyes, and, like Ella, fluffed a shirt that had crumpled against her seatbelt. She stood and complimented Ella's outfit, in turn requesting approval for her own choice of clothing.

"Vanity has always been a problem for me," Beverly admitted and laughed. "Of course, you've known me long enough to know that." She said with a smile.

Ella offered a sly smile. "Getting older doesn't mean we have to get sloppy." She scoffed. "I'd rather be vain than not have pride in my appearance. Besides, we've always been meticulous in our attire, even as kids, but I think you were pickier than I ever was."

"I can't believe we're almost seventy." Beverly declared. "That makes our friendship forty years strong."

"Forty-eight," Ella corrected and smiled. "Can you believe we're that old? I cannot. I have difficulty remembering I am sixty-one as I still feel twenty. It is scary to think that Kelly will be twenty next year, and my darling Sandra would turn thirty-six had she survived that wretched car accident and lived. It makes me so sad that Kelly missed knowing her mother. It just makes my blood boil."

"I hate that you lost your daughter, Ella. It breaks my heart that you suffered such a loss, and I know you still feel the pain today. I am so sorry, I truly am."

"It's best if I don't think about it."

"I understand, but you know I'm always here for you whenever your thoughts stray. I'm sure it must be scary."

"It is damn scary, but having you and Caroline Carter as best friends, well, I couldn't be happier, as you both have helped me so much in life, especially in raising Kelly. Do you remember how useless I was when she came to live with me? Oh my, I was such a terrible custodian, and I had forgotten how to raise a child. If it had not been for you and Caroline, I would have made a mess of things. You have no idea how grateful I am to have such a good friend like you in my life, Beverly, and I truly feel honored to know you, honestly."

"Thank you, Ella," Beverly told her. "Friendship goes both ways, and while you feel lucky, the same applies to me. If not for you, I would have given up years ago. After Thomas passed away, I felt so alone and so lost, not forgetting how heartbroken I was. I never thought I would get through the days, let alone the nights, but your encouragement aided me. Now, look at me. I have a new husband, my children are all grown, each with a fabulous career, and I have more energy now than I did twenty years ago. I swear your health shakes are why, and I hope you consider marketing them one day because they are so good and nutritious and look good on my skin. You'd never believe I was sixty-two."

Ella sighed. "My, aren't we full of compliments today? Let's spend more time together and inflate our egos, as I feel like a million dollars after listening to your gracious words."

Beverly had been Ella's best friend since they would both attend Wellesley College in Massachusetts. The ladies had been in the same classes and were studying for the same degrees; they had even chosen to live in Florida together, and they did until both got married, and reluctantly, the Siamese twins had to separate.

"I love you, Ella. We may not share the same blood, but you're the best sister in the world."

An elevator door opened.

Ella directed Beverly by the hand inside the metal chamber and pressed the button to the ground floor. "I don't have to remind you to watch what you say in front of Kelly, do I?" She asked and grimaced.

The elevator door swung open, and outside, a couple stood impatient, anxious to get to their car and leave.

"You know better than asking me that," Beverly assured. She winked. "Your secrets are safe with me, and mine with you."

"Gran!" Kelly said and ran fast to embrace her grandmother. The drive from Forest Park was smooth traffic, less than ten minutes on the main road.

She did not inform Gran that she had driven fast, dashed from her car, ran along the pathway, and had yet to stop until she reached the elevator. She felt invigorated, as did Bella, who now was panting at her heel; Kelly topped up the plastic bowl with bottled water and rubbed the dog's head.

"You look marvelous," Gran exclaimed as she pulled Kelly closer to examine the young girl who stood before her, who was now a woman. "My, how you have grown, and I see you're wearing makeup," Ella said, then turned to Beverly. "Kelly was a tomboy and vehemently detested all the feminine frills of being a girl." She explained.

"Gran," Kelly said, flushing with color. "It's only been a month that I left."

"It feels like forever to me." Grandma Ella argued. "Beverly, isn't it wonderful that Kelly's now wearing makeup and not dressing like a boy?"

Beverly nodded and smiled. "I think we girls all go through that stage at some point," she said, hugging Kelly. "You've grown into such a beautiful young lady, Kelly. I am so proud of you, especially for caring for that sweet dog, and your school exam results are incredible. You are so smart. I mustn't forget your excellent class marks, or Ella will crucify me." Beverly winked and laughed.

Kelly blushed.

Since childhood, friends had called her beautiful, and while she adored the compliment, she just did not see it, could not accept it, and never understood how easily grownups threw the word around.

In every mirror she had looked, she saw a dull reflection and deep-set eyes that needed mascara and eye makeup to wake them up. Full lips looked clownish with brightly colored lipstick, so she could only wear nude shades or clear gloss, and she did not want to think about how frizzy her hair texture was, particularly in the humid summer months. Pretty is okay, Kelly thought, but beauty was a significant exaggeration.

She tugged on a pair of gold hoop earrings, a comfortable size she wore daily, and thought about Robert Vaughn. If her instincts were right, he would be angry that she brought the cavalry to Gainesville to help him organize his life, and she hoped he would not think of them as snoops.

It was odd that she had done so much today. Odder was that Gran had gone along with it, but when she thought about Robert and how pale he looked lying on the dirty sidewalk. She knew she had made the right decision, and if he complained. She would then reply that she was only trying to help.

Kelly pulled on her blond hair, tucked it behind her ears, and noticed her hands shaking. Now that Gran had arrived, she realized she was nervous, almost afraid of Robert Vaughn, and wished she had never stopped her car, offered help, or minded his dog, instead just driven by as other motorists had.

Such a horrible thought, Kelly scolded herself. Do not hate yourself because you care; embrace your kindness, condemn the wicked who walk amongst us, not those good at heart.

"Oh honey, are you okay?" Grandma Ella asked as she noticed Kelly fidgeting with the dog leash. "You look a little stressed, right Beverly?"

"She looks good to me," Beverly answered. "Too good. It is a sin for a woman to look as gorgeous as you," she added and smiled.

Kelly shrugged awkwardly. She did not answer at once; she could not explain that she doubted herself and her behavior today, regardless of whether she feared Robert Vaughn and how he would react when he met not only Gran but her friend Beverly, too. She felt sure he would be furious, and she dreaded the outcome.

"I feel a bit tired." Said Kelly. She faked a small yawn and sighed. "Gran, I think it's best if you visit first, and I'll wait here with Bella. That way, you can ask the adult questions I can't seem to understand."

"Oh honey, are you okay?" Gran repeated.

Kelly nodded, gritted her teeth, and shrugged.

"We'll go ahead, Kelly," Beverly interrupted. "Come on, Ella, let's get up there and see what's happening. Kelly is right. Staying here with the dog is best. That way, we can sort out all the necessary paperwork." She watched Gran's doubtful face turn inquisitive and held her breath.

Suddenly, Gran sided with Beverly, and Kelly watched both women walk toward the hospital entrance. And she did not relax until she saw them both disappear inside.

Then, and only then, was she able to breathe normally.

Chapter One

SEVEN YEARS LATER...

Kelly Evans slammed the large oak door shut.

The hot and humid night was over. If not outside, it was in her South Beach apartment. A modest two-bedroom, two-bath condominium on the seventh floor of Emerald Isle in Miami Beach, Florida.

Quickly, she secured the lock and turned on the in-house alarm system; only then could she begin to escape the day's problems.

Satisfied she had activated the alarm, Kelly leaned against the sturdy door, inhaled deeply, exhaled loudly, and then dropped to the floor.

Today, she had one of the worst days she had experienced in years.

Early morning, she had recklessly fought with her partner, Josh, over something that was so utterly ridiculous, and yet they had verbally assaulted each other to the brink of destruction. Their latest fight had left her bruised and battered, but fortunately, there were no visible signs for others to see. Still, she knew they were there, and that bothered her the most as she wondered how much more she could take. As the strength of her boyfriend's fist against her lower torso still hurt, and even hours after that, sitting down was hard.

Huddled against the door, Kelly knew that, eventually, Josh would punch her in a place she could not hide, and she cursed herself for sitting on the chilly floor, still foolishly enamored by her boyfriend and his nastiness.

You are pathetic, she thought. You need to be strong and end the madness if you are ever going to get out of this relationship.

More than anything, you must accept that Josh was not a fraction of the man you had believed him to be.

This morning's injury report was proof of that.

Kelly sighed, closed her eyes, and willed all sad things to leave her life. Several minutes later, and despite forcing herself to think positively, she could not stop reasoning about the morning's fiasco, which troubled her deeply.

She longed to talk to someone, to explain the depth of her troubles, but to whom? She had no one.

Which was pathetic.

Then, as if her morning were not bad enough, the afternoon became a complete and utter joke.

Midday, while at Dias Studios in South Miami, she had become aggravated working alongside film star Kyle Jackman. The famous actor was an egomaniac and a know-it-all, and reminding her of Josh, she could not stand his company for one more second. Instead of managing her position professionally, she summoned three employees to take over the assignment and walked off the movie set, and that bothered her as quitting was something she would never usually do. Then, late afternoon, she spotted a man on her trail who was sneakily taking her photo. She wanted to ask him why but pretended not to notice to avoid confrontation. Angered that She had not thought to shield herself as the drama unfolded. She gnawed at her lower lip and cursed herself for not dealing with the opposition. Now, she wanted to kick herself for not holding Josh, Kyle, and the strange camera operator accountable for their actions.

Resting her head in her hands, Kelly remembered her grandmother's lectures about safety.

She was supposed to avoid entering isolated places such as parking garages and alleyways, especially alone. Yet, today, she had broken all the rules.

During the day's madness, she had allowed people to treat her harshly and ignored their suspicious activities, even ignoring the man who trailed her every move.

What did he want?

She did not know but thinking about it chilled her to the bone.

Kelly took another deep breath.

She knew she was not physically able to defend herself, least of all against a man like the photographer, who appeared fit and robust.

Thinking about Gran, her friends and coworkers on the beach, the restaurant and boutique owners whose friendly faces she knew so well, she wondered what they would think if the man had mugged her, or worse killed her and left her in an alleyway, hidden from all.

Suddenly, she sat up and grimaced.

She rubbed her temples and tried to unscramble the thoughts rushing through her mind, yet no matter how she tried, she could not soothe her conscience that something was deathly wrong and something worse would happen.

Kelly shook her head. Your apartment is safe, she told herself, and while nestled on the cold, hard floor, she reminded herself that no one could harm her now that she was home.

Besides, nobody was watching, following, or interested in causing you harm, she argued, concluding that the uncertainty in her mind was just nervous energy.

Yet, deep down, in the pit of her stomach, she felt like a prized pony, on display the entire day, available to the highest bidder at an awful slaughterhouse.

As she scrambled to her feet, she thanked her grandmother, Ella, for her decision to buy an apartment in Emerald Isle. At least Gran had the foresight to think ahead to days when Kelly might feel threatened by a person or ghosts from the past.

The luxurious high-rise stood tall on Ocean Drive; the building's green trim complimented the city's Art Deco vibe, and the tall windows reflected the bright, sunny views.

Emerald Isle security was high-tech; all residents must carry coded Elevator access cards, and each unit's private in-house alarm system added another safety layer, as did security officers Emily Prescott and George Lopez. Most elderly homeowners complained about skyrocketing maintenance costs, comparing residing at the deluxe tower to living in Fort Knox. Yet, at every HOA meeting, they unanimously voted that the amenities brought peace of mind and opted to invest more funding into security.

The glamorous city of Miami Beach is a massive attraction for millions of visitors who travel to Florida annually. The influx of strangers walked the sidewalks day and night; with so much to do, it was seldom quiet.

The city streets boasted models, musicians, and tourists who frequented the trendiest nightclubs, boutiques, restaurants, bars, and coffee shops, all squished together on a tiny island in South Florida.

When the sun went down, the bustling city came alive as crowds ascended the small beach town, prepared to spend top dollars on a fun time.

The small Dade County hot spot appealed to people from all aspects of life, and while daytime activities were fun in the sun, nights were fancy cocktails and raunchy sex. It was the city police department's job to separate good from evil and to keep the people moving along the crowded streets.

Kelly loved the lively atmosphere and jumped at the opportunity to live among the lifestyle that is South Beach, as there was no other place she wanted to be.

Growing up in Fort Lauderdale, Florida, she had dreamed of Miami since childhood. Since styling was her forte, the fashion-forward town offered growth for her custom designs. After getting her fashion degree at twenty-three, Grandma Ella spotted an apartment that Kelly would later call home.

At twelve, she had wanted to be a famous model. Gran had gone with her to a local modeling agency. After signing a contract with The Stevens Model Group in Fort Lauderdale, they assigned her to pose for catalogs, fashion magazines, and runway shows up and down the East Coast.

The work was good, as was the pay.

Still, Kelly became disillusioned with the endless weekend travel and constant dieting. She detested living on a high protein and fruit diet, preferring to go to the shopping mall and savor mouthwatering junk food. Despite wanting to put her modeling career on hold, she loved the industry, the hair, the makeup, and the fashion. Still, she preferred to be behind the camera lens, away from the body image criticism that plagued so many models.

Six months later, she quit modeling and focused on the proper credentials to gain a career in design. Kelly took university seriously. She studied hard and joined after-school classes to get good grades.

Gran proudly bought the condominium in Miami Beach as a graduation gift, rewarding Kelly for her accomplishment in reaching a master's degree in interior design, and Kelly was thrilled.

She loved the seventh-floor flat; the salty air was refreshing, the ocean views magnificent, the sound of waves crashing against the sandy shoreline relaxing, and best, it all belonged to her.

On a clear morning, a large yellow circle with orange and purple hues burst through the glorious skyline, cascading across the seashore. As each new dawn began, Kelly marveled at the morning sun, the brightest and most beautiful she had seen. Moreover, she cherished the days Gran and her had spent browsing home stores for electronics, linens, and furniture.

Suddenly, Kelly's cell phone signaled an incoming call; glancing at the screen, she saw it was her grandmother, Ella Evans, and quickly answered the call.

"Did you just get home, honey?" The doting grandmother asked in a worrisome voice that was always present if Kelly was not home after dark.

Ella had reason to worry, as seventeen years ago, her daughter Sandra and her son-in-law Gerald were driving home when a treacherous storm flooded highways, creating lane changes and low visibility. Amidst the confusion, a drunk driver, Jeremy Garcia, fell asleep at the wheel and struck their car, killing them instantly.

It infuriated Ella that while her daughter perished that day, intoxicated Garcia survived, and the fury still burned deep within her core.

At the trial, a heartbroken Ella sobbed when a responding police officer testified that Garcia's sedan obliterated Sandra's SUV on impact.

Thinking about it today, Ella sniffled, knowing the crash details almost destroyed her, as did the trial's outcome. Though, the judge charged Garcia with two counts of vehicular homicide and sentenced him to life imprisonment. Sadly, the sentencing was not to be since a public defender, a pompous young attorney, cited that during Garcia's arrest, police officers did not read his Miranda Rights, thus taking evidence without a warrant, hence his prompt release.

The vehicular homicide case was an injustice for the victims and their families. To date, Jeremy Garcia walks freely amongst the citizens of Miami, Florida, and that knowledge alone terrified Ella Evans.

"Gran, are you there?" asked Kelly.

"I'm sorry, Kelly. I fell into dreamland. I am so embarrassed. It has been happening quite a lot the past few days, and I cannot figure out why. It is because, well, wait a minute because that is too painful to admit, but I..."

"But what, Gran? You are not making sense and sound so distant, almost drugged. Is everything okay?"

"Oh honey, I didn't mean to worry you. The past few days have been tremendously hard on me, and with the Fourth of July weekend approaching, I have been reminiscing too much. That is all, honey. Nothing more."

"Reminiscing about what? Gran, please tell me." Kelly said, anxious and worried.

Grandmother Ella inhaled and exhaled into the phone, then needing time to think, she paused, wondering the best way to approach her granddaughter and express how the upcoming weekend haunted her every year since her daughter died. "You know I hate to bother you with my sentimental memories, but earlier today, the devil crept into my mind, and the next minute, I was thinking about your mother and father. I am sorry. I know I should not and must move forward, but sometimes this date hurts me, and I find breathing hard. It's just a sad time right now."

Again, Kelly leaned backward against the front door and momentarily closed her eyes. In today's chaos, she had forgotten Independence Day weekend, which was only two days away. No wonder everyone at work was excitedly talking about holiday plans, everyone but her. She had been so focused on her anniversary with her boyfriend Josh that her mind ignored all other activities. She felt horrid inside and winced. "Aw, Gran. I am so sorry. I had forgotten it was July fourth. I feel utterly cruel, cold, and rotten. I am sorry, Granny. I should have telephoned you today. I should have known this would be a beastly day for you to get through, yet I selfishly thought only of my troubles. Can you ever forgive me?"

"Oh, honey. You know I love you more than life itself. I really should not have laid my troubles on your doorstep. I am so sorry, Kelly. So sad. Please ignore my emotional distress. I swear I will not do it again," Ella paused and coughed. "However, now I'm worried sick about you," she continued. "What troubles are you going through?"

"Gran, I'm all right. You know I am a sensible girl. Well, as sensible as any other girl my age. Okay, a little more grown up since you raised me with high morals, which helped me mature faster than others and have a higher level of maturity. I do not know how my real parents would have raised me, but I am not thinking as strict as you, and that is okay. I loved living with you and love you so very much."

"I love you too, my darling granddaughter," Gran replied. "You are the light in the darkest corners of my mind. You are my inspiration during strife. You are the sunshine after a storm and my darling granddaughter who has exceeded all my expectations. I am so proud of you, so proud, Kelly. You have no idea; words can never express how much you've enriched my life."

"Thank you, Gran. It is so good to hear you sound better," Kelly gushed. She paused momentarily. "Gran, was granddad awkward? Are all men annoyingly adorable? I am so stressed with Josh, and I worry he has stopped loving me. I don't know what to do."

Kelly and Gran were quiet.

Grandma Ella spoke first. "Oh honey, your grandfather was the most wonderful man I've ever met. He was charming, kind, and ever so attentive to everyone. Well, everyone but me." After a moment of silence, Ella coughed again; she cleared her throat and continued. "There were so many times I felt invisible and overlooked, but your granddad was a King in times of need. He was a loving man who ensured I had a comfortable home and worked hard to provide all life's finer things."

"So, granddad was not always moaning, like Josh?"

"Oh, he moaned. All men moan. It is what they do best. The key is to find a balanced man. On the downside, Granddad could complain for four solid hours, but on the upside, he was peacefully happy the other twenty hours of the day. I know I taught you that a person's home is their castle, and I taught you that for a good reason. Men are providers, and they will continue to bring stability and worthiness into the home if their home is to their expectations and demands. A woman must know when to push and when to give. If we push too much, we lose the argument, war, call it what you want. I am not saying we must bow down and serve, but we must know when our man needs us emotionally and sexually. And, even after considering all that, I will tell you that Granddad spent many days moaning about situations that had nothing to do with him, and he never stopped talking about world events, but that was Granddad."

"What you are describing sounds a lot like the Civil War. People are always in battle. It cannot be that way every day. Right?"

"It can be," Ella sighed. She looked at a photograph of her deceased husband, James. "I have to tell you something important, Kelly, and that is..."

"What?" Kelly interrupted. "Is it bad news?"

"No," Ella assured her. "I merely want you to realize that you are far too young to suffer in any romantic relationship. If Josh cannot pull himself together and work with you, he is not the man for you. When the right man enters your life, he will bestow peace and harmony, not grief. Does that make sense?"

"I suppose," Kelly told her. "So that you know. I am not marrying Josh. I am merely abusing him until Mr. Right comes along."

"Oh honey, you're so naughty," Ella giggled. "And you always make me smile. I adore our chats so much. You help me see things clearly and make me laugh, too, and considering how depressed I was today, that was a tremendous feat."

"What was?"

"You make me laugh, you silly goose. I feel much better and almost up to joining Caroline on her birthday outing."

"What time are you both going out?"

"She should be arriving any minute."

"Caroline is driving?" Kelly gasped, hating that she sounded astonished, but she was. Kelly could not remember the last time Caroline Carter had driven a car because her aunt was accident-prone. Usually, one of her children takes her to the grocery store, doctor's office, or favorite restaurant.

Ella paused. "No. Caroline is not driving. Bradley is driving. He's escorting us both to the casino."

"What?" Kelly almost laughed aloud. "Since when did the big movie star become a mommy's boy?" She snorted.

"He's a lovely young man," Ella declared. "He's certainly not a mother's boy, as you stated. And, if he was? What is it to you? I think you would be happy he cared for his mother. Glynn helps also, and Cameron would if she hadn't moved away."

"Cameron moved to get away from Aunt Caroline," Kelly argued. "I clearly remember Cam telling me that her mother was forcing her to wed some man she despised. Cameron also worked in another city to avoid a fallout with her mother. She moved to Gainesville, Florida. Somewhere north of here."

"Oh honey, you shouldn't believe everything you hear. Cameron moved away from her mother due to extenuating circumstances that had nothing to do with marriage. If anything, it had to do with a lack of a proposal."

"What do you mean?" Kelly asked. She was intrigued. It was not often gossip about the wonderfully gifted Cameron presented itself on a silver platter.

"I've said enough. I've said more than I promised I would on the discussion of Cameron."

"Come on, Gran. You cannot leave me hanging. You know you want to tell me. You do, don't you?"

"Oh, honey, I can't. I was sworn to secrecy many years ago and I cannot betray Caroline."

"I promise not to tell." Kelly giggled. She enjoyed teasing her grandmother. Besides, Ella needed cheering up, even if at Cameron's expense.

"I will excuse myself and go powder my nose. I am sure Bradley and Caroline will be arriving shortly. Plus, I must dress, as I am still in my loungewear."

"Oh my, we wouldn't want to give Brad Jennings the wrong idea, would we?"

"He's a good man, Kelly. Caroline and I had always hoped you might fall in love, get married, and have children because you would have produced the most gorgeous babies."

"Ew! No chance," Kelly scoffed. "He's such a pretty boy who's squeaky clean, which totally grosses me out. There's no way I would ever date him."

"I'm ending this phone conversation," Ella announced, unzipping a garment bag. "I have to get ready for tonight's event. It would be best if you rested, Kelly. You sound tired."

"I am tired, Gran," Kelly said wearily. "I had a horrid day, and even now, I can't shake the feeling that someone is..."

Suddenly, Ella stopped. Kelly was more important than a dress she had bought for Caroline's party. "Someone is what?" She quizzed.

"Well, I don't want to spoil your evening, but... Never mind, we can talk tomorrow."

"Kelly, what is wrong?"

"Gran," Kelly heaved heavily. "Earlier, I felt like someone was watching me, and I know, I've told you this before, but today, it was so real and so scary I almost went to the police station."

While listening to her granddaughter's concerns, Ella Evans placed the newly purchased dress on a linen chaise lounge chair and walked toward a safe room hidden inside her bedroom closet.

The small panic room is a boxed fortress built deep inside the home cavity and a place Ella would hide in case of danger. Though Ella has never sought protection within the iron bunker, the safe hiding place is perfect for storing pertinent documents away from prying eyes. It was also one of the leading buying points that attracted Ella's husband, James, to buy the home over thirty years ago. James believed the home's earlier owner, a politician, or a diplomat, to be the sole person who commissioned the custom model hidden inside the closet.

Ella tapped the security code at the single control point and watched as the steel-framed, bullet-resistant door swung open to reveal a concrete floor and steel stud walls covered in steel sheets.

Inside the room was a generator, telephone, monitors, and cameras to spy on intruders' movements and could count how many people had invaded the house. A small loveseat sat in a corner with blankets and cushions, and aside from a filing cabinet, provisions of bottled water and medications filled a small refrigerator. A wooden box holding flashlights, weapons, gas masks, and a landline was in the room's far corner. There, Ella sought out a charging cell phone, a device used only in emergencies, and recalling Kelly's dilemma, Ella believed someone had breached security.

"Gran, are you listening to me?" Kelly interrupted.

"Oh, honey. I am so sorry. Of course, I am listening to you. I was merely searching for something inside my closet. Please continue with your description of the day's events. I'd like to hear when and where you were when you first noticed being watched."

As Kelly recounted the day's events, Ella snared the cell phone, wrote a short text message, and sent it to the phone's one stored contact.

The wording was brief and would confuse anyone trying to infiltrate the phone, but after reading the coded message, the recipient would understand the exact course of action to take.

Ella awaited a signal showing that the contact had read CODE 4274, and since she was expecting return correspondence, she tucked the phone into her pocket.

After walking outside the room, she programmed the door to close and watched as the fortified door shut smoothly, giving no evidence of its existence behind the floral wallpaper.

"Kelly, listen to me," Ella said seriously. "I want you to remain home and not venture out for anything or anyone. Do you understand?"

Kelly rounded her shoulders to relieve tension in her neck muscles and sighed again. "Yes, Gran.," she replied, "But what is happening? And why are you suddenly alarmed, yet when I told you last year, I thought someone was following me, you did not seem bothered?"

"Oh honey, last year you didn't seem half as alarmed as you are tonight. I am only being more cautious this time because I am going out for the evening, and last year, I was home for the evening should a turn of events occur. But, Kelly, I need you to promise not to leave your apartment until I contact you later tonight. I do not expect to be out late, and honey, I would cancel my plans, but it is Caroline's birthday, and I just cannot let her down. Do you understand?" Ella explained. She placed her cell phone on the speaker so she could talk while dressing.

The light of the moon cascaded through the windowpanes into Kelly's dim living room, and she contemplated telling Gran more, but she did not want to spoil her evening, so she said nothing.

"Kelly!" Ella sounded frantic. "Are you listening to me?"

Upon hearing the curtness in her grandmother's voice, Kelly froze and sat saddled on the floor, resting an elbow on her knee, and gritting her teeth. "Yes, Gran," she answered nervously. "Of course, I am listening. I'm just feeling more scared now than ever before."

After realizing her abrupt tone had startled Kelly, Ella softened her voice and spoke smoothly. "I promise not to be out too long," she coaxed. "I'll also have my mobile phone, so call anytime you need me. Okay?"

"Yes, Gran. Is there something you are not telling me? Because if there is, I'd prefer to know now rather than after the fact."

"Oh honey, you're my pride and joy. Nothing is going on, and there is no way I would allow you to be in danger, no way at all. I want you to be happy, I would also like to see Caroline knowing you are safe. Kelly, that apartment building is impenetrable, so do not worry that someone can barge in because they cannot. You are safe there, so heed my words and do not leave. Besides, holiday weekends are crazy enough with so many drunk drivers on the roads and city streets. Please stay away from the party scenes, and I promise to stay connected with you this evening. Also, I'll return as soon as I can."

Kelly mustered a smile. "Gran, you're so dramatic," she said, grinning.

Ella fastened the zipper on her dress and peered at her reflection in the mirror. She noted that the sales lady at the trendy boutique was correct in that the dress was perfect for her figure, elegant enough for a birthday party, yet simple enough not to outshine the birthday girl.

"I'm the way I am because I love you, you little goose. Anyway, I need to touch up my makeup and tend to some pressing matters here before I leave, so don't forget, stay home." Ella demanded.

"No worries," Kelly sighed. "I'm not going out tonight. I will enjoy a hot bath, a light dinner, and a long movie."

"That sounds relaxing and rewarding."

"Yes! Okay, Gran. I hope you have a fantastic evening," Kelly said. She rose from the floor and wiped her creased trousers. "Please wish Aunt Caroline a happy birthday for me," she added, then paused. "Do you know if she got the birthday card I sent? I posted it a few days ago to ensure it arrived for her birthday."

"Oh honey, I don't know, but I will ask her and send your regards."

"Thank you, Gran. Remember to drink at least a gallon of coffee, especially around Brad. Can you imagine falling asleep while listening to one of his boring stories? That would be so embarrassing. Good night, Gran."

Ella burst into giggles. "You're such a naughty, wicked girl," she laughed. "Good night. Call me anytime, my darling girl."

"Thank you, Gran, and I'm sorry if my fears caused you to worry. I hope I have not spoilt your evening because I did not mean to. I was just expressing myself. Okay, Gran, I hope you and Caroline have a fun time out. Call me tomorrow. I love you, and I miss you already."

"Oh honey, I love you too. Good night."

The call ended.

Sam Smith was born in Cheshire, England. Her first novel, Run Wild, was published in 2006. She is a keen supporter of human rights and animal welfare. She has lived in Switzerland and Spain and is now settled in Miami, Florida, with her husband, two dogs, and cat.